Totally Bound Publishing books by Faith Ashlin:

Knights and Butterscotch
What You See
Pathfinder
A Slow Process of Understanding

A SLOW PROCESS OF UNDERSTANDING

FAITH ASHLIN

A Slow Process of Understanding
ISBN # 978-1-78430-357-0
©Copyright Faith Ashlin 2014
Cover Art by Posh Gosh ©Copyright November 2014
Interior text design by Claire Siemaszkiewicz
Totally Bound Publishing

A SLOW
PROCESS OF
UNDERSTANDING

Dedication

For Chris, for continuing to put up with me.

Chapter One

'It's not fucking fair,' was all that kept going through Jimmy's mind. Over and over on repeat. It wasn't fucking fair—not fair he was here, not fair he'd be here for weeks, not fucking fair he was being forced to bond with some guy he didn't even know. How could something like that ever be fair?

Okay, so maybe he'd stepped out of line and said things he shouldn't, to people he shouldn't. Said them long and loud. But he'd been drunk, and everyone knew he was an arsehole when he was drunk. He'd just kind of assumed they knew he was he was a friendly, didn't-mean-it kind of arsehole.

And okay, maybe he had hit someone, but he hadn't meant that either. He was the kind of drunk that did stupid things they wouldn't normally—things they didn't mean. Hit people they didn't mean to. It wasn't personal. He hadn't known who the guy was. Just some random kid, who just happened to have a powerful mother.

Was it such a crime to get drunk and say things he shouldn't, in front of people he shouldn't? And hit people he shouldn't?

Yeah, actually even he knew it was a crime, but shit, this was a hell of a punishment.

He was a good guy really, only the authorities hadn't seen it like that, and now he was fucking stuck here. Even the minor celebrity that came with being on a TV show with plastic spaceships hadn't bought him any leeway. But he should have known that, known what a hard, unforgiving bastard The State could be.

Now he had to pay for his stupidity. Nothing else to do now but suck it up and pay his dues.

But it might not be all bad. They'd told him he was going to be bonded with this guy—which was as near as damn it to fucking marriage—but the man would still be Jimmy's slave. Jimmy would own him, be accountable and responsible for him. That was supposed to be part of his punishment. To teach him to be responsible, so in future, he'd act that way toward The State.

Owning a slave. That was a weird concept, but there could be positives.

He wasn't about to treat a slave the way some people did. He'd seen it—at parties, around, hell, on the streets. Slaves bent over and fucked, passed around for anyone's pleasure. Treated as slabs of meat. He wasn't about to do anything like that. He'd be fair, protect him from the perverts. He'd be responsible, just like they wanted, even if it wasn't fair.

They both knew the score, knew there'd have to be sex, but he knew how to treat a person right. Slaves were people, no matter what The State said. He'd take the free, no-strings sex as a bonus. But people, anyone, deserved to be treated right.

He might not have understood the freedom movement, but he could help one man live an easier life. He'd be doing his small part to make the world a more decent place. He'd be responsible and accept his punishment like a man. Once he got through prison.

That made him feel a little better about everything.

He just hoped the guy didn't look like the tail end of a rhinoceros.

Two-and-a-half hours later, just as Jimmy was beginning to think that nothing would ever happen and that the silence would eat his brain away, his cell was unlocked. Three men held the door open for him, the first one pointing to the door. "It's time," he said.

Jimmy was led along numerous corridors, his hands sweating, his belly rolling every step of the way. He knew what was coming. He'd be all right, but still, shit. He rubbed his palms on the back of his jeans but the moisture was replaced as soon as he wiped it away.

On into a court room with more people, all the equipment laid out ready. Hell, this was real. This was really going to happen.

He was taken to the far end, stood in front of a lectern, then a court official murmured to him, "We just have to wait for your slave to be brought in. He needed medical treatment. He'll be here shortly."

Medical treatment?

Then the door at the back opened again, and Jimmy twisted round, straining to see as a group of people made their way forward. Two enormous men were half leading, half carrying a guy who was dragging one leg behind him. Jimmy's eyes were drawn down to where the guy's jeans had been raggedly cut open above his knee. His foot, ankle and lower leg were covered with a thick plaster cast, his bare toes sticking out—his bare, filthy toes. Jimmy wrinkled his nose in disgust as his gaze moved up. The rest of the guy was just as dirty, mud encrusted and grungy. His hair wasn't much better, nor his face, but he sure wasn't bad looking under the dirt.

Maybe this wouldn't be as hard as it could have been.

Before Jimmy could take in anymore there was a commotion and the judge entered. His thick robes and stupid hat may have been over the top and melodramatic, but they had the right effect. They brought an air of seriousness—of things being out of his control and inevitable—and Jimmy felt himself start to shake.

"Verdict has been passed," the judge spoke solemnly, the majesty of the law behind every word. "I'm here to carry out sentence." He studied Jimmy as a small hand-held machine was pushed in front of him. "Sign your name," the judge instructed.

Taking the stylus that was thrust at him, Jimmy fought to keep his hand from shaking. He had to do this right, make his writing legible. This was important. This was permanent.

Permanent.

He exhaled hard, nostrils flaring, and wrote his name.

The judge nodded and turned to an official. "Bring the slave forward." The guy with the cast was hauled forward, his right hand pushed onto the lectern, his fingers splayed. The machine was fitted into place over the back of his hand and a button pressed. He grunted and a flash of pain hit his face, but he quickly pulled himself together, standing as immobile as he could. The only sign of anything wrong was the way his chest heaved.

Permanent.

"Second brand," the judge ordered, and the guy's face went blank.

One of the men who had brought him in now braced the slave on the side with the broken foot. The guy leaned in, gripping on with one hand. He had no choice if he didn't want to fall over, as one of the other men undid his jeans pushing them and his underwear down his thighs. The man moved behind the slave, and Jimmy caught sight of pale freckled skin and a soft belly as his shirt was lifted and held up. Again the machine was brought forward and placed on his left hip, over the pubic bone. When the button was pressed this time, the grunt was deeper but more contained.

The slave's shirt fell down as he was steadied on his feet and he was left to pull the rest of his clothes back into place himself. Someone pushed Jimmy next to him before they were both turned to face the lectern.

"Now for the bonding," the judge spoke to Jimmy. "You will own your slave but, as you are also to be bonded, you will have extra responsibilities, even more than in an equal marriage. Do you understand?"

Jimmy nodded.

"Do you accept this bonding as the right and proper recompense to your benevolent State for your crimes?"

Jimmy knew better than to argue as his heart thumped against his chest. "I do." They really were going to go all the way through with this.

"Raise your hand."

Jimmy held his hand out, palm upwards. His family would kill him.

The judge turned to the slave. "Do you accept?" No niceties or explanations but he had to be heard to say yes.

There was silence and Jimmy couldn't stop himself glancing over. The slave stared straight ahead as he swallowed deep and hard. Then there was a huge hand on the back of his neck, fingers arching and pushing into the vulnerable tendons at the side. Pushing and pushing and…the veins were standing out either side of the fingers, and Jimmy thought he could see the blood held back, pumping just under the surface and… "Yes," the guy said, and the clamp on his neck was lifted away.

"Raise your hand." The judge didn't even look at him anymore — slaves weren't worth the effort.

The guy lifted his hand, holding it palm down just over Jimmy's. The court official moved forward and wrapped a leather cord round their combined hands, pushing them flesh to flesh as the judge enunciated carefully something frighteningly legal. Jimmy couldn't hear it for the rushing of the blood in his ears.

"You are now bonded," the judge said, as the official tied the cord tightly. "You are now mates." A beat pounded in Jimmy's head, his mouth dried out and his belly clamped. His mum would cry for a month.

The judge was already getting up ready to leave. "Take them to their cell. Assessment in…" He consulted his book. "One month."

Jimmy dropped his hand. The warm palm tied to his went with it. The implication of that hit him like a brick, and he thought he might just fall over. But the men who had brought them in were trying to usher them out. With a firm hand pressed to his back, Jimmy took a couple of steps forward and was almost immediately brought to a stop. He glanced round. The guy really was filthy but his eyes were...

"I can't walk properly," his slave said quietly.

"No, right. Of course you can't." Jimmy went to support him on the side of his injured leg but stopped, turned to the court official. "Do I help him? Am I allowed, seeing as he's my slave?"

"No, you're not allowed to give aid or assistance to a slave. Let them do it." The official nodded toward the men around them. Jimmy realized for the first time that they were slaves as well. On the back of their hands, instead of an individual's signature, there was a State department's stamp. They were owned by the state. One moved forward and caught Jimmy's slave's arm over his shoulder, taking his weight.

"You can untie that now." The official pointed to the cord. "But keep it. It's another sign of ownership and bonding. Some people like to tie it round their slave's neck."

Jimmy's fingers fumbled as he fought to undo the knots. He didn't want to tie it anywhere. He stuffed it in his pocket as he followed the slaves out and down more corridors to a prison wing. They stopped outside a metal door with a number twenty-two on it, waiting as it was unlocked. Then it was opened and he was steered inside, his slave was brought in after him and dumped unceremoniously on the floor by the wall. The door was locked behind them.

The banging echoed inside Jimmy's skull. His mum was going to make more noise than that when she found out.

Nothing else to do but make the best of it.

"Well." He walked forward, assessing the space. "I guess as prison cells go this could be worse." The room was rectangular in shape, a small table and two chairs at one end, big bed at the other, a bank of windows along the short end. Off to one side was a door leading to a tiny bathroom. The whole place was scruffy. There were the scrapes and scratches of other occupants everywhere, but clean enough, functional and better than he'd expected. "What do you think?"

When there was no answer, he turned so he could see the man on the floor. "You okay?" Still no answer. "Hey, I asked you a question."

The man had stretched out his injured leg and was rubbing above the plaster cast. He raised his eyes a little, licking at his bottom lip. "I'm sorry. I don't know how this works."

"How what works?"

"My being your slave. Do you really want to know what I think? If I'm okay?"

Jimmy stopped then, suddenly conscious of everything. There were rules for how to treat a slave. They were meant to be followed all the time, whether in private or public. It was his turn to lick at his lips as he turned in a circle, studying the room again in a completely different way. "You think they have a camera or some kind of microphone in here? That they're watching what we do?"

"Are you asking me? Am I meant to answer?" It was said softly, hesitantly.

The question had been more Jimmy thinking out loud than anything else but now he wanted to know. "Yes. How private do you think this place is?"

The man—Jimmy's slave, and that idea still blew his mind—examined the place, ceiling, walls, fittings. Missing nothing. "There's no camera, no mic I can see and no obvious place to hide one. But then, why would they bother hiding it?"

"True. I guess we don't have to watch ourselves all the time then, that's one good thing. I think that..." Again he stopped, hands on hips as he stared down. "I can't carry on like this. What's your name?"

"Nate," the man said simply.

"Nate, Nat, that's nice. I'm Jimmy, Jimmy Stephens." He stuck his arm out, ready to shake hands. Nate stared at it for a moment before holding out his own, palm down.

"I know," Nate said, looking at the back of his hand. Jimmy's eyes were drawn to it as well. There, amid the raised, red, angry looking puffy skin, was his name, clearly visible in black, burnt-in lettering.

Permanent.

"Shit, that looks painful. Your hip must be as bad. Should you do something with it?"

Nate tipped his head slightly and glanced at Jimmy for a moment before dropping his gaze. "Maybe I should wash it. Keep it clean? Cool it down."

"What about antiseptic or a bandage?"

Awkwardly Nate clambered to his feet. "I'm a slave," he said, and that really did sum everything up. He pushed off from the wall, heading toward the bathroom but stopped. "Is this okay with you?"

"What? I... Yes, yes of course it is," Jimmy blustered. "Hey, I know this is weird shit." He followed Nate. "But I'm not one of those owners who beat their slaves or makes them walk round naked and fucks them in the street. I'm not like that." He watched as Nate ran cold water in the sink and carefully cleaned around his hand with soap.

Nate paused for a moment, watching Jimmy in the mirror, before undoing his jeans and pushing them down his thighs. He lifted the waistband of his boxers, carefully raising it over his skin to rest it below the second brand. This one was angrier, more inflamed. But still Jimmy's name was easy to read.

"I'm not," he said, voice full of something even he wasn't sure of. "I'm not going to hurt you or treat you like a hunk of meat. You're a person. I'm a person, I'm... I'm not like that." Now he could hear it for what it was—anger. "Well? Fucking say something."

"You can be whatever you want. You own me." Nate half turned to glance back, holding the wet washcloth in his hand. "You can change whenever you want."

"I'm not a monster. I'm not going to change, I..." But it suddenly hit Jimmy. It didn't matter what he said. This guy, Nate, was right. He could change anytime he liked and there wasn't a damned thing Nate would be able to do about it. He had no reason to believe Jimmy. He drew in a deep breath, exhaling hard. "Instead of dabbing at it like that, why don't you have a shower or a bath? You're filthy."

"Are you telling me to?" He asked the question very quietly.

"No, I'm... Fuck it." Jimmy held up his hands. "If I were you, I'd wash myself and my clothes before I got blood poisoning or something. But you do whatever you want. I don't care." Then he had to walk away as far as he could get. As far as the main room. He threw himself at the chair, sprawling over it as he rubbed at his face.

This was fucking harder than he'd thought. He was a good guy, decent but... Nate didn't know that. He had no reason to believe a damned thing Jimmy said about himself. He was right not to accept Jimmy's word. Jimmy would just have to show him he was that good guy but, fuck, this whole situation was difficult.

His mum really was going to kill him.

No point thinking about that now. He might as well go and talk to his slave, start making him see what was right in front of him.

When Jimmy pushed open the bathroom door, Nate was sat on the bathroom floor, socks, shoes and shirt in a heap. One leg was naked, the other had his jeans and underwear caught in a tight tangle over the cast. Nate was twisted round, desperately trying to pull them off. He was covered in dried mud, his hair spiky with it, his face red and irate. He was also strangely beautiful. Jimmy couldn't help but laugh out loud.

Nate eyes blazed but then he seemed to remember himself and dropped his gaze.

"Oh, for God's sake, give it here before you tie yourself in a knot," Jimmy laughed, pulling at the end of the jeans. They came free with a whoosh and Nate rocked back, spread out naked on the floor. "You want a hand getting in the bath?" Jimmy asked.

"I can do it." Again Nate used a submissive tone.

"Shut up and let me help you, before you fall and break your neck," Jimmy said. He reached down to help Nate to his feet, supporting him as he hopped over to the bath and got in. He rested the injured foot on the edge, and Jimmy got the plastic bag from the garbage bin, wrapping it round the cast. "How'd you get so dirty anyway?"

"Fell over."

"Where?"

"In a river that turned out to be more mud than water."

"And your leg?"

"It got hurt along the way."

"But they fixed it? Set it, right?"

"Yeah," Nate said, sliding down in the bath to wash his hair.

"You don't say much, do you?"

Nate wiped the water from his eyes. "No pain killers but they set the bone."

"Are you in a lot of pain?"

Nate gingerly touched the brand on his hand. "I've had better days but I'll live."

"That's it? You'll live? I mean, shit, I'm having a bad day but yours must be a killer." Jimmy looked at Nate expectantly but he was scrubbing at his hair. "You can talk to me, you know."

There was a brief pause before Nate asked, "So what did you do to end up in prison with a sentence like this?" He stopped suddenly. "That's if you want to say, if I'm allowed to know. I shouldn't have asked."

"You can ask," Jimmy said, folding his arms across his chest as he leaned against the doorframe. "I'm an actor. I've been in a few things. I'm now doing a sci-fi show. I'm a crew-member on a spaceship, set on a different planet each week. Have you seen me?"

"I'm not sure. I don't think so."

"That means no." Jimmy snorted. "No sweat, though, most people haven't, although we do have an amazing fan base. It's kind of a niche thing. Anyway, I got cocky, thought I was more famous and protected than I was. I got drunk at an industry party, ran my mouth off about The State. Maybe hit someone I shouldn't. When I woke up next morning, I was in a police cell, and the shit had truly hit the fan."

Nate glanced up briefly but Jimmy couldn't read his face.

"You know the really dumb thing? I can't even remember what I said or why I hit him. I know I was being mouthy, showing off, but when they were questioning me, demanding to know what I meant by things, I had no idea what I'd said. I'm a stupid asshole."

Again Nate didn't say anything, but Jimmy was sure he could detect a softening of his face.

"What about you? What did you do?" Jimmy asked, but Nate was already trying to get out of the bath. Not easy with one foot stuck out the side. "Let me help."

Even then it wasn't simple, and Nate ended up pulling the plug and waiting for the water to drain away before trying again. He dragged himself upright, balancing on his good leg and Jimmy watched as he reached for a towel. Without the dirt he was even more attractive. Jimmy had the fleeting thought that, if he had to be mated with his slave, he'd sure as hell fallen on his feet.

Even his name on the pale skin of Nate's hip looked good.

Nate tied the towel round his waist and bent to gather up his clothes. Holding onto anything he could reach, he moved over to the sink, dumping the clothes in and turning on the tap.

"I can't see anything getting them properly clean," Jimmy said.

"Better than nothing." Nate rubbed them together.

Jimmy left him to it.

But there was nothing to do in the other room—no TV, games or music, none of his normal creature comforts. Stacked on the side he found a notepad, pens, a pack of playing cards and a copy of the bible. Four walls, a window and that was all he had to occupy himself for at least a month. He felt the frustration itch up his spine already. Might as well talk to Nate. "Can you play cards?" he called out.

"I guess so, a bit. What do you want to play?"

"Poker?"

"I can do that, if you want."

"Yeah, I…" Just then there was the sound of keys, the door was opened, and two guards came into the cell.

"Prison uniform," one said, dropping a bundle of clothes on the table.

"What? No." Jimmy's face fell. "Why can't I wear my own clothes?"

"Because you're in prison, fool." The guard stared him down.

"But that's fucking stupid. I only wear decent things."

"You'll do as you're fucking told." The guard moved closer, menacing.

"I'm not going to…"

Just then Nate came out of the bathroom, holding onto the wall, the towel low on his hips. "That's a piece of luck," he said, and everyone turned to face him. Jimmy couldn't stop his appreciative stare. The cleaner Nate got, the better Jimmy liked him. "My things are ruined," Nate said, glancing at Jimmy with a look on his face Jimmy couldn't interpret.

"Get dressed," the second guard ordered. "Then go out and collect your dinners. You, slave, you get your owner's as well."

"I don't think I can. Sir," Nate added, rubbing his injured leg.

"Can you walk?"

"Not without holding onto something. Sorry."

"Shit." The guard huffed. "Your owner can't carry for you, so I suppose one of the other slaves will have to bring it in."

The guards marched out, and Nate leaned back against the wall, exhaling hard.

"What?" Jimmy questioned.

"Nothing." Nate dropped his eyes.

"For fuck's sake, don't start not talking again. What?"

"I just didn't want to get the prison officers mad. Not so soon."

"You can't help not being able to walk."

"They might not see it that way, not if I can't act as a slave for you. And if they get mad at me, they might get mad at you."

Jimmy made a sound of begrudging acceptance as he examined the pile of clothes. "Oh they can't expect me to wear this crap," he complained, holding up the uniform.

Nate hopped over, taking the smaller set and already starting to get dressed.

"Don't tell me you actually like this?" Jimmy gaped at him.

"It's clean." Nate smiled softly. "Clean is good."

"Clean is overrated. My jacket is Armani, and this is a piece of shit." But Jimmy was already starting to change. It wasn't fair or right that he'd got to go through this just for one stupid mistake. He'd shout at…someone about it when he was released. Or get his mum to. But first he had to get free, and he guessed Nate had a point. It was no good pissing off the authorities. Not now. Not until he got out.

Nate had already dressed and cleaned up, throwing his old clothes in the trash. Now he sat at the table, resting his hands flat on the top. Jimmy noticed absently that he'd gone an odd gray color but he had no idea why. He pushed the thought from his mind and folded up his clothes. They were too good for a place like this anyway. There was no one here who would appreciate style and quality.

He was just about to sit down when the door opened again and a huge, bull-necked man brought in two trays full of food. He slapped them down on the table, none too gently. "Hey," Jimmy complained. But Nate was already smiling up at the guy.

"Thank you," Nate said, his voice low. "I owe you one." He pulled his foot out from under the table, showing his plaster cast to bull-neck. "I think, by the time I get out of here, I'll owe you a whole hell of a lot."

Bull-neck looked at Nate and something Jimmy couldn't catch flickered over his face, before he swatted Nate on the back of the head and left.

"What was that all about?" Jimmy demanded.

"Slave bonding?" Again Nate gave that soft smile, the one that Jimmy was already beginning to learn soothed a situation.

"That middle aged mobster-mountain was a slave?" Jimmy asked.

"Didn't you notice his hand? He's a slave. Remember, the slave goes to prison along with his owner, even if he hasn't done anything wrong."

"Shit." Jimmy hissed. But it wasn't the unfairness of the law that hit him. It was the thought that he could have been bonded with a slave like Bull-neck. That thought made his blood run cold. He sat down to eat. "Fuck it, this is slop. Am I seriously meant to eat it? Haven't they heard of decent food?"

"No," Nate said very faintly. "I don't suppose they have."

* * * *

Jimmy strode about the room uselessly. Dinner had been cleared away, his own clothes removed, the door locked, and now there was nothing but him and this appalling little cell. He knew he had to get used to it, that he had at least a month here. But it was so small, with nothing in it but Nate, and he wasn't being much help in distracting Jimmy from his claustrophobia.

Nate was sitting on the bed, his bad leg stretched out, rubbing at it obsessively. Okay, Jimmy got it probably hurt, but that meant they could both do with a little distraction. Anyway, weren't slaves meant to help their owners?

"Did I tell you about the show I was working on?" Jimmy didn't wait for a reply. "Do you want to hear about it?" He stood near the window, gazing out at the depressing view of the laundry block. "Mine was only meant to be a small part but the show's producers liked me and, more importantly, so did the fans. It got a real Internet buzz, and my part was beefed up massively. It's hard work—really hard work—but fun. I get to run around pretending to be someone else, with a laser gun in my hand and—what the fuck?"

An incomprehensible shout echoed down the corridor and the cell was plunged into darkness.

"I guess it's night time," Nate said.

"So that's it? It's only fucking... They took my watch." Jimmy ran a hand over his face, leaving it there for a long while, breathing into his own palm. "How is this—any of it—fair?" he said at last.

Nate shrugged but didn't say anything.

"So we just have to go to bed?"

"There's not enough light from outside to do anything else, just enough to stop you sleeping properly. I don't think we have much choice."

"This is fucking... Oh, whatever." Jimmy gave into the inevitable.

Nate had already started to take off his prison uniform and was climbing awkwardly under the covers in just his boxers and T-shirt when he stopped. "Is this okay?" he asked.

"What do you mean?"

"I..." Nate started, his voice louder than normal, stronger, but he cut himself off and inhaled sharply. "You own me. We both know what that means. What do you want me to wear in bed, if anything?"

Jimmy hadn't thought about that. He could get Nate to take off his clothes, get to see all that glorious skin again—if he could see anything in this light. But he wasn't like that. He wasn't a bad guy who was going to hurt his slave. That just wasn't him. "It's up to you, man. I'm not making you do anything."

Only they could both hear it, the monster in the room shouting 'but you will have to.'

"We both know what we have to do at the assessment," Jimmy went on. "I figure it's probably better if we try it out before then, give you a chance to... I don't fucking know how to say this to make it any better. I'm a big guy. I'm in proportion all over."

"You want to give me a chance to get used to being fucked up the arse by you." Nate's voice was so low Jimmy couldn't tell what the rasp in it meant.

"You know how it has to be. You want the first time to be hard and fast?"

"No," Nate said and the rasp had gone. "I'd like to be able to walk after."

"Well." Jimmy couldn't help smiling at the irony. "You'll still have the cast on, so I don't suppose you'll be doing much walking."

"True." Nate snorted gently. "And the clothes?"

"I meant that. Whatever does it for you." Jimmy pulled off his own uniform. "I should warn you though, I sweat like a pig. I was going to sleep naked, like normal, but I'm guessing no one here is washing the sheets anytime soon. So I'll leave my T-shirt on to soak it up."

"That's..."

"Kind of me? Gross?" Jimmy got into bed, patting the other side quickly. "Get in before you fall over."

Nate slid in next to him, his hand going immediately under the covers to rub at his leg.

Jimmy stared up—he couldn't even see the ceiling, the light from the curtain-less window casting odd shadows everywhere. Outside there were big floodlights, their glow orange and somehow menacing. This was a prison. Of course there'd be lights to keep everyone in. Lights and guards and locks and... *Think about something else,* he told himself. "How bad is this going to be for you?" he asked.

"What, you sweating? I think I'll cope."

"I didn't mean that." They were both lying flat on their backs, side by side, wide awake. "I meant the sex. I'm mostly gay, although I keep it under wraps. You?"

"Sometimes gay."

"I've had a string of people, always been lucky, never had to try hard to get anyone."

There was a long pause, expectation building. "I've been with...a few."

"Serious relationships? I don't bother with those."

"No, not serious."

"I like guys, because you don't have to hold back with them when you're having sex. You don't have to watch out for them, because they take care of themselves. You prefer girls?"

"I prefer women to girls. No, it's the person I like. Their gender doesn't matter that much to me."

"Let me guess... You like huge tits and a tight arse."

"I wouldn't say no to either, but it's more an honest smile or a sense of humor."

"You ever been fucked before?" Jimmy asked.

There was a quick intake of breath. "Not much but yes."

"That makes things a whole heap easier."

"Not if you're proportional."

"I'm not going to hurt you," Jimmy said, but was met by a silence that spoke volumes. "Okay, maybe at the assessment I will. But I promise I'll try to keep it to a minimum, try to go easy. We can both make it appear hard, without it actually being that way."

"I can do that."

Jimmy knew Nate's tone was guarded, but he guessed that was to be expected. This man, his slave, didn't know that Jimmy was a good guy.

"What can I do to make it easier?"

"Don't..." Nate stopped and took a deep breath before going on, his voice back to the soft sound Jimmy was coming to expect. "Not a lot, I suppose."

"Do you want to do it before the assessment?" And there was that word, 'want'. The monster in the room was screaming again. They both knew what Nate wanted didn't count for shit.

"I don't know. If that's the first time, there won't be any pretending."

"But I won't know what you need, what's the right side of comfortable for you and what isn't."

"You want to do it before." It wasn't a question.

"Hey, man, I don't want to straight out hurt you," Jimmy tried to explain. "If I know what you can take, what you like, then I can at least kid myself I'm not the guy that can keep a hard-on when he knows he's hurting his slave."

It was quiet for a long moment, before Nate spoke again. "I guess we'll do whatever you want."

It suddenly hit Jimmy that that was exactly what Nate thought they'd do all the way along, and Jimmy didn't know how to change his mind, how to prove him wrong. He thought only time would do that. "I just want to make it easier for you now."

"You want to make it 'easier' right now?" Nate asked. "Can you give me a minute? It's going to take a while for me to get my leg moving again. But then I don't suppose you need me to move."

"No, not now. Christ," Jimmy said it harsher than he meant, but he wasn't sure why. No, that was a lie. He knew why. He wouldn't have minded doing it now. Nate was a damned attractive guy, and just Jimmy's type, even if his hair was a bit too short. But he was trying to convince the man he was a decent person— fucking him their first night together wasn't going to prove that.

But he wouldn't have minded one little bit.

"We'll do it before the assessment, but not now. Even I can see you're in some pain."

"Some..." Nate said it so quietly Jimmy knew he wasn't supposed to hear it.

"Anything I can do to help?"

"I don't think you're supposed to help me."

"There's no one here but us." Jimmy pushed one hand under his head.

"How about you talk to me? Take my mind off it. Tell me about your job. What your life is like outside."

"Okay." Jimmy perked up at the idea. "That I can do." That he could do really, really well. He talked long into the night, regaling Nate with stories from the set, when he was young, now he was famous. He

27

talked, making himself laugh, until he fell asleep despite the ever present orange light.

He woke once, pulling the tangled cover free as he rolled onto his side, close to Nate. Without thinking, he reached round and rested his hand on Nate's chest, snuggling into him. He was practically asleep again when he felt Nate lift his arm off and slide over to the very edge of the bed.

It must be his leg hurting him again.

* * * *

They fell into a routine of sorts over the next couple of weeks. At first they'd spent association time in the communal areas, but Jimmy moaned that the other inmates were all thugs, drug dealers and killers. He went on endlessly about how unfair it all was, until he got bored of the sound of his own voice. But that was better than admitting he was scared of at least half of the people.

Instead, they retreated away from the others and, even when they were allowed outside in the fresh air, he kept Nate close. Jimmy would have argued to anyone that it was for Nate's own safety. Prison was a dangerous place, Nate was vulnerable with his busted leg, and Jimmy was a big guy.

But Jimmy had noticed the way some of the other slaves glared at him. How their eyes darkened, their faces setting hard, even though they tried to hide it, when he put a hand on the back of Nate's neck or his thigh. Then Nate would glance their way, and they'd back off.

Jimmy knew Nate got on well with the other slaves, had seen him talking, fast and stealthy, in little groups. They'd help him without complaint. One young, weedy slave even made Nate a crude crutch. He regarded Nate with admiration, as he'd presented it to him and seemed even more pleased when Nate's face had lit up as he thanked him.

Jimmy didn't like that slave.

Next day Jimmy had gone to the senior staff member and managed to arrange for Nate to get a set of proper crutches. At Jimmy's own cost of course, but he thought they were well worth it.

Nate got on with the other slaves better than Jimmy did with any of the other owners. There was one—big and fat with a greasy ponytail—who constantly watched Nate and made disgusting comments. Jimmy was greeted most mornings with a variation on, 'How many times did you fuck him last night?' or 'Can you force your cock all the way down his throat without him gagging yet?'

Jimmy knew it wasn't a joke. Everyone had seen the bruises on ponytail guy's slave, the ring of hand prints round his neck, the way the slave's eyes hardly left the floor anymore, especially when his owner dragged him back into their cell.

Jimmy wasn't going to be that guy.

Which was why he hadn't fucked Nate yet. He wanted to. Hell, every day, every hour he wanted to a little bit more, but he wasn't that guy, wasn't going to turn into him. So, instead they talked. Or rather Jimmy talked, and Nate listened, asking the odd question when Jimmy came to a stop. It was good, easy, between them. Even the silences were comfortable.

One morning Jimmy sat by the window, his feet propped up on the wall in front of him, and watched as Nate folded a sheet before laying it over the small radiator. They'd managed to snag another set of sheets, or rather Nate had. Jimmy wasn't sure how.

The prison only officially washed them once a week at the most, something Jimmy had complained about bitterly. So bitterly he'd almost gotten them into trouble. Next thing, Nate had found sheets and had taken to washing them out most days, ready to put on clean the next morning. Little things like that mattered in a place like this.

Nate smoothed out any creases, his hand sliding over the material. Even at that distance, Jimmy could see where his name was written on the back, even if he couldn't read it. The sight, the thought, warmed his belly in ways he didn't want to think about. He angled his head, considering. Even when he'd first seen Nate, limping and covered in mud, he'd been an attractive man. But over the last few weeks he'd changed, gotten even better. Jimmy tried to work out why.

Nate smiled slightly, his eyes crinkling. "What have I done?" he asked.

"Nothing. Why'd you ask that?"

"Because you're watching me again."

"I was just thinking you seem different, better."

"I am better, I..." But Jimmy interrupted him before he could finish.

"I think it's your hair, that horrible short cut is growing out already. It looks better, softer. You have to let it grow."

"Oh, okay." Nate shrugged. "I thought you meant feeling better."

"Well...are you feeling better?" Then it hit Jimmy. The gray pallor of Nate's skin had gone, along with the tightness in his face and the black circles round his eyes. "Your leg?"

"Yeah." Nate started working again, picking up Jimmy's clothes and folding them. "The leg doesn't ache anymore. Even my hip is fine now."

"What was the matter with your hip?"

"It doesn't matter." Nate collected up the socks and boxers, hopping toward the bathroom. He'd started washing those out as well after Jimmy had complained that they hadn't always gotten their own back.

"Hey," Jimmy called after him. "I asked you a question. What's wrong with your hip?"

Nate turned back, hanging onto the bathroom doorframe. "Your name, branded onto my skin."

"But that was weeks ago. Was it that bad?"

"It was over the bone. It hurt like all fuck." Nate pressed his lips together, holding his breath for a moment. "Not your fault though."

"But?"

"Then it got infected."

"Oh." And yeah, Jimmy had noticed that the skin around it had been raised, red and puffy. "Is it better now?"

"Yeah." Nate nodded. "Marty managed to scrounge me some medication. I'm fine."

"Who's Marty?"

"The big, bald, slave with the dragon tattoo on his bull neck. The one who brings our food every day."

"I didn't know that was his name," Jimmy admitted. "I've only ever heard him called slave."

"We're all only called slave," Nate said with finality and went back into the bathroom.

Jimmy would have to remember to thank Marty. Nate was...better.

* * * *

That night Jimmy could have sworn the lights went out even earlier than normal. He wasn't the least bit

31

tired. There was nothing to do all day except sit on his arse. A couple of laps round the yard hardly counted as exercise. He just thanked fuck that they only had a month in here, otherwise it would take a hell of a lot of effort to get back into shape. He sat up in bed, hands behind his head, and thought about long runs and afternoons spent in the gym.

"Shit." Nate yelped in the bathroom.

"You okay?"

"Yeah." Nate made his way out. "I knocked over the drinking glass in the dark. I'm soaked." He pulled his T-shirt over his head, already searching for a dry one. The orange light from outside reflected off his skin.

"Why don't you leave it off tonight?" Jimmy said, testing the words out on his tongue as he watched Nate's back.

Nate went very still for a long, long moment, the muscles along his spine rippling. Then he refolded the dry T-shirt, putting it back on the small pile. "If you want." He hopped over to the bed in just his boxers and lifted the covers.

"You could take those off as well."

Another, much shorter, pause, and Nate slid them off before getting into bed. He lay on his back, the arm closest to Jimmy folded over his chest.

The monster was back in the room, fierce and huge.

"I just think we ought to try things out. Time's going by."

"The assessment isn't for another eleven days," Nate said, very quietly.

"But if we leave it to the last minute and it doesn't go well... The more we try it, the easier it'll get."

"The more we try..."

Jimmy turned onto his side, running a hand down Nate's arm. "You don't..." He stopped, thinking.

Finding the right words was hard. He couldn't say anything about wanting to, because they had no choice, neither of them. But he didn't want to sound like he was trying to persuade Nate either. That just felt seedy. They had no choice. He only wanted to make it as trouble-free as he could. "I think it will make the assessment easier on both of us. Remember, I have to be able to get it up. That's hard enough with an audience, it'll be even worse if I know you're hurting." He smoothed his palm out across Nate's chest, at last feeling all that skin he'd only seen before.

"I'll take it real slow." He leaned over and kissed Nate, just a light press of lips. "Give you time to get used to everything." Another kiss, a little harder, pressing his tongue to Nate's closed mouth. "I'm good at this." Again with his tongue until Nate opened under him and he pushed inside. It was as good as Jimmy had hoped it would be. He explored Nate's mouth, tipping and tilting his head as Nate let him. "I'm real good at this, baby." He stroked his fingertips down Nate's face. "Relax and let yourself enjoy it."

"I'm not a virginal girl," Nate huffed out. "I know about casual, one-night-stand type sex. Let's just get on with it."

"Fine." Another kiss and another. "I know we have to do this but there's no reason we can't both enjoy ourselves while we're at it."

Nate twisted under him, hand going out to where the big bottle of lube had been sitting since they first got there. "Do you want to get me ready or shall I do it while you get naked?"

Jimmy looked at him and even in the poor light, Nate didn't seem like normal. There was a hard edge to his face and something else, like he was holding himself tight, holding something in. Jimmy wasn't sure he liked it—he wanted his normal Nate back. He guessed it was nerves, but there was no need for that. Jimmy really was good at this. He'd make Nate see that. "You start, and I'll finish it off." He pulled his T-shirt over his head, throwing it onto the floor. "I want to touch you first, run my hands all over that pretty skin."

Nate pressed his lips tightly together and snapped open the bottle.

Jimmy tried to wrestle his boxers off, gave up then stood at the side of the bed, pushing them down as he watched Nate slick his fingers.

"You weren't lying about being proportional, were you?" Nate said, as Jimmy stood there naked. Nate picked up the bottle again and squirted a whole palm full of lube out before reaching down and around.

"I'm not out to hurt you. I'm not like that," Jimmy tried to explain again. But he could see by Nate's face he wasn't believed. The only thing he could do was make Nate understand. Make him by going slow, taking care of him and getting him to enjoy it as well. Yes, he wanted Nate—no point lying about that—but he also wanted him to enjoy it. He wasn't a sadist or one of those notorious slave owners. He wasn't the ponytailed owner a few cells down. He wasn't like that.

"You might not mean to hurt me, but I suspect you're goin—" Nate held himself very still, his breath trapped in his throat. There was a long pause then he exhaled very slowly, very deliberately, relaxing back into the pillows. "I'm sure you'll do your best by me," he said passively. "I'm sure it's all going to be just fine."

"I only want to make it easy for us," Jimmy said as he climbed back onto the bed.

"Okay." Nate smiled up at him. And if the smile didn't reach his eyes... Well, Jimmy understood nerves. "What can I do to help?"

"You could start by kissing me back." Jimmy leaned in, pressing his lips to Nate's and waiting. After the briefest of pauses, Nate opened his mouth, encouraging Jimmy's tongue forward.

Jimmy pushed the covers out of the way and lowered himself down until he was stretched out half over Nate, leaving himself enough room so he could run his hands everywhere he wanted — to entice, to arouse, to excite. He knew what he was doing here as he ran his thumb back and forward over Nate's nipple. Fucking Nate's mouth with his tongue, biting at his neck, licking and lapping at his jaw and, holy shit, it was so good.

He pressed his cock into Nate's hip as his hands ran over Nate's shoulders, down his arms to... But Nate's hand was pressed under his own body, his leg out to the side, foot flat on the bed. "What?" Jimmy asked.

"I'm almost ready," Nate said, his fingers working on himself.

"What's the rush? We got all night." Jimmy smoothed his palm over Nate's belly, but Nate was already turning over, offering his back. Wide shoulders, smooth flesh, a smattering of freckles that made Jimmy want to lick each and every one starting at his neck, running down his spine, to narrow hips and a fucking perfect arse. "Oh, yeah," he puffed the words against Nate's skin. Maybe now was just about the right time.

He ran his palms up Nate's inner thighs, lifting and adjusting him until he was at the perfect angle. Then higher, under his balls, up, finger pressing closer as Nate passed back the lube. Jimmy stopped, squirting out a generous portion, rubbing in, over and around. He pressed a couple of fingers in and, okay, more lube probably had been a good idea. Nate was tight. "You haven't done this for a while, have you?"

"No." The word came short and sharp.

"Let me just..." Jimmy stretched him with two fingers, three—taking his time. Nate didn't make a single sound as he pressed his face into the pillow. Jimmy felt the give of muscle. "You should be okay now." More lube over his cock and Jimmy was ready, lining himself up. "They don't give us condoms, but I know you've been tested, and I don't take chances."

He leaned closer, licking across Nate's back, biting at his skin. "I'll take it slow," he said. Which had to mean he was a fucking angel, because all he wanted to do was thrust in hard and pound away until he couldn't get any deeper. But he knew he was a big guy, and Nate really was tight.

He pressed forward and the resistance was greater than he'd expected. He took a deep breath, counting to five before he let it go, repeating over and over in his head, 'go slow, go slow'. He pushed a little harder and a little more. He was pretty sure a bit more was all it needed. Harder still, and a flash of excitement roared up inside him as he felt the first give. Another push and the head was in and...

"Wait," Nate said, voice clipped and tight.

"No, not now. It'll be okay. Give it a second. I want..."

"I can't take the pressure on my busted leg, I have to move it."

"Oh." Jimmy had no choice but to pull out as Nate moved under him, twisting so he was lying more on his good side, the heavy cast flat on the bed.

"That's better. Go again."

Jimmy blew out a huge breath. It had to be easier this time. He wouldn't have to go so slow. He lined himself up and pushed, pushed, pushed until he was all the way in.

Nate didn't make a sound.

Tightness all around. Tight and hot and all the fucking clichéd things he could think of—and so achingly good. Hard muscle and bone offering itself all for him to take. He gripped the skin on Nate's shoulder between his teeth as he pulled back and thrust in deep, groaning in the glorious pleasure of it. This was amazing, better than anything Jimmy could remember. No one fighting to take control, no demands to go slow or squirming around under him—just an addictive tightness around the full length of his cock as he thrust again and again. This was just fucking perfect—every bit as good as Nate had looked. And Nate must be doing okay, because he wasn't saying a word.

"Oh God, baby, you're perfect, just fucking perfect." Jimmy sighed, as he caught hold of Nate's hips and let himself go, thrusting deep and sweet. He knew exactly where to aim, the effect a cock the size of his could have on that spot, knew what it would do to the man taking it.

He thrust again, once more, and Nate tightened around him. Controlled, rhythmic constrictions that made the blood boil behind Jimmy's eyes, the heat burn in his balls, and his hips snap hard so he could fill Nate deep. Fill him again and again until he had nothing left.

Collapsing, he panted against Nate's back, his dick still reacting with what felt like aftershocks. He hadn't had an orgasm like that, so hard, in ages. He felt like he'd never be able to move again but Nate was shifting under him.

He should give the guy a break. He'd been breathtaking. Jimmy knew he should feel grateful or guilty. Nate had been left to come without Jimmy ever touching his cock.

He held onto Nate's hip as he pulled himself out, feeling him shudder as he did so. He was just about to pull Nate down to tell him how amazing he'd been when Nate dragged himself off the bed. "Hey, where are you going?"

"I need the bathroom," Nate said, voice flat and controlled.

As he walked away, hand on the wall for support, Jimmy saw his cock. Nate hadn't come—he'd never been hard.

Yeah, he should feel guilty.

Nate was in the bathroom for a long time, long enough for Jimmy to calm down, clean up and arrange himself on his back, one hand under his head. When Nate came out, he seemed his normal self but he stopped before getting back into bed. He glanced down at his clothes, then at Jimmy who was still naked, and got in.

"That." Jimmy paused before going on. "Wasn't a good performance by me. I should have helped you out, stroked you off."

"It's okay," Nate said gently.

"But I should have thought more, your leg? Is it hurting?"

"No, it's fine."

"Is that why...?"

"I'm fine. It's no problem."

"Did I hurt you?" Realization slowly dawned. "Shit, man, I'm sorry. I didn't mean to. You just felt so good that I got carried away. I never intended to hurt you, I'm sorry."

"Jimmy." Again Nate's voice was soft. "I'm your slave. You aren't expected to say sorry to me."

"Doesn't mean I shouldn't though." He ran a hand down Nate's arm, stroking over his wrist and across his belly, leaving it there as he moved in closer. "I'm sorry. We'll try again tomorrow night, after you've had a chance to recover. I'll do better then, I promise." He rubbed his nose into Nate's neck, tightening his arm as sleep over took him.

When he woke much later, Nate had rolled to the far side of the bed and was asleep on his belly. He couldn't stop his smile as he traced his fingers down Nate's spine. He really had gotten insanely lucky. He slid over, wrapping an arm round Nate.

Next time he woke, the outside floodlights had been turned off and an early morning gray gloom filled the room. Nate sat in a chair by the window, wrapped in a blanket, staring out at nothing. "Hey," Jimmy called quietly. "Are you okay?"

Nate turned round. "Yeah."

"Are we okay?"

There was a short pause then, "Yeah."

"Sure? You aren't going to kill me in my sleep or anything else dramatic?"

"No." Nate suddenly smiled, natural and warm. "I haven't got the energy for dramatic."

Jimmy instantly decided smiling suited Nate. "Come back to bed? If you want to?"

Nate considered him for a long moment and the smile didn't slip, then he pushed himself up. "Why not? We don't have to be up for hours yet."

Jimmy lifted the covers for him to get in as he dropped the blanket on the floor. "Man, you're freezing. You put your icy feet of death on me and I might just have a heart attack."

"I'll remember that if I ever do want to kill you." Nate sank down, pulling the covers up to his chin as he shivered. "But icy feet of death? That's…"

"Weird? Go on. Say it. Everyone else does. Even my mum thinks I'm weird."

"Different," Nate said. "I'm going with different."

"Chicken."

"Wise. Different can be good." Nate shivered again.

"You really are cold. Do you want to huddle up and get warm?"

Once more Nate considered at him carefully before smiling. "Sure." He rolled onto his side and Jimmy pressed in behind him, wrapping an arm over him.

"I have a theory about this as well," Jimmy said. "This isn't snuggling or cuddling, oh no. You only snuggle with girls. As we're both men, this is most definitely huddling, which is nothing like snuggling at all."

Nate patted Jimmy's hand. "Like I said, different can be good."

Chapter Two

The next night Nate didn't even bother asking about clothes, simply taking his off before he got into bed. When Jimmy got in next to him, Nate passed over the bottle of lube. "Use lots. Lots and lots." His tone was gentle, there was even a vein of humor in it but it didn't reach his eyes. Jimmy wondered about that.

The day had been an all right one, Nate hadn't seemed off with him, like Jimmy had almost expected. In fact he'd smiled and laughed more than normal. Maybe things were all right.

Jimmy looked at the bottle in his hand. Or maybe they weren't.

"I really am sorry. I'm a big guy, I know I am. I should have taken more time, gone slower and... How bad did I hurt you?"

"I'll live."

"No, answer properly. How bad?"

Nate shook his head, smiling again. "On what scale?"

"One to ten? Or 'ouch, I've stubbed my toe' to giving birth."

Nate actually laughed at that, "I've never actually given birth."

"We've all seen the videos and my mum's told me enough times how bad it was."

"Okay." Nate thought about it. "Going to the dentist."

"Root canal treatment or that check-up thing when they poke at your gums with the sharp stick?"

"You're mad." Nate laughed a little more and Jimmy decided he liked that even more than when Nate smiled.

"Yeah, probably. But which?"

"When they give you an injection in your gum."

"You ought to ask for the gel, they put it on first so it doesn't hurt. I know it's meant for kids but I argue why should they be the only ones to get pain-free."

"I'll ask, if I ever need one again."

They lay in silence for a while. "I genuinely didn't mean to hurt you," Jimmy said, as honestly as he knew how. "I got carried away because it was so good, and I wanted you so bad that... Oh shit." He slapped a hand over his mouth, painfully aware that he was starting to blush. They weren't meant to be doing this because he wanted Nate. It was meant to be about practice for the assessment.

"Hey, don't worry. I'd kind of worked out that you wanted me."

"You did?"

"Difficult not to with the way you've been watching me for the last week."

"Hell." Jimmy ducked his head. "I was going for ninja stealthy."

"You missed that by a mile." Nate was smiling again.

"Do I say sorry for fancying the arse off you? That doesn't seem right. It's insulting if anything."

"No, you don't need to say sorry for anything."

"If I'd met you anywhere else, in any other circumstances, I'd still want you as much," Jimmy admitted. "I thought that was a good thing, but I guess I need to...control my excitement, or be less enthusiastic?"

"Just..." Nate chewed at his lip for a moment. "Slow down. Don't go so hard. At least until I get used to the size of you."

"I can do that," Jimmy said, and Nate stared at him. "I can, honestly. Okay, just remind me if I get..."

"Over enthusiastic?"

"Yeah." It was Jimmy's turn to laugh. "You said you thought of this like casual, one-night stand sex. You'd remind me if it were that. Well, do it. Treat it that way and remind me."

"If this was a one-night stand I'd have vetted you before you got into bed. With that thing in your pants, you'd never have passed the ruler test." Nate's words sounded harsh but there was a smile on his face and even a twinkle in his eyes.

"It's not that big, I'm not inhumanly freakish or something. Am I?"

Nate raised an eyebrow in what had to be a practiced move. "On what scale?"

"Oh don't start that again." Jimmy laughed. "I'll get a complex. I promise I'll be slower. I won't go so hard and I'll use lots and lots of lube. Okay?"

"Okay." Nate nodded.

"And you'll remind me if I forget?"

"Okay." Nate nodded again.

"So?" Jimmy said slowly.

"So."

"I suddenly feel like a virgin on her first date."

"You put out on your first date? Man, you were easy." This time they both laughed.

"So…what do we do now?" Jimmy asked.

"Well, I figure you had the basics pretty well worked out last night but how about we start with some kissing?"

"I can do that," Jimmy said enthusiastically. "I could pretty much spend all night kissing you." He leaned in, hand on Nate's shoulder, and kissed him, soft and easy, taking his time. Nate opened immediately to him, tongue pulling Jimmy in, giving Jimmy all the space he could want. Jimmy let his hands roam free, not thinking about his next move, just exploring. "How am I doing?" he asked, pulling back just a fraction.

"Good." Nate tipped his head. "Good."

"Better?"

"Yeah."

"You can touch me as well, you know."

"Okay." Nate lifted a hand, resting it on Jimmy's shoulder.

Jimmy rolled them until Nate was on his back, kissing the whole time. He leaned over, not pressing or holding Nate down but gently running a hand down his side, across his belly. Nate pushed up, angling his hips so their groins pushed together. He moved under Jimmy so Jimmy's cock rubbed over and over his hipbone. Jimmy had pretty much been hard since he'd watched Nate getting undressed – this was all he needed to get him completely ready.

But no, not yet. He could wait.

He caught hold of Nate's waist, pressing him back into the mattress and wriggled his hand in between their bodies. Across Nate's thigh, up, a quick cup and roll of his balls to pull at... Nate's cock was completely soft.

"Give me some time on that one, yeah?" Nate said, out of breath.

Jimmy held still for a moment. All right, maybe Nate was worried about getting hurt again. It was understandable. Jimmy had done a rotten job last night. He'd do better this time. He just had to give Nate a chance to find that out. "Okay, we got all night. We can..." Nate lifted up and kissed him again, and Jimmy forgot what he was going to say.

Kissing and touching, Nate's hands on his back, his shoulders. Nate working his dick with his hip, then his hand. His fingers slick with spit, quickly learning what Jimmy wanted, needed. How to make him groan and gasp, how to make him so hard he felt like his cock was throbbing. But Jimmy had to do better. "Where's the lube?"

"Here." Nate scrabbled round in the creased sheets until he found the bottle, pressing it into Jimmy's hand.

Jimmy squeezed out a palm full, grinned at Nate briefly, and added a load more. "You can never have too much," he said, mouth back on Nate's. "But no rush," he whispered the words close to Nate's ear as he reached down between his thighs.

Making sure the tips of his fingers were coated, he stroked up and over. Round and round, taking his time, playing and testing. A little pressure, just to tease, then away. While stroking with two fingers, he kissed Nate deeper, his other hand rubbing over a nipple. With his hand constantly working, he let one finger slip inside, and he felt Nate stiffen. "Too soon?" he asked.

Nate shook his head. "Slow and careful though, please."

Jimmy nodded, fingers flexing on Nate's shoulder.

Gently, gently, gently, Jimmy kept saying the word over and over in his mind, a constant reminder when the need to pull his fingers out and thrust his cock in got too much. He kept his hand working, only stopping to add more lube—then more still. His fingers started to ache, the hint of cramp there in the background, but he knew he needed three to stretch properly. He kept going, kissing as he went and, hell, that was no hardship. Kissing and stroking Nate inside and out—only problem he had was keeping himself under control. But it was worth it when he felt Nate relax around his hand, the muscle easing its tight grip. Still he kept going, working Nate. He rolled onto his side, just enough to give himself room to slide his other hand in between them but Nate was already turning over. "You ready?" Jimmy asked.

"Yeah."

"Sure?"

"Yeah."

"You don't want to try it on your back? Might be easier."

"No," the word came sharp. It was followed by a quick intake of breath. "I prefer it this way round. Is that okay?"

"Sure, I don't mind. As long as your leg's okay like that."

"It's fine as long as I position it right."

Jimmy got up on his knees, sliding a hand up Nate's spine. Such a beautiful back, such glorious skin and muscle and all his. He rested that hand just below Nate's neck, not holding, no pressure, just resting, and eased him open with the other. Glorious. And all his. "Okay?"

He felt Nate nod.

He pressed in just a little, just the tip, and forced himself to stop.

"Still okay?"

Again the nod.

In a little farther. "Slowly, slowly, slowly," he repeated making his hands stay gentle on Nate's skin. "Slowly, slowly, slowly." He felt a shudder through Nate's back and forced himself to stop again, the blood pulsing in his cock, his chest, his face. "I'm hurting you?"

"No, you're making me laugh with the chanting," Nate said. And Jimmy could hear it. There really was amusement in his voice.

"Just trying to...calm myself down. I can keep going?"

"Yeah, I'm okay. In fact there's so much lube that I'm in danger of slipping off the bed."

"Shut up." Jimmy snorted. Damn, that amusement was contagious. "I just want to do...better."

"Keep going," Nate said, and Jimmy felt him deliberately relax his body even further.

Jimmy pushed, and again, and a little bit more then he was all the way home flush against Nate's skin. The pulsing of his blood multiplied by about a hundred times. He could feel the veins and tendons in his arms and neck, pulling taut, standing proud as his breath came short and shallow. Fuck, he wanted—fucking needed—to pound hard and now, now, now. He sucked in the biggest breath he could manage and forced himself to hold it until his lungs felt like they'd burst. He waited and waited and waited and...again he felt Nate's body relax under him, around him.

"Move," came Nate's voice, muted and lax.

He let the breath go, slow as he knew how, feeling it ghost over his lips as he pulled back, watching. His cock, deep inside Nate's body. The sight was doing nothing to stop his blood pounding. Solid push back in and the muscles in his belly tightened and rippled and the sweat ran down his face. "Slowly, slowly, slowly," he murmured and felt the ripple through Nate's back.

Out and in again and the spectacle was almost too much to take. "Gently, gently, gently." He changed the words but still felt Nate's reaction. "Gently."

"Gently is good," Nate said, and Jimmy couldn't tell how he sounded this time, the blood was pounding too loud in his ears. "But you need faster and I'm okay."

"Sure?"

"Faster." Nate nodded.

Jimmy pulled both hands in to cup Nate's hips, spreading his fingers wide. Even that sight set something off in him, his weathered hands against Nate's pale flesh. His dick in Nate's arse. Too much — if he watched that he wouldn't stay gentle. He ran his hands up Nate's back, leaning over him and gave up just a bit of his control, letting his hips go faster. "Gently," he whispered. "Gently."

He thought he was doing so good, living up to all his promises, when he glanced up at his hands on Nate's shoulder blades.

Both hands on Nate's shoulder blades.

Meaning there weren't any on his cock.

"Shit." He hissed, reaching round immediately. But before he could get his hand where it should already have been, Nate dropped down, pushing his belly into the bed.

He tried to wriggle his hand under but Nate tightened the muscles in his arse, and it felt like Jimmy's dick was being milked. A moment later and the squeezing was in rhythm with his thrusts. "Gentle." He pushed the word out over his teeth, lips against Nate's back. But it was too late to worry about that. There was no time left for gentle or anything else as Nate squeezed again and Jimmy came hard and complete, his whole body pulsing in time with his blood.

His breath was labored as he squeezed his eyes tight shut and held onto Nate's biceps, waiting for the pounding in his chest to ease.

"Better?" he asked, pulling Nate tighter to him as he slipped himself out.

"Yeah." Nate did sound better.

"Did I hurt you?" He pressed his nose into the back of Nate's neck.

"No."

"Sure?" He stroked up Nate's arm, smoothing across his shoulder.

"I'm sure."

"So really okay?"

"You want me to give you a point score?" The amusement was thick in Nate's voice again.

"Shut up." He bit gently at Nate's neck, just below his hairline. "I'm just checking."

"You did okay." Nate rolled back into him.

Jimmy ran his hand down. "And you finished yourself off without letting me touch you and... Jesus." His hand had gone fast across Nate's abdomen before Nate could stop it. Nate wasn't hard. He never had been. "Why didn't you fucking say? I could have..."

"Jimmy, please." Nate pulled away. "Give me a break here, please. I can do whatever...but I can't...please, I can't make myself get it up."

"But I wanted you to enjoy it and—"

"I'm doing my best, honest. Please."

"Okay, okay." Jimmy licked over his lips, reaching out to grab Nate and pull him back in. "Okay." He tucked Nate close to him, back to chest, and wrapped himself over him. "It's okay. Tomorrow we can try..." He felt Nate stiffen.

"Please, Christ, don't," Nate pleaded.

"But I..."

"Don't give me anymore pressure, I'm begging here. Any more pressure and I'll never get it up."

"Okay, no pressure. I can help you out though, can't I?"

"No, not yet, I need..." Nate took a deep breath.

"What do you need?"

"Time, I need a bit of time and no pressure. I'll do whatever you want, just no pressure. Please."

"All right." Jimmy held him tighter. "No pressure but..."

"And no buts. No pressure, no buts and no help. Just give me a bit of space to...not get it up."

Jimmy kissed his shoulder, his neck, the side of his ear. "No pressure, no buts."

But he was going to get Nate to take some pleasure if it killed him.

* * * *

Over the next week Jimmy enjoyed himself enormously, indulging them every night. He tried lots of positions, with varying degrees of success. Nate didn't seem to mind how he was moved around, on his belly, on his knees, smiling as he asked, "Really? You think either of us are that flexible?"

One night he fucked Nate slow and careful standing up against the wall and was mighty pleased with how good it was. Mighty pleased as Nate had started laughing out loud. "Man, that was one hell of a ride." A small, smug smile stared to form on Jimmy's lips, only to fall when Nate added. "Have you any idea how hard it is to keep your balance on one foot when you're getting fucked? I had to hang onto the light fitting all the way through." Then Jimmy knew what all the wriggling and stretching had really been about.

Some nights he had to fight with his own want — his need to fuck hard and deep — to try to give Nate a good time. But Nate pushed his hand away and pressed his belly into the mattress, effectively stopping Jimmy getting near his cock without making it a big deal. Nate didn't want to talk about it either. Later, after, Jimmy realized that Nate turned any conversation as fast and efficiently as he turned his body.

Two nights after that and again Jimmy wanted to try something else. He pushed Nate onto his back when he rolled into his normal position on his belly, kept his hand firm on Nate's chest when he attempted it again. "I don't like…" Nate started.

"Try it." Jimmy kept his hand firm. "Relax, baby, and try it. It can be real good this way round."

Nate opened his legs, crossed his arms over his face and went limp. He barely moved or reacted as Jimmy fucked him every way he knew how — slow and gentle, fast and deep. When Jimmy came with a groan ripped deep from his chest, then pulled out, Nate rolled onto his side and didn't say a word. Jimmy pulled him in close, wrapping an arm over him, and didn't say anything either. Nate had never been anything other than completely soft.

Next night he tried it with Nate bent over the end of the bed. "Good?" he asked, after.

"Yeah." Nate smiled at him. "My leg didn't hurt at all in that position."

Now there were only two days to go before they were back in front of the judge for the assessment. Jimmy had felt the tension building until it tingled across his skin.

"We can't muck up," he said, getting into bed. "We have to do it right, look right. Make it seem like everything they want."

"I know." Nate climbed in next to him and lay on his back. "But we should be able to do it."

Jimmy leaned over, kissing him sweetly, hand holding Nate's face. "I'm going to have to be...not rough, I won't hurt you, but rougher. I have to be seen to dominate you."

"I know that as well. Nothing we can do about it."

"But." Jimmy licked along his jaw line, biting at his collarbone, stroking over Nate's chest. "I want..."

"I know what you want," Nate said, already starting to roll over. Jimmy caught him when he was on his side, holding him in place.

"I don't want it to be bad for you." He kissed Nate's shoulder, his neck.

Nate pushed his hips back, his arse rubbing against Jimmy's already hard cock. "See, told you I knew what you wanted. I always know what you want." Nate reached round, his fingers slick. "I know you don't like waiting." The smile was thick in his voice as he worked himself open. "An eager... I was going to say eager little beaver but eager great big beaver would be more appropriate."

"It shouldn't be like that though." Jimmy licked Nate's shoulder before pressing his mouth to it. He lifted Nate's good leg, pushing it high and forward as he pressed his way in. One, two, three thrusts, and he was already panting hard. "I want you to get something from it."

"I'm not meant to." Nate pushed back. "Not in the assessment."

"But you don't get anything at any time." Jimmy slid his hand round quick, before Nate could do anything about it, and cupped his limp cock.

"I told you," Nate said, gentle and cajoling. "It's okay — more than okay. Don't bother about that."

"But if you'd only relax, baby, it could be so much better." Jimmy thrust in again, doing his best to get it right and time it exactly with his hand.

"I don't need it." Nate eased his hips back, away from Jimmy's hand, onto his dick.

"All right then, I do. I need you to have a good time. All you got to do is relax and let yourself." He squeezed, pushing in gently whilst pulling, equally gentle.

"No, it's okay." Again Nate tried to squirm away. "I don't..."

"I do," Jimmy said firmly as he held a little tighter.

"I can't perform with that kind of pressure. I don't work like that."

"There's no pressure. You just don't give yourself a chance." Jimmy kept up the movement, rolling and squeezing.

"Please." Nate caught hold of Jimmy's wrist, fingers gentle but implication clear. "Not your hand..."

"Then you do it." Jimmy laid a kiss on his ear, another to the column of his neck as he searched for the lube. He squirted out a handful, caught hold of

Nate's hand and smeared it over his palm. Guiding Nate down to his own cock, he kept his hand on top as he made Nate grip and start a slow rhythm. "You can do it, sweetheart. Let yourself go with it. Let yourself feel it. You've loosened up, now lighten up."

"But…"

"Let it go." Jimmy bit his shoulder, upping the pace over Nate's hand. "Feel it. Feel that electricity in your arse, in your dick. Let it roll over you. Give into it." He could feel Nate trying to pull away, but there was nowhere for him to go, no way for him to move. He could also feel him getting hard. "I want this and you want to give it to me." He fucked in again, the angle different as Nate pulled his leg up, his palm working on himself. "Keep going. It's coming." Jimmy wasn't sure who he was talking to. He was pretty sure that if he didn't keep talking, he'd be the one coming first. He caught hold of a mouthful of Nate's hair, pulling it tight, and concentrated on getting his coordination just right.

He could feel Nate's breathing speed up, the exaggerated expansion of his chest, the rippling of the muscles in his belly. He tightened his hand on Nate's, thrusting up and over as Nate heaved against him and…they might just do this. A little faster with cock and hand and Nate mewled. There might have been a hint of a, 'no,' in the sound but he wasn't about to stop, not now, not when they were both so close. So close…the thought of Nate coming while he was buried balls deep in his arse. It was something Jimmy had been thinking about for a while—what Nate would sound like when he came. What it would feel like round his dick.

"Nearly there, nearly there," he whispered, smearing his mouth across Nate's back, lapping at the skin. He pushed in as deep as he could get, pulling Nate's leg out of the way so he could get more, further. Then little thrusts, without pulling out hardly at all. Deeper, deeper, hand fast on Nate's, giving him no space to breathe or think or get away from it. Jimmy could feel his own orgasm pulsing behind his balls—he bit down hard, desperate to stop it. *Not yet, not yet.*

He wanted to feel Nate come on his dick, had been waiting, fantasizing about it. He needed it.

Hang on, hang on... Find that spot that made Nate shudder. Keep his hand ruthlessly moving, keep up the pressure, the rush. Demand that Nate come with dick and hand, milk him of it and... He felt Nate suck in a breath, shallow and fast, then he was coming, warm strings of liquid Jimmy could touch on the upstroke. Feel it in the way Nate's muscles constricted around him, clamping down on his dick, and it was every bit as good as he'd hoped. Wanted. Needed.

He came as hard as he could ever remember doing, his cock throbbing, breath panting. He pushed his face into the back of Nate's neck and let the pleasure roll over him, glorying in it. Grabbing every second of it. "Man, we have to do that again and soon," he said, running his hand up to smear the cum into Nate's belly. Pushing it round in little circles and rubbing it in.

Nate didn't answer.

"You okay?" Dumb question, Jimmy thought. Of course Nate was okay—he'd just had a spectacular orgasm.

"Yeah, sure." Nate moved forward a little, Jimmy's dick twitching inside him. "Could you?"

"Sure." Jimmy repeated the word as he pulled out and rolled onto his back, already reaching for Nate. But Nate was up and off the bed. "Where you going?"

"Bathroom." Nate closed the door behind him before Jimmy could say another word.

It must have been nearly half an hour before he came out again. Half an hour during which Jimmy couldn't swear he hadn't fallen asleep. Nate had taken a shower and was towel drying his hair as he made his way back to the bed. He'd become adept at managing with the heavy plaster cast, even in the shower. Now he steadied himself with a hand on the wall as he moved. He dropped the towel and got back into bed.

In the strange orange light Jimmy thought his face seemed normal. "Are you okay?"

"Yeah." Nate positioned his foot carefully.

"Your leg's not hurting?"

"It aches a bit, I slipped in the bathroom, but I'll live."

"You say that a lot, 'I'll live'."

"Anything wrong with it?"

"No." Jimmy turned onto his side, watching Nate. "But it's not, 'I'm awesome'."

"I don't think I do awesome."

"Not even after an awesome orgasm?" Jimmy propped himself up with a hand under his head. "Nothing else hurting?"

"I'm..." Nate licked over his lips, tongue pressing hard as he went. "I've thought about it and I'm all right. Can we leave it at that?"

"Was the orgasm 'all right'?"

"It was." A smile started on Nate's lips. "A bit more than all right."

"Then we'll leave it at that."

Jimmy thought he was going to try for more than 'all right' the following night.

Nate didn't try to stop him and, at one point, actually let Jimmy jack him. Jimmy figured that meant he'd beaten 'all right', and had actually done really well.

* * * *

The assessment was at two o'clock, and Jimmy felt he'd been waiting years for it to come round. Years of endless pacing and sweating and... This could be his last day in prison. All he had to do was get through the formality of the assessment. Let it go smooth and sweet then he'd be out of here and back to work—after an epic lecture from his mother. But he could take that, all of it, for the thought of decent food, clothes and his freedom. He'd have his driver and the makeup girls and his life back.

All he had to do was get through the assessment—preferably without sweating like a pig. He pulled his shirt out, flapping it to try to get some air on his skin. "I need a shower, another one," he said, already dragging at his clothes.

Nate nodded from his position sitting by the window, staring out, up at the sky. Even that was unnerving Jimmy. Nate was usually moving about doing things. Jimmy wasn't sure what he did, but Nate didn't usually just sit, like now. Maybe he was fed up waiting as well.

A cool shower helped. It would have been even better if Nate had got in with him but that wasn't going to happen. Jimmy had insisted they try it once but it was ridiculous, and pointless. Nate couldn't have sex in the shower, not with his foot wrapped in plastic balanced on the side of the bath. In the end he'd fallen on his fine arse, and Jimmy had laughed out loud until he'd seen the scrapes up Nate's back from the taps. That had to hurt.

A cool shower on his own it would have to be. He came out of the bathroom just in his uniform trousers, rubbing at his hair with a towel. Nate was still sitting in the same place.

"Hey, I got an idea. You could always blow me," Jimmy said, smiling at the thought. They hadn't tried that before because, Jimmy had to admit, he'd gotten a bit obsessed with fucking. But that was easily remedied.

"You think that's a good idea?" Nate's face was strangely blank.

"I think it's a fucking excellent idea." Jimmy rubbed his hands together. "Don't worry, I'll give you a hand job after."

"I was just thinking it might...put extra pressure on you, seeing as you have to fuck me for the assessment in about half an hour. I know how much you like fucking me, but doing it in front of a roomful of people can't be the easiest thing."

"You might be right." Jimmy huffed. "I mean, I'm good, but I might not be that good. Half an hour and the pressure? Not many guys could do that." He reached for a T-shirt to put on.

"You might want to wear a shirt," Nate said softly. "You don't have to get naked, only I do. A shirt will hide more of you than a T-shirt," he explained.

"Thanks." Jimmy dropped the T-shirt and found a prison issue shirt, the biggest one he had. "This is hard on you, isn't it?"

"I'll live." Nate got up and, using his crutch, he made his way toward the bathroom, picking up the bottle of lube as he went. "Is it okay with you if I get myself ready?"

"Shit, yes, of course. Do whatever you have to, to make it easier."

"I talked to the others." Nate stopped, leaning on the crutch. "The other slaves. They said don't do too much, it has to look hard, like you're just taking what's yours."

"I don't want to hurt you."

"I know, and I'm grateful for that. I've seen the ones who have been hurt. Just...let's do this right. Let's make it look real."

* * * *

Make it seem like he was taking what was his.

Jimmy thought about that as he stood watching Nate take his clothes off as soon as they got in the judge's room. Watched him keep his eyes lowered as he did it, noticed everyone else's eyes keen on Nate as the judge went through Jimmy's file. Thought about Nate being his, how no one else should have the right to see him naked. How no one would once they got out. Nate was his, was going to stay that way.

His, all his.

"Well, get on with it." The judge waved an imperious hand at Jimmy. "I haven't got all day."

Nate braced himself against a desk, spreading his feet, shoulders rounding. Jimmy moved up behind him, running a hand down from his shoulder to hold his hip. The other hand undid his zip and pulled his cock out. He hadn't had any trouble getting hard, none at all.

Nate was his and those bastards around the room had no right to see him naked. No right at all.

He lined himself up and could feel all eyes on Nate, wanting to see him get taken.

He reached up, grabbing hold of the back of Nate's neck and forcing his head down as he pushed in. No one had the right to see Nate's face as he got fucked. No one. No one got to see the shudder as Jimmy thrust in hard. He was used to more lube, a hell of a lot more, but this was... His cheeks burned at the thought that he might just like it—taking Nate like this.

But that wasn't him. It wasn't. He was good and decent. He treated Nate right. Would always treat Nate right.

He thrust again and again. Thrusting deep as something close to shame coiled in his gut at the idea that he liked this. Liked taking too much.

Nate wasn't pushing back, wasn't helping, like he normally did. He wasn't pulling away either—that would have been senseless. There was nowhere for him to go. The authorities would simply tie him down if he tried anything. Nate wasn't going to run, never was. Jimmy knew that, even if the rest of the room didn't. But this was Nate playing along, making out that there wasn't already a connection between them—that Jimmy didn't know how to make him come, didn't care if he did.

This was Nate being taken, and it was a heady pleasure.

Too many faces watching them. Watching Nate's cock swing limp, watching him rock with each of Jimmy's thrusts. Watching him take it. Jimmy gripped harder with his hand, holding Nate's head down, keeping as much as he could for himself. He fucked again and again, forgetting rhythm or technique or what anyone liked. He just wanted it over, done, so he could make Nate get dressed, cover him from anyone's eyes but his own.

No one should get near Nate but him. No one. Nate was his — he had the brands on his hand and hip to prove it. Nate belonged to Jimmy. That thought was what it took to push Jimmy over the edge. Making him buck and curse as he bent over Nate, covering him and grabbing him tight enough to his chest to leave marks.

Mine.

He held them there, Nate's hands braced wide, supporting them both, breathing hard into Nate's neck.

"Finished?" The judge raised an eyebrow but wasn't interested in an answer. "Good, then we can get on."

Jimmy pulled out, not as gently as he intended, and steadied Nate as he rocked on his good leg. "Get dressed," he whispered, close to Nate's ear. "Soon as you can."

Nate tugged Jimmy's shirt tails down, covering his cock. Jimmy would be thankful for that, when he thought about it.

"Right." The judge checked his papers. "Everything seems to be in order. You've..." He glanced at Nate who was struggling with his clothes. "Subdued your slave. You've been bonded in the proper fashion to give you a lifelong reminder of your horrendous crimes."

"Horrendous crimes?" Jimmy couldn't help the disbelief showing in his voice as he did up his zipper, eyes still on Nate.

"You don't think they were horrendous?"

"I don't think anything at all. I can't remember what I said."

Nate was having trouble balancing on his good foot.

"So you have no remorse? You don't think your punishment was justified?"

Nate had gone very still and he was staring hard at Jimmy, an expression on his face Jimmy couldn't identify.

"I'm sure my punishment is just hunky-dory, if you say it is." Jimmy shrugged, offhand, eyes and attention on Nate. "It was a fantastic party. I was drunk off my head."

"Hunky-dory?"

"Sure. Those industry parties are something else, I'll try and get you an invite to one. I can't help getting a bit silly — you must be able to see that."

There was a pulse beating in Nate's forehead, his lips were pressed hard together, and if he stared any harder at Jimmy, it looked like his eyes would pop out of his head.

"You think you were 'a bit silly', and you have no remorse," the judge said the words slowly. "I think you need a little longer in here to consider your actions. Reassessment in a week."

"What?" Jimmy pulled his gaze from Nate and stared at the judge. "Whoa, no. You can't do that."

"I most certainly can." The judge was already writing something down.

"No, no, no, I can't stay here another week. I'm an actor, I'm on a show. They need me. We're filming now. I can't miss any more time, I'm important." Vaguely, Jimmy registered Nate's sharp intake of breath. It might have been only vaguely, his mind was fogged with the possibility of staying in prison for another week, but he heard it, and it was enough to make him shut his mouth.

"You're important."

"I...yeah." Again there was a sound from Nate, small, quiet but very sharp. "Look, I know I did wrong, but I mean really...it's half my security guy's fault. It's his job to pull me out before I get stupid."

"It's not even your fault?" The judge put his pen down, tapping his fingers on the desktop. "You really do need to think about what you have done and how lenient The State has been toward you." He closed the folder in front of him with a snap. "Reassessment in another month."

"No," Jimmy cried. "You can't."

"Would you like to make it two months, Mr. Stephens?"

"But that's not fai—" Jimmy stopped as his arm was grabbed. Nate had stumbled, holding on to stop himself falling over his bad foot. His apology was instant, vociferous and effusive. Slaves weren't supposed to touch their owners unless told to do so. But the trip had seemed real, nasty. The potential fall serious. "Get up," he said, pushing Nate back onto his feet.

Nate hung onto him a little longer than was wise, his eyes glued to Jimmy's. Jimmy stared back.

"Are we staying at one month or do you want to go for two?" The judge said, dragging Jimmy's attention back.

"One, please. One. Can't we make it less than—"

But the judge was already leaving and they were being led back down to their cell.

Chapter Three

"That is so not fucking fair," Jimmy said, fist thumping the wall after they'd been put unceremoniously back in their cell. He'd hardly registered the stares of the other slaves, the laughter of the owners. The soft touches to Nate's shoulder and the whispered, 'good luck', as the door was locked behind them.

"Another fucking month, stuck in here with nothing to do." He turned to face Nate, nostrils flaring, shoulders back ready for a fight. "I have things to do, a show to make. He can't treat me like that, the fucking asshole."

Nate's face stayed closed down tight and he didn't say a word as he shuffled across the room.

"Where are you going?" Jimmy demanded.

"Bathroom, I need to…"

"You're not going anywhere, sit down before you fucking fall over again." Jimmy swung around, grabbing a handful of clothes and throwing them at the window. "I was so fucking close to getting out of this shit hole. Doesn't he realize? I have a life. Things to do, people to see, a career. I don't care about fucking state rules. I was drunk, it doesn't count."

Nate sat carefully on the edge of the bed and didn't look at Jimmy.

The ranting went on and on as Jimmy spewed out enough vitriol to fill a football stadium. His anger rolled around the room, consuming the air and bouncing off the surfaces as he stormed about, his size making everything feel that much worse.

Slowly, inch by inch, it began to ease until he sunk onto a chair with a huge sigh and a hand on his face.

"Well, aren't you going to say anything?" he asked at last, voice rough from all the shouting.

"You're upset. It's not fair. I get it," Nate said quietly, hardly lifting his head. "You shouldn't be in here."

"That it? You got anything else?"

Nate glanced up at last. "Can I go to the bathroom now?"

"That's all you can think about after all I've... What's the matter with you?"

"Nothing. Can I?"

Jimmy waved a hand through the air, and Nate pulled himself to his feet, moving slowly. "Are you all right?"

"I'll live." Nate made it to the bathroom.

"Nat," Jimmy's voice was more insistent. "Did I hurt you?"

Nate stopped, turning back awkwardly. "Not enough lube. My fault. But I'll be fine. Just give me a minute."

Nate was a lot longer than a minute, long enough for Jimmy to stop being angry and calm down completely. He was flopped out over the bed, legs spread wide, mumbling to himself, when Nate came out. "Better?" he asked.

"Yeah." Nate managed a small smile. "I'm fine."

"Come here." Jimmy beckoned him over and Nate climbed onto the bed, stretching out on his back in the space Jimmy had left. "Sorry about being so pissed. It's not your fault. It's just..." He sighed again. "I wanted out so badly and now I'm stuck here. It's..."

"Not fair?" Nate offered.

"Oh, fuck it." Jimmy rubbed a hand over his face. "I know I'm feeling fucking sorry for myself, but it isn't fair, getting punished for something I don't even remember doing."

"You have to be..." Nate hesitated for a moment, until Jimmy turned to look at him quizzically. "What I mean is that, if you want to get out, you have to accept it. Play their game. Follow their rules. You can't fight it, not while you're in here. Just go with it, until they let you out."

Jimmy sighed, long and loud. "You're right. I know you are. It's just that I'm not used to being pushed around and bullied. I live a good life — some would say a privileged one — and I'm protected from the real world." He reached out, pulling Nate to him. "My mum always called me her golden boy and, I guess, that's how I've always been treated by her and most other people. I suppose I thought that's how it would always be then this happened. It's hit me hard."

"I know it has. It's been a hell of change for you."

"I'm doing my best though, trying to make the best of it. Trying to stay a decent guy and that's not easy in here."

"I can see it — see you trying."

Jimmy rubbed over Nate's chest, hand possessive. "I'm sorry I hurt you. That's never been my intention."

"I said, I'm fine. Anyway, we had to make it look real," Nate said carefully.

"Shouldn't have hurt you though. This is tough on you as well. You're stuck in here with me. You don't get out until I take you."

"It's okay."

"How can you say that?" He stared at Nate, eyebrows arched. "Having to stay here is fucking awful."

"It doesn't matter much, not to me. At least here I get a lot of things done for me while my leg heals up."

"I suppose so. But I'll get us out next month." He patted Nate, nodding to himself. "I'll treat it as an acting job, being the contrite prisoner who wants to thank his compassionate State for helping him to see the error of his ways."

"You do that," Nate said, settling back.

* * * *

Jimmy had never really been laughed at before—his sheer size put most people off. But the next day he got a full blast of it from the other owners and the prison officers. He knew they were trying to rile him, trying to provoke more anger so he'd end up with an even longer sentence, but he wasn't going to fall for it. All morning it went on, snide and nasty. He couldn't retreat back into their cell—leaving association early would just show weakness. He wasn't ready to do that.

He was damned thankful for the after lunch lock-in. Just him and Nate and relative quiet.

When the door was unlocked again in the late afternoon, Jimmy felt wired and ready to snap.

"Let's stay here," Nate suggested softly. "Too much testosterone out there. It's peaceful inside these walls."

"And do what? I gave all our books back, cleared out the magazines I'd bought. There was no point keeping them. We were meant to be getting out." Jimmy paced around the small room, tension radiating from every pore, increasing with every slammed door and shout.

"What you doing, princess?" One of the owners shouted through their open doorway. "Are you coming out to play or are you gonna take your anger out on your whore's arse?"

"Fuckers." Jimmy hit the wall hard, his hand balled into a fist, the veins and tendons in his neck standing out. There was a big pockmark left in the plaster. "You're a slave, not a whore. How fucking dare they talk about you? You're mine. I'll tell them."

"Jimmy." Again Nate's tone was low, his hand even more gentle where he stroked Jimmy's arm. "Stay, just you and me."

Jimmy glared at him, his eyes angry.

"Close the door. No one can see in, and it'll just be us."

Jimmy stopped, lip caught between his teeth as he considered. "But you can't do anything, not yet. I hurt you yesterday."

"I keep telling you I'm fine."

"I'm not hurting you again. I refuse to be that guy."

"It's okay, I—" But Nate was interrupted by more filthy shouts from outside. Jimmy felt his face tighten once more. "Hey, come on," Nate cajoled. "It doesn't matter what they call me. In here it's just us. Shut the door and…"

"And what?"

"I'm not hurting now. We can do whatever we want."

Jimmy stared at Nate, assessing. Then he reached back and slammed the door shut hard. "You can blow me. That won't hurt you."

"No, it's okay, I can take anything you've got to give me. Honest. You won't hurt me."

"I'll give you a hand job after and, hell, that's a win, win situation for both of us. We haven't done it before and it's about time we did. I mean, man, you have a mouth made for it."

Nate took a step back, his lips setting in a thin line, his eyes narrowing. "We can fuck, I... I like you fucking me. It's good."

"I know it is, baby, and I know how much you like it." Jimmy undid his zip, pushing the material down over his arse. "This will be good too though. You wait and see. Don't know why we've waited so long. Come on." Jimmy grinned. "Get your clothes off. I want to watch you do this naked."

Nate's face changed, a blank, controlled look coming over it. He didn't say a word but he pulled his T-shirt over his head and sat on the edge of the bed to wriggle the rest of his clothes over his injured leg.

"You want to be on the bed or do you want to kneel on the floor between my legs? You'd get real close that way." Jimmy was warming to that idea with every second he thought about it.

"I can't kneel," Nate said. "I can't balance and stop my leg from hurting."

"Fuck that cast," Jimmy moaned, disappointed. "How much longer have you got to have it on?"

"They said about twelve weeks, if it heals right."

"Tell you something. I'm going to fuck you so sweet in the shower when it's gone, that you're going to be wishing it had been a hell of a lot sooner. You remember that." Jimmy sat on the bed, pushing himself up so his back was against the headboard, his legs stretched out in front of him.

"I will." Nate turned round, rolling across the bed until he was face-to-groin with Jimmy.

"I want this," Jimmy said, stroking his hand through Nate's hair, his mouth salivating at the images it provoked. "I get to see all that amazing flesh as you do incredible things to me and—what the hell?" He touched his thumb to the dark bruises round the back of Nate's neck. "Who the fuck did this to you?"

"It's nothing," Nate started to say, but Jimmy wasn't listening.

"You fucking tell me. I'm going to kill the bastard." He caught hold of Nate's hair, holding him tight. "Tell me who bruised you like that."

"You did," Nate said quietly.

"What? No, I wouldn't. I'm not... When?" He let go of Nate.

"At the assessment. When you were fucking me."

"Shit. I didn't mean to, baby." He pulled Nate to him, stroking his hair, his face, bending Nate's head forward so he could kiss the back of his neck. Finger shaped bruises. His fingers. The bruises he'd made at the assessment. He kissed each and every one, softly and gently as he knew how. "I'm sorry. I'm so sorry. It's just they were all looking at you, and I hated it. You're not for them to see. You're mine. Mine."

"It okay," Nate said as Jimmy tried to kiss him. "It's only a few bruises. It doesn't matter."

"I really didn't mean to."

"Don't worry. I'll live. You didn't hurt me."

"But I did. I hurt your neck and your arse, when I said I wouldn't." Jimmy patted and petted, using his hands and his mouth. "It's just as well I saw the marks. To think I could have hurt you again, now. I can't do that."

"So you still want me to blow you?" Nate said carefully.

"Yeah, of course. This will be easier for you. I should have thought of it before." He cupped Nate's face as he kissed him deeply and thoroughly. "This is going to be so good. I'm going to make it worth your while, after, because I just know this is going to be amazing."

Only it wasn't.

At first Nate only took a tiny bit of him in, working just on the tip, until Jimmy encouraged him with a hand on the back of his head. Then he gagged, really gagged, like some kind of wicked parody of a porn film. Jimmy sighed hard, staying quiet while Nate caught his breath. "Try again," he encouraged.

"I'm no good at this, never have been." Nate licked over his lips, trying to wet them.

"You can learn," Jimmy said gently.

Nate took a deep breath and did as he was told, really going for it. But he sucked too hard, went too rough, bobbed his head too fast. "Slow down. It's not a race," Jimmy said. "Okay, so you're not very good at it, which really is a shame. But I can teach you how I like it."

Nate was willing to learn. Jimmy would give him that. He almost seemed downright eager to go as fast as possible but he had no technique, no finesse. When Jimmy was almost, almost, almost there, Nate caught him with his teeth for what felt like the ninety-ninth time. Jimmy groaned in frustration and Nate made a similar noise as he rubbed at his jaw.

But Jimmy really wanted to do this. He wanted to finish it, wanted to come on Nate's pretty face. See his spunk dripping from those long eyelashes.

Only that didn't work either. Right at the crucial moment, just as Jimmy was about to pull out, Nate gave a cock-breaking suck and Jimmy's body gave up and he came. Nate pulled off as soon as Jimmy was done, trying to hide his face as he forced himself to swallow. But he wasn't quick enough and Jimmy saw his grimace and the shudder in his shoulders.

No point getting worked up about it though.

He pulled Nate with a hand to his biceps, dragging him in close. "Well." He tried to laugh it off. "That didn't go quite as I figured. Still, a promise is a promise and you sure as hell tried." He reached down between them and gave Nate's limp cock a squeeze.

Nate's head thumped back against the bed. "Jimmy, please. I know I'm not allowed to ask but do me a big favor—just this once, forget it."

"That exhausted?" Jimmy laughed, rubbing a possessive hand over Nate's chest. "Okay, I'll leave you be. We'll try it again though. You're smart. You'll soon learn, but I owe you one, baby. Next time I fuck you, I'm going to make sure you come sweet and hard."

Nate closed his eyes.

* * * *

Things calmed down from then on. Jimmy learned to ignore the taunting and accepted that there was no option—he had to serve the extra month. He had no idea what was happening on the outside, especially with work. But he figured his ever forceful mother would make sure he wasn't sacked. For once he really appreciated the 'no visitors' rule.

Other owners went home with their slaves—new ones came in to the gay, bonded section of the prison. Some of the slaves looked terrified, and Jimmy noticed Nate would sit with them, talking quietly. A few of the owners seemed pretty scared as well but Jimmy figured they'd soon learn there were benefits to being forced to bond with a slave. He was starting to realize just how lucky he'd been. Okay, so Nate had a cast that was really starting to fucking annoy everyone including Nate, but he was gorgeous, easy to get along with and smarter than Jimmy had first thought.

Yeah, he could have done a lot worse. A hell of a lot worse. Nate made... Nate made his life go smoothly, and his cock throb with want. He wanted him right after he'd just had him. Wanted him all the time, any time, any way he could get him, in any position the damned cast allowed. He hadn't felt that way about someone he'd fucked in... He'd never felt that way about anyone.

He also wanted to cuddle and stroke and pet after sex—all things he would have run screaming from before. He had to admit it—he liked fucking Nate, liked looking at him, liked cuddling with him, liked talking to him.

Liked everyone else knowing he belonged to Jimmy.

Jimmy couldn't seem to get enough of him.

One morning Nate came out of the bathroom with just a towel wrapped around his waist. He pulled it off to rub at his wet hair. "Hey," Jimmy called from the bed. "They left the pittance they laughingly call breakfast while you were in the shower."

Nate picked up half a slice of toast, taking a bite as he went to find clean underwear.

"I've already eaten," Jimmy said, his voice low. "Don't bother getting dressed, sweetheart. After you've finished, I'm going to take you back to bed, fuck you deep and slow, make you come the same way. Make your day start good."

Nate didn't even glance up. Instead he made his way back to the table, sat down and ate his breakfast in silence.

Jimmy also came to another conclusion—one that truly warranted the expression 'took his breath away'. He'd come to expect Nate to take care of all the things involved in their time in prison. The routine of daily life, their dealings with other people, what was happening around them... Jimmy knew he'd never been an observant guy, that he'd always been a bit self-oriented, and he missed a lot of what was going on. Nate took care of all those things now. He steered a clear path for them, so Jimmy didn't have to be bothered by anything he wasn't interested in.

All of that made the new prison officer's arrival even harder to take. Nelson was a relatively small man, with dark floppy hair and beady eyes that always seemed to be watching Nate. At first Nate insisted it wasn't personal, that the staring, the lewd comments, the touching, wasn't just aimed at him. Nelson acted that way with half the slaves. But then, after a few days and endless incidents, he stopped protesting, and Jimmy knew Nate agreed that it most certainly was personal.

Jimmy became very interested in Nelson with his wandering hands that always found their way to Nate's arse, his back, his chest. Interested in the way that Nelson was forever trying to catch Nate on his own, preferably in a dark corner, a secluded corridor. There were other owners who were only too happy to help that happen. Owners who didn't like the fact that Jimmy hadn't marked his slave, hadn't cowed him to the point that he never raised his eyes, let alone his voice.

Owners who told Jimmy that Nate was too pretty for his own good. That he needed to understand what being pretty meant, that he was only good for one thing. Owners who made it clear, in no uncertain terms, that Nate should be shared around.

Jimmy wasn't having that, wasn't having anything like it. Nate was his—his and his alone. He was going to keep what was his, no matter what it took.

Slowly Jimmy noticed that during the outdoor exercise periods, Nate had started to stay close by him, within a touch. Nate was just as aware of the other owners' interest in him and turned to Jimmy for the only protection he could get. At those times, Jimmy made sure he spent longer with his hand possessively on the small of Nate's back or the base of his neck.

Jimmy chose to ignore how good that made him feel. But he did appreciate both the benefits of his size, the effect it could have on other people and the way Nate moved nearer to him.

In the association area late one afternoon, Jimmy was playing checkers with a heavy set guy, while Nate sat, a little way off, talking to another slave. Nate waved to indicate he was going to the communal bathroom and Jimmy watched absently, checking no one was following, as Nate made his way slowly.

No one had needed to follow because, as Jimmy found out later, Nelson was already waiting for Nate when he came out.

It wasn't any single thing that Jimmy could put his finger on that made him aware that something was wrong, more a combination. Nate had taken too long, the other owners were talking too loudly, blocking his view, were too interested in the game he was playing. When he stood up, already scanning for Nate, they moaned and jeered, wanting him to go on playing, taunting him for not doing so.

When he pushed away from the table, knocking the counters from the board and heading down the long room, his destination obvious, the taunts changed. Now they accused him of being led around by his dick, of not putting his slave in his place and keeping him there. Of forgetting who was slave and who was the owner.

But Jimmy hadn't forgotten anything. He couldn't stop the screams of, 'mine, mine, mine,' in his head — wasn't sure he wanted to. All he knew was that he had to find Nate — get to him, before anyone else put their hands on him. He pushed past men, knocking them out of his way, until he rounded the corner.

There was Nate, standing stock still, arms hanging at his sides, his crutches against the wall, staring straight ahead as Nelson licked across his cheek and pushed his hand down the back of Nate's trousers.

"Get your filthy—" Jimmy started to say, but Nate twisted round to stare at him.

"You got something to say to me, Stephens?" Nelson spat the words in Jimmy's direction, hand deliberately moving lower.

"No, Sir," Jimmy forced himself to add the last word. "Just come to look for my missing slave. Nate, get over here." The change in tone was obvious — the last sentence was most definitely an order.

Nate stooped down so Nelson's hand slipped out, then he moved fast to stand next to Jimmy.

"Where the fuck do you think you're going?" Nelson demanded.

Jimmy rested his hand on the back on Nate's neck and pulled him closer. "Right where he should be," Jimmy said, turning to Nate. "I told you not to leave — that I had jobs I need you to do. When I tell you to stay, you fucking stay." Jimmy did his hardest, toughest, owner impression. He was an actor after all.

Nate ducked his head and leaned in as Jimmy tightened his grip.

"Thank you," Jimmy said to Nelson. "Thanks for finding my wandering slave for me. I appreciate that. Don't worry. He won't bother you again. I won't let him out of my sight in the future. Not ever." With that he turned Nate, grabbed the crutches, and got them back to their cell as fast as he could, ignoring all the catcalls from the other men. He pushed Nate inside and slammed the door behind them, standing with his back against it. "Fuck, that was close."

Nate stood a few feet away, trying to catch his breath.

"Did he...?" Jimmy knew what he was asking but didn't know how to say it. "What did he do?"

"No." Nate knew as well. "He didn't get the chance, but he would have." He turned slowly, until he could look up at Jimmy. "Thank you," he said formally, laying the words out with precision. "Maybe I should be, but I wasn't ready for that and...thank you. I appreciate it."

"You don't need to say thank you to me. It's my job." He huffed out a long breath, resting back as he did so. "We were set up. Nelson is after you, but the other owners worked together to make it happen.

"I know." Nate sat on the edge of the bed. "I knew there was some...bad feeling toward us but..." He stopped, staring up at Jimmy again.

"You didn't think they hated us quite so much?"

"Something like that."

Jimmy took another deep breath then pushed himself away from the door, sitting down next to Nate. "Half of them want a crack at you and, if they can't get it, they want to see me hurt you and put you in your place."

"They want me to have bruises?"

"The one with the ponytail? He told me you'd be real pretty with bruises, especially around your throat."

"That's..."

"Sick? Yeah, I think so too." Jimmy sighed, rubbing at his face absently, then he shook himself. "They want you to look, act like, some of the other slaves, all scared shitless and broken. Want to see me dominating you. But they don't get that we're not like that. We're... I don't know." He shrugged again. "I like to think that we're working together to get through this, to make it as easy as possible. So what does that make us? Partners?"

Nate studied him for a long, long moment, face curiously blank. Then he nodded, just once. "Yeah, partners."

Jimmy smiled, warm and affectionate as he reached over, resting his hand on the back of Nate's neck again. "This could have all been so much worse. We could both have been stuck with someone awful. I don't just mean some fat, ugly bastard, although I don't think either of us would have liked that much. I mean you could have got someone who hurt you, and I could have got some whiney, frightened wreck. We're lucky that didn't happen, but even luckier that we get on. Think about it. We've been stuck in here together for weeks already and we haven't got on each other's nerves, haven't killed each other. That's pretty good going."

"Yeah," Nate agreed, and Jimmy could feel him relax, hear the softening of his voice.

"It's a miracle." Jimmy fell backwards onto the bed, pulling Nate with him. They lay there for a while, looking up at nothing, knees bent, feet still on the floor. "I think we're friends," he went on suddenly. "That's what they don't like, the fact that we can have something better than pain and fear."

"I think…"

"Go on. Say it," Jimmy urged. "If we're friends, you should."

Nate hesitated, briefly glancing at Jimmy. "You…you're different, confusing but different from other owners. I think some of them like pain and fear, at least for their slaves."

"I think so too, but I'm not like that. You know that by now, don't you?" He waited for an answer and Nate obliged by nodding. "I don't want to hurt you. I never want to do that. Maybe, at the start, because we were stuck with each other, I was just making the best of things, but it's different now. I like you—you're a nice guy. I think we would have been friends if we'd met on the outside."

"What do we do now?" Nate asked. "Even if we get out at the next assessment, we've still got a lot of time to serve in here with the others and the guards."

Jimmy sighed again. "We've got no choice, even if we're friends, we have to act more like owner and slave when anyone else is around. You have to drop your eyes and run around after me, and I've got to be seen as domineering."

"You want to give me some bruises?"

"No," Jimmy said, suddenly vehement. "I'm not giving you bruises for their benefit or any other reason. I... Oh fuck it." He laughed, just as sudden, rubbing at Nate's skin. "Let's just not go out. Let's stay in this cell until the assessment. I think you got lucky because, not only don't I beat you, but I also have brilliant ideas. You have to admit that was a brilliant idea."

"That it was." Nate nodded.

* * * *

Jimmy thought his plan worked out pretty well. They stayed in the cell as much as possible — playing cards, reading and talking long into the night. Although Jimmy had to admit, he did most of the talking, but Nate was a damned fine listener. He was interested, involved and remembered what Jimmy had said from weeks before, when Jimmy himself had long since forgotten.

It was so unusual for Nate to initiate a new line of conversation that when he did, early one afternoon as they'd just finished lunch, Jimmy was more than a little surprised. He'd been talking about the party that had started this nightmare. The one at which his carefree life had come crashing down.

"Can I ask you something?" Nate said, head tipped to one side, an uncertain look on his face.

"Sure. Friends, remember."

"Did you really just say a bunch of stuff about The State and hit some kid or was there more to it?"

"No, that's pretty much it. Why?"

Nate licked at his lip, paused, then spoke slowly, as though he were picking his words with care, "It's just your punishment doesn't seem to fit the crime. You said some things you shouldn't have, but you can't even remember what they were and everyone agrees you were drunk. I'd expect you to get prison, but a slave and bonding as well? It seems a bit much."

"There was the kid I hit." Jimmy shrugged.

"But you said you didn't hit him hard, didn't do much damage?"

"Yeah, but…" Jimmy swung back on the hind legs of his chair.

"Sorry." Nate ducked his head. "I know I shouldn't have asked."

"No, it's okay. You can know." Jimmy dropped the chair back on all four legs with a bang, staring straight at Nate. "I scared the kid more than anything else, scared everyone else as well. I did the whole giant looming over him thing and got right up in his face. I'm a big guy. I can do intimidating real well and" — he snorted, shaking his head — "I can remember some of the things I said to him. I called him a filthy faggot, as well as some other choice phrases about his sexual practices."

"But you're…"

"Gay? Yeah, only not many people know that. It's not something you spread around when you're an actor starting out."

"I never thought of it like that. But why call him…?" Nate stopped again, his bottom lip caught between his teeth. "Sorry. Not my business, I know."

"Why'd I call him a faggot? I have no idea, apart from the amazing number of tequila shots I'd done. I could have just as easily called him on his ginger hair or spots."

"Ginger hair and spots? Wow."

"Really wow, he had thick glasses as well." Jimmy smiled, leaning back in his chair and relaxing again. "But idiot me had to go for the gay thing."

"It explains why you got given a male slave. I guess to teach you a lesson. But bonding as well? That's still pretty harsh."

"The kid's mother was a State official," Jimmy said simply.

"Oh you—" Nate stopped himself before he said another word.

"Fool? Idiot? Fucking moron?" Jimmy laughed. "Yeah, I've called myself all those and more. Now the whole world gets to know I'm bonded with a male slave. It's kind of a poetic punishment really."

"It does explain things," Nate said cautiously.

"It could have been worse." Jimmy's smile softened and warmed as he glanced over. "Could have been a lot worse."

"Yeah." Nate dropped his eyes. "It could have."

* * * *

Later that week Jimmy suggested Nate blow him again, assuring him that this time it would be better as Nate knew what he liked, how he wanted it. He was wrong again. It was just as bad. Nate couldn't seem to get the knack, no matter how much Jimmy explained. They got there in the end but Jimmy figured Nate couldn't have gotten much more out of it than he had. Such a shame—all the promise of Nate's mouth wasted. Jimmy decided he wouldn't bother trying again until they got out.

With some alcohol inside them both, he was sure things would be better.

They fucked instead—long slow, toe curling sessions that made him want to start again as soon as it was over. He noticed that Nate was enjoying it more as well, his back arching and his cries of pleasure harder to bite back as he spurted into Jimmy's hand.

Jimmy also took the time to learn what Nate liked, what he needed. The guy never said anything but Jimmy could tell from the way Nate hitched himself over to one side, pushed up or down. Yeah, he learnt where Nate liked it, how hard Nate wanted it. How to make his body sing.

There were worse ways to spend a few weeks.

When they did have to mix, Jimmy noticed that the other slaves would congregate around Nate, trying to create a buffer. It wouldn't stop anyone with power who wanted to get at him, but it did create a disturbance, and that gave Jimmy time and a chance to intervene.

Jimmy also did his damnedest to act the menacing owner, using his height and muscles to full advantage on more than one occasion. He'd loomed over one of the other owners, face full of fury, streaming obscenities, and told him what he'd do to him if he ever laid a hand on Nate again. After, his heart had been thumping hard against his ribs as Nate had calmed him back in their cell.

"Thank you. Again," Nate said, as he straddled Jimmy and lowered himself onto Jimmy's cock. "I know you said it's your job, but I need to say it."

Jimmy ran his hands up Nate's thighs and watched as his face closed up until it showed nothing. He figured that position always hurt Nate's leg. "Hell, that's what friends are for," he said as he thrust up.

* * * *

Days dragged on, one blurring into the next with the relentlessness of time, each one seemingly going slower, lasting longer than the one before. The boredom got to Jimmy and he couldn't stop himself taking it out on Nate, moaning at him as he sat, staring out of the window at nothing.

Another week and they'd have their second assessment. Another long, mind-numbing seven days of wasted time.

Jimmy wasn't going to fuck it up—not this time.

One evening they sat at the small table finishing up dinner. Jimmy had eaten all his and was just thinking about stealing the rest of Nate's as he obviously didn't want it. Nate had spent the last five minutes pushing the mashed potato around his plate and sculpting it into odd shapes with his fork. But cold, congealed mashed potato wasn't something Jimmy was desperate for.

He looked at Nate's hand, watching as he made what appeared to be a volcano. He had nice hands, elegant, with tapered fingers and well-shaped nails. But they were surprisingly rough on the underside, as though he'd had to work physically hard over a long period of time. He wondered idly what Nate had been doing before but then his attention was caught by the dark letters of his name on the back. It had healed well, all the redness gone to leave just the outline of the letters, stark and clear.

Jimmy was suddenly pleased that it was so easy to read, that it was his writing, not just printed. It made it more personal.

Everyone would know Nate was his, his and his alone.

"You only have my name on you," he said, breaking the silence.

"'Course I do, you're my owner." Nate shrugged.

"But just one name."

"Better than it being a corporation with a huge long title. It would go half way up my arm or right round my hip."

"Well, yeah, I guess so." Jimmy hadn't thought about that. "But I meant you only have one. Some slaves have a load more, the names of previous owners crossed out. Why don't you?"

Nate regarded him for a long moment, as though he were thinking, maybe deciding on something. "Because I don't have a previous owner."

"You weren't a slave before now? I'm your first? How did you suddenly become a slave at your age?"

Nate's gaze flicked up to Jimmy's face, assessing. "You're my first and only," he said slow and deliberate, voice dark, a wicked grin curling his lips. "My first owner, the first to take me to bed, to mark me, to make me his. Do you like that idea?"

Jimmy didn't have to think about it—he liked that idea a lot, a hell of a lot. The flare of it burned in his belly and on his face. "Yeah." He couldn't stop the quaver in his voice. "I like that."

"Thought you would." Nate's grin grew, the corners of his eyes crinkling.

"Wish I was the first to fuck you though." Jimmy couldn't help admitting it.

Nate pushed the plate away, laying his hand flat on the table and rubbing over Jimmy's name with the tip of his index finger. "Bit late for that, I'm not exactly eighteen anymore. But..." He glanced over, eyes dark. "You are the first to make me come so hard when you do it."

"Honestly?" Jimmy knew he was staring but the answer mattered so much.

"You want honest? I'll give you honest," Nate said. "You're the first to make me do anything other than grit my teeth and get through it when I'm fucked."

"But you..." Jimmy thought about Nate's spunk on his hand, the way his back arched, his hips rocked back into Jimmy. His bitten off moans and curses. "When we...you..."

"When we fuck, I do a lot more than get through it."

* * * *

Three days later and they were back in the assessment room. Jimmy hadn't packed up his things like last time. He didn't want to tempt fate. But he had been true to his word and was treating it as an acting job. He psyched himself up, creating a character of a model, contrite prisoner, determined to be in that character, before they went in and to stay that way. He stood in front of the judge trying to appear like someone who'd learned their lesson, and offered his apologies in his most sincere voice as Nate got undressed.

He hoped Nate had prepared himself just as thoroughly.

"Ah, Mr. Stephens, back here again I see," the judge said, flicking through Jimmy's file. "Have you had any sort of change of heart?"

"Yes, Your Honor," Jimmy said, trying to keep his eyes off Nate. "Most certainly."

"In what way?" The judge folder his hands together, watching Jimmy closely.

"I've had a chance to think about what I did and I realize now how wrong I was, how stupid."

"And?"

Jimmy sucked in a huge breath. "And I've come to see how lucky I am to live in such a benevolent State. How good it's been to me."

The judge gave Nate the barest of glances. "I should say you've been extraordinarily lucky."

"So would I," Jimmy said, and it sounded truly heartfelt, even to his own ears. "I was wrong. Wrong to say what I did, wrong to think it. I can see that now. But The State didn't punish me as hard as it could have. It was kind and understanding and gave me a chance to see what I'd done wrong." He glanced at Nate, who was standing, naked, his hands hanging at his sides, his face purposefully blank. Jimmy looked a lot longer than the judge did, having to force himself to turn back. "My generous and compassionate State even made up for the hardships of being locked up by giving me a prize many would covet. I truly am very lucky."

"And grateful?"

"Oh hell, yeah," Jimmy said so enthusiastically that even the judge smiled.

"Very well." The judge wrote something in the file. "Your punishment didn't quite turn out the way we'd intended but, as you stayed with us an extra month and have a permanent reminder of your crimes, I think we can accept your new attitude as fulfilling the conditions for release. Now." He turned over a page, writing something else and Jimmy moved closer to Nate, resting one hand in the middle of his shoulders, the other going to undo his trousers. "I don't think we need to bother with that." The judge waved his pen at them. "Not after last time. The enthusiasm of your statement was obvious and, I remember, you were also very enthusiastic in subduing your slave at the last assessment. There's nothing left to prove." He laughed, and the rest of the court laughed with him.

"So we don't have to do it again?" Jimmy asked, still holding on.

"No." The judge was completing a form, passing it to a court official.

"But he's just gone to all the effort to get undressed. Do you know how difficult that is for him with his...?" He felt Nate stiffen under his hand, every muscle straining as Nate fought to keep himself under control.

"Are you questioning my reasoning again, Mr. Stephens?" The judge's tone had changed, gone was any trace of amusement.

Nate hitched his shoulders, just a small movement but Jimmy felt it, knew it was meant for him and him alone. Knew what it meant. "No, Your Honor. No, of course not. You're the expert. I'm just the fool that stands before you."

"I'm glad you remembered that. I would have hated to waste taxpayers' money keeping you for a further month."

"I'm sorry, sir. Truly sorry." Jimmy gave his very best apologetic, puppy dog expression, all but hanging his head to look up through his hair while pouting.

"Very well." The judge closed the file. "You will be released tomorrow. You will take your slave with you as you are responsible for him forever now. And, Mr. Stephens, we don't want to see you back in the court system ever again. Do I make myself clear?"

"Yes, sir. Very clear. You won't see me again. That's a promise."

Jimmy stood by Nate's side as he struggled to get dressed without anything to hang on to. When he leaned over into Jimmy's space, desperately trying to balance on one leg, Jimmy whispered a quick, "Thank you," close to his ear. Nate glanced up at him, a small smile just curling the corners of his mouth.

Chapter Four

Jimmy bounced on the balls of his feet, waiting for the small door with the big lock to open. They'd been there for nearly an hour already, sitting on a hard bench that was way too small for him. Now he couldn't sit anymore. He wanted to do something, anything, the anticipation getting to his nerves in a way that was going to drive him insane. Kissing Nate would be a start, bending him over and sliding into him would be even better, but, really, anything to do with Nate could distract him.

But Nate was sitting at the other end of the bench tap, tap, tapping his fingers on his good knee. He was trying really hard to keep his face blank, but that was the problem. He was trying too hard. Jimmy could see the twitch of a muscle under his eye, another on his forehead. He was feeling the strain as much as Jimmy was.

Jimmy took four steps forward and stopped. There was nowhere to go. The door was still locked. He pulled down the hem of his shirt, smoothing out the fabric. That was one good thing, at least he had his own clothes back on now. Decent jeans, a shirt that fit in all the right places and shoes that didn't rub his feet. Fucking bliss. It was a shame about Nate though. He'd thrown the only clothes he had away when they'd first got here. The prison had generously allowed Jimmy to buy him a pair of second — or more likely fourth — hand jeans and a nasty brown shirt. It was either that or his slave would have to walk out naked. Jimmy wasn't about to let that happen, but the clothes didn't do Nate justice. Jimmy would soon sort that out as well. They'd go shopping for some clothes that really suited Nate.

Jimmy's pulse quickened at the thought of how good he'd look — at the envious glances he'd get when he walked into a room with Nate.

He turned, mouth open, ready to tell Nate his plans and, suddenly, there was a prison guard, keys in hand.

"This way," the guard said, already unlocking the door and walking through the last courtyard to the main exit. "Can't you make him hurry up?" He addressed the comment to Jimmy but indicated Nate, who was only just keeping up on his crutches.

"Not a lot I can do." Jimmy shrugged.

"Well." The guard opened the final gate. "It's your problem now." He stood back and Jimmy walked through to freedom, fighting the urge to hold onto Nate as he did so. Jimmy took a deep breath and savored it. No more prison — free.

A moment later and Nate was next to him, looking around at the parked cars. "What do we do now?" Nate asked.

Before Jimmy could answer there was a shrill yell, and an impeccably dressed woman swept in and hugged him tightly.

"Oh, James, my baby boy, it's so good to finally, finally have you back. They kept you for so long—it just wasn't fair. You didn't do anything wrong but they put you in that filthy place with all those awful murderers and terrorists and..." She finally took a breath, holding him by the elbows to inspect him. "How are you? Did they do anything to you? Anything nasty? Anything they shouldn't have? You can tell me. I'm your mother."

"No, Mum." Jimmy laughed. "They didn't do anything nasty to me."

"Except keep you in that awful place. I can't imagine what it must have been like. But never fear. I'm here and I'll take good care of you." She kissed him again, linking her arm through his. "I've made sure everything is ready for you. I've been in touch with your work and insisted there'll be no nonsense there. Your house is ready. I've had food delivered and the place cleaned." She started walking Jimmy toward a very expensive car. "I'll get you home now. I have a little surprise for you and... Why is that man watching us?" She stopped, staring at Nate.

"I have a bit of a surprise for you too," Jimmy said, patting her hand where it rested on his arm. "This is my slave. His name is—"

"Your what?" Her voice rose with imperious incredulity.

"My slave," he repeated simply.

"That is utterly ridiculous." She stopped walking to stare up at her son. "An up and coming actor in your position can't have a slave. The industry's perception of you would change entirely, and I can only imagine how the public would view it. No, that's nonsense— you can't be burdened with the inconvenience. You'll have to sell him immediately—discreetly, of course."

"I can't do that. He was part of my punishment."

"That's over with now. You're out of prison. Their hold on you has gone. We'll sell him in the morning." She waved a dismissive hand in Nate's vague direction, not even bothering to glance his way.

"It's not that simple."

"For goodness sake, why not?"

"Because we're bonded."

She took a step back, her immaculately made up face suddenly paling under the cosmetics. "What have you done?"

"I didn't do anything except accept the inevitable. Part of my sentence was bonding with my slave. You know the law. You know I had no choice but to get on with it. We're bonded."

"My son, bonded with a filthy slave." She shook her head, appalled. "But you can't be. I want a stunning daughter-in-law, beautiful grandchildren."

"It's too late for that." He shrugged. "There never was much chance of a daughter-in-law, anyway. You know I'm mostly gay."

"What you do in your own time is no business of mine or a wife's. I want—"

"It doesn't matter what either of us want. The law is the law. It's done and I'm bonded."

"To a slave." Her lips curled as she said it, as though the word itself was dirty. "The humiliation of it. That's an appallingly severe punishment—one they had no right to exact on my baby or me. A dirty slave, who's no better than an animal."

"His name is—"

"I don't care what his name is. He's nothing but a slave and that's all he should be called." She glanced over at Nate, an expression of complete disgust on her face, before she started moving again, sorting through her handbag for the car keys. "Get in the car and bring him with you." She opened the driver's door, glancing back to see what was taking them so long. "Good God, you have a disabled slave. I am so disappointed in you." With that, she got in, slamming the door after her.

Jimmy raised a rueful eyebrow and whispered, "That's my mum."

Nate just nodded.

For the first half of the journey, Mrs. Stephens didn't speak but kept sending Jimmy looks that could have curdled milk. Then she started to talk, moaning at him endlessly about how he'd ruined everything, how he'd let her and himself down, how he only had himself to blame, after she'd given him everything.

Jimmy sat in the passenger seat and took it all as she told him how he'd have to hide his slave from the world, seeing as they couldn't sell him. The only time he said anything was when she suggested they arrange for a little accident before word got out. Then Jimmy simply said no—a very firm, very uncompromising no. She shrugged and admitted The State probably wouldn't like it anyway, seeing as it was part of Jimmy's sentence.

Nate sat in the back and didn't say a word.

They pulled into Jimmy's street, one that he always thought quietly and discreetly spoke of money in every manicured lawn and beautifully painted door. Mrs. Stephens stopped in front of his house, which was set a little apart from the others. She was just about to turn off the engine when a look of horror appeared on her face. "We can't let anyone see…him." Derision dripped from the last word as she gunned the engine and sped up the driveway much too quickly. "You can sneak him in the back door."

Jimmy didn't argue with her. He had too much sense and experience for that. Instead, he got out and discreetly nudged Nate's crutches to him, away from his mother's watching eye, as Nate pulled himself out. He followed her into the house, showing Nate the way without saying a word.

Going through the back door into the kitchen felt weirder than he expected. It was home, that was for sure, but it also felt like he'd been away for more like two years than two months. The walls seemed a brighter color, the cupboards too large for the space, the room smaller than he remembered. Weird. He took a long moment to orientate himself as Nate came up behind him. "She won't stay long," he said quietly. "Then I'll show you round and—"

The door to the main room suddenly opened and there was a cry of, "Surprise!" as a dozen or so people pushed their way into the kitchen.

"I organized a little homecoming gathering for you." His mother smiled brightly. "Just family and a few of your closest friends."

Jimmy stared round. There was an aunt and uncle or two, his older sister, Molly, her husband, a couple of his drinking buddies, a guy he knew quite well from the gym and... Jimmy realized he didn't have close friends, not really close ones. He had mates that were more than acquaintances, people he slept with, but no one he talked to, not like he talked to Nate. He smiled, wide as he could at them all, as a bottle of beer was thrust into his hand. "It's really great to see everyone," he said as he was pulled into the throng.

An hour or two later and Jimmy couldn't count how many times he'd been told he looked great, that prison hadn't changed that. How it had all been so unfair, and he hadn't deserved to be locked up for so long, but that no one could say something like that in public. How it was good to have him back and now everything could return to normal.

He escaped to the relative peace of the kitchen.

Molly was making herself a long, highly alcoholic drink whilst tucking into a plateful of chicken. "How you doing, baby brother?" she asked, wiping barbeque sauce from her chin.

"Not so bad." He smiled. They'd always got on well, although they hadn't seen that much of each other since she'd gotten married, even less since he left home.

"No psychological scarring from being locked up for a couple of months?"

"No, no scarring."

"I guess you had something to keep you occupied."

"You mean…"

"Your slave."

"His name's Nate," Jimmy said carefully.

"I know. I asked him."

Jimmy nodded at that.

"He's very good looking."

He nodded again.

"Do you know where he is now?"

"I left him sitting in the other room." Irritation itched up his spine. She was staring at him as though he were a little kid who'd forgotten to let his dog out.

"I gave him a plate of food and a can of Cola. He seemed hungry."

That stung like a slap to the face, but what could he say? She'd done what he hadn't thought to do.

"You know mum is really pissed off about him? I mean seriously pissed off."

"I had to drive home with her. Trust me. I know." He poured himself a glass of neat whiskey, enjoying the burn as it went down.

"You also know she's slightly drunk? She'd argue you drove her to it. She'd planned a big Hollywood wedding for you with all the paparazzi she could muster."

"Who was I supposed to marry?"

"I don't think that mattered, as long as she was stunning and could help you move up in the business."

"I didn't want that."

"You aren't going to get it, not now. Not with him in tow." Molly offered him a chicken wing. "What's he like? Apart from pretty."

"He's nice." Jimmy smiled, leaning on the counter as he ate. "A good guy, easy to talk to, to get along with. Easy to be around."

"What's the matter with his leg?"

"He busted it just before he went in."

"How?"

Jimmy shook his head. "I don't really know. He never said, but it should heal okay."

"When does the cast come off? Is he seeing a doctor?"

"I don't think so. I don't know," he had to admit. "I guess that's down to me now. I'll arrange something in the morning."

"It's your responsibility, little brother. I think that's the point of the sentence. You have to deal with the responsibility forever. It might make you grow up."

"You don't think I've grown up? Look at the size of me." He stood up straight, stretching his arms out to the sides.

"I think physically, you're every inch a man, and that's a lot of inches. But inside..." She shrugged. "You're a little kid that's had everything done for you, and you've never had to worry about a thing. Now you have someone else to take care of."

"And I will. I'll take real good care of him."

"I hope so." She smiled. "Now I'm going to find my husband and make sure he doesn't get as drunk as my mother." She headed back into the living room, pushing open the connecting door.

As it opened Jimmy could hear his mother's voice — authoritative, angry and slightly slurred. "If we're to be burdened with you, it's only right that we get to see what we have to deal with. To see what you have to offer my son to make him bother with you at all."

Jimmy pushed passed Molly into the throng of people. All the talking had stopped and everyone was staring intently at the corner of the room behind Jimmy. He turned, following their gaze. Nate was standing up, half naked, the nasty brown shirt on the chair behind him, the button on his jeans already undone, one hand pulling the zipper down as the other started to push them off his hips.

"Stop that, right now." Jimmy knew he was too loud but he couldn't help it. "What the hell are you doing?"

Nate stood still, his face impassive.

"I asked you a question. What are you doing?"

"What I'm told to."

"What the fu—" Jimmy spun round, searching all the faces that stared at him.

His mother stepped forward. "We want to see what you've been forced to bond with, what you can possibly see in that thing." She waved a derisive hand in Nate's direction. "Why you didn't dump it as soon as you got out of prison."

"He's not a thing or an it or a piece of meat—he's a man. He has a name."

"I don't care what his name is. I want him gone, and if I can't have that then I want to see what he is. You," she spat the word at Nate. "Take your clothes off so we can all see."

Nate's hand went back to his zip fly.

"Don't you dare," Jimmy snarled. "You only do what I say."

"If we're to be saddled with the inconvenience and responsibility of him, then we should get to see. Remind him what he is now—nothing but a cheap piece of meat for us to do with as we want." Mrs. Stephens snarled just as effectively as her son.

"He is not your responsibility and you don't get to do anything with him." Jimmy towered over his mother. "He's mine and only mine. You have nothing to do with him. Now get out, all of you," he spat. "Everyone, out. Right now."

"But you can't—" Mrs. Stephens started, but Jimmy didn't let her finish.

"Get out of my house. You too, Mum."

Quickly, everyone gathered up their things, mumbled a few words and headed for the doors. Molly squeezed Jimmy's arm as she passed, whispering, "She's drunk and disappointed. She doesn't mean it. You know that. Take care." Then she ushered her mother out with calming, pacifying words.

It was just Jimmy and Nate left amid the mess.

Jimmy pressed his lips together for a moment and sighed before looking at Nate. "Get dressed," he said gently.

Nate tipped his head to one side. "But I thought you liked me naked."

* * * *

"That's the switch for turning off the last of the downstairs lights." Jimmy pointed it out before starting to climb the stairs. "Are you going to be able to get up these?" he asked Nate.

"Yeah." Nate pulled himself up the first one. "It's just going to take me a while."

"Okay." At the top Jimmy stopped, giving Nate time to catch up. "Down there" — he indicated one passage way — "is my office-cum-junk room, and the spare bedroom. This way" — he turned, going in the other direction — "is the family bathroom and my bedroom. You can sleep on the same side of the bed as we did in prison, okay?"

Nate glanced at the darkened rooms at the other side of the house then squared his shoulders and followed Jimmy.

Jimmy only fucked Nate once that night and if Nate didn't come that hard, it was only to be expected. It had been a rough day for everyone.

Coming out of the bathroom in the early hours of the morning, Jimmy stopped before turning off the light in the en suite. He stood in the doorway, simply staring for long minutes. Nate was fast asleep. He looked good, impossibly good, in Jimmy's bed, laying half on his side, one hand hanging off the edge of the bed, long eyelashes soft against his face.

Jimmy thought the picture was as right as anything he'd ever seen. Right man, in the right place. A feeling washed over him, huge and complete, traveling from the soles of his feet to his hair and back again.

He wanted to keep Nate there, against his dark blue sheets. There, in his bed where he belonged.

* * * *

"I phoned work while you were in the shower," Jimmy said, as Nate slid plates of food along the kitchen counter onto the breakfast bar where Jimmy sat, waiting. "They said they want me to go in tomorrow, but it will be at least a few days before I start filming again. There's a whole load of stuff they want me to do first. I bet none of it's fun but at least... What are you smiling about?"

"I've got it sussed." Nate's grin grew. "The first cup of coffee I tried to carry over there ended up down the front of my jeans but, if I slide it, I can manage just fine. Plus the counter top is just the right height for me to lean against, so I have two hands free to do stuff."

Stuff? Jimmy thought about it. "Can you cook?"

"No idea, never even tried to boil an egg."

"Well, there are some cookbooks over there that...someone gave me. Maybe it's time to learn. It would be good to come home to something other than take out. Something healthy. There's a decent organic food shop not far from here." He watched as Nate sat opposite him, arranging his foot carefully. "Anyway, seeing as I don't have to go to work and I've rang my mum so she isn't breathing down my neck, we have the day free. I think the top priority has to be getting you some decent clothes."

"What's wrong with this?" Nate looked down at his prison second-hand clothes. "I could do with something else to wear while I wash these, but they're fine."

"Fine?" Jimmy snorted. "They're at least ten years out of date—that's if they were ever in. No, you need something worthy of you. I know a great shop. What else do we need to do?"

"I sure need a haircut," Nate said, pulling at it. "Although I can do that myself if you have some clippers."

"No way." Jimmy laughed, his eyes lighting up. "You're even more gorgeous now your hair is getting longer. We can get it properly shaped, but let's not cut it. You look really good. No, first clothes—I think a baby pink shirt would really suit you—and then we should find a doctor for your leg. I know someone I can ask."

Nate picked up his cup and drank the coffee slowly. "Thank you. A doctor would be good."

"You're my responsibility now. I'm going to remember that and take it seriously. I'll get you a great doctor."

* * * *

Jimmy felt like a kid in a candy store when they went shopping. He found some pretty amazing things for himself—jeans that showed off his arse perfectly, making his legs seem even longer. There was also a shirt that smoothed beautifully across his shoulders and outlined his muscles. But even better was getting Nate to try things on. The man looked wonderful in almost everything Jimmy got him to try, and now his hair was cut properly? Perfect.

He ended up buying much more than he'd expected but what the hell. It was worth it. Nate was worth it.

He even rang around for doctor recommendations, making sure he got the best. He made an appointment for a couple of days' time, as he waited for Nate to try on a pastel striped shirt. He was getting good at this responsibility thing, even if he did say so himself. And if Nate didn't seem as excited by shopping as he was? Well, not all men enjoyed it and he was probably tired from hauling that heavy cast around.

Going into work the next day felt strange. The car called for him as normal, but he didn't like leaving Nate. He knew Nate wouldn't run, very few slaves did—the consequences were so severe. Even fewer who could hardly walk, let alone run. Still, Jimmy did wonder. He rang Nate from the backseat just as they were pulling into the studio parking lot.

He wondered again while his agent, the lawyers and the TV show producers went through all the effects of his time away. Jimmy figured he was in trouble with them, but not that bad. What were they going to do, when it was The State that had kept him from work?

He let it all wash over him, confident that his people would sort out everything, and thought about what Nate would cook for dinner that evening. He'd left a pile of cookbooks on the kitchen counter and a note saying, *Order any ingredients that aren't in the cupboards.* When the meeting was over, as he was going down to wardrobe to sweet talk them into a decent time for his fitting, he rang home again. Just to check. Nate answered sounding breathless.

"What were you doing?" Jimmy couldn't help his slight tone.

"The sun was shining, so I was in the garden trying to fix that broken chair," Nate said, his voice sounding light and bright. "I was sitting on my butt on the grass. It took me ages to get up, get into the house and make it to the phone."

"Take a phone with you next time. Better still, forget the chair. I'll buy new garden furniture."

"But I can easily fix that. It's no problem."

"Fuck the chair. It's not important."

"Fine," Nate said carefully. "It's your money."

When Jimmy got home there were pizza boxes on the breakfast bar and a trash can full of burnt and spoiled things.

"Sorry," Nate said, his voice still measured. "The cooking thing is harder than it looks."

"Is there cold beer?" Jimmy slung himself onto a stool.

"A whole fridge full."

"Then I guess the world is still a happy place." Jimmy smiled, and Nate joined him to eat.

It was good to have someone to come home to, someone to talk to. The unexpected warmth in his belly made Jimmy smile. The world really did feel like a happy place. It was good to have Nate to come home to. He liked it, liked the fact, liked knowing he'd have it tomorrow, the next day and forever. "So, what else did you do today? Apart from burning half the contents of the kitchen?"

Nate glanced over his shoulder at the trash can for a moment, turning back with a grin. "I tried to work out how to use your washing machine but, as I don't have a degree in rocket science, I gave up. Then I tried watching TV, but that made my brain start to rot after twenty minutes, so I fixed the garden chair, the door upstairs that squeaked all night and put the handle back on the kitchen drawer. That's when I found the instructions for the washing machine. There should be clean underwear, but they may be odd colors."

"Man, you did good for one day." Jimmy raised his bottle in salute. "You didn't have time to shave though."

Nate ran a hand over his chin. "You don't like stubble?"

"I think you look better without it," Jimmy said. "Why don't you shave it in the morning? What else are you going to do tomorrow?"

"Well, I thought I might make something that's actually edible."

"Health food would be good."

"I wouldn't hold your breath." Nate gave a small, rather forced smile. "I figured I'd start with ready meals. How hard can it be to take something out of the freezer and put it in the microwave? How'd your day go?"

"Okay, I guess. The bosses are pissed off with me for being away so long. Even more pissed off that it was two months, not one. They were getting really difficult about it, until I kind of told them the extra time was your fault, not mine. Sorry."

"Doesn't matter to me. I don't have to work with them." Nate got out another bottle of beer and slid it over.

Jimmy drank half of it before picking up another slice of pizza. "Don't you want another beer?" he asked. "I told you last night...take what you want. This is your home now."

"I'm okay." Nate carried on eating. "One's enough for me."

* * * *

The doctor's office was cool and bright, done out in expensive looking, muted tones of beige and coffee. Jimmy expected no less. He didn't see why he should sit in some dingy, public hospital that smelled of sickness and sweat when he didn't have to. He liked things nice and Nate deserved the best.

As arranged, he'd sent Nate in earlier, by taxi, so he could be examined and have any tests done that were needed. The receptionist had explained that, of course, all discussions and results would be with the owner, never the slave himself. She said that they could phone Jimmy, but he'd figured that, as he had nothing to do and Nate needed a ride home, he'd come in himself.

Now the rather pretty young doctor was going through the sheaves of papers one last time before pushing them to the side. "From what we can tell, Mr. Stephens, your slave had a rather nasty break. But it's healing well, and there shouldn't be any problems when the cast comes off in another couple of weeks. After that, he'll have to wear a brace for a while afterwards, to support the leg whilst it gains back its strength."

"A brace?"

"Yes."

"For how long?"

"A few weeks. He'll be able to take it off when necessary and won't have to wear it at night. But he must be careful not to put too much strain on the leg at first."

Jimmy nodded. "At least we don't have to put up with it all the time."

"Quite," she said. "Then there's the question of physiotherapy."

"Physiotherapy?"

"Whether he receives any depends on how mobile you want your slave to be. With none, he'll have a marked limp and restricted movement."

"And with it?"

"We can get him back to full health. There are two options—standard care, which is perfectly adequate, but may leave the leg a little weaker than before, or there is the premium service. That would probably leave him better than ever but it involves many more frequent sessions, it's expensive and not necessary for a slave."

Jimmy glanced over. Nate had his eyes down, watching his hand as he rubbed over and over the knee on his bad leg, his face blank. "Book him in for the premium service. I want him back to full health." There really wasn't any other option, no matter what his mother would say.

The doctor opened her mouth to protest but shrugged instead. "As you wish."

* * * *

Two and a half weeks later the cast was cut off and a buckle-on brace fitted. Nate came home and they sat on the sofa after removing the brace, both of his feet resting on the coffee table. They looked at the newly revealed skin. It was greyish and pasty, wrinkled and flaking in places.

Nate scrunched up his nose. "That's not pretty," he said, scratching at his leg.

Jimmy automatically reached over and took Nate's hand away. There were now long red marks on the pale flesh, over the scars above the anklebone. "Have a bath, get some air on it. It'll soon look better."

"My legs don't match." Nate tipped his head to one side, studying them. "I have non-matching legs. One's a man's leg, the other"—he scratched at it once more—"belongs to a skinny teenager."

"That's because they pulled half the hair off with the cast. I bet it hurt. Must have been like getting it waxed.

Molly used to holler when she got her legs waxed." Again he lifted Nate's hand away.

"How do you know that?" Nate stopped scratching for a moment to glance at Jimmy.

"Because I used to go with her sometimes."

"I'm not asking." Nate rubbed at his leg with the heel of his hand rather than his nails. "It hurt like a bitch."

"How does it feel now?"

"Like a son of a bitch."

"Take some pain meds." He grabbed Nate's hand one more time and sat on it.

"That would involve putting the brace back on so I can walk out to the kitchen, and I officially hate the brace as much as the cast."

"You can't go that far without it?"

"It's as weak as a kitten. I feel pathetic."

"Nat, sweetheart." Jimmy pulled him into a hug as Nate started to scratch with the other hand. "You are many things but, trust me, pathetic isn't one of them."

"I have pathetic, non-matching legs," Nate said, sliding down under Jimmy's insisting hand, until his head rested in Jimmy's lap. He twisted round, stretching up to push the hair from Jimmy's eyes. "I want matching man legs."

"Stop whining, work hard at the physio and you'll get them. You heard the doctor." Jimmy grabbed both of Nate's hands as he started to scratch again.

"I was not whin—" Nate laughed, free and easy. "Yep, I've turned into a whiney, non-matching bitch. Good job I have you to call me on it."

"What are friends for?" Jimmy said, tucking both of Nate's hands under his arm and reaching for the remote control.

Nate glanced up at him quickly, a soft shake of his head. "Man, you're confusing," he said very, very quietly.

"Not confusing at all. Everyone needs a *Starsky and Hutch* marathon when they're recuperating from non-matching, itchy leg syndrome."

The cast was finally gone and Jimmy decided that was reason to celebrate. He took a bottle of fine champagne to bed with them that night but, although he didn't really like it, he ended up drinking most of it himself.

He fell asleep not completely sure if they'd fucked or not—something he thought was a crying shame.

If he was lucky enough to fuck Nate, he should at least remember it.

* * * *

Next day came the first session of physiotherapy. Nate got back to the house with his face gray and strained and his fingers pressing too hard against his thigh. Jimmy suggested he sit down and rest the leg but Nate hobbled out to the kitchen, returning with beer for them both. Jimmy took his bottle, looking at the pills in Nate's hand. "Should you have alcohol with pain meds?"

"The quicker I learn how to move in this thing, the more I do the exercises and push at them, the quicker I'll be able to get rid of the brace," Nate said.

"What's the rush? We have all the time in the world, and I don't want you getting sick."

"Maybe but I…" Nate took the pills with a swig of beer and heaved in a deep breath. "I hate this brace as much as the cast. I hate not being able to move properly."

"So do I, but go easy on yourself. You'll get there. There's time and I want you healthy."

Nate stared at him, letting his eyes linger on Jimmy in a way he rarely did. Then his face softened and he eased himself down onto the sofa next to Jimmy. "You're right."

"I always am." Jimmy kissed the side of his head. "Now pass the remote. I want to watch *Die Hard*."

"Again?"

"Yeah, I figure if I watch it enough, eventually the German terrorist might actually win and beat Bruce Willis. I like Hermann the German, his accent is cool."

"His name's Hans…you're…" Nate stopped, laughing very softly as he shook his head, but Jimmy felt him slowly begin to relax.

"Go on. Admit it." Jimmy nudged him. "You'd like to see Brucie-baby taken down just as much as I would." This time, he sensed Nate's soft snort of laughter, rather than heard it, as Nate leaned in. Slipping an arm around Nate, he kissed the side of his head again as they settled to watch the movie. "Put your foot up on the table. You know what the doctor said."

Nate huffed and did as he was told.

"What?" Jimmy asked.

"Nothing." Nate exhaled slowly, supporting himself on Jimmy's knee. "Maybe my punishment wasn't as bad as it could have been."

"Baby?"

Nate shook his head. "Go on. Put the movie on. I want to watch Hermann the German."

Chapter Five

Jimmy got home from work early, the car dropping him off in the driveway as usual. It had been a long hard week, topped off by such a bitch of a day that he leaned back against the door, after he'd closed it on the world, sighing. He felt beyond grateful to be here, in the blessed peace and quiet. He sighed again, deep and hard, before pushing himself to his feet and calling out to Nate.

"Down here," Nate called back, his voice sounding muffled.

"What the hell?" Jimmy stared around at the mess. It seemed like the contents of half the kitchen cupboards were strewn over the floor. Things he didn't remember buying and was sure he didn't know what they were for.

"The sink was leaking," came Nate's voice, his head and shoulders still inside a cupboard. "I might know fuck all about plumbing, but I figured, if I can master the microwave, I can sure as hell take on a leaking pipe." He pulled himself out, looking up at Jimmy with a face full of delight. "All I have to do now is reconnect that..." He waved a hand. "That roundy thing, work out what to do with the washer that's left over and I've cracked it. No more leaking sink."

Jimmy sighed, his body heavy with weariness, his mind craving the one solace he needed. "Come to bed."

"What? Now?" The expression on Nate's face changed.

"Yes, now."

"But I haven't finished, things are pretty critical and..." Nate stopped as Jimmy continued to stare at him, his face bleak.

"Now, baby. I need..."

"Yeah, I know what you need. Same thing you usually need." Nate searched round for a rag to wipe his hands on, before he pulled himself upright, using the counter top for leverage. "Let me just make sure the water's turned off properly or the place will be flooded by the time you're finished."

"I don't mean to drag you away in the middle of something. It's just that..." Jimmy sighed, heavy and heartfelt, his shoulders dropping, his back rounding. "I really need you. I feel like shit and I need... I just need you. You make things better."

"Yeah, I get it. All right, I get it. I'm coming." Nate dropped the rag and headed for the downstairs bathroom.

"You don't have to wash or anything," Jimmy said, his voice drawn out and thin. "Just come to bed."

Nate came out and started to make his slow way up the stairs. "I was checking the stopcock."

"It's in there?" Jimmy followed behind him.

"At the back of the toilet."

"I didn't know."

"I figured," Nate said, pulling his T-shirt up over his head and dropping it on a chair in the bedroom. "What way do you want me?"

"Can we make it slow and gentle, please? I need to hold you as much as anything."

"Bet you fuck me though." Nate gave a snort of a laugh, his mouth curling up in a smile that didn't reach his eyes.

Jimmy let his clothes fall to the floor, pulling the covers back and climbing onto the bed, before holding out a hand to Nate. "I just want to lose myself in you for as long as I can," he said in a wistful voice.

"Sure." Nate crawled in next to him, and the smile he gave Jimmy this time was gentler but more real.

Jimmy took his time, using his hands to soothe himself on Nate's skin, his mouth to taste and take Nate's. He could feel the tension evaporate from his pores with each press of his skin to Nate's, every time he combed through Nate's growing hair. He loved the feel of it as it ran across his palm, as he held on tight. Loved the heat of Nate's flesh, loved the feel of Nate's breath on his skin, loved the look of Nate's long eyelashes.

He took his time, luxuriating in the pleasure of everything he loved to do, to feel, to see.

When he fucked Nate, he did it as leisurely as possible. Counting into each thrust, holding his breath so he could truly feel when he reached his deepest. He clung on tight at each pull back, never wanting to let go. Never wanting to leave the safety of Nate's body.

He went as slowly as he knew how, but still the end came too quickly, his release pulled from his body long before he was ready. He could admit it—it was long before his need was satisfied, even if his body was sated.

He pressed his nose into the back of Nate's neck, his mouth open wide, arms wrapped tight around Nate, gripping hard. His breath heaved in his throat, his heart thumped against his ribs and he spread his hands, trying to feel as much as he could at one time. His finger touched the tip of Nate's cock.

He hadn't come. Jimmy had taken all he could and he hadn't even bothered to make sure that Nate came.

Rolling Nate onto his back he slid over him. "Sorry," he whispered, mouth on Nate's shoulder, his cheek, his lips. "Not fair...so not fair." He stroked down Nate's arms, over his chest, his belly, out to his hips. "I'm sorry." Kisses to Nate's neck, licking at the base of his throat. There was so much more to taste and touch, even if his own body couldn't do, take, anymore. There was more than one way to lose himself in Nate. He bobbed his head down quickly, catching Nate's dick between his lips and sucking it in.

He felt Nate hiss, sharp between his teeth, his muscles pull and tense in his belly, his thighs. "You're not supposed to do that."

"I can do anything I want." He slid his lips down and Nate cursed, hissing again, pushing his hips back into the mattress.

"But no one expects you to bother..."

"I want to. There's no one to stop me."

"But you don't need to. I don't need, don't want... I..." They both knew a slave didn't say what they wanted.

"I want to do this."

"But I don't think..."

Jimmy looked along the line of Nate's body. "I want to do this for you, so just hold still and let it happen." He knew there was nothing Nate could say to that.

Before he went back to his task, Jimmy watched as Nate closed his eyes and threw his arm across them.

Sucking just how he himself liked it, Jimmy pulled upwards with his lips, and Nate heaved under him, whole body tensing. Again, and he could feel Nate fighting himself to keep his hips down. This was new. Nate could be responsive, sweating and moaning, before he came hard in Jimmy's hand. But not usually this quick, this potent. Jimmy felt a strange, comforting warmth spreading across his chest. One to make him stop and think.

This was a different power he had over Nate, a different control. It wasn't about slavery or ownership—it was about two people. He was going to make the most of it.

He spread his hands wide over Nate's hips, holding him, and went to work on his cock. Sucking, rubbing, making it ride the roof of his mouth. Nate groaned, a litany of swear words pushed over his lips, even as Jimmy felt him try to stay quiet. Jimmy just sucked harder, faster, ruthlessly pushing Nate, until he was shaking under his hands. Until Nate lost any semblance of a rhythm, leaving it to Jimmy to do whatever he wanted with him. Until he had no choice but to come.

Jimmy swallowed the first load, spat the second back onto Nate's groin, leaving a smear across his lips which he licked off carefully. He ran a finger through the sticky mess of Nate's pubic hair, rubbing it in as he spread it out. Nate had his hands over his eyes, mumbling, "Shit, shit," over and over, just under his breath, as the heaving of his chest started to calm.

With a last pat to Nate's thigh, Jimmy rolled onto his back, pushing himself up the bed until they were lying side by side, a small gap between them. "You okay?" he asked, after a long, long moment.

"Yeah, I guess." Nate blew out a long stream of air. "You?"

"Yeah." Jimmy couldn't help an ironic snort that didn't really sound like laughter. "You always make things better. Well, better than they were at least."

Nate turned his head on the pillow, hands still up by his head. "Bad day at work?"

"You could say that."

"Tell me about it."

"I..." Jimmy didn't know where to start.

"What happened?" Nate asked, voice low and concerned.

"Things have been strange since I got back. I didn't really notice it at first, I'm not always the most observant of guys but...there was an atmosphere. I've always got on with everyone, been well liked. Because of that people would do stuff for me, make allowances or just laugh it off if I made mistakes." He stopped, the words drifting away.

"But something happened today? You know you can talk to me."

"I kept fucking up," Jimmy said quietly. "There was this stupid scene, with dialog that had to be delivered just right as I worked a couple of props. I couldn't get the timing, kept saying the line in the wrong place or doing the wrong thing. It was a difficult scene but the more I tried, the more I fucked up."

"And? What was the reaction?"

"Normally, before, everyone would have laughed, called me an idiot."

"But not today?"

"Oh they called me an idiot all right, but they weren't laughing. No one was laughing, especially the crew. Then it all started to come out...how pissed off everyone is with me. First I was going to be away a month, and that was bad enough. It screwed up schedules and when other actors were booked. But they sort of managed to change things around and only wasted a few days. Then it was another month, with no warning. There was nothing they could do. Filming had to be canceled. Everything shut down for a while. Some actors lost work, but most were okay. It was the crew that really got hit. They didn't get paid."

"There was nothing you could do," Nate said, gently.

"But it was my fault. Even though I'd lied through my teeth and told them the extra month was your doing, they didn't care. They didn't believe me. I offered to compensate them but most turned me down, said they didn't want my money. I tried to make it right but..." He ran a hand quickly over his eyes, brushing his hair out of the way. "The atmosphere has changed and no one bothers to hide it anymore. I'm not the golden boy or even the class clown. I'm just the guy who cost them time and money."

"Then you have to make them change their minds."

"How the hell do I do that?" Jimmy raised a disbelieving eyebrow. "The pay packet is a powerful thing."

"Work hard. Make them see that you're really trying to do your best to make up for it. Be helpful and willing, always be on time and professional, do whatever you can to go the extra mile and help things go well."

"You really think that would make a difference?"

"It would to me, if I saw someone was really trying. But you have to do it right."

"What do you mean, 'do it right'?"

Nate took a deep breath, holding it while he stared at Jimmy. Then he let it out slowly. "You have to be tactful, sensitive and discreet. Sometimes you…"

"Go on. Say it. After what I've had thrown at me today, nothing you say can be that bad," Jimmy said, meaning it.

"Sometimes you don't always think things through before you say them." Nate's voice softened further still, until it was warm, intimate. "When you offered them money, did you do it quietly, in private, where it wouldn't hurt a man's pride?"

Jimmy stared at the ceiling, thinking through the day's events. "I shouted it at them, in a room full of people. I may have used the words mother and fuckers, I certainly did it at the top of my lungs."

"See." Nate touched his shoulder, making Jimmy glance back at him. Nate was smiling, crinkles marking the corners of his eyes. "Not the most diplomatic way of offering."

"No."

"You have to make them see that you really mean it when you say you're sorry."

"Am I though? I'm not sure I'm that good a person."

"Of course you are. You're sorry for losing them money, for wasting time."

"I guess so, maybe."

"Do right by them, without shouting and flashing your money about, and they'll come round. It'll take an effort but you can do it. I know you can."

Jimmy looked at him. Nate's hair was mussed—the effect more pronounced now it was longer. He had pillow creases down the side of one cheek, dirt from his attempts at plumbing on his forehead and a bite mark on his shoulder. "I love you," Jimmy said out of nowhere but suddenly, fiercely, aware of how much he meant it. "I really do, and I've never said it to anyone before. Never been in love, not properly. Not like this."

There was a long moment of silence when Nate's face went blank. Then his smile was back, warm and full of humor. "You just want me to clean up the mess in the kitchen."

"No I don't. I mean it."

"And you're hungry." Nate sat up, searching round for his underwear.

"No, I…"

"Don't give me that." Nate laughed. "I know that look on your face. You saw the steak in the fridge. You're hoping for that, salad and the whole God damned works." He got up and pulled his clothes back on. "And a beer. Lots of beer. Lots of very cold beer. Well, you'll have to wait a while. I've got to fix the sink, before I can do anything else. I'll put the water back on first then you can go and have a shower. I should have things started by the time you're done." He leaned back over the bed and dropped a quick kiss on Jimmy's lips. "Go, wash off the whole rotten day. I got work to do."

Jimmy wished the kiss hadn't been quite so quick. "You don't have to. Call a plumber."

"What for? I can fix it, I think. At least it'll prove to your momma that I'm not as useless as she says I am. She called again."

"Did she call you as many names as the time I heard her?" Jimmy sat up on his elbows.

"She has an amazing vocabulary. I don't know what half of them mean."

"But they're all rude." He wasn't asking. He knew they were.

"I'm guessing so, from the way she says them." Nate's grin grew.

"I'll talk to her. Again." Jimmy sighed. "Doesn't mean we can't call a plumber though."

"Don't bother. I like the challenge. I will not be beaten by a sink, and it's not like I have much else to do."

"Hey." An idea suddenly occurred to Jimmy. "It's a long weekend. How do you fancy going away?"

Nate turned to face him up, clearly interested. "What are you thinking of?"

"I've got a cabin by a lake. It's about an hour and a half from here. I bought it as an investment and..." It was Jimmy's turn to grin. "As somewhere to hide out when my army of fans got too much to handle. I haven't been there much but it's nice."

"Sounds good. I'd like to get out of here for a while."

"Good, we'll go after dinner. I could do with getting away as well."

"Dinner." Nate's face scrunched up. "That means washing things. In the sink." He headed for the door. "I've have things to fix."

* * * *

Nate stacked a bag by the back door and returned for the last one, full of food. Jimmy had said to take enough to last them through breakfast, that they could go shopping after that. He'd also reminded Nate just how much he liked to eat for breakfast.

Jimmy came in through the back way, letting the cooler night air in with him. "I've brought the car right up to the door. It'll be easier to load it that way."

"How come you don't use the front door?" Nate asked, passing over a bag. "Your mum told me very specifically that, under no circumstances, was I ever to use it — that the front door was for 'decent people only'. So why don't you?"

Jimmy grinned at him as he took the bag. "Because I'm not decent. Because it's easier to use this door. Because it really fucking annoys her. Because I'm really petty and make a point of never using it, especially if she's around."

"Sometimes you're not nice to your mum." Nate got the last bag, heaving it over his shoulder as he switched off the lights.

"What do you care? She's never nice to you."

"Know what she said to me today? That I wasn't really human, what with being a slave and all. I asked her what I was then and it took her ages to come up with sub-human. Sub-human? Was that really the best she could do? I was kind of disappointed."

"I'm glad you can take her like you do. Me? I'd want to kill her." Jimmy locked the door behind Nate, throwing his bag into the back of the car.

Nate shrugged and didn't say a word as he got in.

The drive was quiet, peaceful. Jimmy marveled at just how easy it was to be with Nate, just how comfortable he felt in his company. He didn't have to pretend to be happy and upbeat all the time, didn't have to pretend at all. Nate accepted him just as he was. He didn't have to make an effort with Nate — it all came naturally. It was just about perfect.

The roads were clear, the car ran faultlessly. Jimmy eased back in his seat, one hand on the wheel and enjoyed himself as the blackness rushed past them. He put on some music, soft country that he always loved. "Okay?" he looked over at Nate.

"Yeah." Nate smiled, closing his eyes and stretching out in the seat.

They made good time, turning into the narrow drive to the cabin well before midnight. Jimmy roused Nate with a hand on his arm then went to open up.

Nate followed him up onto the porch with a bag on one shoulder. "I can't see anything."

"You won't. There's no other people and no lights for at least a mile. You'll have to wait until morning to see the lake and everything else. But the cabin is comfortable and soon"—he opened the door, switching on lights as he went inside—"it'll be nice and warm."

Outside there was a large verandah running the length of the cabin, with wicker chairs and a table. Inside, it had wooden walls and comfortable, but old, furniture. There was a large, over-stuffed sofa, mismatched armchairs, an archway through to a small but serviceable kitchen, even a small fireplace. Nate dropped his bag on the floor and stared around him.

"I know it's not the most glamorous place," Jimmy said, bringing in the last of the bags, "but the previous owner left all their furniture and I've never got round to replacing it. I should, and get it redecorated, make it a bit more modern looking."

"Do you have to?" Nate smiled over at him. "It's perfect just as it is. It looks like a place you can really relax in."

"It is. See that door?" Jimmy pointed. "It's a utility room, where you can dump all your muddy clothes and boots."

"So no worrying about spoiling the rugs?"

"Nope."

"What does your mum think of it?"

"She came once. She's never been back. She hated it." Nate's grin grew huge and Jimmy couldn't help but laugh. "There are two bedrooms, a small one I use for junk and ours, which has a huge bed with the most amazing mattress ever. You're going to love it. Bed?"

"Yeah, okay." Nate nodded, glancing round once more. "I like the feel of this place."

* * * *

When Jimmy woke the next morning, the bed was empty, but there was a wonderful smell coming from the kitchen. He threw on some old clothes and went down to investigate.

"Morning." Nate was already dressed. "I am officially amazing. I made bacon sandwiches for breakfast without burning them."

"Wow, you're getting good." Jimmy slid onto a chair at the table. "I missed waking up with you, though."

"The sun was shining, the birds were doing that early morning singing thing. It was too good a day to waste in bed." Nate sat opposite him with the plate of sandwiches.

"Trust me, being in bed with you is never a waste."

"Can we go out and explore a bit?"

"Can you walk far?"

"I'm doing better now. With the brace and a walking stick, I can go farther than before. Maybe we could go round the lake?"

Jimmy nearly choked on his food as he laughed. "Nat, baby, the lake is huge. It'd take us over a day to do all of it."

"Oh." Nate took another bite of his sandwich. "I've never been much of a country guy. I don't know much about it."

"We can go for a walk this morning, see how far you can manage on rough ground. Then we'll go into town for lunch and supplies. If I could get the fireplace to work without filling the place with smoke, we could spend the evening naked in front of the fire. Seeing as I can't, we'll just have to spend the time in bed."

Nate stopped, his food half way to his mouth. "Are there bears in the woods? I heard some weird noises in the night."

"No, no bears. Those are just country noises."

"I'm not sure I like them."

"Now you sound like my mum."

Nate glared at him, his face full of mock anger. "I'm not sure I like you."

* * * *

Outside the air was clear, crisp and clean tasting. From the verandah to the edge of the lake was only about a hundred yards and the view was gorgeous. The sunlight glistened off the water, which had little ripples on it, caused by the breeze. There were trees and plants along the edge with an open, cleared patch in front of the cabin.

Jimmy pointed out a small shed at the back. "There's a Canadian style canoe in there." He looked at Nate as his eyebrows knitted together. "Can you swim?"

"Yeah, can we go out in it?"

"Let's wait until you've got rid of the brace. If you fall in now, you'd sink to the bottom." Jimmy took a deep breath, inhaling the atmosphere of the place, the atmosphere between them. "It's different now, isn't it?"

"What, this place compared to the city? Very different," Nate agreed.

"No, I didn't mean that. I meant us — the way things are between us. It's changed since we got out of prison. Things feel..." He wasn't quite sure what he meant. "I feel like we're more us, Jimmy and Nate, less the roles The State expects us to play. It's different, good. It's...better." Jimmy nodded, pleased to have found a word he liked. "Now, half the time I forget you're a slave. You're just Nate, Nat—the man I share my life with. Things are more balanced. Everything feels more natural." He turned to face at Nate. "Don't you think so?"

Nate licked at his bottom lip, eyes glued to the view in front of them. "It is better than when we first got thrown together. Anything would be better than that," he finished softly. Then he exhaled hard and looked at Jimmy expectantly. "Are we going to explore?"

Behind the cabin the woods were thick, tall trees that pointed to the sky, with narrow paths leading in all directions. They walked along by the lake shore where the ground was flatter and easier to manage with Nate's stick. The birds sang, the sun shone and Jimmy had to admit it had been a great idea to come here. He could feel all the tension of the previous day ooze out of him. He could even see the possibility of doing what Nate had suggested and making it up to the people he worked with. He resolved to do better when he got back, to make everyone smile at him again. To smile like Nate was now.

He watched as Nate kept stopping to pick up stones and throw them out into the lake, trying to make them bounce. He almost turned round in circles, trying to see everything, as he took big gulps of air and relaxed alongside Jimmy.

"What kind of tree is that?" Nate asked. "What animal made those tracks?"

"I have no idea." Jimmy shrugged. "A little one?"

"We need a book," Nate pronounced. "If we're going to be mountain-men, we ought to know this stuff."

"We're going to be mountain-men?"

It was Nate's turn to shrug. "Well, just while we're here."

"Whatever you say." Right then Jimmy would have given him anything he wanted. "I do love you."

"You just like the idea of me with a big beard and a dead raccoon over my shoulder." Nate laughed.

Jimmy frowned. "You can forget the big beard. It would spoil your face, and it would tickle. As for the dead raccoon..."

Nate stopped still and shook his head, a small movement that Jimmy didn't understand. "You're one perplexing guy. One minute you're..." Then he huffed, shaking his head again, before fixing a grin on his face. "You'd prefer a dead polecat?"

"I don't even know what a polecat is." It was Jimmy's turn to laugh.

"We need a book, man. I'm telling you...a book with lots of detail."

"And food, lots of food. Come on, let's go shopping."

As far as Jimmy was concerned, the weekend was pretty much perfect. They walked, as much as Nate could manage, they talked and ate. Then they made up weird stories about the animals that could be living in the woods.

As they were both so relaxed, Jimmy thought it would be good to try out blow jobs again but, despite his perseverance, Nate wasn't any better. Jimmy tried adding a bit of alcohol to the mix, but Nate didn't seem to like it much and always stopped at a glass or two. When Jimmy pushed, hoping to relax Nate further, he'd ended up drunker than Nate. He'd woken with a thick head to find Nate fast asleep, face squashed into the back of the sofa, bad foot hanging off the edge.

He'd left him like that and had gone to throw up in the toilet. Nate came into the bathroom a while later, still sleep mussed and, obligingly, rubbed Jimmy's back and handed him cool flannels. When Jimmy put on his best puppy-dog face and looked up unexpectedly, Nate was watching him with a fond expression. That stirred something in Jimmy's belly that he didn't want to name, didn't want to think about. But he locked it away to keep it close when Nate's face changed to his more normal, respectful caring expression.

They even thought about going swimming, but Jimmy chickened out on that one after putting his foot in. It was ball-shrinkingly cold. Instead they made up for it with a long, long shower together that had him sighing in contentment and thinking just how damned lucky he was.

He forgot all about work and his problems there until the drive back on Sunday night. Then Nate rested a hand on his thigh and smiled over at him. "You'll win them back round," he said gently, "if you take your time and make an effort. I have confidence in you."

Nate had confidence in him. He really couldn't lose with backing like that.

The weekend had been good for them both. "Thanks." He nodded, the tension easing again. "You want to go back to the lake cabin sometime?"

Nate lay back in his seat. "I'd like to go back real soon. That's one great place."

"Maybe I could leave you there, if I only have to come back for a couple of days' work."

"No, no point." Nate closed his eyes and yawned. "Not as much fun if you're not there."

Jimmy stared the engine and drove away with a last look in the rear view mirror. "Then we'll both come back soon."

* * * *

The phone rang eleven times before it was answered. Eleven—Jimmy had counted them. *What could Nate be doing that it would take so long?*

"Hello," Nate answered, breathless.

"It's me."

"Oh, hi, you just caught me."

"Where are you going?" He didn't like the thought of Nate going out without him.

"Physio. Again. But it's working so I shouldn't complain. Did you need something or are you just checking up on me?"

"I just wanted to warn you. My mum rang. She said she'll be dropping some stuff over there this afternoon."

"Shit." The expletive sounded only too heartfelt. "Thanks for the notice. I... Shit."

"Is she still that bad?" Jimmy asked. "I thought she'd got better with you."

"That's..." There was real hesitation in Nate's voice.

"Tell me," Jimmy demanded.

"I don't like telling tales."

"Tell me, otherwise I can't protect you, and you are my responsibility. Isn't she better?"

"Only when you're around. When it's just the two of us, she's just the same," Nate admitted, then sucked in a deep breath before going on. "Jimmy, you have to tell me how I'm to handle it."

"What do you mean?"

"She says stuff, makes me do stuff. I can't say no to her. She's your mum. But I don't want you walking in and I'm standing there butt naked. You..." Nate laughed, an odd sound without humor. "You wouldn't take it well."

"What has she done to you?" Jimmy could feel his chest tighten up with something close to anger. She was his mum but Nate was just *his*.

"Nothing." Nate was quick to reassure. "Not yet, and I'm real good at making sure I'm not alone with her, but it's going to happen sooner or later. I should know what you want me to do when it does."

"She can't... I'm not having anyone touching... Fucking hell..." Jimmy's temper was rising fast. "I'll fucking talk to her. Tonight. I can't do it now, I have to be on set in a couple of minutes, but I'll talk to her then. In the meantime..." He didn't know what to suggest.

"I'll have a cup of coffee at the hospital after physio. Then go and get some food in. We're running short."

"Good idea. Take your time and I'll meet you outside the supermarket. We'll come home together, just in case she's still at the house."

"Okay." The smile was back in Nate's voice. "Take care."

"And you." Jimmy was just starting to realize how many times Nate helped him out or just plain rescued him from difficult situations.

That night Nate sat on the bottom of the stairs watching Jimmy as he tried to get a word in edgeways with his mum on the telephone. "No, you're not listening to me," Jimmy said for about the hundredth time, exasperation dripping from every word as he ran a hand through his hair. "Just stop talking and listen. And don't call him that." He watched as Nate scrunched his face up in mock disgust, his eyes twinkling as he fought not to laugh out loud. "He is none of those things and you shouldn't even know words like that. Plus, that last one isn't even physically possible—at least I don't think it is." Nate put his hand over his mouth.

Nate—his beautiful Nate with his shaggy hair and his laughter crinkles around his eyes.

"No." He changed his tone to one with a hard edge to it. "I'm telling you, both of you—he's sitting right in front of me—he is never to take his clothes off when you're around, no matter what you say. I own him. I make the rules, not you. He doesn't do what you say, no matter how insistent you are, if he knows I won't like it. He knows how I feel, and I'm telling you straight out, I don't want anyone else touching him or him to touch anyone else. No tricks, Mum. No, twisting my words to fit in with whatever crackpot theory you have going to justify yourself. You don't do anything or say anything to him that you wouldn't say out loud in front of me. I don't care what you think. That's the way it is."

There was a brief silence in which Jimmy stared straight at Nate, as he only half listened to the vitriol that spewed from his mother's mouth. Nate's laughter had gone, his face registering the seriousness of Jimmy's voice and words. "He's mine and no one else gets to look or touch, not even you. If you don't like that, then don't come here anymore. You're not welcome." Jimmy switched off the phone. "You think she got the message?"

"I would have but..."

"Yeah, I know." Jimmy blew out a breath, the hard edge gone. "She's my mum and she plays by her own rules."

"Something like that," Nate said. "But... I don't think you're meant to side with your slave over your own mother."

"Nat, sweetheart." Jimmy sighed. "I didn't think about it. It's a done deal. I'll choose you over her any day."

"I..." Nate tilted his head to the side and regarded Jimmy, an expression on his face that Jimmy didn't quite dare to think he'd interpreted right. "Thanks, you very confusing man."

"Why am I confusing?"

"No reason, just thank you for saving me from your mother. And if that doesn't make me sound as lame as a school kid, I don't know what would." Nate laughed.

"You don't have to thank me – it's just the way it is." Jimmy grinned, wide and infectious. "How about I promise never to leave you alone with her?"

"That will do me just fine," Nate said, and he seemed like he meant it.

* * * *

Jimmy thought about passing it off as an impulse buy, something he saw in a shop window and liked. With a wave of his hand, he could say he hadn't thought about the significance of it, that he thought it would just look good on Nate, but that would have been missing the point. He could say all that to other people, but it was important that Nate knew the truth – knew what it really meant, the intention behind it.

But he didn't want to make a ceremony out of it, one full of clichés and scenes from bad movies. No, Nate was a man—a big strapping, six-foot-plus man, with strong shoulders and workman's hands. He didn't deserve to be treated like a woman. He deserved more, much more. Jimmy was hoping he could prove that. Hoping he could show Nate just how much he thought of him. How much Nate meant to him, what he would do for him. If this didn't prove it, he couldn't think of anything else that would.

* * * *

He planned it carefully, a quiet evening when there was no rush to do anything, no place to be, and no chance of being interrupted. They'd just finished dinner. Nate's cooking skills were improving—sort of—and Nate had plonked a bowl down on the table. "I made pudding," he said, eminently pleased with himself.

"What is it?" Jimmy stared. It was pink-ish and wobbly.

"Not sure. It was meant to be a custard thing but we didn't have half the ingredients and then I found a bottle of red food dye in the back of the cupboard so I added it. I thought it would come out like blood but it's more like mashed Barbie." He shrugged, serving it up. "Still it's got a ton of sugar and cream in it, so it should taste good."

"Good, but maybe not healthy. We're supposed to be eating healthy." Jimmy tried it. It wasn't bad for a pink-ish, wobbly thing.

"Knock yourself out and do what you want for the night." Nate tucked in with gusto.

Do what you want.

There was one thing Jimmy very much wanted to do.

He watched Nate eat for a long moment then reached into his jacket pocket. "I bought you something."

"Can I eat it? Is it steak?"

"No, to both of those. You wear it."

"Oh, okay. Another pink shirt?"

"No, not a shirt. It's a... Here, see for yourself." He pushed the small blue box across the gap between them.

Nate picked it up and stared at it before glancing up at Jimmy, his face curiously blank. Then he opened it.

"I searched everywhere for it—shops, the Internet, everywhere. I wanted something just perfect. It's antique silver, not from here. I got it sent over, had it resized, which was pretty damned hard without letting you know. I wanted something with a history, something with meaning to it. The pattern on it is intertwining branches, it's about unity and two becoming one and..." He sucked in a lung full of air, letting it out slowly. "I wanted something that would have meaning for me, us. I wanted you to understand how I feel about you."

Nate lifted the silver ring from the box. "Thank you," he said carefully, evenly, laying the words out. He turned it round, before holding it ready to put on.

"No," Jimmy said quickly. "Don't. I have to do that. I want to put it on you and see it there every day and for you to know what it means. What you mean to me." He took the ring back, holding it carefully, with reverence, before he lifted Nate's hand. He licked at his lips, mouth suddenly dry. He wanted this so much. Wanted it and wanted it to be right. "I know we're bonded but that wasn't by choice. I wouldn't have done it, not if I could have got out of it, not back then. This is all about choice, about free will. I want this. I want to do it. I want to bond us together, want it with every atom of my body and soul." He pushed the ring on Nate's finger.

It fit flawlessly. Looked perfect.

He glanced up, desperately needing to know that Nate understood just how much he meant every word he'd said.

Nate was biting at his bottom lip. A nerve flicking up high above his eye and he was very obviously fighting for control. "Thank you," he said again, the words clipped, tight.

Maybe Nate did know after all.

* * * *

They went to the lake cabin the following weekend, driving down on Friday night, as Nate was so keen. He was up really early the following morning, breakfast on the table, jacket and boots ready by the door, big grin on his face.

"What?" he asked, the grin growing, as Jimmy yawned and scowled. "All that walking last time did wonders for my leg. We have to do it again."

"Can't we do it later?"

"We could but if we go now, we have the rest of the day for other things."

"Other things?"

"I thought we'd go swimming in the lake this afternoon."

"Are you fucking nuts? It's still freezing and… You're joking, right?" Jimmy glanced over, Nate's grin was almost manic. "I hate you."

"No you don't." Nate laughed. "Come. Walk. It'll be good."

And Nate was right, it was good, fun. Walking in the crisp morning air, with the dew still on the grass, talking about unimportant things, laughing at nothing, enjoying the comfortable silences. Jimmy started to daydream about the 'other things' they could do all afternoon. He'd have to get a hot tub fitted, maybe a steam room, then those other things could happen in even more wonderful places. It was good until he had become aware that the silence had gone on too long and turned over to see that Nate's face was pinched and gray. "What's the matter?" he asked.

"Maybe I got a bit overconfident." Nate took a deep breath. "Maybe I walked a bit too far."

"Shit, baby, are you in pain?" He caught hold of Nate's arm, easing him down to sit on a fallen tree.

"A bit," Nate admitted, wincing as the angle of his ankle changed in the brace. "But I'll live."

"More like a lot. Why didn't you say something?"

"Because I was enjoying myself?" Nate sounded apologetic.

"You're not now though." Jimmy looked around them. They were in the middle of nowhere, no roads or tracks in sight. "There's no way I can get the car here. We're going to have to make our own way back."

"I'll be okay." Nate didn't sound it. "Just let me rest here for a while and I'll be able to walk back. I'll be fine."

Only he wasn't fine. By the time they made it to the cabin, Jimmy was practically carrying him, and Nate was covered in a cold sweat and holding his leg in a fierce grip. The 'other things' Jimmy had in mind disappeared as he spent the rest of the day watching Nate sleep off the effects of all the extra strong pain meds he'd taken. Even when he woke up in the early evening, he was groggy and still rubbing at his leg. Jimmy made him eat some pizza, but he had more sense than to force a beer on him.

He ignored Nate's thanks for taking care of him and pressed Nate back to bed for more sleep.

In the middle of the night Jimmy woke to a dream-like image of Nate standing at the side of the bed staring down at him. He was just about to reach out a hand when Nate pulled up the covers, tucking them securely around Jimmy and smoothing the hair out of his eyes. Before he knew what was happening, Jimmy was asleep again. When he woke once more, properly this time, it was to an empty bed. He didn't like that, so he went to find Nate. He was sitting by the window, watching as the night turned into early morning gray.

"I missed you," Jimmy said, resting a hand on the back of his neck, caressing slowly.

"My leg ached. Nothing bad, but I couldn't settle. Not after sleeping all day. I didn't want to disturb you. You seemed so comfortable."

"How about tomorrow, today," Jimmy amended. "We sleep late and take things easy."

"Sounds like a plan."

"Come back to bed when you're ready." Jimmy stroked across Nate's shoulder, down his arm. "We have all day to relax and enjoy this place."

"Can we come back again? I haven't put you off?" Nate stared up, his eyes wide in the gloom.

"Course you haven't put me off." Jimmy smiled. "I like it here. I like you even better when we're here. We'll come as often as we can."

It was a promise he would keep.

* * * *

When Jimmy got in late the following Thursday, Nate was whistling, off tune, to a melody he didn't recognize. "Hi. You sound in a good mood." He gave Nate a quick kiss on the cheek.

"I am. You know the long running war I've been having with your washing machine?"

"Our washing machine," Jimmy corrected, getting a beer from the fridge and offering Nate one. When he shook his head, Jimmy put it back. "I've heard about it. To be honest, in more detail than I really wanted."

"Well, today I won. Not just the battle, the whole war. I have that bitch tamed." Nate grinned. "I found the black sock that was jammed in it. I had to take the back off the machine but, shit, I tanned its arse. We both know who's boss now. That's if it still works."

"And if it doesn't, we'll buy a new one." Jimmy sat at the table.

"Like hell you will. I am not letting it win."

"Whatever." Jimmy rubbed at his neck. "We're going to have to put back going to the lake cabin. I have to work Saturday, make up some time that was lost. I should get Monday off, so we can go Sunday, come back then. If not, we'll have to make it the following weekend."

"Okay," Nate said, pulling plates out of the cupboard.

"I know you're disappointed but it can't be helped."

"Really, it's okay."

"You know what I love about you?" Jimmy smiled up at him. "You're so damned easy going. I've been with guys and girls that are really high maintenance but you? You're just about perfect."

Nate looked at him for a moment then shrugged, his face showing nothing. "You still having poker night here Friday?"

"Yeah. You want to play this time?"

"No. They're your friends." Nate opened the freezer door, rooting around inside. "I'll stay upstairs."

"You don't have to. You're welcome down here."

"And get pawed all night? I'm happy to read and watch TV."

"They paw you?" Jimmy drank the last of his beer. "I warned them off."

"They don't." Nate turned round grinning, wide and infectious. "But you do."

"Can't help it." It was Jimmy's turn to shrug. "I like people to know you're mine."

"I know you do. You want steak pie that 'looks and tastes like mum makes'?" Nate read from the packet.

"Not if it's my mum. She can't cook to save her life."

"And yet she'd happily spend hours telling me how crap I am."

"You two are about equal when it comes to cooking."

"Sweet Jesus, save me now." Nate laughed, his eyes crinkling up. "I'm being compared to his momma."

"Shit, you really are in a good mood. What brought that on?"

"I'm in love with my physiotherapist."

"What?" Something dark and nasty rolled in Jimmy's belly as his chest tightened.

"Sven, the Swedish sadist, has left. I now have Susan, who has soft hands, a gentle voice and doesn't bully me. But she gets the job done, one flutter of her eyelashes, and I'm begging to be allowed to do another set of exercises. Man, she's good. I come out feeling like I've worked my arse off but thanking her for the privilege. I'd have fallen in love with her for that but today she said I can leave the brace off most of the time, that it was the weight of dragging the damned thing around that made me hurt so much up at the lake cabin. She says I should be going for a walk every day without it. I am finally, finally almost free of the fucking thing. A bit more physio to get my muscles back to full strength and I'm good to go."

"You can't sleep with her," Jimmy said quietly.

"What?" Nate stood with the half open frozen pie packet in his hand, a confused expression on his face.

"I said you can't sleep with your physiotherapist. Your new love."

"It was a joke." Nate shook his head. "She's married with four kids, a cat and an obsession with her garden."

"Doesn't matter. You can't sleep with anyone but me."

Nate shut the freezer door with great care and deliberation. "Don't worry, I know the rules. They were made extremely clear to me when I became a slave."

"I…" Jimmy sucked in a huge breath, fighting down the whirlwind in his belly. "I couldn't stand it. I just… You can't sleep with anyone else. No one but me."

"I know." Nate turned his back, switching on the oven. "Mash potato with the pie?"

"Yeah, whatever you want." But Jimmy had to force himself to say it in a normal voice.

* * * *

The scene at the lake cabin the following weekend was exceptionally beautiful. The sun literally sparkled on the water, making the whole place look picture perfect. The birds sang, the wind scarcely moved the leaves on the trees and the light was bright, clean and glowing. Even Jimmy was happy to get up early the first morning. There was something in the air that made him want to be outside enjoying it. They walked round part of the lake and Nate's leg didn't hurt at all, even without the brace.

Three weeks later they were back again and Nate could walk all morning, a picnic on his back, returning through the woods in the afternoon, and his leg didn't even tighten up. The sun was hotter, making the flowers Jimmy didn't know the name of, bloom, making Nate smile and warming the ground and their butts when they sat down.

Jimmy liked watching Nate smile, and he did it so much more often at the lake cabin. The atmosphere seemed to suit him, relaxation oozing through every pore, and Jimmy couldn't get enough. Couldn't get enough of watching as Nate seemed to regain full health before his eyes, as he stretched and tested his leg, tested Jimmy's walking stamina as well.

Exercising in the gym was one thing, this was altogether different.

Walking, taking the canoe for long trips to explore the far edges of the lake. Swimming in the now warm water until his muscles ached. Eating breakfast on the verandah as the day came to life, eating dinner out there watching the sun set, slow and easy over the tree tops. It was a beautiful way to spend a weekend.

Snatched, quick sessions outside in the long grass, long, slow ones in the huge bed with the windows flung open wide, so they could hear the rustle of the trees, the sound of the wind. Taking his time to fuck slowly and thoroughly, holding Nate against his chest as he thrust into him. Nate's breath coming sluggish and rasping, his sweat slick under Jimmy's hand, his heart thumping hard, his head thrown back. His hand reaching for Jimmy.

All good.

Just as good as a fast and frantic session in the shower, with Nate pressed against the glass. Or the rare occasion when he took Nate's cock into his mouth and Nate's reaction took his breath away. Even those sloppy times when Nate returned the favor. Jimmy could forgive the poor technique and lack of finesse. It was worth it to see Nate's mouth wrapped around his dick.

Jimmy couldn't get enough of any of it. He was happy, truly happy. Happier than he'd ever been before in his life and almost all of it was down to Nate. Nate made him see the beauty of the lake cabin, made him relax. Made him realize that nothing else was really important—not work, not what his mother thought. Watching Nate made him happy. Nate made him happy.

Jimmy stretched out on the crumpled sheets and pulled Nate tighter against him. "Remember how I told the judge at our last assessment that I'd been damned lucky with my punishment? Well, it wasn't a lie, I was damned lucky. I got you and was made to take the time to get to know you, really know you. That's not a punishment. That's a privilege." He kissed Nate's hair, inhaling his scent as he did so. "I thought I was suffering, when really my golden boy luck was working just as well as it ever has."

Nate patted Jimmy's thigh and Jimmy felt him fall asleep.

* * * *

Nate came home from physiotherapy almost dancing. "I am formally released. My leg has been declared as good as it was and I feel fine, like my old self. No more physio. I am officially healed." He slapped the paperwork down on the sofa next to Jimmy with a huge flourish.

"That's excellent news." Jimmy really did feel as excited about it as Nate. "What do you want to do to celebrate? We could go out, somewhere fancy? Or." He waggled his eyebrows. "We could stay in."

"You know what I'd really like?" Nate said, suddenly serious. "Can we go to the lake for a couple of days, just for... I'd like that."

"Really? That's all you want?"

"Yeah. Just you and me and a couple of days peace and quiet to let it all sink in."

"Sure, man. If that's what you want."

"Can we go this weekend? I don't want to leave it too long."

"Yeah, I was thinking of going anyway. It doesn't seem like much of a treat though."

"It is." Nate smiled. "Trust me. It is."

* * * *

It turned out that Jimmy thought it was a treat as well. It was probably the nicest weekend they'd had there so far. The weather stayed good. Nate's cooking stayed edible. They finally got the rhythm of paddling the Canadian canoe together and life felt great. He pushed thoughts of the increased workload that was coming from his mind. There was a new story line and he was in the thick of it, which would mean a lot longer hours for quite a while. But it was a good story, something he wanted to be a part of – a challenge. He still hadn't made his peace with everyone but, at Nate's gentle insistence, he was trying, putting in a real effort. A couple of the directors didn't like him, one writer almost went out of her way to make life difficult for him and half the crew weren't keen but... Maybe he was being overly optimistic, maybe there was a monster waiting around the corner for him, but he was doing his best to make things better, and that's what Nate said counted.

Even more challenging was his mother. She'd phoned again just before they'd left and some of the things she said, some of her suggestions regarding Nate, had him reeling. He didn't want to have to deal with her. He would, eventually. He knew he'd only put things off, but it had been good to shut the door on that part of his life and leave. At the lake cabin everything seemed so much less complicated.

Yeah, it was a treat going to there. Time alone to fuck and not to fuck. Time to hold Nate tight, to walk and to talk. To smile as Nate reached for his hand, a gentle glow on his face.

On Sunday night, Nate seemed as reluctant to leave as Jimmy was. He stood by the car looking around at the growing darkness and felt thankful he had this place to come back to. There were bad things back in the real world, he could almost feel their tentacles reaching for him, but here, now, life was good.

Nate stood even longer, leaning on the open car door, one foot already inside, gazing back at the lake and the cabin with an expression a little like longing on his face.

"We can come back soon," Jimmy reassured him. Nate just smiled before he got in, closing the door with a bang.

* * * *

The shoot was running over again, much to Jimmy's annoyance. At least it had stopped raining but it was cold, the gray light of dawn spoiling the night effect the director had wanted. They would call it a wrap in a while and Jimmy could go home, slipping into a warm bed, and an even warmer Nate.

The thought made him smile. He'd promised Nate he'd be home early. Nate had wanted to surprise him, or talk to him or something. But that was the great thing about Nate. Jimmy could break promises and he would understand. He never complained.

He'd make it up to Nate though—fuck him sweet and slow, take him deep and make it last for hours.

He was just thinking that thought through, his cock growing, when his attention was caught by a noise. Three big, powerful cars were pulling up, people he didn't recognize climbing out. How the hell had that happened? This was a closed set. No one got in who wasn't meant to be there. Not his problem though. Security would take care of it. Then he saw Nate get out of the passenger seat of the lead car.

"Hey, baby, what are you doing here?" he called over. Nate had never come to the set before. Jimmy was surprised he felt confident enough to do so now. That wasn't like Nate. But… "What the hell have you done to yourself? I didn't say you could cut your hair, you know I like it long. And what's with the awful clothes? They don't do you justice."

"Do you know who that is?"

Jimmy spun round at the question. It came from one of the young technicians—lighting, he thought. The guy was standing there now, eyes stretched wide, mouth hanging open, staring at Nate.

"Of course I know." Jimmy couldn't help the pissed off tone of his voice, Nate was his. No one else was allowed to stare at him like that. "That's Nat, my bonded mate."

"That's your mate?" The technician was staring at Jimmy now, his eyes even more shocked. "But you can't be bonded with him, he's..."

"Who?" Jimmy didn't understand. "What?"

"He's one of the leaders of the freedom movement. You must know that. How can you not?"

"Nat?" It was Jimmy's turn to stare at Nate.

Nate sighed. "My name isn't Nat or baby or sweetheart," he said levelly. "It's Nathan Fletcher, and these are other members of the freedom movement." He drew a semicircle in the air, indicating the other people, who had followed him out of the cars and now stood, a little way back, in an arc around him.

"You're a freedom fighter?"

"He's one of the best," the technician cut in. "One of the best fighters. I saw him in action a year or so ago, getting slaves off a farm where they were being beaten half way to death. He was amazing. I'd have stormed the barricades right then if he'd asked me to." The technician took a step closer to Nate, something like hero worship on his face. "When The State went after the freedom movement, no one knew who was still alive and who was just in hiding. I prayed they'd come back and they have, stronger. We might just get a revolution. But I never thought he'd... You'd... Shit, what a way to hide out."

"Shut up," Jimmy shouted at him, before turning his attention back to Nate. "Is any of that true?"

"It's all true," Nate said. "Can we go and talk? Please."

"Holy fuck." Jimmy felt the color drain from his face as his belly rolled and his brain tried to catch up. "You were hiding with me?"

Nate shrugged—a slight hitch of one shoulder. "It was as good a place as any. I was safe and fed. Plus it wasn't exactly hiding. The State knew where I was— they put me there. They knew I couldn't run, not with a busted leg."

"They knew who you were?"

"Let's go and talk about this somewhere else where we can—"

"No." Jimmy shook his head. He could feel his hands shaking, his chest, his everything. "You tell me now."

"Of course they knew." Nate took a couple of steps forward, stopping as the other people moved in closer behind him. "How do you think I got the broken ankle?" he asked, his voice quiet. "After they caught me, they hit me with a baseball bat to stop me going anywhere. I was just lucky they didn't break both legs. But that was their mistake, underestimating us."

"Why didn't you tell me?" Jimmy demanded. "Why didn't you tell me any of this? Who you are... What they'd done."

"You never asked," Nate's voice dropped lower.

"But you could have told me."

"When we were in prison, you never stopped talking long enough for me to get a word in. You were too busy moaning about how your life sucked. Later...it didn't matter to you."

"That's not fucking fair, I—"

"Jimmy," Nate interrupted him. "Let's take this somewhere private. We don't need an audience."

"Take what private?"

"I need to talk to you. I waited at the house until the last minute, but you didn't come and now I have to go."

"Go? Where the fuck are you going?" Jimmy couldn't think, couldn't breathe, couldn't understand what was happening.

"Back to work," Nate said gently. "Back to my life, back to what's important."

"You can't go anywhere, not without my say so. Don't forget, I own you." Then Jimmy watched at Nate's face closed up, the softness draining away to leave an inflexibility Jimmy wasn't used to.

"Let's talk about this in private." Nate scanned the area, moving toward Jimmy's trailer.

"No, I'm not going anywhere." Jimmy couldn't stop himself shouting. "Neither are you. You're my slave. You'll do what I tell you. I fucking own you."

"I don't do what anyone tells me, not anymore," Nate said, stopping where he was, voice very controlled. "Thank you for the chance to heal up but I'm leaving now. I only came to say goodbye. I figured I owed you the courtesy of an explanation." Then he was turning, hand reaching out for the car door, leaving, and Jimmy couldn't stand it.

"The courtesy of an explanation?" Jimmy felt his face go tight, every tendon standing out proud in his neck. Nate was his—his. "You bastard, after all the hours we've spent making love, all you owe me is that?"

"Making love?" Nate's voice changed in an instant. Now it was icy cold, his face hard. The others had moved into a closer pattern of support around him as Jimmy had shouted.

"What the fuck else would you call it?"

"We've never made love. We haven't even fucked much." Nate's hands had balled into fists at his side. "Don't lie to yourself. I was your slave all right. I had no choice. You raped me. Yeah, maybe I learned to get something out of it but it was rape, nothing else."

"Rape? I didn't..." Jimmy took a step back, feeling like he'd been punched.

"What, you think I liked being fucked five ways to Sunday?"

"But you never said... You let me think..."

"You fucking owned me." Nate's voice rose dangerously. "What could I say? No? Don't? Then you'd have probably beaten me and there wouldn't have been a damned thing I could have done about it. Instead I kept you sweet, let you think whatever you wanted to think. That way I didn't get hurt and even got off myself. I'd have run if I could, but I had to stay put until my leg healed. No point making the wait worse than it had to be."

"But we're bonded, married." Jimmy couldn't think straight, couldn't work out what was happening.

"Bonded?" Nate raised an incredulous eyebrow as he pulled the ring from his finger. "It doesn't count if someone is threatening to break your neck if you don't say yes." He threw the ring up in the air, catching it easily. "Here." This time he threw it at Jimmy, who didn't even attempt to catch it and it landed at his feet. "I might not be able to get rid of this." Nate rubbed over the brand on the back of his hand. "But I sure as hell don't have to wear that piece of crap anymore. I used to take it off every fucking time you walked out the door. I hated it so much."

"But I bought it so you'd know how I felt—about you, about us, about everything. That wasn't forced."

"Wasn't forced?" Nate's eyes turned hard, nasty. "Remember when you stuck it on my finger, gave me a shit speech about free will and choice? Well, it sure as fuck wasn't my free will, my choice. You never even asked me how I felt about it—you just tried to brand me all over again. Have you any idea how close I came to hitting you that night? It took every ounce of self-control I had not to beat that crap out of your mouth. Free will? You didn't even think about it and you sure as hell didn't get a ring for yourself. Understand this… I'm not your slave anymore and we were never bonded. I'm walking away and, if the freedom movement wins, I'll make sure no other poor sucker has to go through this shit."

"But…"

"What, what now?" Nate stared at him and Jimmy couldn't work out if it was disgust, contempt or pity he saw in his eyes.

"I love you," he whispered.

"Jimmy." Nate pulled himself up to stand straighter, taller. "You don't even know me." The scorn dripped from his voice.

Jimmy stood and stared as Nate walked away, watched as he started to climb back into the car, the other people going with him. Nate stopped then, looking back, and again Jimmy couldn't read his face. "I might like taking it up the arse from you at times but I also like giving it just as much and"—he paused, making sure Jimmy was watching—"I truly fucking hate sucking cock."

Then the door closed, the cars drove away, and Jimmy was left standing in the middle of a group of people who were all staring at him.

Chapter Six

Jimmy closed the front door and stopped for a minute, his palm flat against it. He was so fucking glad to be able to shut the world out. He closed his eyes and took a couple of deep breaths, slow and precise. He felt utterly exhausted—exhausted to the point of falling down.

Another day over, another to get through tomorrow.

Since Nate had left, each one had been the same.

So many on set had witnessed the scene of Nate leaving, had heard everything he'd said, that Jimmy couldn't hide from it. Those that hadn't soon got it from someone else, word spreading like wildfire, until the whole world knew. At least that's what it felt like.

His mother had called that first night, her vitriol boiling over. How could Nate have done it, shaming him like that? Slaves didn't know how lucky they were these days. They needed putting in their place. He should have beat Nate more, made him understand that he was nothing. Made him understand just how goddamned lucky he had been to have an owner as decent as Jimmy. At the end of the phone call, the only thing Jimmy could think was how glad he was he'd never told his mother how much he loved Nate.

How much he still loved him.

Jimmy felt like the one who had been put in his place.

Others had said the same sorts of things as his mum. He should have beaten Nate, lent him out to other people to fuck. That would have shown him who was boss. He should have done this, done that, he should have... Endless things he should have done when all he wanted to do was love Nate.

Now people stopped talking when he came into a room, whispering behind their hands, eyes always tracking him, watching.

The false normality that wasn't normal at all.

Just about everyone regarded him differently.

Some felt sorry for him, offering sincere — or insincere — remorse. Others, more, looked at him with something in the back of their eyes. They'd heard Nate's words, heard how Jimmy had raped him.

Rape — what was he meant to think when a word like that was thrown around?

Jimmy thought... It had actually taken endless nights lying awake staring at the ceiling to work out what he thought. What he'd been thinking back then. Soul searching that had taken weeks and sapped the energy from him. It had been damned hard to see himself in the bright, florescent light of Nate's gaze.

Seen what he'd been, who he really was.

And looking that hard hurt. Hurt in ways he hadn't imagined. But then he never had been very good at imagining or thinking things through truthfully.

He'd thought then — back at the start when they'd first met — that they were both doing what they'd had to do to get by, to get through a system that was punishing them. Nate had been no fool. He'd known that Jimmy had to fuck him, had to be seen to do it. That they had to do it like it was a regular act between them. He'd known and gone with it, because, really, what other choice had there been?

Then, after, when it was just the two of them... Jimmy had honestly thought it had grown into something else. At first, maybe, he'd known that it was just about them both getting off but, hell, there was nothing wrong with that.

Nothing wrong with sex just for the fun of it, and that's what Jimmy had thought it had been.

But Nate hadn't and, honestly, Jimmy had never bothered to stop and think about what Nate wanted, what he thought. Never thought about how Nate reacted to sex, to the suggestion of sex.

Nate had never ever initiated sex without an ulterior motive.

That revelation took Jimmy ages to arrive at, and when he did, it hurt more than any of the 'rapist' stares he got. They were bad, those people who now thought of him as a rapist. Were they right? Everyone knew Jimmy had been bonded against his will to his slave, that he'd had no choice either.

But...a slave. Everyone also knew Nate was a slave. What did they think was going on?

Maybe they were as naïve as Jimmy. Maybe they thought it was love as well. Maybe the world was as stupid as he was.

But no, everyone looked at him differently, acted differently around him and he had no response to any of it. So he slunk off home as fast as he could, hiding out in the house, taking the phone off the hook more often than not. This had been his place of safety and comfort. Coming home to Nate and…

All that had been a lie and the sooner he got his head round the idea, the better. Got used to it and moved on. But how did he move on, when everything of Nate's was still here except the man himself? His clothes were still in the wardrobe, his mug on the rack, his boots in the hall, his toothbrush in the pot, the magazine he was reading still open at the same page on the coffee table. His smell lingering on the clothes Jimmy wouldn't wash.

He hadn't taken a damned thing.

Yeah, maybe Jimmy should have gotten rid of it all by now. It had been long enough, but… It was no good, he could lie to the whole world, putting on a brave face about worthless slaves, but there was no point lying to himself. He loved Nate. Loved him now as much as he had that day when he'd left for work. The day everything had changed.

He ached for Nate every morning when he woke up, every night as he tried desperately to fall asleep.

Nate, who said he'd raped him. Jimmy let the word wrap around his mind again, tried to match it to the thought of them in bed together. Him, buried deep inside Nate, Nate calling out his pleasure and, yes, it had been pleasure. Jimmy was sure of that. Nate had gotten something from it.

But had he made himself get something from it? He hadn't wanted to do it, but since he had to, he might as well get some pleasure from the act? That was so scarily real that Jimmy had reeled from the idea for days.

Slowly he was starting to accept that maybe that's all it had ever been, at least on Nate's side. Getting pleasure from the physical act.

And Jimmy had pushed him, forced him, to do that as well. Jimmy could remember only too well, back in prison, when Nate hadn't wanted Jimmy's hand on his cock. Hadn't wanted to come. He hadn't wanted it and Jimmy had made him. Jimmy felt sick at the thought of it.

He'd bet Nate didn't ache for him now. Didn't feel like there was a hole a mile wide, like half his life was missing.

Nate had said Jimmy didn't know him and he was right. He didn't.

After he'd left, Jimmy had hit the Internet hard, finding out about both the freedom movement and Nate. What he'd found had shocked him. He'd known about the movement, in the same way he knew about global warming. He knew it was out there, knew someone else was taking care of it. He'd never thought about it, never really thought about slavery, except in a kind of abstract fashion.

He'd never considered the right and wrong of it. It just was—had been for generations—those men and women taken and owned.

He'd always thought no one could do anything about something like that. Only it turned out people could and some people were. Heidi Allott, the tiny, blonde, charismatic leader of the movement, who always seemed to be covered in dirt. Vinny Reitz, Paulo Campbell and Lizzy Palmer—names he'd vaguely heard before, but now he could put a face to them. Could put Nate's name alongside theirs.

He'd thought about slavery since though. No longer abstract, someone else's problem, like hurricanes in a remote part of the world. This was real—Nate was real. So were those that he was fighting with. Names and places and dates had come up when he'd

Googled, following one link after another. Things that he'd kind of heard about. They'd been on the news, and he'd been watching, only not properly, not with his full attention.

Now he knew about these people, what they were doing. They were getting stronger every day. The freedom movement had come back and hit The State hard, gathering a wild momentum. People all over the country had been surprised by how thankful and relieved they'd been to see the movement back and had joined.

Nate was part of it all, had been from early on. Not at the very top level, not one of the main leaders, but certainly a deputy, lieutenant... However it was said. Jimmy might not know what to call him, but he knew Nate was close to those at the top, worked with the leaders. His name came up all the time. He was dug in deep. He was important. Very important.

His bond-mate was a freedom fighter. He always had been one, and Jimmy had never had an idea. He'd never known anything about Nate, because he'd never bothered to ask. That was one thing Nate was right about. It had never occurred to Jimmy to ask. Because he hadn't cared who Nate was, who he'd been before? Because he'd been just a slave? Maybe. Instead he'd owned Nate, had grown comfortable with the idea. Kept him hidden away from the world, all for himself.

Nate had gone along with the hiding to keep his identity from Jimmy — that made sense.

Jimmy had grown comfortable acting like an owner — he accepted that now. Accepted it but wasn't proud of it. Appalled was the right description. How had he let himself become like that? He'd spent many nights trying to figure that one out but in the end, it didn't matter. He couldn't change what had happened. He'd turned into someone he didn't recognize and didn't like.

Now he had to accept it and get on with his life.

Easier said than done.

The thought of an empty house, of eating a half-cooked microwave meal in front of the TV, really didn't appeal. Going out or seeing other people was even less attractive. Tomorrow he'd get his driver to stop and pick up a pizza on the way home.

It was a plan, of sorts.

* * * *

It was pitch dark when he got home. He had to balance the pizza box on one hand, while he searched his pockets for his keys. That was the trouble with always using the garden door to the house — no street lamps, only the small security light that came on when it detected movement. He waved his free hand high up in the air and it clicked on, illuminating the door and a small area around it. But he still couldn't find the right key, couldn't fit it in the lock, couldn't...

There was a rustling noise off by the bushes, farther into the garden. No, not a noise, movement. There was someone or something there and, fuck, what was he meant to do? Throw a meat feast pizza at an intruder?

"Is there someone there?" he called out. "Because if there is, you can just fuck off." Then it suddenly hit him who it probably was. Colleagues of Nate's. Other freedom fighters who weren't taking too kindly to the way he'd acted, what he'd done. Rape. It was a hell of a word. The movement was strong enough now that they could settle old debts. "Look. I know who you are and maybe you feel like you have a right to scare the shit out of me and maybe you do but it's only going to cause more trouble and no one wants that. So why don't you just fuck off and I won't call the police. You won't beat my skull in and we'll all be happy. Well, maybe not happy but at least..."

"Christ," came an exasperated sound from the darkness. "Just shut up."

"Nate?" Jimmy's belly did a double back somersault then dropped down to his feet. "Is that you?"

"You always did talk too much." Nate stepped out of the shadows.

"I..."

"Wow, that's a first. You've actually run out of words."

"What are you doing here?" Jimmy felt like he'd been hit with something hard, something that made his head spin. He took a step back then two forward, reaching out a hand.

Nate didn't move. "That's close enough," he said, voice stiff.

"Sorry, I..." Jimmy noticed he still had his hand out, palm up, fingers reaching and he felt a fool. He dropped it to his side, rubbing along the seam of his jeans. They stood like that for a long time, the pizza box making Jimmy's other wrist ache. But he didn't want to put it down, didn't want to take his eyes from Nate. The silence went on and Jimmy realized that Nate wasn't going to speak.

But if he didn't speak he'd leave and... "How are you?"

"Okay," came the reply.

"You're looking good, rugged. Are you eating enough? Getting enough sleep?"

"Jimmy, stop it. You're not my mother."

"No. Sorry." Jimmy didn't know what to do. He knew he was rambling, but he wasn't prepared for this. He honestly hadn't thought he'd ever see Nate again, except maybe on the Internet or TV. The damned pizza was heavy in his hand, the grease permeating the cardboard to slick his fingers and he didn't know what to do with it or with anything else. "Hey, I got pizza, you want to come in and have something to eat? There's enough for a family, let alone two."

Maybe it was a dumb thing to say, but he didn't expect the reaction it got. "This isn't a fucking social call." Now Nate sounded angry and Jimmy didn't know why, didn't know what had changed.

"What is it then?" he said at last, when the silence was becoming painful. "Why did you come?"

"I have no idea." The anger was gone, replaced with... What? Confusion? Despondency? Emptiness? Jimmy couldn't read it, didn't trust his own judgment.

"I shouldn't have come," Nate said, already turning, heading back into the darkness.

"Will you come again?" Jimmy called after him.

"I don't think so. No, I won't be back."

Jimmy heard a faint rustle of foliage then it was silent and still. It wasn't until the security light clicked off and he was left in darkness that he tried the door again.

Standing in the kitchen, he hadn't the heart to put the light on. He felt as if something would break, a spell or fantasy, something, if he did.

He threw the pizza in the trash and sat in the living room staring out of the window into the garden long into the night.

* * * *

Nate had said he wouldn't be back, but nine days later, as Jimmy was opening the back door, he sensed, rather than heard or saw, Nate in the darkness. He stopped, sliding the keys back into his jacket pocket and waited. The silence went on, but he knew, in ways he could never explain, that Nate was there.

This time it didn't come as quite such a shock and the wait gave him a chance to catch his breath and calm himself down. But waits could go on too long. "Are you going to take off if I turn round?" he asked quietly.

"I'm not a horse you have to avoid spooking," Nate said, his voice light, as though there were a vein of humor in it. Jimmy hoped there was.

"I'll turn slowly just to be on the safe side." He twisted on his heels. He waited and, eventually, Nate stepped into the light. Jimmy could see him better this time. He had a thick wash of stubble over his face, a weather beaten look to his skin and it seemed like more creases at the corners of his eyes.

He took Jimmy's breath away.

"You came back." It wasn't a question, wasn't meant as one. Just something to say.

"Yeah." Nate nodded.

"You said you wouldn't."

"I didn't think I would."

"Do you want to come in?" Jimmy gestured toward the door, but Nate was already shaking his head.

"No."

Should he risk it? Jimmy couldn't see what he had to lose. "So why did you come?"

"Because." Nate dropped his eyes from Jimmy's face for the first time. Jimmy watched as he squared his shoulders and made himself lift his gaze. "Because I didn't do what I came for last time."

"I thought you didn't know why you came?"

"I did. I had a motive, but then I got here and..." Nate shrugged and Jimmy saw he was smiling with embarrassment. "I kind of forgot the purpose."

"I guess that's what happens when you get old." Jimmy smiled right back at him. "Your memory goes."

"Yeah, maybe." Then the silence was in danger of growing too long again. Jimmy didn't want that.

"What did you come for last time?" he asked at last, not sure if he wanted to know the answer.

"I meant to say sorry but" — he shrugged again — "I don't know."

"Sorry for what?" Jimmy asked incredulously. "I think I should be the one saying sorry."

Nate ignored that. "Sorry for not talking to you the way I'd intended before I left. For doing it in public, in front of all those people you work with. That wasn't fair, but I guess I lost my temper. I shouldn't have done that. I'm meant to have better control."

"You don't have to apologize." Jimmy started then stopped. "Well, maybe it would have been better if it wasn't out in the open like that, but I deserved it."

"No, you didn't. You deserved a quiet, private conversation, not us shouting at each other like a couple of banshees."

"I didn't mean to shout." Jimmy wanted to move closer, wanted to reach out and touch. "It all came as such a shock — everything you said, the truth. I didn't think and... I guess that was my problem all along. I didn't think."

Nate pushed his hands into his pockets, standing easy and more confident than Jimmy ever remembered seeing him. Confident — that was it. Nate was confident, sure of himself, sure in his own skin. It changed everything about him, from the way he stood, now with an effortless gait, to the slope of his shoulders, to the tilt of his head. A man at peace with himself.

Jimmy was suddenly ferociously glad of the limited light as his cheeks flared. He wanted. Damn whatever had gone on before between them, he wanted Nate more than he ever had. Wanted with every atom, every ounce of his soul.

"You thinking now?" Nate asked, tone low.

"Done nothing but think since you left."

"What do you think?"

That I want to throw you down and fuck you so hard you scream my name. That I want to claim you and shout how you're mine. Jimmy thought but he had the sense not to let anything like that out of his mouth. "That I let it all get way out of hand. That I acted like someone I didn't know, don't like. That I'm sorry, sorry for a lot of things."

"We all have things to be sorry for." Nate stared at him levelly, showing the intelligence he'd always kept hidden. "What's your number one, top of your list?"

Jimmy knew how important his answer was, how so much could depend on it. He could carefully think out an answer, try to pick the right one. The one Nate wanted — or he could be completely honest. He went on instinct and did the latter. "I'm sorry I forgot the difference between right and wrong."

Nate didn't exactly smile, but his whole face softened and his body relaxed. "I'm sorry too." He pulled his hands out of his pockets, turning to go. "I'll see you around, Jimmy Stephens." He even raised a palm as he left.

Jimmy slept easier that night than he had in a long time.

* * * *

Jimmy had only just managed to get his heart rate back under control the next time Nate appeared, when Nate's phone rang and he said he had to go. Jimmy tried to say something about staying, about coming back, but his voice stuttered and Nate was already melting into the shadows.

That visit had been as much of a surprise as the first. He hadn't known what, 'I'll see you around', meant, didn't want to think too much. It was a casual phrase, right? One that didn't mean a damned thing.

But Nate had come back, done it after he'd made his peace with Jimmy. He'd had no reason to be there that time other than... Jimmy wasn't going to think about that either.

Less than a fortnight later Nate was there again and, yeah, maybe Jimmy had been watching for him every night when he got home. Watching, but not hoping. He was starting to work out that if he hoped too much, he didn't get. He'd even admitted to himself that wanting to leave a note under the pot by the door listing his shooting schedule was maybe going too far. He figured, if Nate wanted to know what time he'd get home, he'd have ways of finding out.

"Hi." Nate spoke first for once.

Jimmy let the feeling of relief sweep over him, before he looked up. Nate was sitting on the wooden patio table, feet on a chair. He seemed relaxed but tired. "Hi, yourself." Jimmy nodded to one of the other chairs. "Can I?"

"Knock yourself out." Nate pushed it closer to him with his foot. "It's your house, your chair."

Jimmy wanted to say it was Nate's home as well but he kept his mouth shut. He sat down, pulling his jacket tight around himself and stuck his hands in his armpits. If they were going to keep having late night meetings in the garden, he was going to start wearing a thicker coat. "Man, it's cold."

"You want to go in? I can go."

"Didn't say that, just commenting. It's been a long day."

"You and me both," Nate said, but didn't go on.

"I've been chasing make-believe aliens in my spaceship. What have you been doing?"

Nate looked at him for a long, long moment and Jimmy wasn't sure if he was going to answer. "Freed a bunch of slaves in one of the small towns out in the middle of nowhere."

"Sounds more important and rewarding than my job."

"We tried to do it by changing opinions rather than hitting and threatening people. Let me tell you, it's a damned sight harder."

"I bet it is. Did you manage it?"

"Well." Nate reached into his pocket, pulling out a half full bottle of whiskey and taking a mouthful. "The slaves are free and no one shopped us to the police. Can't say all the owners were happy about it or that there wasn't a hint of a threat, but it wasn't bad."

"Why did you bother? Changing opinions, I mean."

"Because Heidi says if we're actually going to transform the freedom movement into a freedom revolution, we have to take as many of the people as we can along with us." He drank some more then held the bottle out for Jimmy. "She's right, of course. That woman is always right. Can't have a revolution without support, but it's damned hard."

Jimmy took the bottle from him and drank. "You think it's really possible? To create a revolution?"

"I don't know. The momentum is building. I can feel the thing getting bigger every day. The State made a huge mistake when they hit us hard but didn't kill us off. We had time to recuperate and rebuild, to come back more potent. But it's more than that. The support out there is much, much stronger and more widespread." He held his hand out for the bottle, rolling it between his palms before drinking again. "Heidi and the others say it's now or never, and I think they're right," he said softly.

"I hope so," Jimmy said, unexpectedly conscious of how much he meant it. "Even if you can't stop it, you're changing perceptions." Nate watched him as Jimmy reached for the bottle again. "It's like with big gas-guzzler cars," he went on. "Everybody used to think they were okay, even a status symbol. Now it's all changed, with global warming and everything. It's gone beyond questioning the right or wrong of having one, to looking down on someone that does. The same thing is happening with slaves, people used to brag about owning one. Now they keep their mouths shut, even hide it."

"Really?" Nate said cautiously. "It's hard to tell from the inside."

"Yeah, really," Jimmy said. "I've spent a lot of time slowing down and trying to see what's was really going on. It started with the past, what happened between us, but I guess it's a habit you get into— trying to see the truth. Take it from someone on the wrong side of slavery. You're changing things. You're making a difference."

"We'll keep going then," Nate said, and held his hand out for the bottle before getting up to leave.

* * * *

Nate started turning up about once a week after that. Nothing regular, nothing planned, sometimes it would only be a couple of days between visits, other times longer. They'd talk about what Nate was doing, Jimmy's work, anything. It was simpler to talk than Jimmy had expected—sitting outside on the patio furniture, coats pulled tight around them, conversation seemed to come easy.

Conversations unlike any they'd had before. This was real, honest. Nate didn't try to please, didn't always agree with Jimmy or sugar-coat his words. When Jimmy realized that's what Nate had always done before, it had come like another slap to the face.

Nate had always said what he thought, knew, Jimmy wanted to hear. Now he didn't. Now he said what he meant. Surprisingly they agreed on more than Jimmy expected, but... Nate didn't have to and that was the whole point.

One night there was a lull and Jimmy decided it was time to take a chance. "Nate," he asked, suddenly serious. "Tell me about us, before. I think back to then and I can't work it out. How we got there. How we got to here. I've been trying to work out what happened then and...I don't understand it."

It was silent for a long time and Jimmy thought he might have pushed too hard.

"When you first saw me, saw who you were going to be bonded to, what did you think?" Nate said at last.

Jimmy thought all the way back to the start. "You were covered in mud, filthy except for the cast on your leg. I..." What had he thought? "I thought you were fucking gorgeous. You washed up even better. I thought I'd got real lucky." Nate stayed silent so Jimmy asked, "What did you think?"

"I never even considered what you looked like. I just thought you were a man-mountain, that you could hurt me with a flick of your wrist. In a fair fight I could take you any time, but it was never going to be that. I was your slave. You were allowed to hurt me and there was nothing I could do about it." He paused for a moment. "I wanted to get out of prison alive."

"I never thought of it like that."

"No, and that's the point... You never thought." Nate sat back in his chair, rubbing his hands together, his legs spread wide, his eyes on Jimmy's face, unwavering. "Remember, in prison, when I asked you about your sentence? I said it didn't seem right, didn't fit your crime, and you told me all the details." Jimmy nodded, and Nate went on. "Well, up until then I couldn't work out why I'd got you as a punishment. I was freedom movement. Slavery I could understand, but not bonding to a man. Then you told me about the homophobic insults, about hitting that guy for, what seemed to everyone else, being gay. Then it made sense. They thought you were going to beat the shit out of me, especially as you had to fuck me. You'd fuck me and beat me and it'd go on forever — that was a fitting punishment for someone in the movement. That's what they thought. That's what I thought as well."

"But I wouldn't... I didn't..." Jimmy stopped, appalled.

"That what I was waiting for." Nate's eyes never moved from his. "You kept saying you were decent and you seemed okay but I fully expected you to fuck me that first night."

"I couldn't. You were in pain and I never would..."

"You thought about it," Nate said quietly. Not softly, not like he used to talk, but quiet, deadly.

Jimmy pressed his lips together. No point lying, not now. "Okay, maybe I did, but I didn't go through with it."

"But you did let me think we wouldn't be doing anything until near the assessment and you were happy for me to do all the work around the place, while you sat on your butt—for me to be the slave." Nate went on, "Then you wanted sex and, no, it had nothing to do with practicing."

"You're right." Jimmy stared down at his feet, but he owed Nate more than that. He made himself look up. "I wanted you, plain and simple. I know the first night we fucked was a disaster. I was so concerned with enjoying myself that I didn't even think about you, about if you were getting anything from it." He took a deep breath and stared Nate straight in the eye. "I didn't care if you were. I was only interested in myself."

"I know," Nate said carefully. "But at least you can admit it now."

"Admit it to both of us. I wouldn't have, not back then, not even to myself."

"That's something. But." Nate studied him and Jimmy felt like a specimen under a microscope. "Are you ready to take the next step, admit the next thing?"

Jimmy's mouth suddenly felt so parched he had to fight to swallow. "Tell me?"

"Fucking me in the courtroom wasn't just me being raped. We had to do it, both of us. It didn't matter if you wanted to or not, so really you were being raped as well. Sex without consent is rape. But doing it when you wanted to and I didn't, when you didn't even bother to ask if I wanted it—that was rape."

And there it was, that word again. Out there, clear and forceful, with no place to hide from it. But it was better like that, better when it was there where they could both see it, face it, deal with it.

"I've thought about it a lot, going over everything that happened since you first said the word to me in the parking lot and…"

"And?" Nate pressed him. He wasn't going to get away with not thinking or hiding anymore. Nate wasn't going to let him.

"Yeah." Jimmy nodded. "That first night was rape, even if I convinced myself it wasn't, that it was just practicing. The second night though, we talked and…it seemed different, not just the sex, everything. Am I wrong in that?"

"No." Nate swung back on the legs of the chair before putting them down again. "You're not wrong. But it wasn't the sex that was different, it was me."

"How come?"

"It wasn't anything you said, wasn't really about you. I'd sat up the night before, thinking. You kept…" He shrugged. "You kept pawing at me in bed, not for sex, just hanging on to me."

"And you didn't like it?" That was a surprise.

"No, but then the next day I was looking at the other slaves. So many of them had bruises or shadows in their eyes. We all knew what was going on. Some talked about it, some didn't, but we knew anyway. A lot were getting hurt real bad. I wasn't and you could have so easily. I decided to just get on with it and make it as easy as possible for myself. If I could keep you happy, I wouldn't get away with it easy. Then you started talking, saying sorry, promising not to hurt me again, and I figured maybe I'd got lucky. I talked myself down then round to a different attitude."

"So the next night was better? And those that came after?"

"Better."

"But?" Jimmy stared at him. "Fuck, I can hear it, a huge great but... I honestly thought it was better. Not at first but slowly, over the next few days, weeks, it got better. We talked about how to make it good for you, about you telling me if I was going too hard. I kept encouraging you to get something out of it, to take. I tried to help, when you'd let me, I tried to make it good for you. Hell, I even admitted how much I wanted you."

"But you never thought to ask if the feeling was mutual."

"I..." Holy fuck—that made Jimmy stop and think again. "You're saying what I thought was rape, in the courtroom, wasn't just you being raped, it was me as well. But what I thought was different, better, was... It was all rape and I didn't know it. You never wanted me."

"You kept talking about making it good but never, not once, was there even a possibility of me saying no, I don't want sex with you." Nate kept his eyes fixed on Jimmy's. "Being forced to enjoy it felt like...it felt like more abuse. I wasn't even allowed the luxury of telling myself I was getting nothing from it. You wanted sex, so we fucked. You wanted me to come, so I had to, and that really got to me. What I wanted never came into the equation."

Jimmy couldn't take his eyes away and he had to ask. Had to. "Have you ever wanted me?"

"There were enough times after we got out of prison when it was good, when I enjoyed the sex. After I'd stopped getting so uptight about everything and relaxed."

"But wanted, actually wanted?"

"I don't know. It's hard to tell if you want something when you've got no choice in it."

"But." Jimmy felt like his skin was too tight, his blood pounding too hard, too close to the surface. "Sometimes you initiated sex?" He knew he was fooling himself, but he had to ask.

"When you were being a dick, when you were about to get us into trouble again, in prison. To calm you down or to stop you nosing into things I didn't want you anywhere near and, sometimes, just to shut you up."

"That's...horrendous."

"What did you think it was about?"

"I don't know, I...I loved you, I thought... I hoped...not that you loved me but maybe that you wanted me?"

"I never had a choice. Never. How could I tell if I wanted you when that fact made me want to put my fist through the wall, I was so angry?"

"I was raping you and I didn't realize." Jimmy closed his eyes for a moment, holding his breath as he thought back. "When you came, when you moaned and groaned and fucked back onto me... I really believed you were enjoying yourself, that you were getting something out of it. I never thought about rape."

"There were times when you pushed for sex, even though you knew damned well I didn't want it, but..." Nate paused for a long moment, licking at his lips. "Usually I hid that and maybe I was complicit in it." He sounded hesitant for the first time. "I made sure you saw what you wanted to see and I'd be fucking lying if I said I didn't get anything out of it. No wonder you couldn't see the truth. But all I kept thinking was, 'I have no choice', and I made myself despise you for that."

Jimmy swallowed hard, the tendons working in his neck. "Tell me the rest. Tell me the worst. What else did you think?"

"What did I think?" Nate shrugged. "At first, that you were a prize dick, who was nothing but a trouble magnet. That you were self-absorbed to the point that you couldn't see reality and that, when it came crashing down, you'd take me with you. I was right. You fucked up and we both had to stay an extra month."

"You said you didn't care about that?"

"What the hell else was I going to say? Bawl you out for it and get smacked for my trouble? You owned me — there was nothing else I could do. But truth was, I didn't really care. I needed to wait for my leg to heal and I was safe enough in there with both you and the other slaves watching out for me."

"They were watching out?" Jimmy had to rethink that one as well. "I thought they wanted you."

"You thought a lot of things that were wrong."

"They knew who you were?"

"Some did. They told those that needed to know. It's why we got an easy ride inside."

"So they knew and the guards knew?"

"Most, not all."

"How come I didn't?" Jimmy had to ask.

"Because you didn't see what was going on right in front of you. Because I didn't want you to know and made sure you didn't find out."

"Why not? Why couldn't you have told me then or later, when we were free?"

Nate studied him critically, eyes so sharp that Jimmy felt like squirming away. "Because you'd got yourself a slave and you thought everything in the garden was perfect. You were loving it. I didn't know what you'd do if you knew I was one of those fighting to take it all away from you."

"You're right, of course." Jimmy hung his head for a moment. "I don't know what I would have done either. I like to think it would have been the right thing but..." He took a deep breath before going on. "So you stopped me getting into trouble and smoothed things out for us."

"Somebody had to—you had no idea what you were doing. Then, later on, I just thought you were an idiot. One minute you'd act one way toward me, the next you were completely different, and you were always saying such stupid things."

"Like what?"

"Like..." Nate seemed to think about it, then his face suddenly lit up. "One time you congratulated me, saying you loved me because I was so low maintenance, unlike most of the other people you'd been with. I was your fucking slave. What did you expect? I had no choice. Of course I didn't complain."

"Okay, you're right." Jimmy rubbed his hands over his face. He figured he'd thought all this out but he'd only scratched the surface. "So what did you hate about me, about being with me?"

"Hate's a big word. There's not much I hated. You weren't that bad."

"So what didn't you like? What pissed you off?"

"Pissed me off?" Nate's eyebrows rose. "I can do a list of those. You want it alphabetically or by how pissed I was?"

"Anyway you like, just start at the top."

Nate pushed himself forward, counting things off on his fingers as he said them. "Being called baby or sweetheart really fucking annoyed me. I'm not a woman. I didn't like Nat either, not from you. But if you'd called me Natalie I probably wouldn't have been able to stop myself laying you out. Lucky you didn't do that one. Then there were the appalling clothes. I mean, for God's sake, pink? And the health food and expecting me to cook and clean and be the perfect little housewife. The stupid TV programs you watch and the way you used to stroke me like some kind of pet in front of other people. The way you were always messing with my head. I tried so hard to pin you down and read you, but I was never quite sure where you were coming from. You never lied to me but, one minute you'd be decent and loving, the next you'd pull the owner card. Then there was always having to be in a good mood, while trying to coax you out of a bad one, just like a little kid. Oh and being nice to your mother and... How far down the list do you want me to go?"

"I think I get the idea." Jimmy pressed his lips together for a moment but he'd started this, better to keep going. "You said there wasn't much you hated. That means there were some things. What?"

Nate sat back in his chair, sighing. "I really hated the ring."

"Why that out of everything?"

"Because it meant so much to you. A ring ought to mean a lot, ought to be important, ought to be about commitment. It was to you but you never thought about me, how I felt about it. A ring should be about joint commitment, not about you sticking it on my finger and saying I was yours all over again."

"You're right, of course." Jimmy wasn't sure how many more home truths he could take. "What else?"

"Mostly, not having a choice in anything. Not being allowed an opinion or to say anything. Never being asked, not even on the little things."

"I asked you about stuff—asked what you wanted, what you thought."

"No you didn't, not really. You might have said, 'what color bed sheets shall we get?' But you only wanted the answer that agreed with you. That's not asking."

Jimmy hung his head as he rounded his shoulders again, but once more he made himself look up. "And in bed I never asked at all, did I?"

"No," Nate said simply. "And I'll tell you one thing that I really do hate and that's sucking dick. It has nothing to do with you and the size of your cock. I hate sucking any dick. For years I've heard about my amazing cock-sucking lips. How men want to see them wrapped around their dick. Seems ironic that people feel like that about them, when I plain don't like the taste, the feel, the...anything about it."

"I used to like the look of my dick in your mouth," Jimmy said quietly.

"I know you did. But at least you didn't force me to take more than I wanted. I'm...grateful for that."

"Grateful?" Jimmy snorted. "That I didn't rape your mouth any harder? You shouldn't be grateful. You should be mad. Why didn't you tell me?"

"Because you didn't want to know and you wouldn't have listened anyway. You liked it too much." Nate laid the words out flat and stark.

"Jesus." Jimmy thrust his way out of the chair, hands on his face as he took a couple of strides into the darkness. "You're right. I wouldn't have listened. You must hate my fucking guts."

Nate raised a shoulder, letting it fall casually. "Like I said, hate's a big word."

"Is there anything you like about me?" Jimmy really didn't know if he wanted to hear the answer.

"Well." Nate stretched out in the chair, knees falling open wide again. "You're funny. You're generous—thanks for paying for all the physio by the way. They did a great job. I don't have any problems with my leg now." He started counting things on his fingers again. "You're weird but in a good way. You're loyal—hell, you even defended me against your mum. You're easy to be around. You're mostly the happiest person I've met and I think you're intrinsically kind and probably decent. Also..." He looked up at Jimmy, humor in his eyes. "When you calm down and concentrate, you really do know how to fuck."

"What?" Jimmy wasn't sure he heard the last one right. He dropped back onto the chair.

"That was another thing I've never liked much, being fucked. If I was with a guy, it was usually me doing the fucking. But you, you really know your way around...well, around me or my insides or something equally as gross sounding."

"I know you said you liked it, and I thought you did, but I figured that was just you saying what I wanted to hear. You actually mean it?" Jimmy asked.

Nate glanced over at him, holding his eyes, a smile on his lips. "Seeing we're being honest here, I guess it's only right you get the good as well as the bad. When I calmed down as well, stopped freaking out over being forced into sex and let myself have a good time, I realized pretty quickly that I've only ever really enjoyed being fucked by you. You sure do know where to put that monster in me."

"You're insane," Jimmy said, astonished.

"Probably, but you have to admit it did make the nights more pleasurable."

"Yeah but…" He couldn't help staring at Nate.

"And you're fucking good at sucking cock. I can't, hand-on-heart, say it's fair, seeing as I hate it so much. But, man, I loved it when you sucked my cock, even if you didn't do it that often."

"I didn't know you liked it that much."

Nate tipped his head, considering him. "Yeah, you did. You knew just how much I liked it. That's why I wouldn't let you do it very much."

"I don't understand. Explain that."

"You knew how much I liked it, how I lost control when you did it," Nate said quietly, laying the words and implications out. "You enjoyed me losing control. But more than that, you enjoyed being in control, having that power over me. It's why I stopped you most of the time."

"You stopped me? I don't remember it like that."

"You're real easy to distract, to get going in another direction. And if you were persistent? Hell, I'd just offer to blow you. That worked. It's why I wouldn't get drunk with you."

"Wait. You said you didn't like alcohol?"

Again Nate angled his head, watching. "I said a lot of things that aren't true."

"So why wouldn't you get drunk with me? Didn't you trust me to look after you?"

"I wasn't sure what you'd do if I was out of it. You did like the power."

"I wouldn't have hurt you." Jimmy sat forward, face closer to Nate. "Don't you know that?"

"Maybe not hurt but..." He hesitated for a moment, bottom lip caught between his teeth. "I think you might have taken advantage of the situation."

"Christ." Jimmy hissed. He thought he might have as well.

"Anyway," Nate went on. "I didn't trust myself to get drunk. I might have let slip something that you weren't to know."

"I really had no idea what was going on, did I?"

"Not a lot." Nate shrugged. "But I'll tell you one thing, if the acting ever falls through, you could make a career out of sucking cock—and fucking."

"I don't know how you can be so calm about it all, be so..." He searched around for the right word. "Lighthearted."

"Because I knew what was going on and you didn't." Nate sat back, oozing confidence and self-assurance. "It hasn't come as a shock to me. I've had all the time we've know each other to work things out and you're still rolling around in the dirt."

Rolling around in the dirt. Jimmy liked that way of putting things. It summed up how he felt pretty perfectly. He was rolling in the dirt, trying to figure which way was up.

But at least he knew it now.

Chapter Seven

After the night when they had really talked about the past, it was nearly three weeks before Nate came again. Jimmy had started to get scared that he would never return. But, when the television news showed reports of freedom movement activity at the other end of the country, he stopped worrying if Nate was coming back and started worrying whether he was even alive.

The State was hitting the movement harder than ever before.

Whatever happened though, Jimmy made sure he always came home alone, always sent his driver away before he came round the back of the house. Always waited for a moment before he pushed his disappointment down and went inside.

Late one night, when he'd already given up any hope, Nate called out a hushed, "Hey," just as Jimmy was about to open the back door. Nate was panting, face flushed as though he'd been running.

"Hi," Jimmy said.

"I didn't think I'd catch you before you went indoors."

"You could always knock?"

"No." Nate did up his jacket, pulling up the collar before sitting down and making himself comfortable.

Jimmy thought about asking why not, but he wasn't sure he wanted to hear the answer. Instead he nodded, accepting. "You're not dead then. I was...beginning to wonder."

"Yeah." Nate stretched his legs out. "Not dead, even though it's been a tough few weeks."

"That bad?"

"Depends what you mean by bad." Nate shrugged. "We did our thing. Some people joined us. Some did their damnedest to stop us. It was hard but..."

"But?"

"No, no but. Hard but necessary and we made progress. Another step in the right direction, as Heidi would say."

Jimmy bounced the keys in his hand, eyes fixed on Nate. "If you had been dead, I'd never have known, would I? Not unless it was on the news."

"I doubt I'm important enough for that." Nate shrugged again. "You'd find out eventually though."

"Yeah?" Jimmy raised a disbelieving eyebrow. "Who'd bother to tell me?"

"Well." A slow grin crept across Nate's face. "You are still my legal owner. The State would send you the bill for getting rid of my body."

"Oh shut the fuck up." Jimmy turned away, rubbing a hand over his mouth before looking back. "Can I ask you a question?"

"Sure. Not guaranteeing I'll answer it, but ask away."

"Why do you come back here?" Jimmy asked. "I mean, why do you come and see me?"

Nate hesitated for a long, long moment, studying Jimmy. "I don't know. I don't understand it myself really. I shouldn't want to. Everyone says I shouldn't but…" He shrugged.

"You don't understand why?"

Nate chewed at his lip, eyes still on Jimmy. "The whole wanting to come here thing fucking scares me and I don't get it and…"

"Come on, gut reaction. Why are you here right now?"

Again Nate shrugged, an odd hitch of one shoulder. "Because I know where I am with you?" he said at last. "Because you've never lied to me."

"I've never lied…" The concept left Jimmy gasping and he had to sit down. "But? That's fucking madness."

"No it's not. You lied to yourself." Nate tipped his head toward him. "You saw what you wanted to see, thought what you wanted, but you were always straight up with me. Even when you were being a possessive mother-fucker, you always did it honestly, openly. You didn't hide anything from me or play games. I hate games." He sat up a little, clearly warming to the idea. "At first I thought it was because you were too stupid to do anything else, too stupid to hide stuff, but you can. You can act. I've seen you play a part for other people, only you never did it to me."

"But, I…" Jimmy didn't know what to say, what to think. "You…"

"Trust me, I'm right, I always did have more sense than you. You used to confuse the fuck out of me by changing from affectionate and loving to a controlling, possessive owner. But even then, after a while, when

I'd got used to you, I knew where you were coming from. I understood you, understood each mood, even if I didn't know how they fitted together. I knew where I stood with you and I think I still do. I..." He stopped for a moment. "I appreciate honesty. There's not a lot of it around."

"But there must be in the freedom movement, those you fight alongside?" Jimmy said, still trying to comprehend what Nate had said.

"Yeah, they're honest but..." Nate scratched his head this time, forehead wrinkling. "So many of them have agendas and that's all they think about. Ask a question and the answer is always shaped by it. Talk about something else and they aren't interested. They're going to get the job done. They're a hell of a lot more focused and useful than me only..."

"You don't always want to think about the fight?"

"Sometimes I don't want to think at all," Nate admitted.

"So talking to me is a break?"

"Here I don't have to... I don't know." He made an indistinct gesture in the air with his hand. "I don't have to be anything—not a freedom fighter, not strong or determined. I don't have to keep my game face on all the time. I used to act a part with you, but I don't anymore. I'm not pretending, not now and you know that. I can just be me and that's a relief."

"I'm glad I can help," Jimmy said softly. "You're welcome here anytime."

Nate looked at him sharply but didn't say a word.

* * * *

The next time Nate was sprawled out on the patio chair, legs spread, hands hanging by his sides, when

Jimmy got in late from work. If Jimmy didn't know better, he would have thought he was asleep. "Man, you look tired," he said, finding the bottle he'd taken to hiding under the forsythia bush before sitting opposite. "Bad day?"

"Bad few days," Nate admitted, taking the bottle and drinking after he yawned.

"Why?" Jimmy asked. Nate was talking to him about things that mattered. He realized it had never happened before Nate left. Nate had never talked and he'd never listened.

Jimmy enjoyed listening now.

"A load of things. The State is coming after us even harder. We freed another bunch of slaves and... Fuck." He sat forward, his head hanging between his shoulders. "I knew there was some sick shit going on out there but, hell, it's bad. What some people do to their slaves. Hearing about it is one thing, seeing it is completely another."

"Nate." Jimmy couldn't stop the concern showing in his voice.

"I'm okay. They aren't, but I am." Nate drank more of the whiskey before wiping his mouth with the back of his hand.

"But you're exhausted." Jimmy glanced around, seeing the situation properly. The legs of Nate's chair had sunk into the soggy grass, there was an empty potato chip packet underneath it, a discarded can of Coke by the bushes. "You've been out here hours, haven't you?"

"You were meant to be back at seven."

Jimmy thought about it. "How do you know that?"

"Ways and means, man." Nate snorted. "We have friends everywhere."

It was now almost ten. How many times had he waited like that before? "I'm sorry I was late. I..." He stopped, shaking his head. What else could he say? If he was tired, God only knew how Nate felt. A sudden shiver ran through him and he pulled his jacket closer. "Will you do me a favor, a big one? At least consider it?" He watched Nate.

"What?"

"Will you come inside?"

"How's my coming inside doing you a favor?" Nate asked, his voice level.

Jimmy closed his eyes, sighing before he opened them again. "Because I'm cold down to my bones and I'm hungry. I bet you're even worse. Please?" The silence stretched on and Jimmy wasn't sure if he'd asked too much. "Is it such a big risk just to come into the house? Can't you trust me on that?"

"Trust you?" Nate narrowed his eyes. "Don't you realize how much I already trust you by coming here?"

No, Jimmy hadn't really thought about it at all. "Tell me."

"If you talk to anyone, word will get back to the State Police, and I disappear. You wouldn't even have to give me up to them, just run your mouth a bit, and I know how you like to talk. If I was lucky I'd get a bullet in the head, if not... I've seen what they do to runaway slaves like me, let alone freedom fighters. I'm trusting you with my life already."

Jimmy felt like he'd been sucker punched. No, he hadn't thought it through. Worst still, it was the same crime he'd been guilty of before and he'd done it again. Right when he was congratulating himself on thinking, on having more sense. Nate was taking all kinds of risks coming here and he hadn't thought about it. Nate was also making a habit of knocking him sideways by the things he said. "I won't let you down or disappoint you."

"Disappoint me?" Nate stared at him, his eyes deadly serious. "The others all tell me not to trust you but I do, hell knows why. Tell you something though. I can understand why you acted like an owner and I can forgive what happened back then. But you break my trust now and I'd never get beyond that. That's what would…make me disappointed in you."

Another sucker punch. Not just that Nate trusted him, but how much making sure Nate wasn't disappointed in him mattered. "I won't," Jimmy said it with complete and utter conviction. He wouldn't let Nate down — not now, not ever. "Please, come inside."

"Okay." Nate nodded.

Jimmy sat Nate down in the living room, close to the patio doors that led out into the garden, and made a show of unlocking them. It seemed appropriate. He turned the heating up a notch then went into the kitchen. If he needed food, Nate probably did as well.

Nate was right. The State's control was slipping. He could feel it in the air, see it in people's eyes. Change was happening. Censorship was crumbling — the news was more balanced. There had even been a TV documentary about the people involved in the freedom movement a few nights ago.

A reporter had gained unparalleled access to some of the top members, following them around, filming them no matter what they were doing. Everything from hanging around wherever their base happened to be that week to impromptu rallies on mountainsides or empty car parks.

Jimmy had recorded it, watching it over and over again obsessively.

Heidi and the others had taken center stage—working, living, spreading the message. Nate hadn't been one of those featured prominently but he was often there, in the background, laughing and joking with his peers, coming back looking exhausted and bloody from raids, fights. Whatever a freedom fighter did—Jimmy wasn't sure.

When Jimmy had first seen it, he'd thought that there were two Nates. The one from Before—a word that definitely needed a capital letter—and the one on the TV screen.

During one part of the program Nate was off to the side, playing air drums and singing along to heavy rock music with a couple of the others. He was obviously enjoying himself and at ease. Before, Jimmy had thought Nate liked the same sort of soft country music he did.

That was another thing Nate was right about—Jimmy didn't know him.

Nate liked his hair short, his face stubbly, his clothes dark and non-descript. Jimmy would have got every one of those wrong. The realization had hit him hard. All the things he thought Nate liked were his preferences, how he liked Nate to be. Nothing had come from the man himself.

Nate knocked back shots with his friends, happy to get drunk with them. He was louder and so much more self-assured, sure in his own skin, of his own power. Nothing like the Nate that, only a few months ago, Jimmy would have sworn he knew so well.

At one point Nate gave the cameraman a glare and the lens had dropped, the man obviously moving out of his way without a word being spoken. Jimmy thought he would have moved just as fast.

Nate handled a gun and a knife like he'd been born with one in his hand. Just from watching him play fight, Jimmy could tell he knew exactly what he was doing — every movement was easy, controlled, deadly. Even his voice was different. No more soft supplication and pacification. Nate's voice was deeper, warm and confident, whether he was dancing along to the radio with one of the women, giving orders or laughing at a joke or an accident.

Jimmy had never seen him dance, hardly seen him laugh.

He stood differently as well. At first Jimmy couldn't pinpoint what it was but in the end he realized it all came from Nate's innate sense of purpose, of self-belief. He believed in his own ability, whether that was to raise and control a crowd or handle himself in a fight. He believed in what he was fighting for, knew his cause was right, whatever the cost.

No, before Jimmy hadn't known the real Nate at all.

But now he knew that even that wasn't all there was to Nate. There were three Nates — the one from before, the one on the TV and the one with no barriers. The man he talked to in the back garden late at night, the man who was open and honest and wouldn't put on an act, not for Jimmy. Not anymore.

The man currently sitting on his sofa in the living room.

He wanted to know that Nate. With every fiber in his body, Jimmy wanted to know the real man. Know what he thought, how he felt. What made his face light up and his eyes crinkle when he laughed.

Jimmy really wanted to be there when Nate laughed.

He put the plate of sandwiches and a coffee mug down on the small table in front of Nate. There was only a side light on and the room was blanketed in shadows, but Jimmy could still see the dark smudges under Nate's eyes, the exhaustion in his face. He sat at an angle, their knees almost brushing, and pushed the plate closer, so Nate wouldn't have to stretch to reach. "I saw the TV program about you all, watched it on repeat," he admitted as Nate looked at him, assessing.

"I..."

"You were right, what you said when you left. You were right. I don't know you. That program made me see that everything I thought I knew was wrong. Back before, I saw what I wanted to see. No, that isn't right." He shook his head, explaining just as much to himself as Nate. "I saw what I'd made you, how I wanted you to be. My fantasy of you."

"No, if we're being honest we both have to do it," Nate said, resting back into the sofa, sandwich in hand. "You saw what I wanted you to see. I took your fantasy of me and made it real for you. I let you think I was how you wanted so that I got an easy life."

"But I should have realized, should have looked closer. Hell, we lived together in one small room twenty-four hours a day for two months, lived here together for a damned sight longer. I should have had some inkling of what you're really like after that."

"Maybe I'm just really good at pretending."

"I should at least have had an idea that you were lying."

"Why?" Nate watched him as he ate. "At the beginning you felt like you'd been hit by a truck with all that'd happened. You were trying to make the best of it and I was trying hard to give you what you wanted, and I really am very good at most things I do."

"I feel like a child that's just woken up to an adult world and realized what a fool he is," Jimmy admitted.

"You're not a child, you just…you just had everything easy. It stopped you from questioning things. Stopped you seeing the questions."

"But I don't know a thing about you."

"That used to really bug me. You'd say you loved me but how could you when you didn't know me? When it was all an act. But then maybe you do know a lot about me." Nate watched at him, his expression soft. "You know how I react when I come, the noise I make when you hit just the right spot, how my hair stands up in the morning, how cantankerous I get when I'm bored…" He stopped, the softness slipping away. "No, you don't know that one, do you? I hid that. Maybe you don't know as much as I thought."

"And I want to know." Jimmy felt stretched tight, thin and transparent. "I really want to know all the things I missed."

"Where do you want to start?" Nate asked.

"I don't know. What sort of music do you like?"

"You want a list of bands?"

"Maybe, I…" Jimmy shrugged. "I don't know how to begin. I know nothing about your background, your family, how you got to be where you are, what you like, why you're still fighting."

Nate pushed the last of his sandwich into his mouth, drank half the cup of coffee and brushed the crumbs off his lap before looking at Jimmy. "I like really loud, crowd pleasing rock music that makes you want to shout and dance. My mum is the only family I have left—she's really old and lives in a little village in the back end of nowhere. I'm the total epitome of grumpiness when I'm bored and I was really fucking bored a hell of a lot of the time." He took a deep breath, holding it for a moment before going on. "I like seafood, but it makes me sick, and I'm still fighting because I believe it's the only thing I can do. Slavery has to stop because it's wrong and, yes, I really think it's as simple as that."

"Is it a cause worth dying for?" Jimmy knew how The State's attitude had changed. The freedom movement had long stopped being a nuisance, transforming into a threat to be hunted down and eradicated. How they must regret not wiping them out when they'd hit them last time. What they'd done was force the movement to change their tactics and come back a whole hell of a lot stronger.

Their mistake and underestimation was the freedom movement's – and Jimmy's – gain.

"Yes, it's worth it. We'll either change things or I'll die trying."

"And me? What do you think of me?"

"You?" Nate shook his head, the movement small, the question behind it much bigger. "You've always confused me, even though you were always straight up and honest with me. Sometimes you're so decent it's almost painful to watch, and I know you cared about me, I could see that. But then you'd act the owner and..." He shook his head again. "Toward the end of the time we spent together, I figured you didn't know how you felt. I think you wanted to love me as though I were free, but you also liked the control, knowing I was yours."

Jimmy inhaled sharply, his nostrils flaring as he tried to work that out. "I hadn't thought about it like that but..." Again he took a deep breath, holding it a moment. "You're right. I wanted – no, I kidded myself that we had – a normal, equal relationship. But, yes, I liked knowing you couldn't leave, liked having ultimate control. What power does to you is a scary thing," he admitted. "So how did you feel about me?"

"How did I feel about you?" Nate pulled a face, silly and scrunched up, and so typically him it took Jimmy's breath away. "That's even more confusing than working out who you were. Back at the start it was easy—I hated your guts. Later... I wanted to hate you, thought it was only right that I did, and I really do try to do the right thing. Only I didn't. That confused the fuck out of me, made me angry with myself."

"And now? What do you think now?"

"Give me a break here"—Nate huffed, shaking his head again—"because I'm struggling." He took a deep breath before letting it out slowly. "The others see you as my abuser. Paulo says I should still hate you. Me? I just... I find myself coming back and I don't know why and don't want to think about it. Not now, when there's so much else going on. I just...shit. I don't think I want to know."

Jimmy really didn't want to press him on it, not when Nate seemed so wrung out and tired, when there were so many more important things happening. Not when, if he pushed, he might get an answer he didn't want. But there were some things he needed to know. "But how do you feel about someone like me? Someone who slipped into making you his slave without even realizing I'd changed. I was so sure I wasn't like that."

"I played you so I'd get an easy life but..." Nate picked up another sandwich, twisting it round and round rather than eating. "Maybe how I acted had something to do with what you became. In those first few days, weeks, we were together, I didn't know what kind of owner you were." He shrugged. "The decent kind, the beating kind, the sicko pervert kind. So I acted the slave to keep you sweet. I didn't realize you didn't know what you were either. I let you turn into an owner but, no, no, Jimmy. No one can be allowed to act like that." He stared over, gaze sharp. "I want to help create a world in which that's not allowed. You went along with it because it's a slippery slope, not knowing where to draw the line, to say that's enough, it's wrong. You did it because it was acceptable, but it isn't. It's not acceptable now, wasn't then. We have to make sure everyone knows that it isn't going to be tolerated."

"You're right and…" Jimmy chewed at his lip for a moment as he tried to get the words right in his head. "I know that it's wrong. I know it down to my bones but…that's not what's scaring me now. I know that's true. It's other, more personal truths I'm having trouble with."

"Like what?"

Jimmy rubbed a hand over his face. This was stupid, a stupid question. He knew it. But he had to know and he had no one else to ask. No one else he could admit it to. "Do I love you?"

Nate shrugged, his face creasing up with a smile this time. "I don't know. Do you?"

"I feel like I do." Jimmy had to look away, anywhere but at Nate. "Every atom in my body is screaming that I do, but how can I when I don't know you?"

"I think." Nate eased back in the chair, his posture shouting out his exhaustion. "That's something you have to figure out on your own. I can't help you." He closed his eyes, already halfway to sleep. "Just be brutally, totally honest with yourself. You can lie to the rest of the world, but don't do it to yourself."

Jimmy sat forward, collecting up the plate and mugs, watching Nate. "I won't," he murmured. "I won't lie to myself and, I promise, I won't lie to you."

Nate opened his eyes just a fraction, his gaze fixed on Jimmy. "I'd appreciate that." Then his eyes slid shut again. "Is it okay if I just stay here for a bit, not long? I'll just get a little rest then I'll go."

"Of course you can stay. Don't be stupid. Why don't you go to bed, get some proper sleep? The spare room is actually tidy."

"No." Nate shook his head. "Can't stay. I'll only be a while."

"At least take your coat off," Jimmy said, but it was too late, Nate was already asleep.

When Jimmy got back with blankets and a decent pillow, Nate was in exactly the same position. Jimmy tried to ease him round so he could stretch out properly without waking completely, but half way Nate caught hold of his sleeve. "I can't stay. It isn't safe."

"No one knows you're here."

"I can't sleep if I don't feel safe." Nate's gaze flicked to the door then the windows before they were back on Jimmy. "Watch my back?"

"Of course." Jimmy pulled the blankets over him. "I'll keep you safe." He wasn't sure exactly what Nate expected but staying awake, sitting in the chair opposite, seemed like a really good idea.

The pitch black of night faded into the gray of pre-dawn and the birds began to sing as he watched Nate sleep. He thought about who he'd been, back when they'd first met, who he was now. How much he'd changed. How much they'd changed.

When Jimmy woke at five thirty, his neck screaming in protest, his back sore and his hands frozen, Nate had already gone. The blankets were neatly folded, the pillow stacked on top. Jimmy scratched and stretched as he stood up.

He wished Nate had stayed for breakfast.

* * * *

Four days later Nate was back, a soft familiar, "Hi," coming from the shadows.

"I wasn't sure if I'd see you for a while," Jimmy said. "I saw the news on the TV. Things are really heating up." The freedom movement was gaining support all over the country. In some places they were in control freeing all slaves by whatever means proved necessary.

"Heidi and Vinny are pushing as hard as they can." Nate stepped into the light. "The end is getting closer. I'm not sure which way it'll go but it's coming." He was filthy and looked just as tired as last time.

"You can't lose, not now when... Do we have to go back to this, talking in the garden?" Jimmy asked. "Can't we go inside — eat, drink, get warm?"

Nate glanced down at himself, lifting his dirt-ingrained hands. "You sure you want me in there?"

"Eat, warm up and wash?" Jimmy offered. "I have a totally amazing shower?"

Nate's face softened. "Yeah, you do."

"Come on." Jimmy led the way inside, relieved when Nate followed. At the bathroom door, Jimmy stopped. "I'll find you some clean towels." When there was no reply, he turned, Nate was standing at the top of the stairs, staring around him.

"You haven't changed anything. It's all just as I remember it."

"What would I change?" Jimmy shrugged.

"I thought you'd get rid of my things for a start." Nate touched at the jacket he used to wear, hanging in an alcove, with his boots on the shelf underneath.

"I…" Jimmy hesitated, not quite sure why he hadn't done it. "I didn't have the heart to." Yeah, he did know. Deep down he knew.

"You should have moved on," Nate said, and Jimmy couldn't read his tone.

"Maybe."

"My coming back is probably stopping you," Nate said, his face unreadable, his hand on the bathroom doorframe.

"I don't think it's that, but my lack of impetus has one positive side effect. There are clean clothes that'll fit you. I know they're not to your taste, but will they do while what you're wearing is in the washing machine?"

Nate suddenly smiled, bright and warm in his dirty face. "I am not wearing the stupid shirts, but a T-shirt and… Oh, have you still got that old dark green hoodie? Man, I loved that."

"Yeah, it's in the cupboard." Jimmy smiled back. "And it was washed with added fabric conditioner — makes it extra soft."

"What more could anyone want?" Nate laughed as he took the towels from Jimmy, closing the bathroom door behind him as he went to shower.

What else indeed? Jimmy thought as he left clean clothes for Nate in the hall and went down to the kitchen. He'd made pasta by the time Nate came in, showered and shaved.

"My razor was still in the pot," Nate said. "You don't mind?"

"Knock yourself out." Jimmy put the food on the table and they sat down. It all felt weirdly normal.

Only it wasn't.

Whilst Nate had been upstairs, Jimmy had closed all the curtains, putting on a minimum of lights. He'd switched off his mobile and left a message on the house answer phone saying he was tired, was off to bed and he'd ring back in the morning. No one could know Nate was there. No one. Then a thought hit him.

"Did you say before that the other freedom fighters tell you not to trust me?"

Nate lifted his gaze, his mouth full, and nodded.

"Then they know you come here?"

"Some do, not all." Nate nodded again. "Heidi obviously, she has to know everything. But I also told Lizzy and Paulo."

"Why?"

"What? Why did I tell them or why don't they trust you?"

"The first," Jimmy said. "I know why they don't trust me. Hell, if I were them, I wouldn't trust me."

"Why wouldn't you?"

"No." Jimmy had to laugh at the absurdity of the circular conversation. "You answer my question first. Why did you tell them?"

"Because I have faith in them, because they're my friends." Nate started eating again. "Because I refuse to be ashamed of anything I do."

"Is that what you think you should feel? What they say you should feel about seeing me?" Jimmy put his fork down, shaken.

Nate shrugged. "Lizzy says she worries about me. Paulo is a bit more...up front."

"What does he say?"

"That I'm fucking insane coming back to my abuser. That I have Stockholm Syndrome or some other such shit." He glanced over but only briefly, laying the words out for Jimmy. "That I come back because I don't have to think around you. That you take away all the decisions for me."

"But that's not true," Jimmy said, appalled at the idea.

"I know."

"They think we slip back into old patterns, that we act like we used to? Owner and slave?"

"I guess so."

"But you wouldn't stand for that, not when you have a choice."

"And that." Nate studied at him properly. "Is why I don't bother explaining to them. You understand that and they don't. A year ago I would have sworn it would be the other way round, that they'd always understand me and you would never get it. I was wrong." He pushed the rest of his pasta into a pile, scooping it up and adding it to the top. "You're not the only one that's learned things."

"Thank you," Jimmy said formally. "Thank you for letting me show you I've changed."

Nate tilted his head to one side. "Not so much changed as shown me who you really are."

The statement left Jimmy gasping. It humbled him to his very core. "That's how I feel about you. I see the real you."

"But what you see now isn't as easy on your eye as the version you tried to create, is it?"

"No." Jimmy stared at him, stripped bare of any pretense. "It's better."

Nate looked up momentarily, a strange half smile on his lips. "Fuck, you're still a confusing bastard. Paulo is right. I should hate you and half the time I want to but—" He stopped talking abruptly, as though he hadn't meant to say any of that out loud, before he carried on eating.

After dinner followed, dessert and coffee—nothing like a formal, planned, dinner party, more an impromptu meeting of friends, easy and comfortable as they cleared up together. Jimmy was just about to offer the spare room again, the sofa if that was all Nate would take, when Nate made a phone call then said he had to go.

Jimmy didn't protest. "Do you want any of your old things that are still here?" he offered. "Some of the clothes could be useful or maybe the books or magazines?"

Nate pursed his lips, thinking. "No, it's okay. I'm good."

"All right." Jimmy turned away. "I'll dry your clothes once they're washed. Should I send them somewhere?"

Nate paused at the back door. "Don't bother. I'll pick them up next time."

Next time. It was the first promise of a next time Jimmy had ever had.

* * * *

As Jimmy was locking up for the night, there was a soft tap at the back door. When he opened it, Nate was leaning against the frame.

"I know. I'm dirty as all shit again," he said, a smirk on his lips. "But can I crash on your sofa like last time? If I don't get some proper sleep, I'm going to fall over."

"Yeah, sure." Jimmy opened the door wider, ushering him in. "But for fuck's sake, sleep in the spare bed. It'll be a damned sight easier to wash the sheets, if nothing else."

"Maybe. I..." Nate hesitated. "If..."

"I'll watch your back," Jimmy cut in.

Nate nodded his appreciation.

"You want something to eat first? A shower?"

"I can hardly keep my eyes open. I haven't had more than two hours sleep in days, haven't been in a bed in...ages."

"Sleep then. Do the rest in the morning." He locked the door behind Nate, sliding the deadbolt in place and leading the way to the stairs. In the hallway he opened a small, discreet cupboard and flicked a switch. Nate raised a questioning eyebrow. "New alarm system," Jimmy explained. "Top of the range and very sensitive to anyone anywhere near the house."

"Why?"

Jimmy paused then said simply, "Because I'm bound to fall asleep again while you're here."

"You didn't have to do..." Nate stopped. "Thanks," he said, already heading into the spare room and sitting on the bed to take off his shoes. "At least now you can go to bed yourself."

"I'll see you in the morning." He closed the door to save Nate getting up again.

Jimmy left the door to the living room open and settled down on the sofa to go over his lines for the next few days. He wasn't intending to stay up all night but... He fell asleep at about three in the morning, waking up again after an hour or two.

At dawn he went up to sort out his things for work and slipped into a clean V-necked T-shirt and fresh jeans. He could shower at the studio. When he headed back downstairs, Nate's door was open, the bed carefully made, his used towels folded on top of the laundry basket in the bathroom.

At first Jimmy thought Nate had gone but he hadn't. He was in the kitchen making breakfast.

"Here," Nate said, putting a plate of food down on the table, before going back to the counter to get his own. "I remember how you like to eat as soon as you wake up."

"Thanks." Jimmy slid into a chair, already reaching for a fork.

"I actually feel human again after a decent night's sleep and a shower," Nate said, coming back to the table. "I…" He stopped and Jimmy heard his breath catch. "You kept it." Nate's fingertip ghosted over the bonding ring he'd worn for so long, now hanging around Jimmy's neck.

"I couldn't get rid of it." Jimmy acknowledged quietly.

He'd picked the ring up after Nate had thrown it at him on that awful day.

Held it in his hand and stared at it whilst everyone else on the set had stared at him. He'd closed his fingers round it while the panic had washed over him. Squeezed his hand tight shut while he'd tried to work out how the world had turned upside down.

He'd kept hold of it while he demanded to be taken home, his fingers clutching ever harder on the unbearable journey, until he found some semblance of peace inside the house.

Inside the house, where all Nate's things were, just as they had been when Jimmy had gone to work. He'd moved round, touching a book here, a cup there, Nate's coat on the back of the chair, his comb by the sofa.

He remembered back to the horror and confusion he'd felt then.

Nate hadn't meant any of those awful things he'd said. He couldn't. It was some kind of twisted joke. Yeah, that had to be it. Nate had been made to do it by some of Jimmy's friends — he certainly wouldn't have done it out of choice. No way.

Only Nate didn't have any contact with Jimmy's friends. Jimmy had barely had any himself since he'd been let out of prison — there'd been work and Nate.

Nate. He'd been so wrapped up in Nate that he hadn't thought about anyone else.

Jimmy had sat at the empty table and thought about how Nate had looked at his friends strangely when he couldn't hide in the kitchen or upstairs and was forced to see them. Even at the time he'd thought it had been odd but he'd only worked it out later, after Nate had left. Was it disdain? Contempt? Disgust? Almost certainly a mixture of all three.

They hadn't put Nate up to anything. But he'd said those things, all his stuff was still here, only he wasn't and…and…and…

And Jimmy hadn't known what to think. He'd sat there as the day passed, as it got dark again outside, and waited. Nate hadn't come back that night or in the morning.

When Jimmy had finally got up, the bonding ring had still been in his hand. He'd searched for somewhere to put it, somewhere safe. In the bedroom there was a box on top of the chest of drawers in which he kept odd things, special things. He could put it there, only he didn't want to put it down, didn't want to let it go — even though that was stupid.

He'd opened the lid and there inside had been the leather cord their hands had been tied with when they'd first been bonded. Instinctively he'd picked up the cord, threaded the ring on it and tied it round his neck.

He'd never taken it off.

"And the cord?" Nate asked, bringing Jimmy back to the present.

"Our bonding one."

Nate tapped the edge of the ring again, never touching Jimmy's skin. "It looks..." He shook his head, turning his attention to his food. "Paulo rang earlier. We're going north next."

Jimmy was acutely aware that it was the first time Nate had told him anything about what he would be doing. "Is that good or bad?"

"I don't think it's either, just another job that has to be done." Nate started eating. "It's colder up there, which is a bastard if we have to sleep rough but support's been growing there for a while."

"I was thinking," Jimmy said as he ate. "I can't do anything to help, not really, and I'd like to. One thing I can do is give money. How should I do it? Do I just give it to you?"

"No." Nate had stopped, his forkful of food in his hand.

"No, I don't give it to you?"

"No, you don't give any at all."

"Why not? The freedom movement must need every bit they can get."

"They do, but not from you."

Jimmy felt his face drain. "My money isn't good enough? Is it tainted because I used to be an owner?"

"Legally you're still an owner." Nate put his fork down and laid his palm flat on the table between them. Jimmy's name was stark on the back of his hand. "You own me."

"So that's why you don't want my money?"

"No, that's why you can't give it. From what we've managed to find out, The State Police have dismissed you as a threat, mainly because of the humiliating way I treated you when I left. I hadn't meant to act like that but being so vicious, calling you those things and doing it in public turned out to be the best thing I could have done to protect you."

"I don't understand." Jimmy shook his head.

"The police think you hate my guts, must want me dead. Thank Christ you never said anything about loving me to anyone else. If you had..." He let the implication hang. "Me walking out in that stupid show of macho crap meant that the police don't think there's a connection between us now." Nate suddenly gripped Jimmy's T-shirt sleeve, twisting it painfully tight. "You listen to me—you don't do anything that could make them change their minds. There's no connection between us, none between you and the movement. You understand?"

Jimmy nodded.

"I'm not the only one I put at risk when I come here," Nate said soberly. "Remember that."

Jimmy nodded again. "You've checked up on me, on how The State Police view me." It wasn't a question— it was Jimmy working things out.

"Wanted to make sure you're as safe as can be. Paulo said... He says a lot of things, but I need to know you're as safe as we can make you. I shouldn't come here, I put you at risk and..."

"I'm glad you come," Jimmy interrupted him. "I don't want you to stop. I would have liked to help though," he said softly, frighteningly conscious of Nate's skin so close to his own through the thin fabric of his T-shirt. Conscious of the emotions Nate was fighting hard to control.

"But you do help." Nate went back to his food, his eyes dropping to his plate. "You keep me sane when the world is going mad around me."

Jimmy tucked that idea away and kept it close.

* * * *

Jimmy flicked through the channels on the TV, desperate to find something that would grab his attention and hold it. But he knew he wasn't ready for that, not yet. His mum had phoned him, going on for nearly half an hour, nothing but anger and threats, and all about Nate. Always about Nate. Before he went to prison he hadn't realized that she was that bad—that bigoted and downright disgusting. What she wanted to do to Nate went beyond sickening into frightening, and he hadn't known she could be like that. Not until Nate.

He couldn't tell her about that, though. Couldn't defend Nate or try to talk some sense into her. Nate was right. He did talk too much, and if he tried to argue with her, he might just let something slip. *Don't talk about Nate, don't ever, ever, ever mention the visits,* he repeated to himself. That the thought was seared into his brain like nothing else. *Keep Nate safe.*

The call had been over two hours ago and still he still didn't feel right. His mum's bile had a tendency to linger.

He flicked the TV again. Cooking—no. Renovating your house—again, no. A cop show from twenty years ago—maybe. It was then he heard a loud knock on the back door, more like something banging against it. Immediately his adrenaline rushed and his belly rolled. Had the State Police discovered the visits? Were they currently surrounding the house? He listened again, hearing nothing but the rain that had been lashing down for hours. Then... another bang, like the garden chair outside had been knocked over.

The State Police didn't make that kind of rudimentary mistake.

He went to the back door and opened it cautiously and the rain immediately found a way in. The security light came on and Jimmy could see there was nothing there, then Nate stepped round the corner from the garden.

Nate—looking like Jimmy had never seen him before. Soaked to the skin in only a thin shirt and jeans, hair plastered to his head as the rain ran down his face. Jimmy stared, unable to pull his gaze away from the pain on Nate's face.

Nate didn't move, didn't try to protect himself from the merciless rain, and Jimmy could only focus on the hurt in his eyes. Then Nate turned his head, and Jimmy saw the blood on his cheek.

Blood on his cheek.

Jimmy didn't have to think. He was outside without collecting shoes or a coat, hands already reaching for Nate. "What the fuck? Are you okay? Where are you hurt? What happened?" The questions tumbled out of his mouth without thought. "There's blood—is it bad?" Again he reached for Nate, hand going up to his head.

He wasn't prepared for the way Nate recoiled, as though his hand were on fire. As though it were diseased.

"I... You, you fucking... It's not right." Nate threw his arms wide, then reined them back in, and Jimmy saw the blood on the back of his knuckles.

"Nate." He couldn't stop the barked shout, but it caught Nate's attention, made his gaze snap round. "What happened? Are you...? No. Come in the house, out of this rain." Jimmy took a step to the side, giving Nate room to pass by him. But Nate just stood there, water dripping from his eyelashes, his hair, his nose. His whole body slumped in on itself, confusion and pain oozing from every pore.

Jimmy wanted to run to him, to hold him and promise everything would be all right. He had more sense now. "Come inside," he said again, softer, keeping things simple.

Still Nate stayed there, but now he was staring at Jimmy, his eyes wide and round.

"You know I won't hurt you," Jimmy said. "You know you can trust me." But Nate didn't move, his gaze fixed on Jimmy, and Jimmy began to waver. "You do know that, don't you?" And so much seemed to depend on the answer.

Nate stood and looked, his whole body still, the moment drawing out until it felt pained, tight. Jimmy could feel his own breathing slow, become more labored, until suddenly Nate roused himself and nodded. One brief, hesitant nod. Then he walked into the kitchen, and Jimmy had never been so grateful to close the door behind them.

Now Jimmy wanted to go into full panic mode. He started firing questions again. "Tell me what happened? Where are you hurt?" But already, in the light, without the awful rain, he could see it wasn't as bad as he'd first thought. Nate hadn't been beaten. "Were you in a fight? Was it The State Police?"

Nate shook his head. "Give me some fucking whiskey," he demanded, voice hoarse. Then he added an appeasing, "Please."

Jimmy took the bottle and passed it over as Nate grabbed a mug from the drainer, poured in a slug and knocked it back.

"Better?" Jimmy asked, and Nate nodded. "Do you need a doctor? Do you want me to clean up your face and hands?"

Nate was already shaking his head again. "It's not that bad. I've had a hell of a lot worse."

"Are you going to tell me what happened?"

"Like you said, I got in a fight."

"Who with?" The rain was soaking through Jimmy's shirt, making his skin cold, but he wasn't going anywhere.

"Paulo."

"Paulo Campbell?" Jimmy exclaimed. "But I thought you were best friends?"

"We are." Nate poured and drank some more.

"And he hit you?"

"Only after I hit him. Hard."

"Wow." Jimmy held his hand out and drank straight from the bottle when Nate passed it over. "What made you do that?"

Nate sucked in a huge breath, his body immediately tensing as he turned away.

"Nate?" Jimmy pushed. "You don't hit friends. Why'd you do it?"

"Because he wouldn't fucking shut up." Nate spat the words out, anger thick in his voice, but also something else, something he was trying to hide.

"What was he saying?"

"That... That I... Fuck it." He slammed a fist into the wall and the nearby window reverberated under the force. "The fucking bastard keeps going on at me, saying stuff, messing with my head."

"What does he say?" Jimmy asked gently. He'd never seen Nate like this before—not this worked up over anything. Not this angry. It was as if the subservient, smooth-edged Nate had never existed and all Jimmy could see was an intimidating fighter.

"Trust me. You don't want to fucking know."

"So it's about me, right?" Jimmy shrugged, even though Nate still had his back toward him. "Can't be that bad."

"Can't it?" Nate turned round, his face as wrecked as ever.

"Can't be worse than what my mum says about you." Jimmy watched as Nate reacted to that—the tension in his body smoothing out just a notch, as he gave an ironic snort. One that might have had a grain of humor in it. A notch in the right direction, at least. Jimmy pushed on. "What does he call me?"

Nate's face tightened again, but maybe not quite as badly. "A rapist, an abuser, an evil bastard. An owner."

"So what?" Jimmy shrugged again, taking another swig of whiskey before holding the bottle out to Nate. "You've called me all that and more. And it's true."

"I never called you evil." Nate snatched the bottle, giving up on the mug to follow Jimmy's example and drank straight from it.

"Bet you thought it, back when we were in prison."

"That's different." Nate grimaced as he swallowed.

"What else did he say?" Jimmy asked, his tone low as he dropped into a chair by the table. "Was it all about me?"

"No... I... He's a fucking bastard." He slammed the wall again, with the flat of his hand this time, and Jimmy thought that was progress.

"Tell me."

Nate took a step closer, looming over Jimmy. "He said I've gone fucking nuts, that I need a head doctor, that my coming back here proves it." His hand shook where it grasped the bottle, the rain still dripping from his hair. "He said you've indoctrinated me, infected my brain with your hold over me, until I can't see straight."

Jimmy pressed his lips together for a moment, and thought his own hand might shake if he lifted it from the table top. "What do you think? Is that true?"

"I don't know what I think." Nate managed to say, as he heaved in a breath and seemed more shattered than ever. "He took everything I said and twisted it until I don't know anything anymore. He keeps on saying I have Stockholm Syndrome. He showed me all this stuff he found about it. That it was wrong and evil and… He said it was a psychological condition. That I need help." He stopped, breathing hard as he stared at Jimmy, his mouth slightly open. "You, now, you're nothing like the man I met in prison. The way we talk, the way we are together? None of it's like then or when we lived here. It's different, it's all different, but I can't make him see that."

"If you know, then what does it matter what he thinks?"

"What if I'm wrong?" Nate said, the words splintering round the edges. "I don't want to be the cliché guy with a syndrome. I refuse to be him, but I'm so fucking scared that I am and I can't see it. I want…"

"What do you want?" Jimmy asked, low and hushed.

Nate inhaled slowly, holding it for a moment. "I want to trust my own instincts. I want to understand what I'm doing and I'm not sure I do." Any last color drained from Nate's face.

Jimmy stuck his hand out for the bottle, drinking as soon as it was passed over. "I don't pretend to know much about psychological anything, but, do you think I'm still the man that abused you?"

"I wouldn't be here if you were," Nate said, with real confidence in his voice. "Only..."

"What?"

"What if...? Fuck it." Nate grabbed the bottle again, drinking without breathing properly until it made him splutter. He slammed it back on the table and wiped a hand over his mouth.

"Why do you come back?" It was the only question Jimmy knew to ask, even if he had asked it before. "Why did you at the beginning?"

Nate took a few steps away, then back again, breathing hard. "The first time it was genuinely to say sorry but you looked so...such a mess that I ran. Then I came back to actually say it and this time you looked, I don't know, still a mess but different." He waved the bottle toward Jimmy, voice and face a little more steady. "Then you said stuff about starting to think, about right and wrong, and you sounded different. After that I didn't analyze why. I just came. But I guess I could see you change. Every time I came you were different, like something evolving, and I wanted to see it. See what you became as you thought about each little thing I threw at you. I told you the truth and watched how you reacted."

"And now... Why do you come back now?"

"Because." Nate hesitated, his gaze flickering to Jimmy, away, then back again. "Because I can talk to this new you, because I can let my guard down with you. Because it's easy and comfortable being here. Because what I feel about you..."

Jimmy didn't have the guts to ask about that one. Instead he sat, watching Nate, and waited. Nate didn't finish the sentence, although he did go on. "But what if all of that is some syndrome, like Paulo says? What if I'm wrong?"

"Are you?" Jimmy asked. "I trust your judgment, always have. Do you?"

Then, suddenly, there was nothing else but the weight of Nate's gaze on him, the expression on Nate's face pinning him in place, fixing him, holding him—burning through him like he could see right inside the flesh and bone.

The clock on the wall ticked, the fridge hummed, the rain still spattered against the window, but all that was important was Nate. Nate standing, wet and dripping, in his own bubble of tension, in the middle of Jimmy's kitchen, watching him.

For long, long moments nothing moved, nothing else seemed to exist but the weight of Nate's stare.

Then Nate huffed, his whole body relaxed and the bubble burst as he smiled.

"My judgment says I should stop acting like a fucking girl." He smiled again, and it really did seem to reach his eyes. "Can I borrow your shower? I'm meant to be somewhere, but I refuse to go wet and freezing."

"What? Yeah." Jimmy shook himself, trying to catch up. Trying to work out what had happened. "I can put your clothes in the dryer while you wash, but what...?"

"Thanks." Nate was already heading for the living room. "Don't bother making any food. I really have to run. Heidi is going to kick my butt for being this late."

Jimmy was left watching, with his mouth open, as the door closed behind Nate.

Chapter Eight

Jimmy put his bag by the backdoor, laying his thick coat on top. That was it. He was all ready. He opened the door, turning off the lights before he stepped out, bag in hand. Friday night and he'd had enough of everything. Work was hard. He felt disconnected from it, from the people, what they were doing. There he was, running around pretending to be a hero, when he came home only to watch people doing it for real on the TV. The freedom movement was on the news every night—reports of rallies, the freeing of slaves, fights and, worst of all to watch, police action to track them down.

But things were changing fast—they'd gone from being mere 'criminals' to 'murderous extremists' and even 'terrorists'. Now, sometimes, even the mainstream news reports called them 'Freedom Fighters'.

There was a lot in a word, even more in a name.

Jimmy knew there was something big going on in the north of the country again. Nate hadn't mentioned details, for which Jimmy was grateful—if he didn't know he couldn't tell, even by accident. But it was on the TV, radio and in the newspapers. He just hoped Nate was okay.

He turned to lock the back door just as there was a rustle near the bushes. He glanced up. "Hi, I didn't expect to see you. I thought you'd be too busy," he said, as Nate stepped into the light. "Hey, has something else happened? You look awful."

"I'm okay," Nate said, but he didn't sound it, didn't look it. Not in the way of his last visit, there was no blood for a start. But he seemed... Jimmy wasn't sure. Not the hurt after the fight with Paulo, but something was wrong. "You going somewhere?" he stared pointedly at Jimmy's bag.

"I was going up to the lake. I haven't been there for ages." He gave a snort and a shrug of his shoulders. "Too many memories at first, but it's been a long week. I'm going to come back for work on Monday morning. But don't worry," he added quickly. "I can go another weekend. Come in, have something to eat, sleep, shower. I think you need it and I can always—"

"Can I come with you?" Nate said.

"I..." Jimmy was taken aback by the request, but Nate seemed to take it as hesitation.

"No, sorry. Stupid idea. It came out of my mouth before I thought."

"Of course you can come," Jimmy said louder than he intended, but he truly meant it. He wanted Nate to go, really wanted him to.

"You sure?" Nate wrinkled his nose in uncertainty. "You haven't got someone going with you?"

"I'm going to get away from people, not to see them," Jimmy assured. "Just me and the wildlife."

"Then you don't want me there." Nate took a step backwards.

"Hey," Jimmy called. "You want honest and I promised it to you. I want you to come. Now shut the fuck up and get in the car."

"Sure?"

"I'm sure." Jimmy locked the door and walked to the car, throwing his bag on the backseat before going round and getting in. He pushed the passenger door open for Nate and waited.

Eventually Nate got in as well.

Jimmy reached for the key but stopped before he turned the car on. "Are we going to talk about your last visit?"

"What about it?" Nate gave an out of place, cheesy smile. "Can't think what there is to say except that I might not understand how I feel, but I trust my own judgment when it comes to you." He shrugged as he said it.

"I guess not then." Jimmy shook his head and started the engine.

They drove out of the town in silence. Jimmy offered Nate free choice on the radio but he said no and went back to staring out of the window. It was about forty minutes before Jimmy spoke. "I didn't think to ask if you need anything. You haven't got any stuff with you, but it doesn't matter. Your old clothes are still there. You'll have something to wear."

"Thanks," was the only reply before the silence was back.

Jimmy thought it was like having a weight lifted when he got to the cabin—no people, no other houses in sight, no noise except the ones made by nature. There wasn't even a light visible anywhere as he turned up the tiny path Nate seemed to feel it too. "I like it here," Nate said quietly, almost to himself.

The State Police wouldn't be able to get near the place without them hearing them coming from a long way off. The cabin was secluded, protected and perfect. They both relaxed as they got out of the car.

Inside, Jimmy got the heating going and Nate volunteered to make something for them to eat. They sat down in front of the fire to a pile of toasted sandwiches and bags of savory snacks. "A feast fit for kings," Jimmy declared and, after taking a look at Nate's tight face, found a bottle of whiskey to go with it.

He knew Nate wouldn't get drunk but he meant to get him mellow, to take the edge off the strain that was so obviously stretching him thin. But after an hour or two, he realized he was the more smashed of the two of them, not Nate. He wasn't falling down drunk but his tongue was looser, his brain had less of a filter.

It was another hour before he became aware that Nate was pushing him, goading him. It was as though Nate wanted a fight but didn't want to start it.

"What's your problem tonight?" Jimmy asked after another snide remark that could have been innocent but really wasn't.

"Why do I have to have a problem?"

"Because I haven't, so it must be you."

"No, you can't have a problem, because you're fucking perfect — fucking perfect little actor boy, who's always kind and helpful and understanding with his runaway slave. Saint Jimmy."

"Whoa." Jimmy stared at him wide eyed. "Where the hell did that come from?"

"True though, isn't it? You're always so damned nice with me now." Nate laced the word with real venom. "Does it go all the way through you, or is it just an act, actor boy?"

"Is what an act?"

"The way you are with me, so caring and considerate. Come on. What do you think about the real me?"

"What do you want me to say?"

"The truth would be nice. You promised me it, but I don't suppose I'll get it, not this time. You'll just lie and say you think nice thoughts about me all the time."

And Nate had done it—maybe Jimmy had drunk more than he'd meant to but, in his intoxicated state, Nate had gone too far, pushed too hard. "No, I don't think nice thoughts about you all the time." Jimmy stared at him through narrowed eyes. "Sometimes I want to scream at you that your place isn't out there saving the world. It should be under me, with your legs open. But what the fuck good would that do either of us? It'd turn me back into a rapist owner and you into my whore of a slave."

"Is that what you think I was—a whore?"

"You said yourself that you did whatever you had to, to keep me happy and quiet. I never had to hold you down, even if you didn't have a choice."

"Is that what you think I still am?"

"No. I'm not fucking stupid." Jimmy pushed a hand through his hair, unable to work out what was going on, why he was saying all this stuff. "You asked if I always thought nice thoughts. Well sometimes, even though I never imagined admitting it out loud, I don't. You created a fantasy world for me and, yeah, sometimes I'd like that back—a world in which I could actually touch you, where you wouldn't flinch if I got too close, where—"

"I don't flinch."

"How do you know? Because, apart from your last visit when you recoiled in horror from my hand, I'm careful never to get that close. I can't take that again. But I want to touch you and fuck you and take comfort in your body. I want you to want me. I want it to be real. There are times when it's so bad, when I'm so desperate, that I lose it and I'd like to have the power again to make you. Most of all I want to stop feeling guilty for ever thinking that, but I can't, because it'll never be right. So no, I'm not perfect or Saint Jimmy or anything else you called me."

He heaved in an enormous breath, holding it in his lungs deliberately before letting it go slowly. "But you pushing me to say all that crap hasn't done either of us a bit of good. It's just left us in deeper shit, because I don't feel like that when I'm being rational. I don't want to be a rapist or you to be a whore. I like the you I've got to know over the last few months, better than the fantasy one, even if he was more willing to spread his legs, because you're real and he wasn't." He took another deep breath, watching Nate's ashen face as he stared back at Jimmy. "I'm also trying to like myself a bit better, because I'm truly ashamed of the old me. But it's a rocky road and I don't need you throwing it in my face. You come to see me. I don't make you, much as a small, shameful part of me would like to."

Pulling himself up, Jimmy stood glaring down at Nate. "I get that things are shit for you right now, but don't take it out on me — at least not when you've deliberately got me half drunk. I can't take it. I want you and it's fucking hard to control when I'm not sober." He huffed, soft and deliberate, shaking his head at no one. "I'm going to bed. Make sure you lock up before you do."

He didn't look back as he walked out and, for the first time, he didn't attempt to stay awake while Nate slept. At two in the morning he woke up panicking about that before a rational voice in his head reminded him that Nate had said it was safe here. If Nate said it was safe then it had to be.

* * * *

Next morning Nate had made breakfast when Jimmy came into the kitchen. "You're still here then," Jimmy said, taking a couple of slices of toast from the pile. "I thought you'd probably leave in the night."

"No." Nate pushed over a mug of coffee and Jimmy drank most of it in one go.

"I'm going for a walk by the lake to clear my head. I'll see you when I get back." Jimmy had his boots laced up and his jacket on, when Nate came out into the hall.

"Would you mind if I came with you?" Nate asked.

"Depends if you're going to give me more shit."

"No." Nate shook his head. "No more shit."

"Come if you want then." Jimmy shrugged.

They walked for ages, staying close to the tree line rather than down by the water's edge. It was cold. The wind had a real bite to it, but it felt good on Jimmy's face, fresh and clean and healing. The last of the bad feeling from the previous night evaporated with the stretch of his legs and the ache in his muscles.

Although he stayed quiet, Nate seemed to be enjoying it as well, tipping his face up into the bright but cold winter sunshine.

After an hour or two, Jimmy sat on a fallen tree trunk and threw stones into the water, watching as the circles expanded before fading. "I like it here," he said at last. "It's peaceful."

Nate sat next to him, throwing the stone Jimmy had given him up into the air and catching it again.

"I could live here or somewhere like it," Jimmy went on. "Somewhere with lots of trees and no people."

"My mum died," Nate said abruptly.

"God, I'm sorry." Jimmy turned to him. "When?"

"Last week." Nate glanced down at his hands. "I wasn't there, didn't even find out for a couple of days."

"That's awful, not being able to say goodbye."

"It was my fault," Nate said, his voice small, broken.

"No, don't think that. It can't be your fault if you weren't there."

"The State Police were questioning her, even though I made sure I didn't go anywhere near the place since I got out of prison. She was old when she had me and worrying about me had made her even older than her years. She was a bit..." He fought to find the right word. "She was a bit eccentric, a bit dizzy. She didn't understand a lot of things and they kept badgering her."

"What happened?" Jimmy asked, when he thought Nate had stopped talking for good.

"She had a heart attack, died in minutes."

"There are worse ways to go," Jimmy said quietly.

"Than dying whilst being questioned by The State Police?" Nate stared at him but they both knew Jimmy was right.

"I'm sorry. I really am. I know she was your only family."

"I hadn't seen her for so long. Hardly seen her at all in the last few years but... I miss her."

"Of course you do. You love her."

"I do," Nate whispered. "She used to wear silly hats and clothes that were thirty years out of date. The other kids thought she was mad but I adored her, was proud of her."

"And I bet you she was proud of you."

"She was."

"Which means you can't blame yourself for what happened. She wouldn't have wanted that."

"She would be cross with me if she knew." Nate's head hung down low as he sagged in on himself. "She never told me off but I'd see it in her face. She'd be disappointed with me and I could never stand that. I always wanted to make her smile, make her..." His voice broke and he raised a hand to cover his face as he slowly slid sideways, until he rested against Jimmy's side. Then he very deliberately turned his head to bury his face in Jimmy's neck.

Jimmy fought hard to control his belly as it rolled and tipped, before he slipped an arm round Nate's shoulders, drawing him gently in.

It was the first time he'd touched Nate since the morning Nate had left. It felt like a million years and the most natural thing in the world.

They stayed like that for a long time, until Nate's breathing calmed completely and the shaking in his shoulders stopped. Eventually he wiped his face but didn't raise his head. "I came to see you last night because...because I couldn't think of anywhere else I wanted to be," he finished simply.

"I'm glad you did." Jimmy sighed, knowing it would sound lame but wanting to say it anyway. "I'm proud of you, as well. Proud to know you."

"Proud when I kick off like a four year old?" And there was a smile in Nate's voice as he said it.

"Well, I could do without that, but I'll let it go."

"Is that how you really feel? Those things you said last night, about wanting me and sometimes not caring if I have a choice."

Jimmy huffed out a breath, glad Nate hadn't moved, that he couldn't see Jimmy's face. "I promised you honesty and I'm doing my best to give it to you, but it isn't easy. It's damned hard to admit things you're ashamed of. Yeah, I want you and sometimes I think it would all be so simple if you didn't have the luxury of choice. I'm no saint. But that's not who you are or who I want to be."

"You aren't doing so bad." Nate looked up, although he didn't move. "You know those award shows for bravery? Bravest fire-fighter, bravest child."

"Yeah." Jimmy nodded, but he didn't know where this was going.

"Half the time I think they're a con. Not that the people haven't done amazing things. They have. But it isn't brave if you don't have a choice. The kid fighting cancer is wonderful and remarkable but not brave. They didn't choose to have cancer — they just did what they had to do. The man who rescues the toddler from an oncoming car is brave because he did have a choice. He could have just let it happen. You had a choice — you could have stayed as you were. After I started coming to see you, you could have brought me back in chains as a runaway slave — could have restrained me and fucked me and... But you didn't. You're choosing to change, even though you know what it's like when you're in total control. You're fighting your own deep, dark thoughts. That's brave." He very carefully, very deliberately laid his hand on Jimmy's knee. "You're not doing so bad."

"I..." Jimmy didn't know what to say, how to say it.

"It's one reason I came to you. You're not perfect, none of us are, but you're brave. I don't need perfect, I need...real."

"I'm real and you have me," Jimmy said, his voice sounding like it was dragged over broken glass, as he fought to control his breathing. "You'll always have me. See, it says so right here—you have me." He rubbed his thumb over his name, where it stood out dark on the back of Nate's hand. He didn't know if it was a good thing to say, or even the right one, but Nate looked up again and smiled and Jimmy thought it would do.

"Yeah, I guess I do," Nate said and went back to staring at the water.

* * * *

The rest of the weekend was just about perfect as far as Jimmy was concerned. They walked endlessly. They ate—weird and wonderful concoctions as they refused point blank to go into town to buy more food. If it wasn't in the cupboard or freezer, they would do without. It made for interesting combinations. They talked. They stayed silent. A comfortable easy silence that had Nate smiling softly as Jimmy watched.

"Does this mean we're friends now?" Jimmy asked suddenly, on Sunday morning, peering over the top of his book. "I mean proper friends? Not like I thought in prison but friends who really know each other. After all, you know all my deep, dark secrets and I know a few of yours."

"Yeah, I guess it does." Nate adjusted his feet where they were propped on the coffee table and pushed back into the sofa.

"Good. I like that." Jimmy closed the book. It was time for a nap.

* * * *

On Sunday night they packed up the car, ready for a very early start the next day. Jimmy opened a bottle of wine with dinner and they both drank enough to ease the edges but no more. Next morning it was still dark as they left.

"I'm sorry to go," Nate said, as they drove back along the small track. "I like it here better than..." He snorted, laughing at himself. "Better than anywhere else."

"We can come again, whenever we want," Jimmy assured him, and Nate seemed content with that. "What are you going to do now?"

"I don't know. I'll call the boss, see what she says."

"Don't stay away too long," Jimmy said softly. "Please."

Nate nodded.

* * * *

Nine days later there was a soft tap on the back door very late at night and, when he opened it, Nate was standing there, looking as exhausted as ever. He made to go inside but Jimmy stopped him.

"You can't come in. Not today."

"Okay." Nate was already taking two steps backwards.

"Hey." Jimmy called after him in a whispered hiss. "It's not that I don't want you to—of course I do. It's just that my mum turned up to stay, unannounced.

She still isn't your greatest fan. You really don't want her to see you."

"Okay." Nate repeated, already in the shadows, moving fast. "I get it."

"Hey, please." Jimmy thought he might just be begging, but he didn't care, this mattered too much. "Please, man, come back soon."

"It's okay," Nate said for the third time, slowing down as his voice dropped to a gentle hum. "I'll come back," he reassured. "And I really do appreciate you warning me. I can do without your mum. I'll see you soon."

Jimmy just hoped to God that he meant it.

* * * *

When his phone rang four days later, and caller display showed an unknown number, Jimmy almost, very nearly, didn't answer it. He'd had enough crank calls when news had first spread about who Nate was, for him to be wary. But some instinct kicked in and he was glad it did. It was Nate.

"Hi," he said, and Jimmy knew who it was, just from that one word.

"Hi, N—"

"Don't say it," Nate instructed. "No names, please. People can listen in on these things."

"Sorry, force of habit. I'm not used to you calling."

"For the same reason."

"Of course." Jimmy knew all the implications. "But you're ringing now. Shit, is there something wrong?"

"Well, there is if your mum's still there." There was lightness and humor running through Nate's voice.

"No, she went yesterday."

"I thought she might, you never could take her for long."

"It's even worse now," Jimmy admitted. "You should hear some of the things she said this time about... No, you really don't want to know."

"I can guess."

"Are you going to come by soon?"

"Yeah, I'd like to." There was something else in his tone that Jimmy wasn't completely sure about but he knew it was good.

* * * *

The tap at the door came in the early evening on Jimmy's day off. It was already dark but Jimmy still hadn't expected it that early. Nate usually waited until much later. He opened the door, ushering Nate into the living room. "You want something to eat? A drink?"

"I've eaten thanks but a beer would be nice." Nate looked around at the mess. "What are you doing?"

"I thought it was about time I did something with all your old things." He handed a bottle to Nate. "So I collected it all up, began to sort it and then didn't know what to do with it." There were black sacks of clothes, magazines and even the brace Nate had worn when he first got out of plaster.

"Why now?"

Jimmy shrugged, sitting down cross legged on the floor in the middle of the chaos. "I was thinking...this stuff is all about the fantasy-Nate I tried to create and—"

"We created," Nate said. "We made him together."

"Okay, maybe. The fantasy-Nate we created. Maybe I hung onto this stuff because I wanted to remember him. I don't now."

"You want to forget him?"

"Real is better than fake."

Nate held up a pink striped shirt. "Anything is better than this. Did you really like me in it?" His eyes were sparkling, the skin at the corners crinkled up as he said it.

"Shut the fuck up." Jimmy snatched it from his hand, laughing. "It went with your skin, eyes. Something."

"It went with the blush of embarrassment I got when I wore it."

"Whatever." Jimmy stared at the mess. "I know you said you don't want anything but what do I do with it? Give it to charity? Store it in the garage? Throw it away? My mum gave me a really hard time over it."

"You should burn the monster's clothes?"

"Something like that," Jimmy said, the laughter falling away. "Man, the vileness of the things she said, what she'd have done to you when—not if—you're caught."

"I can imagine."

"No, you probably can't. She wants you deliberately crippled, so you can't get away again."

"I've seen people it's been done to," Nate said.

"God." Jimmy sucked in a breath. "I thought things like that were just stories told to frighten slaves. I never thought..." He glanced over at Nate. "That's the trouble, isn't it? I didn't think, nor did a lot of the population. By not thinking, we let it happen."

"That's why we're trying to make sure everyone knows what really goes on."

"I don't watch or read any of it," Jimmy admitted. "When there are reports about it on the TV, in the newspapers, I deliberately don't look because I don't want to know. Because of you. If it happened to you…"

"Let's hope it doesn't."

"Stop it." Jimmy stared at Nate. "Stop it so no one else gets hurt."

"We're doing our best." Nate rubbed his hands together as he sat forward on the sofa. "But first you have to clear all this up."

"How?" Jimmy grimaced. "I thought I should ask you before I did anything. I don't know what's the right thing is to do with it."

Nate pursed his lips as he thought. "Would you mind stashing it all back and putting up with fantasy-boy for a while longer?"

"Why?"

"Because things are getting real close." Nate folded the shirt before putting it back in the bag. "I don't want anyone, especially The State Police, to have any reason to look at you. If all my old things suddenly hit the charity shops, they may just come asking why. If someone casually mentions to the wrong person that you've got rid of all this crap, you could get the same result."

"I'd just say I'd moved on."

"But why say anything?" Nate looked at him cautiously. "The more anyone says to the police, the more likely they are to slip up. Don't talk to them. Don't appear on their radar. Don't do anything to make them notice you—not now, not when the end is so near."

"Is it that close?"

Nate nodded. "Yeah, I think so. One way or another, I think the fight will be over soon."

"I'm scared," Jimmy confessed.

"So am I," Nate said quietly.

"You have so much more to lose than me."

"I plan on going out fighting." He tilted his head, eyes soft on Jimmy. "I can't go back to being a slave. I won't."

"Not even mine? It wouldn't be like before. I wouldn't let it. Or do you think I'd slip back into those old ways?"

"I know you wouldn't. Even so, I still couldn't do it."

"But I could protect you, keep you safe."

"No one could." Nate shook his head. "Not when we've come this far. If we lose now, it'll be a blood bath. They'll wipe us all out."

"Then don't lose."

"We plan not to."

"And now." Jimmy straightened his shoulders, sitting upright. "You can help me put all this back."

* * * *

Reports about the freedom movement and the growing unrest, dominated the television news and the papers. Rallies and riots all over the country, programs about the horrors of slavery, the misery caused by the terrorists—it all depended on which channel he watched.

It seemed like everyone was choosing sides.

Jimmy's mother had picked hers. He hardly left the house except for work.

Nate turned up more frequently but stayed for less time. His eyes gleaming, his body wrung out with fatigue. Jimmy fed him, stuck him in the shower, watched over him whilst he slept then sent him on his way. He felt he was doing something, albeit small, for the cause. Nate wouldn't let him do anything else.

* * * *

Jimmy's ordinary life felt like it plodded on as relentlessly as ever. The following Friday he was about as relieved to be finished work for the week as he'd ever been. He was going to have a bath, a proper long one, with bubbles and everything. He couldn't remember the last time he'd done that. A bath, a take away, sitting on the sofa in front of the TV, doing nothing while he forgot everything for a while.

As he walked round the back of the house, he saw a familiar figure sitting on the patio chair.

Doing nothing whilst sitting on the sofa with Nate would be even better. If he could get him to stay that long.

"How you doing?" he asked as he unlocked the door.

"Okay, I'm good." Nate followed him into the kitchen.

"Want a beer?"

"Yeah, but…"

"What?" Jimmy passed the bottle over. "You can only stay twenty minutes and you need to shower and eat in that time? It's all right, I can cook while you wash."

"No, not that." Nate went quiet for a moment, hesitation in his voice that Jimmy wasn't used to anymore.

"What?" He asked again.

"I have the whole weekend off. Last chance to catch our breath before..."

"Wow," Jimmy said, astonished. "And you came here?"

"Yeah, but... Can we go to the lake cabin? You and me, for the weekend? If you don't mind?"

"Mind? Have you gone completely insane? No, I don't mind." He had to stop grinning like a fool, before his face stuck like that. "That's a brilliant idea, I'll just..." He looked at Nate, still grinning. "Fuck it, there's stuff up at the cabin, and if it isn't there, we don't need it. Let's just go, right now."

"I hoped you'd say that." Nate smiled back.

* * * *

It was cold when they pulled up in front of the cabin. The frost was thick on the ground, sparkling in the headlights, on the branches and leaves. Even the water seemed to glitter and glisten.

Inside they sat on the floor in front of the fireplace that Jimmy had finally had cleaned, watching the wood crackle and burn, eating pizza they'd picked up along the way straight from the box, beer in the other hand. The flames danced and Jimmy could just about hear the occasional animal sound from outside. He felt secluded, protected from the world—sheltered in a little bubble of peace. He knew it wouldn't last long, but for now it was perfect. He couldn't think of anything else he wanted.

"Let's go for a long walk tomorrow," he said. "If we headed for the mountains, we wouldn't see another living soul all day."

"Sounds like a plan." Nate kicked his shoes off and stretched his legs out closer to the fire. "I'd have liked to go for a swim, if it wasn't fucking freezing. But I'm not breaking ice to get in the water."

"We can, next summer." Jimmy thought about the idea. "If we're still here and we still have the cabin. If the..."

"Let's not think about that now. This is almost certainly the last bit of calm for a while, let's enjoy it."

"That soon?" Jimmy watched him.

"Yeah, probably."

"Okay." Jimmy nodded. "Then it's walk, eat, more eating and tons and tons of sleep."

"Speaking of which." Nate pulled himself to his feet. "I'm going to bed." He stared down at Jimmy, the firelight reflected on his face. "Do you want to come with me?"

Jimmy's jaw fell open as his head went back to rest on the seat of the sofa. "Do I want to sleep with you?"

"Well." Nate's smile was warm, affectionate. "I was hoping for sex but if you just want to sleep, I guess we can do that."

"No, no." Jimmy was on his feet even though he had no idea how he got there. "I want sex, lots and lots of it. Masses of it then more sex and..."

"Come on then." Nate caught hold of his cuff and pulled him toward his bedroom. But inside the door, Jimmy stopped. "Have you changed your mind?" Nate said carefully. "That's okay. We don't have to do this. You have to really want it."

"I do." Jimmy exhaled hard. "Oh God, I do."

"But?"

"You have to really want it as well."

"You think I'd have got you up here if I didn't?"

Jimmy held onto Nate's sleeves, so surprised with himself that he was saying this, when he'd just been offered everything he hadn't even dared to hope for.

"Do you just want an easy fuck before the end comes? A last bit of pleasure before all-out war? I can do that. I just have to know what it is."

Nate's face softened. "I can get easy anywhere. With you it's not easy—you're more complicated than any other fuck in the world. But I'm here and I'm asking you."

"Good, that's really good." Jimmy nodded again. "But...?"

"What?"

"Does this mean something?"

"It does to me," Nate said. "If you want time to work out what it means to you, then we can—"

"No, no," Jimmy was quick to say. "I just need to know what's going on in your head right now. Where I stand. What you think of me."

"I..." Nate looked up at him and exhaled, hard and slow. "Everyone still says I should hate you. No, they just expect me to. Those that know I don't feel like that still worry about me. But I'm not here to prove anything to them or myself. I'm here because...because I want to be where you are. Because you make me think. Because the thought of touching you, seeing you smile, warms my belly and gets me through the bad times. Because I want to do this again." He reached up and brushed the hair from Jimmy's eyes. "Because if this is the pause before the storm or even if it's the end, there's no one else I want to be with. Because... I want to," he finished simply.

"That's good enough for me," Jimmy said. "There's no one else I want to be with, either."

"So?" Nate leaned forward, tipping his head back so their breath mingled.

"Fuck." Jimmy's laugh barked out of him along with the word. "I'm as nervous as a virgin. I want..."

"What? What do you want?"

"I want it to be different."

"Oh it will be. Trust me."

"But I want it to be epic and amazing and… I don't know what to do or how to do it or…"

"Shut up." Nate reached up, caught hold of Jimmy's hair and pulled him down, kissing him.

Kissing Nate this time was nothing like any other occasion Jimmy had done it. No submission, no 'letting' Jimmy or moving into a position Jimmy wanted. This was the real Nate kissing the real Jimmy — strong, capable, knowing exactly what he wanted and going for it. Not trying to take control but giving every bit he took.

Equal for equal.

Jimmy had never had a kiss like it. He never wanted anything else.

"Sex now, please," he said, when Nate let him go long enough to speak. "Now, now, now."

"Okay." Nate laughed as he eased Jimmy's thick shirt off his shoulders and smoothed down his arms, before going for the T-shirt underneath.

Skin on skin.

Nate's rough palms over his biceps. It felt different and perfect and everything Jimmy needed. Only Nate's hands weren't enough. He needed more, now. But Nate was kissing him again and it was hard to think when that happened, even harder to coordinate his hands to get some of Nate's clothes off. Then Nate pulled Jimmy's T-shirt over his head and the kiss had to break, just for a moment. He managed to find a way under Nate's layers and started to lift them up, running his fingers over flesh that was so familiar it felt burned into his memory.

Familiar yet different, and not just because the man inside wasn't acting anymore.

Jimmy pulled away, dragging Nate's tops off him. "What's this?" he asked, thumb rubbing over a mark under Nate's rib cage.

"Not as bad as you think it is," Nate reassured. He caught Jimmy's wrist, holding it in place against his skin. "Life's been tough. You know that. But not so bad. I've got a few bumps and bruises, nothing else. Nothing to bother about." With his other hand he flicked the button on Jimmy's jeans, wriggling the zipper down. "Let's forget it. We have better things to concentrate on."

As Nate pushed inside, sliding under the elastic of his underwear, Jimmy groaned. He caught the back of Nate's head and pulled him in for another kiss, deep and demanding. He ran his tongue across Nate's teeth, further in, before slowly and thoroughly fucking his mouth as Nate jacked him.

As Nate jacked him. As he fucked Nate's mouth.

No, that wasn't how it was going to be. Not even if the kiss and the touch felt different. That was what they'd done before. He wasn't going back there. He pulled back again, further this time, face clouding over as he took a step away. That was owner and slave and this was—this had to be—different. Only he wasn't sure how to guarantee that, to make certain there were no slip ups. No going back. Hesitation hit him hard for a moment.

"Hey?" Nate stared at him with questioning eyes. "Come back here."

Then Jimmy looked down and, hell...the same man, same body as he knew so well, only it wasn't. Nate was different, real, and it radiated through every one of his pores.

"I will, just got to get out of these." Jimmy forced himself to move again, pulling the rest of his clothes off before starting on Nate's, easing them off as carefully as his shaking hands allowed. He wanted so much that it physically hurt. But he wanted to do it right. If he messed this up, if he never got to feel Nate under his hands, never tasted his mouth again, never...

He had to do it right.

"Stop thinking and get over here," Nate said, holding out a hand.

Jimmy wasn't a fool—he did as he was told. Climbing onto the bed beside Nate, stroking a hand up his chest, he leaned over to kiss him. The kiss went on and on, Nate tugging on his hair to hold him in place, grinding his cock against Jimmy's hip, panting into his mouth, hand skimming over Jimmy. Nate wanted this—that was one thing Jimmy was pretty damned sure about.

"Now." Nate huffed into his mouth. "Do it now."

"What?" Jimmy's mind felt clouded.

"Do me now. Which way do you want me?"

"No." Yet again Jimmy pulled away.

"You don't want to fuck me?" It was Nate's turn to look confused. "But you always want to fuck me."

"No. Yes. Fuck, I..." Jimmy took a deep breath and tried again. "Yes, I want to fuck you. Yes, I always want to fuck you but not now."

"Why not?"

"Because...because... Jesus shit, I'm struggling here." Jimmy sat up, rubbing a hand over his face. "I want to but, more than anything, I want it to be different from before. We had sex so often we'd got into a rhythm and it was all based on what I liked. I don't want that now."

"But I like getting fucked by you. I told you that."

"I know. But you also told me you hate sucking cock. That's burned into my brain. Only I'd never have known if you hadn't said. You're a fucking good actor. I don't know what you really liked and what was an act. I don't know what's real and I really, really want to. I want..." He glanced round the room, reaching out for something that wasn't there.

"What do you want?"

"I want real. I want to start again from scratch."

"I can't make what happened — all those memories — disappear, but I can give you real," Nate said carefully.

"But I can't tell, not when my brain is fogged with sex and we're doing something I know so well. Does that make any sense?"

"Yeah, I guess so." Nate nodded. "So what do you want to do?

"I want to do something we didn't do before. I want you to fuck me," Jimmy said, making sure he held Nate's eyes the whole time.

Nate licked slowly across his lips. "You been fucked before?"

"Yes, but not for a very long time. Do you want to do it?"

"Hell yes." The eagerness that Nate said it with made Jimmy laugh.

"What are we waiting for then?"

"Go get the lube out of my jacket pocket," Nate demanded. "I came prepared."

Jimmy rolled off the bed, grabbing Nate's coat and fishing in the pocket. He turned back to face the bed, the laughter gone from his face, leaving soft acceptance. "Should I find a condom?"

"I don't know, should you?"

"Not for me, we don't. But I understand if…"

"Not for me either." Nate stopped him.

Jimmy felt a warmth flood over him, rising up from the soles of his feet to the ends of his hair. "Good." He smiled. He crawled back up the bed to loom over Nate. "I know you don't like sucking cock but how do you really feel about having yours sucked?"

"By you?" Nate grinned up at him. "I already told you."

"Maybe, but tell me again now, when I can really believe you. What's your deep down opinion?"

"I fucking love it."

"I hoped so." Jimmy kissed him, deeply and thoroughly, before trailing his tongue down Nate's chest to swirl it across his belly as Nate hissed.

Sucking Nate's cock wasn't anything like it had been on the few occasions he'd done it before. It tasted different, felt different in his mouth. It seemed to swell in flavor, texture, pleasure, to overwhelm, overpower him. Engulfing him in all that was Nate.

If he thought he loved Nate before, it had nothing on now.

The thought hit him like a tidal wave, drowning him in the knowledge. Before he'd been in love with Nate's body, even more than the idea of him. It had been good, really good. Now? Now he was in love with the man himself.

He'd give up the sex if it meant he got to keep the man.

That thought left him breathless, choking on the cock in his mouth.

"Are you okay?" Nate panted down at him.

"Yeah." Jimmy knew his voice sounded as raw as his throat.

"No you're not. Come up here." Nate tried to pull him.

"Not a fucking chance." Jimmy went back to his task. Right now he did have it all, even if it only lasted the night. Right now he could have everything.

He swallowed Nate back in, taking him deep, sucking hard.

If the taste was different, it had nothing on the reactions of the man himself. Nate bucked up into the pleasure, gasping, breathless and erratic. And Jimmy knew what it was, knew the difference. Before Nate had always fought to stay in control, even when he was caught in an orgasm, when he was coming. Now he was letting himself go, giving himself over to Jimmy's care. Jimmy recognized the importance of the gesture. He wouldn't let Nate down.

He sucked again, smoothing over Nate's hipbones, drawing circles on the flesh with his thumbs.

Again, letting Nate fuck as deep into his mouth as he wanted.

Again, riding and glorying in the taste, the feel of Nate losing control.

Again and Nate was pulling at his shoulder, his hair.

"Please." Nate begged. "If you still want me to fuck you, you have to stop right this second. It's your choice."

"I want." Jimmy let the cock slip from between his lips, squeezing at the base to take the edge off.

"Sure? I don't care either way." Nate sounded wrung out, flayed open.

"I want it, need it. But first I need to do this." He pushed Nate's legs further apart, settling his shoulders between them and licked down Nate's dick, ignoring the man's deep-pitched moans. Down over his balls, taking them into his mouth, leaning and testing the texture, the weight and taste in ways he'd never bothered to before.

Down even lower, letting his tongue slip and slide before focusing in on that one place.

"You don't have..." Nate tried to say but Jimmy wouldn't let him.

"Shut up. Don't you dare say anything stupid, not now. I want to do this. You want me to as well." He didn't give Nate a chance to argue, pushing his face back in, lapping and prodding with his tongue. Learning a part of Nate he'd never known before. Learning how Nate responded to it and, God, it was a wonderful thing.

Nate tried to fight for any control with little bitten off groans. But then he gave into it, pressing into Jimmy's face, making stark, broken noises. Then he was pulling himself away, hands fisted in the sheet as he dragged his body backwards.

"Fucking—you said you wanted fucking. You have to stop if we're going to have a hope in hell of doing that now. Unless you've changed your mind?"

"No." Jimmy pulled him back down, kissing his neck, his face, his mouth. "Fucking now. But we have to do that again and soon."

Nate gave an almost pitiful moan.

Jimmy rolled over onto his back, dragging Nate with him. He spread his legs, pushing Nate until he was between them. Nate was still panting, mouth hanging open. He pushed the lube into Nate's hand. "Are you going to make me do all the work?"

"It's about time you did." Nate huffed, his mouth against Jimmy's chest. He heaved in another huge breath then pulled himself off Jimmy, looking down. "But you always did make me do everything." It was nothing but a stupid joke about a time that was past.

Jimmy felt another spark flower in his chest. He knew that, knew it, accepted it, could laugh along with it, make jokes of his own like it. All because they both knew that time was gone. This was now and it was completely different.

"You just want to see me finger myself open," Jimmy said, as he watched Nate's eyes go impossibly wide and dark.

"You'd better do it quickly because, so help me, God, I need to fuck you so hard you won't be able to stand up."

"Need?" Jimmy took the lube, squeezing it onto his own fingers and reaching down between them.

"Need—not want. I need it so bad my dick is in danger of exploding."

"That would be a real shame." Jimmy's face registered it as he pushed two fingers in.

"Fuck, I have got to see this." Nate scooted back onto his knees, eyes intent on the juncture between Jimmy's fingers and his arse. "Oh sweet hell, that's good. Please, I'm begging here, tell me you aren't going to need long? I have got to get in there."

"Got to get in there? When the hell did you get such a way with words?" Jimmy pushed in a third finger and Nate's eyes went ridiculously round. He twisted his hand, staring up. "I'm done. You ready?"

"I am so ready I'm..." Nate crawled back over him, arranging legs and arms as he went. He leaned down and kissed Jimmy, not hard, but thorough and filling. "I... You..." There was something in Nate's eyes that Jimmy couldn't quite read. But before he had a chance to think about it, Nate was kissing him again and pushing in. Not slow and careful like fantasy-Nate might have done, but sure and capable.

It was Jimmy's turn to melt, giving up any attempt at control as he mewled into the feeling. He hadn't been fucked for a long time, but it had never, not ever, felt like this. Faultless. He reached up, twisting his arms round Nate's neck and hanging on as he gave over everything he had. Opening himself up and not just physically. Canting his hips, back into every thrust, squeezing to hold Nate inside, to give him more pleasure, more of Jimmy.

More reason to return.

Jimmy felt himself pushed up the bed and gloried in it. Felt his body filled to its limit and ached for more. He'd never imagined the slide of a cock in his arse could feel anything like this good.

If he died now, his only regret would be that he hadn't got to do it again.

He matched Nate's every stroke, fucking himself on Nate's dick, wanting more. Then there was a hand on his cock and it wasn't what he wanted. He wanted, needed, it to go on forever, but the pull of fingers, the press in deep wouldn't let him. He came shouting into the air, his hands biting into Nate's neck and shoulders.

Then he hung there, lost in that between worlds before coming back down as Nate kept going. Deep and deeper still as Jimmy's muscles relaxed, and that was good, so very good. Then he could feel Nate coming, the spasming of his dick, the warmth inside, the shuddering of his body. He locked his arms round Nate and rocked him through it, keeping him there, until they both caught their breath.

Nate pulled out but didn't move away, for which Jimmy was profoundly grateful. He needed all the contact he could get right then.

"That was..." Nate stroked across Jimmy's shoulder.

"The word you're looking for is awesome. It was awesome."

"Yeah." Nate drawled the word, lazy and content.

"And we have to do it again real soon."

"My turn next though."

"Your turn at?"

"Being fucked."

"You've had lots of turns." Jimmy snorted. "I've got to catch up."

"Your fault for not asking for it sooner. My turn next," Nate insisted.

Jimmy suddenly laughed, holding onto Nate's shoulder. "You realize we're arguing about who gets to take it up the arse?"

"I'm not arguing." Nate rubbed his nose into Jimmy's skin. "It's my turn."

"Fuck, you're a pushy bastard."

There was a long pause as they both caught their breath. "What was the hesitation at the start all about?" Nate asked eventually.

"I had a...bit of a moment," Jimmy confessed.

"Tell me."

"It hit me that, even if everything goes shit upwards and you, we, lose, I don't want you back as my slave."

"You don't?"

"I think, back then, I was in love with your body as well as the fantasy of you. Now I want you as you really are. If I can't have that, I don't want the slave. I don't even want your body if I can't have you as my friend."

"Jesus, man." Nate sucked in a huge breath, holding it for a sharp moment. "You've come so far, changed so much. I am so fucking amazed by you."

"You're amazed by me? It was you that let me change. More than that, you let yourself see it. I..."

Jimmy licked at his lips, hand soft on Nate's belly. "I don't think I would have, if I was you," he admitted. "I'd have been so angry, so bitter. I couldn't have forgiven me."

"Yeah, you would." Nate kissed Jimmy's neck, leaving his face buried for a moment. "Because you're deep down good and kind and decent, although you forgot it for a while."

"Won't forget to keep trying," Jimmy said honestly. "Even if this is the last time we see each other." He acknowledged the unspoken truth.

"If it is, it'll be the last and the best." Nate rolled until he was crushed into Jimmy's side, head under his chin.

"Isn't that the truth." Jimmy wrapped a hand round the back of Nate's head and held him tighter. "Tell me. Did you plan that we'd end up in bed when you suggested we come up here?"

"Sort of," Nate said. "I planned for the possibility, if it felt right."

"You wanted something good, before the firestorm started?"

"Yeah, maybe. But it was more than that. I wanted to see how good we could be together. There might not be another chance and, if it all goes arse up, I wanted to know. No point hanging onto possibilities. I wanted to know about us."

"And what do you think about us now?"

"I tell you what I think." Nate looked up. "I think we should spend this weekend having as much sex as we possibly can in as many positions and places as we can think of."

Jimmy's laugh made his whole body rock. "God, I knew there was a reason I loved you so much."

Nate burrowed in deeper, a smug grin on his face.

* * * *

Next morning Jimmy took one look at the rain thundering against the window, shivered over dramatically as Nate laughed at him, and retreated back to bed with a pile of food. He propped Nate against the headboard, slid in next to him, and pulled up the covers as far as they could. "This is a morning, if not a whole day, to be spent in bed," he announced as he tried to balance his coffee cup on his knee.

"I couldn't agree more," Nate said, taking everything he was offered then dumping the dirty dishes over the side of the bed. After they'd eaten Jimmy spent the rest of the morning relearning Nate's body with fingers, mouth and tongue, and Nate did the same. What felt like hours later, Jimmy pressed up against Nate's back, his cock hard. Nate pushed back, rocking against him as both their breathing quickened. "Are you going to fuck me now?" he asked.

"Only if you want me to."

"About time." Nate reached back, holding Jimmy to him. "You made me wait long enough."

"Stop moaning." Jimmy found the lube, slicking his fingers up.

"Wait." Twisting his head to a ridiculous angle Nate kissed him, soft and wet.

Jimmy sighed into it, it was all so good. Then Nate turned some more until they were pressed chest to chest. "Do you want to do it this way round?"

"But I thought you preferred it from... That was another part of the act, wasn't it?"

"Not so much an act. More that I didn't want you to see my face."

"Why?"

"Because it's hard to keep the right expression in the middle of an orgasm." Nate hitched a shoulder. "Only now I want you to see me. More important, I want to see you."

"I… Thank you." Jimmy combed his fingers through Nate's hair, pushing him onto his back.

Nate opened his legs and pulled Jimmy on top of him.

Kissing the real Nate had been different—fucking him was like a whole new world. He thrust back, grabbing Jimmy hard, not afraid to leave marks and demand, 'more', 'harder', 'faster', 'over a bit', 'right there', 'keep it going'.

The real Nate was bossy but gave so much more. His chest heaved, a mottled red stain growing across the pale skin as he let go—a response Jimmy had never seen before—hadn't thought possible, as Nate bit at his mouth, his shoulder. As his back arched and his hips moved constantly.

Jimmy had wanted something different from the sex they used to have and he gotten it in every breathy moan, every sigh and plea for more. They'd never had sex like this before, not even close. Jimmy had wanted to start again with a clean slate. This went further than anything he'd thought possible.

Jimmy laughed at his own excitement and eagerness, knowing he was acting like a teenager, even as they started again, a slow and thorough exploration of skin and their reactions as the world went on outside without them. They kept constantly touching, because now they could. Now it meant something.

* * * *

Very early Monday morning, when it was still dark outside, Nate pulled Jimmy on top of him, holding on tight to his hair and kissing him softly. Jimmy lifted Nate's leg, fucking into him just as softly, just as gently making it last as long as he possibly could. He stroked Nate's shoulder, fingertips ghosting patterns and shapes, joining up freckles. Somehow he coordinated his body, pushing in with his tongue in time with his cock, velvety thrusts with minimum force as he savored every second, storing the sensations, the memories away.

Inevitably it had to end and Nate came as he cradled Jimmy's head between his hands, mouth pressed to Jimmy's cheek as his breath puffed out against his skin. Jimmy thought it was perfect, so perfect it drew him over the edge as he held Nate tighter. They stayed locked together, ignoring the cooling mess between them, until the blackness outside turned gray with the first hint of morning.

In the shower, Jimmy ran his hands over Nate's body, memorizing new muscle, old freckles. When it all got too much, too intense, Nate turned him round, washing Jimmy's hair, his back. His hands were gentle, the rough pads on his fingertips sliding over Jimmy's skin with such care it made Jimmy's belly roll and catch. Afterwards, Nate took him back to bed and fucked into him again with just as much care, until Jimmy couldn't think, could barely breathe.

Then it was time for the calm before the final storm to end.

After packing up the few things they wanted to take with them, they threw their bags into the back seat of the car and looked back at the cabin. "We'll be back soon," Nate said with false confidence.

Faith Ashlin

"Yeah." Jimmy went along with him. There was nothing else he could do. "We'll be back."

He dropped Nate at a street corner soon after they got to the city. As he got out of the car, Jimmy caught hold of his cuff, pulling him back. "Just remember, I really do love you. The real you."

"I know." Nate smiled softly, his fingers gentle on Jimmy's face, and kissed him quickly before walking away.

Pursing his lips, he watched in the rear-view mirror as Nate crossed the road, got into a dark blue car and drove off.

He had no idea when they'd see each other again.

Chapter Nine

It happened slowly at first, a few days calm before the tornado hit full force and the world seemed to shudder and gasp, holding itself on a knife-edge.

It was here—whatever it was. Jimmy thought 'revolution' sounded over the top and melodramatic, but what else could he call something like this? Something so momentous and important. The country was about to change, or maybe it would stay the same. That was the truly scary thing—they might have come this far and got to this, only for it all to fall away.

For two long days and three even longer nights, everyone held their breath and was caught in the most significant period of history Jimmy could remember.

Filming shut down, everywhere bosses sent workers home—those that had been brave enough to leave their families and go into work in the first place. Cinemas, theaters, shopping malls closed as The State tried to ban public gatherings. Many people were too frightened to go out on the streets, but there was still panic buying as they barricaded themselves in their homes.

On the television Jimmy watched uncensored news reports of protests, some peaceful, some more like riots as huge numbers of people stared down The State Police. At first, the protestors were mainly young, those still idealistic and with hope. But something wonderful happened on the second day, when it seemed like The State would regain control. A TV news film of Heidi Allott was shown everywhere, her face grimy and exhausted, her normally golden hair matted with dirt. She stood in an empty car park, her shoulders down and defeated, and pleaded with ordinary people to come out and make a difference.

To help the children who were being made into slaves, to stop the system.

The tears streaming down her face were as unusual and unexpected as they were effective. If Heidi Allott was begging, it was time to take sides.

Jimmy was just putting his jacket on ready to go, when he spotted Nate in the background. He was getting into his car when he got the phone call. "You leave the house and I'll hunt you down and kill you myself," Nate said.

"But I—"

"No, no buts—not this time. Please, please, just do as I ask."

Jimmy locked himself inside the house and put the television back on.

He might not have answered the call to help but thousands did, and many of them were astonishing. Men and women, old and young. Middle aged, middle income, women with their round figures and homely faces stood next to thick-necked young men with tattoos and work roughened hands. Hippy girls with 'eat vegetarian' badges and grubby feet next to old men with their walking sticks and caps. The only thing they had in common was how determined they seemed.

They confronted The State Police in a gentle, non-threatening way — sitting down in front of them and refusing to go. To move them would have meant a bloodbath, to do it in front of uncensored cameras would have been suicide for The State's leaders.

The standoff lasted all that night and most of the next day. Then came the announcement that the former leaders of The State would be standing down.

They were already on a plane heading for another country before the TV reported the news.

It was over.

They had won.

There was no more slavery, no more slaves.

Now there was just chaos as everyone tried to work out who was in control. People celebrated in the streets as the new order tried to work out who they could trust, who was really on their side. That was a difficult task — an easier one was deciding on the police.

The division between The State Police, that controlled slavery, and the ordinary civil police, concerned with law and order, had always been clear cut — a fact the freedom movement were profoundly grateful for, Nate had told Jimmy in one of his many, but brief, phone calls. They had a body they could trust and they needed that.

At the end of each call, Nate always finished the same way. "Please, help me out by staying safe. I... I can't worry about you. Not now. I'll see you as soon as I can."

Jimmy could live with that.

Slowly things calmed down, fear turning into festivity, even if life was far from normal. The studio had no plans to reopen, but there was food in the shops, electricity when the lights were switched on — although that had gone at one point. Now the freedom movement was out to consolidate the change. Slaves were free. Slavery would never be allowed to happen again. A rally was going to be held in the city's athletic stadium. All the leaders would be there — everyone was welcome to come and party with them.

This was one time Jimmy thought he could go.

Then came the inevitable phone call from Nate. "About the rally tomorrow," Nate started.

"Oh come on, man. I can go to that. It's safe. Hell, the woman in the corner store is taking her grandkids. If they can go, I can. Please, let me go."

"Well, if you want to go with Grandma you can. I was going to suggest you come with me, but if you have a better offer..."

"Seriously? You mean it?"

"Sure, if you want to go."

"If I want to go? You fucking bastard, of course I want to go with you." Jimmy couldn't help the unadulterated delight in his voice.

"I'm glad. I'll pick you up at six." Nate just sounded smug.

At ten to six Jimmy was bouncing in front of the back door, waiting — which meant he had to race through the house when the front door bell rang. When he opened it, Nate was standing on the step, looking fucking gorgeous and jangling his keys. "What the hell?" Jimmy demanded.

"Got no reason to hide anymore." Nate's smile made him look even more gorgeous. "You need to close your mouth though. You remind me of a fish that's just been dumped on the quayside." Then, bold as brass, he leaned in and kissed Jimmy, warm and thorough, right there, right on the door step.

Jimmy sighed and melted into the touch.

"Ready to go?" Nate asked as he pulled back. Jimmy had to open his eyes and start thinking again before he could nod. "Come on then." Nate caught hold of his hand, drawing him out of the house, waiting as he locked the door behind him, then walking down the short driveway.

"You want to use my car?" Jimmy asked when he could get his brain to catch up.

"No, I got one."

"Where is it?"

"I parked on the street."

"Why?"

"So everyone will see us as we walk out hand in hand, of course." Nate grinned at him.

"I… That…that's fucking awesome." Jimmy pushed in closer and Nate obligingly kissed him again.

* * * *

When they reached the stadium, there was already a big crowd, but Nate was waved through a high security gate to a parking place at the back. He didn't bother locking the car. "We're late," Nate said. "It's my fault but things will start soon. I'll introduce you to the others now, if you'd like."

"Actually." Jimmy held back. "Do you mind if I don't?"

"You don't want to meet them?"

Jimmy shrugged, feeling foolish. "I do, just… Not now? Now I just want to wallow in the fact it's over, that you're free. That I can say 'I know him', rather than 'I own him'. Is that stupid?"

"No, not stupid." Nate's face softened. "We got time—all the time in the world now."

"Thanks." It was Jimmy's turn to initiate the kiss. It felt wild, audacious, to be kissing there, where so many of the freedom movement could see them, where the world could see them.

"Come on, I'll find you somewhere to stand at the side of the stage. You don't have to talk to anyone if you don't want to."

"I..." Again Jimmy hesitated.

"What?" Nate laughed.

"I want to watch from the crowd, out with everyone else. I want to watch my hero on stage, even if he is at the back."

"Your hero?"

"Why not?"

"Stupid asshole," Nate laughed. "Okay, if you want to get crushed, be my guest. I'll ring you after, then we can go home and celebrate properly."

"Sounds like a plan." Jimmy followed as Nate led the way. "Where will you be standing? I want to be on the correct side, up close, so I can actually see you."

"I'll be on the right. If I let you out there you'll be near the stage, albeit on the wrong side of the fence. Stay as far to the right as you can get."

Jimmy did just has he'd been instructed, pushing his way through the crowd to a spot on the grass, a few feet away from a post supporting the chain fence. When the speakers came on, he got a great view of the side of their heads but that didn't matter. He could hear what they said, feel the buzz and rise of emotion from the crowd, see Nate right off at the side. He was standing, arms folded over his chest, smile a million miles wide—obviously so proud of all that had happened, but keeping out of the spotlight. Several times he scanned the crowd. Jimmy hoped it was in an effort to spot him. It was, of course, impossible and Nate laughed, shaking his head and smiling as Lizzy Palmer stopped to talk to him on her way by.

It was a wonderful evening, cold but crisp, with a feeling of hope in the air, a real carnival atmosphere. It lasted until something was thrown over from the other side of the huge crowd. It didn't make it onto the stage, Jimmy wasn't sure it was intended to, landing instead among the people and a howl of protest went up. Another missile was hurled and another, then the crowd surged, forwards, backwards — away.

Jimmy pushed his way forward, not interested in the riot that was threatening to break out but trying to get to the fence, to get to Nate. Then he was there, fingers curling around the wire.

Everyone on the stage was looking toward the trouble. Heidi had taken the microphone, was appealing for calm. No one was watching the group of men that had come round the other way. No one stopped them as they moved closer, as they knocked out two guys, caught a girl by the throat and threw her off the stage. Jimmy shouted, loud as he knew how, but the roar from the crowd drowned everything else out. He yelled again, his throat burning as they moved in on Nate at the side of the stage, grabbing him by his hair and yanking him backwards.

Jimmy screamed warning after warning, clawing at the fence as he tried to climb it, but it was no use. It was never going to be any use, not with the stack of speakers in the way, all the noise and everyone's attention fixed elsewhere. The men bunched around Nate, pushing him up against the speakers so hard his head bounced off them. He tried to fight, fists flying, legs kicking, but, pushed face first against something so solid it was obvious there was little he could do.

When they ripped his jeans down he fought even harder, hurting himself as he thrashed and struck out. But hands were holding him in place — too many hands, too many fists to his back, his sides.

Jimmy screamed when a man moved toward Nate's back, his cock out. Screamed, but not at Nate. He knew what was coming and there was nothing he could do that he hadn't already tried. Jimmy screamed at the other freedom fighters, at anyone else who might hear, who might help.

No one did.

He kicked at the fence with everything he had but it bounced back, intact. Again he tried to climb it, blood trickling down his palms, but it was too high, the gaps too small for his feet.

He yelled again, louder, more desperate.

One of the group surrounding Nate turned slightly and Jimmy saw the exact moment a cock shoved viciously into Nate, saw him rear up and recoil. But all the hands holding down simply pushed harder, not allowing him to move more than an inch.

There'd be no escape.

It was as fast as it was ruthless, the man biting at Nate's shoulder through his jacket as he thrust into him. Then he was pulling away and Jimmy could see Nate's flesh, naked from the small of his back to his thighs. Flesh he'd gotten to know all over again. Then it was gone from sight and another man thrust in and Nate fought again, pushing and shoving and...did Jimmy hear him call out in pain?

It wasn't possible but he was sure he had.

He couldn't watch anymore, couldn't stand it. He threw himself at the fence — fuck the consequences.

Only the fence didn't buckle or break. It absorbed his force and pitched him back. He screamed, picking up a discarded bottle from the ground and throwing it at the freedom fighters over the other side of the stage as he tried the fence again. None of it worked, not until there was the sound of gunfire over the loud speaker system and the crowd fell silent for a moment. Jimmy shouted louder than he ever had in his life, throwing everything he could reach.

And this time it worked.

An empty Coke can hit the man on the stage closest to him and he turned. Jimmy shouted again, pointing furiously from where he was hanging half way up the fence. The man spotted Nate's head between the bodies surrounding him, called out to the other fighters and the next second they stormed across the stage.

Jimmy offered up a silent prayer to any deity that was listening. The men around Nate realized rescue was coming and started to run for the edge of the stage. Jimmy watched as the rapist pulled out from Nate. He thought Nate would fall when he was free, but instead he twisted round, one hand dragging up his jeans as he lunged toward his attacker. That was when Jimmy's world started moving in slow motion.

The first man who'd raped Nate raised the bat he'd been carrying and swung. Slowly it cut a line through the air and Jimmy knew where it would land, what it would hit, moments before it did. He couldn't hear the sound as it connected with the side of Nate's head, but he thought he could feel it.

Nate's neck snapped backwards. His whole body lifted off his feet with the force. As he flew through the air to land hard on his back, limbs sprawling everyway, until he was completely still.

Jimmy screamed and screamed Nate's name, fought even harder to get to him, but all he could see was a motionless body and a face covered by blood.

He screamed again, tearing at the fence with bloodied hands, but a pack of freedom fighters blocked his view.

* * * *

Jimmy sat on the hard concrete outside the hospital and stared at his hands. They were torn and bloody — he figured they must hurt, but he couldn't feel anything. He looked up — the sky was dark, the dead of night.

He had no idea where to go or what to do. He didn't even know if Nate was alive.

He'd tried to get to him but there was no way. The people around Nate, protecting him, had called for help and Nate had been carried away by paramedics. Still Jimmy couldn't reach him. He'd shouted, screamed, but the place was chaos and no one was listening.

He'd pulled out his phone but he had no numbers to call.

As people cleared out of the stadium, he'd tried to get through the back, but every way was barred and not a soul would talk to him. Even if they had, what could he say? 'I own Nate — or at least I used to, before you changed everything'.

He'd kept trying until the place was empty and there was no hope. Then he went to the hospitals. He didn't know which Nate had been taken to, but it had to be one of them. There was so much blood.

Unless they needed a morgue rather than a hospital.

That thought chilled him to the bone.

But none of the hospitals would tell him if Nate was there. The woman behind the desk in this last one had said she wouldn't tell him even if Nate were in the building. That made him walk away, but there was nowhere to go, nothing more to do.

So he'd sat down and he was still here.

Maybe, when it was daylight, he could go to the movement's headquarters. Maybe he could make someone there tell him if Nate was alive at least. Maybe, maybe, maybe.

His phone rang. Maybe Nate wasn't as badly hurt as he thought, maybe... He didn't recognize the number but answered automatically.

"Hello," came a low female voice. "Is that Jimmy?"

Jimmy made a noise of confirmation.

"You don't know me, but I'm Lizzy Palmer. I work with Nate and..."

"I know who you are. Is he alive?"

"Yes," she said, and Jimmy could have cried, very nearly did as he gripped the phone tighter. "He's alive and just come out of surgery. The doctors think he's going to be all right."

"Surgery?"

"His head, he... Jimmy, do you know what happened?"

Jimmy sucked in a huge breath, holding it as he squeezed his eyes closed. But that didn't help, the scene played like a movie reel inside his head. "I saw it, all of it. I shouted and tried to get to him but I couldn't and no one could hear me and..."

"It's okay. He's safe now."

Jimmy clung to those words, his breathing ragged.

"Do you want to see him?" she asked.

"See him? Of course I do." He was already pushing himself to his feet.

"He's in St. John's. Do you know where it is?"

He looked round. Wrong hospital. "I'll be there in fifteen minutes."

"Ask for me at the desk, I'll get you in. You..." She hesitated, and he could hear her gentle breathing. "You do care about him, don't you? I mean, not just as your slave or ex-slave now."

"He hasn't been my slave for a long time," Jimmy said, meaning every word of it. "And no, I don't just care about him. I love him, the real him."

"I'll be waiting for you," she said and hung up.

* * * *

True to her word, Lizzy was waiting at the desk when Jimmy arrived. Completely bypassing the staff, she took him further into the hospital, not stopping until she stood in front of a door. His eyes widened as he saw the sign next to it.

"He's just come out of surgery so he's in intensive care but that's normal. It's serious. Any surgery to the head is. But it's not as bad as it could have been," she said.

"I want to see him now."

"And you will, just let me explain first. I'm pretty sure you won't be listening to me when you see him." She rested a hand on his arm, soft and very feminine. "He had a depressed fractured skull. They had to operate to fix that. But his brain isn't swelling and that was the main concern. He's on a ventilator and sedated to give his body a chance to recover. There are a lot of machines and..." She stared at him, her face gray. "It scared the hell out of me but the doctors assured me it's all normal and nothing to panic about."

"Okay, I get it." He nodded, already making for the door.

"Jimmy." Her hand was a little firmer now. "Do you know what else happened to him? Before he was hit?"

Jimmy took a step back, turning to face her directly and her hand fell away. "He was raped, two men. One right after the other."

The word sat there like a huge monster between them. Lizzy tried to smother it. "You know. It's good you do. But..."

"What? You thought I wouldn't be here if I knew? That only I'm allowed to rape him?"

"I didn't say that."

"You really don't fucking understand at all, do you?" He tried to push past her and this time she let him go. "I want to see him now."

"All right, I'll show you."

But Jimmy stopped at the door, suddenly frightened. "Did they...? How badly did they hurt him when he was raped?"

"Not too badly," she reassured quickly. "Nothing that needed treatment physically. But you needed to know."

"Why? So we can compare notes on how he was raped? This was different. He let me rape him." He pushed the door open and she scrambled to catch up, leading him along to a room at the far end.

A nurse stood by the bed, blocking the view but already Jimmy felt panic. There were machines everywhere, some making noises, others with lights, more still dripping liquids through thin tubes, all leading to the figure in the bed. Then the nurse moved and Jimmy caught sight of Nate.

A thick dressing covered his head—down to his neck on one side, over half his cheek, with a small tuff of hair sticking out the top. His gray-tinged skin was pulled tight across his face, and covered with flecks of dried blood. His eyes were closed, and his lids seemed thin, almost transparent, the veins in them standing out like rivers on a map. He had a tube in his mouth, many more going into his hands, his arms, wires leading under the stark white hospital sheet. Dozens and dozens of tubes, wires and cannulas with filters and ports to allow even more tubes to be attached, laid all over his chest.

But he was alive.

He'd never looked more beautiful.

Jimmy pushed round to the side of the bed, catching hold of the hand with the least wires going into it.

Lizzy was talking to him, the nurse saying something that he knew deep down in his bones was important, but he couldn't hear either of them. The only thought in his head was that Nate was alive. He was alive. He stared down at their joined hands, his dark with dirt and blood, Nate's pale and soft. He thought about how they'd felt on his skin, touching him with care, with desire.

Every instinct he had told him never to let go.

"Jimmy." Lizzy touched his shoulder. "He really is going to be all right. The nurse said the doctors have just left—they're all pleased with his test results. They're going to keep him sedated for a while." Her face softened as she watched at him. "Have you heard anything I said?"

"Keep him sedated. Going to be okay."

"He is." She caught hold of a chair, sliding it to Jimmy. "Sit down before you fall down." He did and she stood by his side. "I want to stay. I really do, but I can't. There's so much to be done. I never thought what it would be like after we won. It seemed too much like tempting fate. It's crazy, so many people to deal with, so many things that need doing and all of them screaming for top priority. We're all working as hard as we can but..." She rested a hand on Nate's shin, stroking it through the sheet. "We can't leave him alone — not now."

"Is that why you called me?" Jimmy demanded, accusation in his eyes. "Not because you thought I might need to see him, not because he might want me, but because none of you could spare the time?"

"I didn't mean it like that. We called his mother but there was no answer and..."

"She died weeks ago."

"Oh God." Lizzy clamped a hand over her mouth. "He told me but I forgot. He told you?"

"We spent the weekend at my lake cabin. He told me then."

"That's where he was," she said, more to herself than anyone else. "I did wonder. He went away broken, came back like normal. That was you?"

"Is it so hard to believe?"

"Yes, actually it is." She turned to face Jimmy, capturing his attention with her clear blue eyes. "When he first left you and came back to us, Paulo was all for going after you, but Nate wouldn't let him, made him swear he wouldn't hurt you in any way. Then, when he said he was seeing you...I didn't understand it, I couldn't work out why, and I was worried about him. Paulo thought you had some kind of hold over him. We all expected him to hate you — thought it was the only thing he could feel about you. But he... He wouldn't talk about you, seemed as though he didn't know what he felt. Or maybe he did know, and he couldn't admit it to anyone, including himself. We didn't know how you felt about him but we figured we could guess. He's an attractive man."

"I love him. That's all. Why can't you see that?"

"Because you owned him. Because you didn't know him." She crouched down so they were at eye level. "Jimmy, we were in contact when I was still in hiding, when he was still living with you, waiting for his leg to heal. Do you remember the first day you went back to work after getting out of prison? Paulo and I were waiting on the other side of the road for your car to pull away, waiting to go in and see him."

"You were at my house?"

"A lot of the time you weren't there, we were with him, either at your house or we'd pick him up if we had to go somewhere else. Paulo even tried to teach him how to cook for your sake. It was..." She hesitated, her face clouding. "Weird. Not good—not good at all. We'd be there and he was the same man I'd known for years, then you were due home and he'd change. Everything—the way he dressed, the way he wore his hair, the way he stood, spoke, everything. He said it was easier, easier to handle you that way. I left him like that, knowing he was going to have to have sex with you, whether he wanted it or not." She pressed her lips tight together, breathing hard. "After—when he'd left—he said you loved him. But how could you? You didn't know what he was really like." She paused, licking at her lips. "Yes, we were worried when he started seeing you again."

"You're right. I didn't know him, not then." Jimmy's attention went back to Nate. "I was in love with his body, with the fantasy he created for me. But I do know him now, really know him and I love him."

"I love him too. He's the brother I never had," she said quietly. "But I've known him a lot longer than you have. We've practically grown up together in the movement."

He gripped Nate's hand tighter as he turned to stare her in the eye. "You might have only got me here because there was no one else to stay with him, but I'm not leaving. Not unless he tells me to go."

She nodded, just once, crisply and briskly, as she stood up. "I think there's more to you than any of us realized, but Nate saw that. Stay, take care of him. What happens after that is up to him. I promise I'll even do my best to keep Paulo off your back, when he's finished with the men who did this to Nate."

"You caught them then?"

"Oh yes. They were never going to get out of that stadium."

"Have you found out why they did it?"

"What do you mean? They wanted to hit the movement." She looked at him, confusion in her eyes.

"No, it wasn't that random. They went straight for Nate. They knew what they were doing, who they were after."

"We didn't know that," she admitted. "I'll tell Paulo." She looked at Nate once more. "He won't wake up for a while, but they said it might help if someone is here, someone he knows. Someone he trusts."

"He trusts me." Jimmy's attention was back on the bed.

"You're that sure?"

"He'd never would have kept on seeing me if he didn't."

Again she nodded. "You're right. Take care."

Jimmy didn't know if she meant him or Nate, but he knew he'd do his damnedest to keep Nate safe. He didn't need her to tell him to do that. He didn't need anyone to tell him.

* * * *

It was a long night. The ventilator kept up its steady murmur as it breathed for Nate, the other machines bleeping, proving he was still alive. Healing. Jimmy kept hold of his hand, resting his chin on top as he stared up at Nate. Why now? Why did everything have to go so wrong when it was just starting to be good? When there was, at last, hope? When... He could destroy himself with thoughts like that. He closed his eyes and prayed with all he had that Nate would wake soon, whole and well.

The nurse was a constant presence that he blocked out most of the time, until she placed a hand on his shoulder. "I've got you some food," she said in that hushed, patient tone of all night nurses. "But let me clean your hands first."

Jimmy stared at where his hand covered Nate's. He couldn't imagine moving it. "They're okay."

"No, they're not," she said. "You have cuts all over them and they're dirty." He didn't move and she played her trump card. "Mr. Fletcher doesn't need to catch an infection from you." There was no way he was going to argue with that. He offered up his hands and she washed and dressed them, then made him eat, before he had a chance to protest.

Finally she pulled over a high-backed chair, positioning it as close to the bed as possible and encouraged him into it. When he fell asleep in the gray light of early dawn, his hands curled around Nate's, she covered him with a blanket.

* * * *

The next day was much like the night. The doctors came round, talking amongst themselves, talking to Jimmy with words and jargon he didn't understand. The new day nurse stopped by his chair when they'd gone, talking in low tones. Nate was doing better, all the signs and tests were positive. They'd be waking him up soon, maybe even tonight. It was good. He had to stay positive.

He did his very best but it was hard. He had to keep reminding himself Nate was in a drug-induced coma. He wasn't like that because he was sick.

Many members of the freedom movement turned up throughout the day — people Jimmy had seen on the television, in newspapers, had heard Nate talk about. Mostly they ignored him, the odd one giving him a brief nod, the majority glaring at him with disdain if not outright contempt and anger. Paulo came twice, his presence filling the room to a bursting point. Lizzy was with him, and she deliberately made sure she was always between him and Jimmy.

Paulo didn't say a word to him.

Heidi did. She said a gentle, "Thank you." Then she stroked Nate's face with the back of her hand. She mumbled a quiet, "It shouldn't have been him," before she smiled at Jimmy and was bustled out, the group around her telling her about all the things she needed to deal with.

Jimmy thought that under any other circumstances, he would have been mesmerized by her presence, now he just wanted everyone to leave, so he could focus on Nate.

That evening, when the night nurse came back on duty, she took one look at Jimmy and ordered him into the shower. "I don't need it," he protested.

"Sure you do," she insisted. "I have no intention of spending another night with you smelling so bad. Now go. It'll only take you a few minutes. Think yourself lucky I don't make you go home. I would in most cases." She softened, moving closer to Nate. "I promise I won't leave his side until you get back."

* * * *

Doctor's rounds were appallingly early the next morning, but Jimmy was already awake, already waiting. It was decided that it was time to wake Nate and his medication was duly adjusted. Jimmy spent the next hour talking to him about nothing, obsessively rubbing the back of his hand and watching his face. Lizzy arrived, standing close, telling Nate how much they missed him, how much they needed him back. How much everyone cared about him.

Jimmy bowed his head low, feeling he didn't belong, even though his gut instinct told him it was important that he was there. Suddenly he felt Nate stir. He looked up to see Nate's frightened eyes searching the room. They passed over Lizzy and the nurse who was trying to soothe him as he became more frantic. Then Nate caught sight of Jimmy and his hand shot out, grabbing a handful of Jimmy's hair and pulling hard as he could, dragging him closer.

Both Lizzy and the nurse tried to free him but Jimmy was having none of it. Nate needed him. He wasn't about to argue. He moved nearer, face inches from Nate's. "It's okay. You're okay." He smoothed a hand over Nate's hair, his shoulder. "You were hurt but you're doing better. You're going to be fine."

"It's all right, Nate," Lizzy said, moving closer. Nate didn't even glance in her direction.

Nate stared at Jimmy, drug clouded eyes full of panic.

"It's okay. I'm here."

Nate tightened his grip on Jimmy's hair, pulling out strands.

"I'm not going anywhere." Jimmy tried to set his mind at rest. "You need to calm down and stop fighting the ventilator. It's breathing for you. Let it do its job."

Again Nate pulled at his hair, obviously the only response he could manage.

Jimmy hoped he knew what it meant. "I'm not going anywhere," he said again, and the pressure in Nate's fingers lessened. Maybe he did know.

The nurse moved into Nate's line of sight then. "I'm going to talk to the doctors, see if we can take out the ventilator. I'm sure you'll feel better then."

Nate clung on until the doctors arrived. Even then he tried to keep a grip on Jimmy's sleeve, but Jimmy was moved unceremoniously out of the way.

Jimmy settled for staying in Nate's line of sight. He even managed to keep watching through most of the procedure to remove the breathing tube. That was nasty. Then the doctors closed in for more tests, more discussion, until Nate was pronounced as well as could be hoped for at that point. He was told in no uncertain terms not to move, not to get agitated and to sleep as much as could.

When they'd finished, the nurse took over, checking or replacing his dressings, giving him something to drink. At last she turned away with a smile at Jimmy. "All yours now."

Jimmy wondered if that would ever be true.

"How do you feel?" he asked, sitting back in his chair.

"Been better but I'll live."

Jimmy had heard that phrase before. This time, he hoped to God it was true as well.

Nate fumbled around on the sheet until he found Jimmy's hand, holding onto the wrist, his fingers curling tight. Then he closed his eyes and Jimmy thought he'd fallen asleep, but he opened them again a minute or two later. "My head... I don't remember."

"They hit you with a bat. It fractured your skull, but they've repaired it. Paulo caught the men that did it."

Again there was a long pause as Nate stared at the ceiling. "I remember before that." He let go of Jimmy, his hand moving away. "You should know, they..." His face creased up with scarcely checked emotion and Jimmy had to stop it.

"It's okay. I know what they did," Jimmy said, catching hold of Nate's hand again. He wasn't letting go. He'd never let go.

"And you're still here? I didn't think you would be if you knew."

"Of course I'm still here. There's nowhere else for me to be but here."

Nate made a little cut-off huff of sound but didn't say anything as his eyes started to flutter closed. Jimmy stroked his wrist, easing him into sleep but, abruptly, he opened them one more time. "Will you be here when I wake up?"

"Nate." Jimmy held tighter. "I'm not leaving until you tell me to go."

Nate stared at him for a long moment, his face solemn, then he drifted off to sleep.

* * * *

Half an hour later the nurse was back at his side. "He's going to be out for a while. You're not going to go home, are you?"

"No." Jimmy shook his head. "He might want me here, but I'm not sure the others would let me back in if I left."

She considered that. "All right. But change into some clean clothes, have a proper meal, a shower and then get some decent sleep, even if it is in the chair. You can't have had more than a couple of hours. I'll wake you if he does."

But it wasn't the nurse that woke Jimmy—it was Paulo and Lizzy returning. They sat the other side of the bed and called for the doctor, asking all the intelligent questions Jimmy hadn't thought of. The doctor left just before Nate stirred, once more looking for Jimmy as soon as he was conscious. The nurse fussed and checked, finally propping him up a little in the bed.

"Hey, man, it's good to see you again," Paulo said, gripping Nate's shoulder. "You scared the shit out of me there."

"Scared the shit out of myself." Nate indicated he wanted a drink and Jimmy got it. When he passed it over, Nate caught hold of his sleeve, keeping him close. "Am I safe now?" he asked.

"Hell yes," Paulo said emphatically. "We have this place locked down tight. No one is getting near you, unless we say so."

Faith Ashlin

"He is." Nate pointed at Jimmy, staring Paulo straight in the eye. "I don't want to fall asleep only to find him gone when I wake up."

"Hey, we can talk about—"

"No," Nate said. "No talking, no buts, no reasons. He stays. I need to be sure of that."

Paulo gave Jimmy a contemptuous glance. "Fine. I think you're fucking insane, but if you want him, you get him."

"Good." Nate settled back against the pillows but didn't let go of Jimmy's sleeve. "Am I safe when I leave here?"

"You mean the people that attacked you? Yeah, we have them. We found out why as well." This time, when he gave Jimmy a fleeting glance, it was with a look of grudging thanks on his face.

"Why?" Nate demanded.

"They wanted to hit us, hit us in a way that would really hurt, but they knew they couldn't do any real damage. The uprising is done. There's no going back but..." Paulo paused, looking at Nate. "They wanted to teach you, and everyone like you, a lesson because you're the only one of us that was still technically a slave, albeit a runaway one."

"They came after me specifically?"

"Yeah, it was planned. They organized the diversion on the other side of the crowd, were already waiting." He licked his lips, shrugging in a gesture of incomprehension and anger. "They said they wanted to put you 'back in your place'. To remind everyone what a slave is for." Again he paused, hand on Nate's shoulder. "I'm sorry. That's fucking lunacy, but we've made sure they won't hurt you or anyone else ever again."

Nate sank farther into the pillows, closing his eyes and breathing deeply. "My head hurts," he said at last, without opening his eyes. "Come back tomorrow. I need to sleep."

Lizzy and Paulo gathered their things, before she dropped a gentle kiss on his uninjured cheek. "Take care. Rest well," she murmured then smiled in Jimmy's direction.

Jimmy followed them, showing them out of the door.

"Not you," Nate said, when they'd gone, eyes now wide open. "I..." He chewed at his lip as though unsure of what he was saying. "I need you to stay."

"I told you, I'm not going anywhere. I was just going to sit outside for a while to let you sleep."

"I'm not tired. I just wanted them to go. Too many people make my head hurt. You don't," Nate said curtly.

"Sure?"

Nate exhaled hard. "I can't explain it to them, don't want to. I'm not sure I can explain it to myself, but I... I need you here." He wouldn't look at Jimmy as he went on. "I need you to want to be here, especially now you know me and what happened. You have to want to be here, because you're honest and—"

"Shut up," Jimmy said, the affection and warmth thick in his voice. "I told you I'm staying and it's not just because you want me to. Hell, I'd sit outside if you threw me out. I'm here because I want to be."

Nate faced him then, an odd expression on his face. "Thank you."

"Shut up again," Jimmy repeated, sitting back down next to the bed. "But I'm sorry."

"What for? You didn't hit me."

"But I made you a slave."

"No, the old government did that."

"I just went along with it way too enthusiastically."

"Agreed."

"And I made you a runaway."

"No, you didn't. I'd have left no matter who they'd put me with, however nice they acted." Jimmy stared at him uncertainly as Nate continued, "I had work to do, soon as I was well enough I was going to leave, no question about it."

"I still feel like I got you into this."

"You didn't make me a slave," Nate said, emphatically. "You didn't ra—"

"Rape you? Yeah, I did. I know that's true because you told me. I remember how much it hurt when you forced me to see what I'd done."

"I didn't mean to hurt you."

"Yes you did, at the time." Jimmy smiled softly at him. "But it's all right. At least it is now. I needed that punch to start my brain working. I think, if our positions were reversed, I'd have been a damned sight more vicious."

"The whole thing was so fucking complicated that…"

"It makes your head hurt?" Jimmy smiled again. "Then stop thinking about it."

Nate rested his eyes closed for a moment, sighing. "Thinking about any of it makes my head hurt. Any of it, all of it. What happened."

"Give yourself a break. You've only just woken up. You've had head surgery. Forget all of it for a while and concentrate on getting better."

"It's hard when it's slapped in my face."

"No one is slapping anything in your face." Jimmy pulled the sheet up, smoothing it out over Nate's chest, over the tubes and wires so he couldn't see them.

"Yeah, they are." Nate turned his head, face close to Jimmy's, watching him. "Lizzy, Paulo, it's there in their eyes every time they look at me. They're disgusted I was raped. They pity me for it."

"They don't. They…" Jimmy started, hand still clutching the sheet. But maybe Nate could see things he couldn't.

"You don't though, do you?" And there was a thick edge of uncertainty in Nate's voice.

"You know something?" He stared Nate straight in the eye. "Even when we first met, I never thought you were stupid. I'll admit I didn't realize you were as smart as you turned out to be, but I never thought you were stupid. Please don't prove me wrong now by being that dumb. I don't think of you any differently."

For a long, long while Nate studied Jimmy's eyes then he nodded, just once. "Okay, but they do."

"I'm not sure you're right, but is that why you wanted them to go?"

"I don't know, I just… Everyone knows. I can't get away from it and never will."

"Does it matter that much?"

"I…" Nate sucked in a breath, holding it as he thought. "No, I guess not really. I'm sure I'm not the only one in the movement that's been raped. There are lots of other ex-slaves, even if there were no runaways at the rally. But, somehow, being raped as a slave is different from that. What happened with you is different. I felt in some sort of control and…fuck it, no." He rubbed at his face, the tubes in the back of his hand moving with it. "I'm not thinking about this. Not now."

"You know something?" Jimmy smiled. "You're a big fat liar, Nate Fletcher," he said, smoothing the hair back from Nate's face on the side that wasn't covered with bandages. "You are tired, totally exhausted. Go to sleep. I'll be here when you wake up."

* * * *

Nate was moved from the intensive care department to another room the next day, one with far less machinery to scare the hell out of Jimmy. The nurse went with them as his bed was wheeled along the corridor. She talked quietly with Nate before she left, then squeezed Jimmy's arm as she reached the door.

"I've told the new nurses all about you." She smiled. "They're going to take real good care of both of you."

Jimmy didn't know why anyone had to take care of him, but he was more than grateful when he was made comfortable in the corner and no one asked him to leave.

That afternoon two nurses came in to remove the dressings on Nate's head, before the doctors came to see him. For once, Jimmy actually thought he might like to be made to leave, but again they worked around him. Slowly, carefully they took off each piece and the full extent of the damage was slowly revealed.

A section of Nate's hair above his ear had been shaved, the rest around it cut off at odd lengths and angles. Vicious staples held together the exposed, pure white skin. The nurse explained quietly that they worked better than stitches and that soon they could be removed. Jimmy winced at the thought but the nurse reassured him that it would heal soon and Nate's hair would grow back to cover everything.

Less easy to hide would be the scarring that ran down from Nate's hairline. One thick line with a second branching from it, an area of puckered skin in between them. There were a few stitches at the top, black cord that looked obscene where it went into Nate's skin, the flesh pink around them. That damage had been caused when the bat used to hit Nate had cracked and half of it had broken off.

Jimmy didn't want to think about the force that would be needed to cause something like that — force that had been used on Nate's skull. He didn't want to think about it, but he couldn't stop the idea going round and round in his head.

He was brought back to the moment when Nate spoke. "Can I see?"

"Are you sure you want to?" the nurse asked. "It's at its worse now. Maybe you should wait for the staples and stitches to come out and the swelling to go down."

"No, I need to see it now. See how bad it is."

"I thought you might say that." She reached into the pack of equipment she'd brought with her, then handed him a mirror.

His face closed up tight as he examined himself, with no emotion showing. "How bad will it be in a year's time? Be honest."

"Honestly? Your hair will cover a great deal and the rest of the scars will fade, the skin will smooth out a lot but, very likely, you'll always be able to see them. They will fade over time though."

"Okay," he said, handing back the mirror.

"Makes you seem more rugged and handsome." She patted his arm just as the doctors arrived.

They spent a long time checking Nate over very thoroughly, assessing his mental state as well as his physical recovery. In the end they pronounced him as well as could be expected, said that he was healing nicely and would hopefully continue to do so.

When they'd gone, the nurse put new dressings on the wounds. Jimmy thought he wasn't as thankful for that as he'd expected. He'd...maybe not got used to Nate's injuries, but they had lost the worst of their shock value.

"Well?" Nate said when they were at last left alone.

"Well, judging at the state of your face, I think that whole thing has left you exhausted. You need to sleep now."

"That's not what I meant and you know it."

"Okay." Jimmy exhaled hard, hands on his hips. "I think we're incredibly fucking lucky, seeing the damage has made me understand just how bad it was. It's like the doctor said... If the bat hadn't cracked— spreading the force... If it had caught you just a little bit higher, we'd be burying you now."

"The bat cracking did different damage," Nate said quietly.

"You've got a few scars. So what? Fuck, man, you're alive and I can't..." Jimmy wiped a hand over his mouth, desperate to hold everything in.

"But I look like Frankenstein's monster."

"It'll heal."

"Not all of it."

"It doesn't matter."

"Maybe it does."

"Jesus, are you trying to pick a fight?" Jimmy challenged. "You'll have a few scars. So fucking what? It doesn't matter, you're alive, I don't give a shit about anything else. I was so scared for a while that I..." Again he sucked in a deep breath, holding it for a long moment before going on. "You'll have scars. They're on your face where you'll see them every time you look in the mirror and everyone else will see them. You can't hide from them, but they'll fade and you'll get used to them. That's the reality of it. You're alive. Be as grateful for that as I am and get on with life."

"Maybe," Nate mumbled, turning away from Jimmy as he eased back, getting comfortable. Jimmy suddenly realized that he might, just might, have unexpectedly won that battle.

He couldn't help his gasp of surprise. "Really?"

"I am grateful. The scars don't matter to me. But..." Still he wouldn't look at Jimmy. "I want you to... I need... You're important...you... Oh fuck it, I don't know what I'm saying or what I think."

"Go to sleep, man," Jimmy said, as his throat constricted and his heart thudded. "Before your poor brain explodes."

Chapter Ten

Ten days later Nate was let out of hospital.

Although, Jimmy thought, 'let out' wasn't quite the right phrase to use. Nate had nagged, bullied and badgered to leave, until the medical staff had had enough of him. Jimmy had started going home at night after Nate had been moved to the new room. He still spent most of the day at the hospital, after running any errands Nate needed. He got there one morning, just after breakfast, to hear another row coming from the room.

He was going to have to apologize to everyone yet again. The day before he'd even had to say sorry to the cleaning staff.

As he went in, the nurse was just leaving, her face flushed. He patted her arm and she gave him a weak smile. Nate stood by the window, staring out, his hand at his mouth.

"You've upset her again," he said gently, putting his bag on the bed and moving to stand next to Nate. "That's not fair. It's not her fault."

"I know," Nate admitted. "I just..." Then his voice broke.

"Hey." Jimmy put an arm around Nate's shoulder, pulling him in tight. He was used to angry Nate, in control Nate and self-assured Nate. He wasn't used to him close to tears. "It's okay. It's all going to be okay."

Nate leaned in, his hand fisting in the front of Jimmy's shirt. "I can't stand it in here anymore. I need to get out."

"The doctors said it'll be soon." He squeezed Nate's shoulder over and over.

"What are they keeping me for? The stitches and staples are out, my hair is starting to grow back. I feel... I don't know. I feel better — as well as I'm going to get in hospital. I can't stand it here and I don't know why I have to stay."

"I know Lizzy and Paulo are worried about you. They're running around trying to do so much and I guess they feel you're safe here."

"So I have to stay for their sake?" Nate stared at him. The possibility of tears might have passed, but he didn't seem much better. "Please, talk to the doctors. They won't listen to me. Get me out of here."

"All right." Jimmy held him tighter. "Let me see what I can arrange."

Nate finally relaxed against him, breathing hard.

But it wasn't that easy. Jimmy talked to the nurses but there was nothing they could do. It was never going to be their decision, no matter what they might think. He asked to see a doctor. He asked again an hour later, when Nate started moaning once more. Eventually a junior doctor arrived but, as Jimmy expected as soon as he saw him, he couldn't make the decision either.

It wasn't until late afternoon that a senior doctor came to see them. She pushed her small glasses up the bridge of her nose and peered at Nate. "I don't see why you shouldn't stay for a while longer," she said.

"And I don't see why I should." Nate was starting out bullish.

"It wasn't long ago since you had surgery."

"But I'm doing better. You aren't treating me for anything anymore. I just need to rest. There's no reason I have to do that here."

"But you can't take care of yourself."

"Yes I can. I'm not an invalid." They stood almost nose to nose, talking fast, neither giving an inch.

"No, but you need looking after."

"I can stay in a hotel. They'll do everything for me."

"You don't have your own house? No, I don't suppose you do. It doesn't make any difference though. You'd still do too much."

"I'm not an idiot either. If you tell me not to do something, I won't."

Again she peered at Nate. "I doubt that immensely. But there has to be someone to make sure you take things easy and rest, someone to make sure you don't relapse. A hotel, on your own, is not the place for you. You need proper care."

"But I can't stay here."

"Yes, I rather think you can." She started to turn away, the request rejected. "Here or a nursing home."

"That's fucking ridiculous. You can't make me stay. I'm walking out and—"

"How about he comes and stays with me?" Jimmy interrupted, before things got ugly.

They both turned to stare at him.

"Nate?" Jimmy asked quietly. He wasn't making any assumptions, taking anything for granted.

Nate gave an almost imperceptible nod. It was sorted.

"You have somewhere decent?" the doctor asked. "I know how these freedom fighters have been living."

"I'm not a freedom fighter. I have a house with a garden and everything he'll need."

"Do you work?" It was Jimmy's turn to be peered at over the top of her glasses. "He shouldn't be left alone all day."

"Yes, I have a job, but it's stopped at the moment, because of the uprising. I'm not going back anytime soon, so I'll be there, I can take care of him."

"Well..." She looked from one to the other.

"I want to take care of him."

"All right." She turned to Nate. "I am not discharging you fully. I'm releasing you into his care."

Then it was Jimmy's turn. "You are to bring him back immediately if there is any change for the worse in his condition. You must make sure he attends all the appointments we give him—that he takes any medication prescribed." She listed the conditions. "You must see to it that he eats regularly and healthily, that he takes appropriate exercise, that he doesn't do too much. Oh, and fresh air would be a good idea."

"Hell, I don't need a nursemaid," Nate protested. But Jimmy held up a hand stopping him.

"Agreed," Jimmy said. "I'll do all that, even the fresh air. When can I take him home?"

She studied Nate. "Do you agree to all these conditions?"

"Do I have a choice?"

"Nate," Jimmy warned. "If you want to get out of here, shut your mouth and just say yes to the nice lady."

Nate scowled at them both. "Yes," he finally said, surrendering.

"In the morning, you may take him home then."

"Oh come on, that's fucking—"

Jimmy clamped a hand over Nate's mouth.

"His speech is a bit slurred." Jimmy grinned. "He actually said thank you very much. Everyone here has been wonderful." He didn't remove his hand, until the door had shut firmly behind her.

"So you're going to be my nursemaid?" Nate sneered.

"No, I think I'm going to be more your jailer than anything else." Jimmy stared him down. "She was right about one thing—you were never going to take things easy if you were on your own."

"I would…"

"No, you wouldn't, because you don't want to face how sick you were, how long it's going to take to get back to full fitness." Jimmy inhaled sharply, letting it go much slower. "I know how hard you find it, but I need you to let me do this. I was so scared when I thought… Let me do this. Indulge me. Let me take care of you, just for a while."

As he hoped, Nate gave in to that.

* * * *

Paulo was no happier that Nate was leaving the hospital than the doctor had been. He got even angrier when he found out Nate was going back to Jimmy's house. He turned a nasty red color and shouted. "If he thinks he can act like he fucking owns Nate, I'm going to—"

"You're not going to do anything." Lizzy pushed him back into the corner. "He doesn't act like an owner. Even you have to admit he hasn't."

"But that's because we're here. Who knows what he's going to do, once he gets Nate somewhere on their own."

Lizzy sighed. "Can't you see Jimmy isn't like that anymore? Nate knows it or he wouldn't trust him, I can see it as well."

"You both think the best of people and you're both insane."

"Hey, hello here." Nate waved from the other side of the hospital room. "I have a mouth. If I don't like what's going on, I'll sure as hell make damned sure Jimmy knows it."

"Not if he's got you tied up or something."

"Oh for fuck's sake," Nate said, exasperated.

"What? You're not on top form. He could overpower you."

"But he's not going to," Lizzy cut in. "Hey," she held up a hand, trying to calm them all down. She faced Paulo. "You ring Nate every day. Check he's okay."

"But he might…"

"Now what? Jimmy's threatening him, making him say it?" She stared at Paulo, incredulous. "Come on. This is Nate we're talking about. I've never managed to get him to do anything he didn't want, and I've tried threatening him. If you're still worried, go and see him every day. You'll soon know if anything is wrong." She took a deep breath, turning to include them all in her gaze. "I think this is a good thing. It would be the right place for Nate, even if we had the option of taking care of him. Jimmy." Again her focus changed. "You ask us for any help you need. And Nate? I know you, at least try and be a good patient."

After that, they were allowed out.

Nate moaned all the way out in the wheelchair, as the car was brought right up to the door of the hospital, at the fuss made getting him into the house and settled on the sofa. Then he fell fast asleep and didn't wake for a three hours.

"Are you okay to take over from here?" Lizzy asked Jimmy. He nodded and she left and they were on their own at last, just the two of them in Jimmy's house.

Jimmy suddenly felt the weight of responsibility. It was huge and overwhelming but one he really, really wanted to take on. He wouldn't let Nate down. He checked on him one more time, and then went upstairs to make sure everything was ready. He'd done everything he could think of to prepare, but he needed this to be right.

* * * *

Jimmy thought it was a pretty perfect evening. They ate off trays on their laps, started watching a film but gave up on it and put on a game show instead, laughing when neither of them got the questions right. They talked, easily and comfortably, and cleared up together. They didn't have to hide or keep to the shadows. There was no one chasing them, and they didn't have to check over their shoulders. The sense of freedom was intoxicating, making Jimmy want to throw open the curtains so everyone could see them.

But the privacy was just as wonderful—no nurses coming in, no unexpected visitors. Most important of all, there were no deadlines. Nate didn't have to disappear before the sun rose. No appointments, no other places to be.

The relief was almost palpable.

As it got later, Jimmy insisted Nate went to bed, but he stood back and let him climb the stairs at his own, slow, pace. "Wrong way," he said as Nate turned toward the guest room. Nate didn't say anything, watching him closely. "You're in my room and I'll sleep in the other room. Don't argue. The bed is bigger, the mattress better. You need it, I don't."

Nate pressed his lips together for a moment and Jimmy thought he was going to disagree. Instead he nodded once and turned the other way.

Jimmy made sure Nate was settled, that he had everything he needed or could possibly want, before he got ready for bed himself. Then he went back and stood in the doorway of the main bedroom.

"What's the matter?" Nate asked, already comfortable in bed.

"I won't be able to hear you if you need me. The spare room is too far away."

"I'll shout, loudly. But I have half the house in here. There's nothing for you to get me."

"What if you don't feel well? What if you're dizzy or feel sick or..."

"I'm fine. Honestly I am."

"You don't look fine. The journey home shattered you and you have black circles under your eyes."

"Oh gee, thanks. Way to make me feel better. Get a bell I can ring or something and stop fussing."

Jimmy spent the next ten minutes looking for a bell before he gave and pushed the fold up bed into Nate's new room.

"What the hell?" Nate stared at him.

"There's no point getting a bell or a buzzer, I'd only lay awake all night to make sure I heard it. If I sleep on this at the end of your bed, I'll know as soon as there's a problem."

"There isn't going to be a problem. I'm only getting worked up because you're fussing. Just go to bed."

"I..." Jimmy stood with his hands hanging at his sides, face forlorn. "Please? I'm going to drive myself crazy in there. Let me stay here so I can actually get some sleep."

"Fine. Just... Just...fine." Nate gave up and rolled over in bed.

Jimmy made up his own bed and settled down, happy at last.

Nate woke him in the early hours, shouting out odd words in the throes of a desperate nightmare.

He thrashed around in the bed, the cover catching him around the legs, making him move evermore frantically as he called out nothing to no one. Jimmy tried to wake him, but he couldn't, not at first, and he got frightened that Nate would hurt himself, maybe even reopen a wound. He knelt at the side of the bed and pulled Nate onto his good side, holding his biceps and said any soothing nonsense he could think of.

Eventually Nate came round, breathing hard. Opening his eyes, he stared at Jimmy before rolling onto his back, looking up into nothing.

"How are you doing?" Jimmy asked, sitting on the floor.

"Don't know." Nate exhaled hard. "That was..."

"What? What was the nightmare about?"

"I don't even know if it was a nightmare, I..." Nate rubbed a hand over the healthy side of his face. "I couldn't work out where I was, which is really strange, seeing as I've slept in this bed more than any other, since I joined the movement. You'd think I'd know about being here."

"But you were in the hospital for a while. Maybe you got used to it."

"Which is why I needed to get out." Again Nate blew out a long breath. "When I worked out where I was, I didn't know when it was."

"What do you mean?"

"I couldn't tell if it was before, when I lived here, before the uprising. I didn't know if we were still fighting or if it was over."

"Must feel good to know you won."

"Yeah." There was warmth in Nate's voice as he said it. "That feels really good." He glanced at Jimmy, an unreadable expression on his face. "Good to know a lot of things have changed. I... Thank you. Thank you for letting me come here. For being... Thank you."

"It's my pleasure. Hey, you realize something?" Jimmy said, settling where he was. "It's not my job anymore to take care of you. I'm doing it because I want to. You think I've grown up at last?"

"I think you're... I think you're doing all right, Jimmy Stephens."

* * * *

Jimmy woke up during the following night for a completely different reason. At first he wasn't sure what it was and he lay there listening carefully. Then he understood. Nate was crying—quiet sobs that were tightly controlled and pushed into the pillow.

He got up and crawled across the bed on top of the covers and held Nate from behind, his chest pressed to Nate's back. At first Nate tried to pull away, but Jimmy wouldn't let him, holding on tighter. He stroked down from Nate's shoulder to his elbow. "My grandma used to say that nasty things are better out than in. She meant trapped wind and was forever burping and farting, the older she got. My mum didn't agree with her one little bit, but I figure she was right. The more you let out, the better you'll feel."

Slowly the sobs gained force and lost any semblance of control as Nate gave into them. He gave in to Jimmy as well, as Jimmy tucked him in closer to his body, cradling him. Jimmy stayed like that until the tears had run their course and eventually Nate fell asleep. Then he pulled the cover up to Nate's chin, checked he wasn't resting on any wounds, and went back to his own bed.

* * * *

Slowly they developed a routine of sorts, mostly based around the meals Jimmy made sure Nate ate. They tended to go out into the garden in the mornings, Nate in the knitted ski cap he'd taken to habitually wearing. It covered the worst of the damage and made him appear softer than the extra short haircut he'd had in an attempt to match with the newly grown hair.

Jimmy had decided that they'd take up gardening, seeing as his old gardener had run off during the uprising. The only problem was neither of them knew a thing about it and really didn't care. So they chopped down overgrown plants, which, Nate declared, fulfilled their exercise quota as well.

In the afternoons, they'd watch TV or read the newspapers, but both were difficult. After the initial euphoria of the uprising, the country was descending toward disorder. There were more supporters of slavery in the administration and civil police than the freedom movement had at first thought. When they'd gotten rid of them, there was no one to run things or keep order.

Jimmy knew Nate wasn't ready to deal with that. He thought Nate knew it as well, but, if he were faced with it all the time, he'd want to help, feel obliged to do so. So, by silent agreement, they avoided any mention of it that they could. But it was hard, really hard.

Other members of the movement would turn up at any time of the day or evening, wanting to see Nate. Jimmy would let them in, register their exhausted faces, offer food and drink, then keep out of the way while they talked. The only time he stopped someone coming in was if Nate was asleep.

He didn't wake Nate for anyone, not even Paulo at his most intimidating.

Often, when it was just the two of them, Jimmy would stop in the doorway or simply glance up from where he sat reading and just look at Nate. He was alive, the fighting was finished and, Paulo assured him, the danger was over. There might just be a future.

Jimmy would smile softly and Nate would stop, scowling. "What?" he demanded.

"Nothing," Jimmy said, and carried on with what he was doing.

Days blended into each other, easy and comfortable, and Jimmy did his damnedest to keep them that way. Most of the time he wanted to take the phone off the hook, but he figured people would only turn up on his doorstep if they couldn't contact him. He didn't want that, so he compromised, switching on the answering machine and making sure he called people back.

They'd just listened to another message from his bosses, saying the studio was staying closed for the foreseeable future, when Nate stared at him from the sofa, perplexed. "What have you done with your mother?"

Jimmy was just as confused. "I haven't done anything with her."

"Then why isn't she here, hitting me with her own baseball bat?"

"What?"

"Come on. She hated me enough before. Now she must be just about bursting with it. Hell, did she turn up at the hospital and try and pull all the tubes out of me?"

"No. Don't be stupid."

"Why not? I bet she wanted to."

"Because I wouldn't let her hurt you."

Nate studied him, eyes narrowing but full of laughter. "Did Paulo have to stop her? Shit, I'd like to have seen that."

"No, he didn't have to. She hasn't been anywhere near you."

The laughter slipped away from Nate's face. "She didn't turn up at the hospital. She hasn't been here. You won't leave me alone to go out. She hasn't even phoned... What's going on? Did you really do something?"

"I didn't do anything to her," Jimmy said carefully.

"So what have you done? You couldn't keep me a secret, not now, not for this long."

Jimmy stared at him. "I had no intention of keeping you a secret, not after the old government fell and you were safe."

"What did you do?"

"Soon as you weren't at risk, I went to see her," Jimmy said evenly. "I told her everything, how I love you, how you'd been coming here, about going to the lake cabin."

"Wow," Nate said, sounding shocked. "What did she say?"

"I didn't give her a chance to say anything. I told her I didn't trust her to be decent to you, so I didn't want to see her, to talk to her and that if she came here, I'd throw her out. My sister, Molly, is going to tell me if she ever has a real change of heart. I doubt it'll happen, but I'm not having any contact until it does."

"That's..." Nate stopped, licking at his lips. "She's your mum."

"She's a hate filled bigot and I don't want her near either of us."

"But you can't... You can't stop seeing your mum because of me. It's not..."

"It's got nothing to do with you. That's why I didn't tell you," Jimmy interrupted him. "She's my mum. It's my decision. She allowed me, encouraged me, to think in ways that aren't right. If she changes, I'll see her. If not, that's her decision." He shrugged. "She knows how things stand."

"But..."

"No, no buts." Jimmy got up, collecting the scatter of coffee mugs. "My mum, my rules — this is one thing you don't get a say in."

Afterwards, when Jimmy thought back on it, even though he knew he was right, he couldn't quite believe he'd stood up to both his mother and Nate. Maybe he was learning after all.

* * * *

Jimmy sat on the bottom step of the stairs and listed to the thump, thump, thump of the bathroom cabinet door being slammed over and over again. Nate had woken up in one of 'those' moods — bad-tempered and just bursting for a fight. They'd happened a few times but Jimmy had always managed to avoid the worst of them. Paulo had caught the full force of the last one, which had been a real doozie. Nate had shouted at him, Paulo had tried to defend himself with reason and logic, so Nate had shouted louder, making no sense but getting more worked up.

In the end Paulo had admitted defeat and left. He'd even stopped by the back door and thrown Jimmy a sympathetic glance. "Good luck, man. You're going to fucking need it."

But Jimmy hadn't. Nate had burnt out all his fury on Paulo and had been sitting, calmly watching an old movie on TV when he'd gone in.

This time there was no one else to take the flak and it was building. Jimmy thought he genuinely felt sorry for the bathroom cabinet, although he had no idea what it had done to upset Nate. In the end he decided there was no other choice. He had to go up and see what he could do. He wasn't sure if he was trying to save Nate from himself or just protect the cabinet.

"Are you all right?" he asked, standing just inside the bathroom.

"Do I look all right?" Nate demanded, staring at himself in the mirror.

Jimmy decided to take him seriously and really consider it. Nate was naked after his shower, except for a towel wrapped round his waist. In the mirror Jimmy could see the reflection of the other side of his head and it was the same as before the attack. It was only on the side nearest to him that anything was different, shocking. But Jimmy had long since got used to the sight of Nate's injuries. They didn't bother him anymore. It was...just Nate.

Jimmy could see how much Nate's appearance had improved. His face was no longer swollen, the angry redness had gone, although the scars on his cheek were still nasty. The really scary patch of white, white skin with its awful wound on his head had gone from sight as well. New hair was already growing, silly tuffs that were soft and funny.

"Yeah, you look fine."

"Fine?" Nate turned to him. "You call this fine?" He waved a hand toward his head. "I'm a freak."

"I didn't think you'd be that bothered. You were never that comfortable with your appearance, the reaction it caused."

"It's one thing to look ordinary," Nate said low and controlled. "Another to look like a monster."

"You don't look like a monster." Jimmy had heard enough of this. It was stupid. "You've got a few scars. So what? Many people have a lot worse. It doesn't matter to me."

"Doesn't matter to you," Nate repeated, deliberating on the words. "No, I guess you like it. Means no one else will want me, so you might get me by default."

"That's not fair," Jimmy said softly.

Nate ignored him. "Is it a price worth paying though? Because I know you thought I was pretty. You like pretty because it turns you on and made you want to fuck me just that bit harder—even when I didn't want it. Is getting me worth giving up on pretty?"

Jimmy felt his face flame with the viciousness and suddenness of the attack. It was just as if he'd been hit, hit hard. He opened his mouth to speak but closed it again with a snap, turned on his heels and walked out. He didn't stop when he got downstairs, when he got to the back door, when he got to the edge of the driveway. He had to stop and think then. His car keys were on the hall table and he wasn't going back inside. Not now.

He walked down the street, his pace increasing until he was running flat out, feet pounding on the pavement, lungs straining fit to burst.

Eventually he stopped and stared around him, trying to decide what to do next. There was a rundown park nearby with a large pond. A young mother was feeding the ducks with two little girls. She glanced at him as he sat down on a bench near the water, her face registering surprise and a little alarm.

He guessed it was warranted. He must look like a mad man.

But the mother didn't move away, didn't even call back her daughter when she came over to Jimmy and offered him some bread. "Do you want to feed the ducks as well?" the girl asked. "The greedy ones at the front are taking it all and the babies at the back don't get any. You're tall. You can throw it further out that I can."

"Sure I will." Jimmy smiled at her as she held out some bread for him. There, on the back of her hand in dark letters, was a signature. He couldn't read the name but it didn't matter, they all knew what it meant.

And he could read the one on Nate's hand.

"You don't have to." The mother rested a palm on the little girl's shoulder.

"No, it's okay." Jimmy got up, taking the bread, breaking off a chunk and throwing it to the ducks at the back. "It's nice here. A nice thing to do."

"It's one of my favorite places," she agreed. "We weren't allowed to come before and then, for a while, everywhere felt too dangerous, but now..." She shrugged and they both looked at the matching signature on the back of her hand. "Everything is different now," she went on. "Now we're free."

"It must be wonderful."

"Yes, I suppose it must be." She smiled at him, soft and compliant. The same way Nate had, back in prison. Back when he acted like a slave.

Jimmy couldn't stand to see it. "Tell me?" he asked, fighting down the urge to demand it. "Tell me what it's like for you now. I... I need to know."

She studied him appraisingly then tipped her head. "I'm not sure about wonderful but it is...better."

"Why not wonderful?"

"It's not easy, suddenly being free. It's more confusing than I expected." She passed him more bread, giving some to the girls. "All of a sudden you have choices that you never had before. What you do, what you wear or eat or who you're with. All those decisions and changes are confusing, scary, even if they're good ones." She suddenly smiled, warm and infectious. "But I wouldn't change a single thing. I have so much to be grateful for."

"Thank you," he said formally. "Thank you for telling me."

"I hope I helped." She touched his arm briefly before gathering up her children. "Whatever it is that's bothering you, is it really that bad? We have a new world. Anything is possible, but we're all going to have to work at it."

Jimmy sat there for a long while after the family had gone, simply staring out over the water. It a small way it reminded him of the lake cabin, the way the light reflected off the surface, the birds flying low over it, the ripple and flow of the water. Even the sound of the wind through the leaves was comforting, familiar.

Everything was different now, and such massive changes took some getting used to. For everyone.

He pulled himself to his feet and started the long walk home. After all, Nate was there and Jimmy wasn't going anywhere else.

When he got in, Nate was sitting on the edge of the sofa, hands tap, tap, tapping on his knees. He looked like he'd been there a long time, but the television wasn't on and there was no book nearby. Jimmy wondered if he'd actually been watching the door.

He went and sat in the armchair opposite. He hadn't thought about what he was going to say, hadn't thought about how he felt. Now he just let the words come.

"That—what you said—really hurt."

"I'm sorry, for what it's worth, I truly am. I didn't mean it." Nate sat forward, squeezing his knees. "I was just hitting out and I don't even know why. You're right. I know it's not that bad. I look in the mirror and I can see it healing day by day. When my hair grows back and it settles, it won't be bad at all." He scrunched up his face as though there were a bad smell. "But I'll always be able to see it and, I might not care what I look like, but it'll always be a reminder."

This time he stared at Jimmy properly, the effort of saying the words showing on his face. "It will always remind me what happened, all of it. I'm never going to get away from it."

"But that doesn't mean you can take it out on me." Jimmy laid the words out carefully. "I know you're angry, that you're hurting, and I can only imagine what that must feel like. But it isn't fair to do that to me."

"You know I didn't mean it."

"Do I?"

"Oh come on. I see it in your face every day. I know you don't care how I look. You just..." He shrugged. "You just see me and that's why I'm here."

"That's not all you said about me though."

"What? That I said you liked pretty?" Nate seemed genuinely confused. "You used to bathe the wounds and you didn't flinch. You only moaned, because the antiseptic stuff made your fingers smell. That's not someone who only cares about pretty."

"But I did care about it," Jimmy said flatly and Nate gaped at him, wide-eyed.

Jimmy sucked in a huge breath and held it for a moment before going on. "Back then I liked you pretty. I liked it when you appeared soft, even if I knew you didn't. And I'll admit that sometimes I knew you didn't want sex, even if you did your damnedest to hide it. I knew and I made it happen anyway because you were so damned pretty. Knowing I'm capable of that is scary. What you said brought it all back to the surface and it frightens the shit out of me. Back then, I liked you pretty way too much."

"Do you feel that way about me now or are you secretly glad I'm not pretty anymore?" Nate asked seriously.

"Don't you get it?" Jimmy said, shaking his head. "I don't feel either of those things. To me you're just as damned pretty as you ever were. No..." Again he shook his head, desperate to get it right. "Not pretty or gorgeous or even attractive. The scars aren't that bad, but even if they were, it wouldn't matter. To me you're just Nate and you're beautiful. I wouldn't have cared if your whole face had been disfigured. You'd still be beautiful to me."

"How can you be worried that you haven't changed?" Nate sat even farther forward, scarcely on the seat. "God, listen to yourself. You may have fucked me because I was pretty but you're not like that now. Now you're decent and kind and I—" He stopped, eyes wide and round.

"But I was like that," Jimmy said quietly. "I don't want to go back to that."

"You can't, because you weren't thinking then and I've made you think, made you so you can't help but do it. Now you question everything—what happened, me, yourself and that's all good. You'll never go back, never be that person again."

"Won't I? Are you so sure? What if I were in the right circumstances, if everyone around me was telling me it's okay to be like that? If I've done it once. How can you be so sure I wouldn't do it again?"

"Do you trust me?" Nate asked. "Truly trust me."

"Yes," Jimmy said simply, with no hesitation.

"I've had to learn to be a good judge of people and I know you. Knew you then, know you now. Believe me, you'll never go back to being that person. You wouldn't let yourself. I'm so fucking proud of you."

"I hope you're right." Jimmy rubbed his hands together before pressing them between his knees, breathing hard. "Someone said to me today that big changes are scary, even if they're good ones."

"You've made huge changes. No wonder you get scared, but you can come to me anytime and I'll do my best to help."

"Does it work both ways?" Jimmy said, watching Nate closely.

"What do you mean?"

"Are you going to come to me next time you get scared by all the changes? Because that's why you lost it today and, frankly, I can't take that again. Not being slapped so hard with what I did."

"I guess." Nate rubbed at his face and Jimmy could see his hand shaking. "I guess it's about time I started thinking as well. I won't say anything like that again and" — he shook his head, before resettling the knitted hat needlessly — "I'll come to you if I get scared."

Jimmy knew just how much that admission had cost Nate. "Then maybe, just maybe, we have a chance of not driving ourselves mad," he said, patting Nate's knee and leaving his hand there.

"I'm not so sure." Nate snorted. "If I stay in the house much longer, hiding from the world, I'll probably go mad anyway."

"Then don't," Jimmy said, the idea suddenly hitting him. "Let's go up to the lake cabin. You're well enough now that you don't have to be so close to the hospital. Let's just pack a bag and go. What do you think?"

"I think." Nate actually managed a small smile for the first time that day. "That you're a genius. Let's go now?"

"No, not now." Jimmy had to laugh. "It'll be dark soon. I want to check with your doctor and…"

"But we'll go early in the morning, right?"

"I promise we'll go early, before Paulo finds out at least. He's going to go fucking ape-shit and accuse me of kidnapping you."

"No he won't." Nate laughed with him. "He'll just… Yeah, actually he probably will."

"We'll go before he knows anything about it."

"And I won't call him until we're there."

"Sounds like a plan," Jimmy said.

Chapter Eleven

Jimmy pulled up outside the cabin and switched off the car. Already it felt good to be here – somehow the very air was different. He got out, collected their bags and stacked them on the verandah before unlocking the front door.

"It's just as well we brought food with us. There can't be much left in the freezer," he said, aiming the words over his shoulder to Nate. There was no answer.

Nate had walked down toward the lake and was standing perfectly still, hands in his pockets, gazing out over the water. Jimmy went after him. "Are you okay?" he asked.

"Yeah, you know I actually think I am," Nate said. "This place... It must be magic or something, but I feel... I don't know. It's weird. I feel more like myself than I have since I got hurt."

"That's real good but don't push yourself too hard."

"I know. I'm not..." He shrugged. "I'm not right yet, but I can think here. I feel like..." He took a deep breath. "If I can sort it all out in my mind then I'll get right, get better. Does that make sense?" He tilted his head, watching Jimmy expectantly.

"Yeah." Jimmy nodded. He could see it already in the way Nate held himself, in his breathing. The tension was easing from his shoulders, his stance — at long last he was beginning to truly relax. If this place had done that so quickly, then Jimmy almost wished he'd brought Nate here earlier. But before anything else, Nate had needed to recover physically. Now he was a long way down that road. If he could sort out what he thought, he could heal in every way. Jimmy knew that was what was holding him back. He had to accept and move on.

Easier said than done, but they'd made a start.

"That makes perfect sense and we've got all the time we need for it to happen, now that there's nothing nasty waiting round the corner for us."

"I like this place." Nate went back to staring out over the lake. "I'm glad you bought it."

Jimmy had to agree with him — he was damned glad he'd bought it too.

* * * *

A couple of days later they heard the sound of a vehicle coming up their small track and went out onto the verandah to see a scruffy black car stop in front of the cabin. Paulo climbed out from behind the driver's wheel and, as soon as he saw Nate, sprinted up the steps, pulling him into a bear hug.

"I knew I couldn't stop you coming," Nate said, when he was allowed to breathe again. "I knew you'd freak and turn up here, ready to rescue me."

"I did not freak." Paulo let go of Nate, albeit a little reluctantly. "I just needed to make sure you were all right."

"I'm all right, just like I told you on the phone yesterday and the day before and the one before that and—"

"Shut up." Paulo turned away from Nate to square up to Jimmy. "Who gave you the fucking right to bring him up here?"

Jimmy hadn't even opened his mouth to defend himself before Nate cut in. "I did. I wanted to come because I like it here. There aren't any noisy idiots shouting their heads off for a start. And look—" He pointed and Paulo dutifully turned to follow the direction of his finger. "Those tall things are trees—the flappy animals in them are birds. It's nature, man. It makes me feel better."

Paulo stared back at Nate, considering. "You're really all right?" he said, much more quietly.

"Yeah, I'm really all right."

"You'd tell me if you weren't?"

"Yes." Nate nodded. "I'd tell you."

"So why didn't you tell me you were coming?"

Nate scrunched his face up, like a naughty school kid, caught doing something he knew he shouldn't. "Because I know you worry, because I figured you'd freak, just like this."

"But you can understand why I freak, can't you?"

This time Nate sighed, rubbing a hand over his eyes. "Sit." He pulled out a chair, flopping into it as the other two copied him. "Yes, I understand why you worry. I guess I'd do the same if our positions were reversed."

"And him?" Paulo waved a hand dismissively at Jimmy. "You can understand why I freak about you being with him?"

"I get it. Honestly I do. Again, I'd be the same if I were you but…" Nate wiped a hand over his face once more. Jimmy thought he suddenly looked exhausted, practically gray around the edges, but he had more sense than to say anything. "Listen to me," Nate went on. "Don't just hear the words, really listen to what I'm saying. I get that you're worried but I've lived on my wits, my instincts, my judgment for a very long time. I trust them. I'm telling you he's changed and he's all right now."

"Next you'll be telling me he's one of the good guys," Paulo said, defiantly.

"He is now." Nate stared him down.

"Maybe." Paulo huffed, giving in. "So he's changed, but there are a lot of good guys around. Why have you got to be with him?"

"I'm here with him because I want to be. I wouldn't be otherwise," Nate said with certainty in his voice. "No one — not even you — is making me do anything I don't want. Never again. Nor are they going to stop me doing what I do want. I'll go out fighting before I'll be told how to live. Are you hearing me?"

"Yeah, I hear you. I just…" Paulo huffed out a deep breath as he sat forward in his chair to get closer to Nate.

"And that means if I want to see Jimmy, I will."

"But why him, of all people?" Paulo asked. "You could have anyone you want."

"Don't want anyone else," Nate said simply. "He's… I don't have to be anything I'm not with him."

"You don't with me either."

"But I don't want to go to bed with you any more than you want to go to bed with me."

"So that's it? That's what you like about him? Sex?" Paulo demanded.

"I like the sex but that's not it. I like that we're easy together, that there are no secrets. I like his strength, his decency and I like the way he makes me feel. He makes me feel good."

"Decency?" Paulo's eyebrows rose. "He owned you, abused you."

"For fuck's sake, listen to me. He's not like that now, hasn't been for a long time, and even when he was I..." Nate made an odd, 'humph' sound. "You, and everyone else, expect me to hate him. Hell, for long enough I expected me to hate him. It was how I was supposed to feel. Only I didn't—don't hate him—and I'm not going to apologize for that."

Again he stopped, obviously thinking. "You keep telling me that growing to like your captor is an age old cliché and I fucking refuse to be one of those. But even being friends with him isn't seen as acceptable, because people think I've been taken in by him, or he still has some kind of power over me or... I can see it in your face that you can't believe we've gone from what we were to being friends. I'll admit, at times, that makes me wonder. You've been my best buddy forever, and if you can't believe it then maybe I should question it but..."

He glanced at Jimmy, just for a moment before his attention was back on Paulo. "I feel right when he's around, wrong when he's not. He doesn't expect anything from me, he accepts me as I really am and just goes with it. I feel... I don't know. I only know I'm happy here with him. He's changed and he's amazing and I need him and his honesty. He makes me glad I'm still alive. Isn't that a good enough reason?"

Paulo stared between them, his gaze finally coming back to rest on Nate. "Yeah, that's good enough," he said, then immediately swung round to stare at Jimmy. "If you ever try anything with him, I'll break your fucking legs off and make you eat them." He glanced back at Nate, grinning. "Or I'll hold everyone back while Nate does it."

Jimmy knew down to his bones that, although he might be bigger than both of them and have more muscle, either of them could do it anytime they wanted. He nodded, not trusting himself to say anything.

* * * *

Sitting for hours on the verandah, wrapped in Jimmy's grandma's homemade quilt, had become Nate's favorite place to be. He said he liked watching life go on around the lake as it always had, but Jimmy knew he was thinking more than watching. Sometimes Nate would stay there long past when he should, until the evening was turning fast into night. Jimmy would always try to entice him in before that happened. But for the last couple of days Nate had wanted to get back out there as often as he could.

Jimmy brought out a cup of coffee, good and hot, placing it in on the table where Nate had his feet propped up. He might have been wrapped in the huge quilt, but it was cold and Nate had been sitting out there all afternoon, watching the birds fly low over the water.

His face was pinched, drawn, but Jimmy knew that wasn't because of the chill.

Some days Nate seemed to forget everything and lived in the moment, others he tried to work through all that had happened.

"Drink it." Jimmy pushed the cup closer. "We don't need you getting sick."

Nate didn't react—his focus still out past the reeds and grasses, watching...nothing. Jimmy touched his shoulder briefly then turned to go back inside. If there was anyone that needed room, even an idiot like him could see that Nate was a prime example. He'd just reached the door when Nate spoke without warning.

"I'm glad we had that weekend."

"Which?" Jimmy asked, coming back and sitting on the chair near Nate. He clasped his hands between his knees, rubbing them together to keep warm. "The last weekend we had up here? When we slept together?"

"When we made love." Nate said it flatly, as though he were stating an obvious fact. "I'm glad we did that before I was hurt."

"Why? What happened isn't going to change who we are."

"No, not change but..." Nate pulled the quilt tighter round himself. "If we hadn't and then I was raped and..." He stopped for a long moment, until Jimmy wasn't sure if was going to go on. "If I felt like I do now, I might have settled. What we had, before, when we lived together after we first got out of prison, it wasn't so bad. It was good compared to being raped in anger and hate. If I didn't know what we could be like, then now, after being raped at the rally, I might have thought back to that and I...might have settled for it."

He looked at Jimmy then for the first time, his eyes clear. "I'm glad I didn't. I'm glad I knew something better."

Jimmy felt like his breath had been stolen. He'd had no idea what Nate had been thinking. That he might have settled for so little. "I..." His voice came out scratched thin. "I'm glad you didn't settle as well. Glad I didn't either."

Nate stared at him for a long moment, sure and steady, then went back to watching the water.

Jimmy sat there for a while, soaking in the peace and comfort, soaking in just being close to Nate, before he went back inside to think about dinner.

* * * *

Over the next couple of weeks they walked for miles, took the boat out and tried fishing, but gave that up as a bad idea when they didn't catch a single thing in two whole days. Jimmy slept more than he had in years but he figured that was good if it made Nate do the same. After the first few days, he gave up on fresh air and exercise as an excuse and admitted he liked a nap — whenever, wherever he could get one.

They went into the small town about once a week, buying all the food they'd need and renting armfuls of DVDs. There was no arguing over what to choose — they got everything and watched old fashioned westerns followed by the latest thriller on days that it poured with rain. But mostly they wrapped up warm and went out, no matter how cold it got, letting the air, the trees and the peace work its magic.

They talked about things they saw as they walked — animals, birds and insects, about the weather, the political situation, the struggle that faced the new government. Jimmy watched as the color came back into Nate's face, the light into his eyes, the strength in his step. Every day he was getting better, stronger. Soon he'd be ready to go back to the real world.

Jimmy wasn't sure he'd ever want this to end.

* * * *

They'd walked all morning but Jimmy had known Nate would sit outside in the big wicker chairs after they'd eaten.

"Hey," he said, going out to find Nate. "You left before the cake. Lunch isn't complete without cake." He put a plate laden with moist carrot cake on the table, taking a slice for himself as he sat down.

"I've been thinking," Nate said.

"I could tell." Jimmy smiled around his mouthful.

"Can I ask you a question?" He sounded very serious.

"Of course."

"Do you still love me?"

Jimmy wiped the crumbs from his hands, his face. This wasn't time for a flippant answer or even a, 'you know I do', type. Nate wanted a proper one. "You want the intelligent, long answer or the honest simple one?"

"Honest. I always want honest from you, more than I want anything else."

"Okay, honestly then. Yes, I still love you."

"And it's as easy as that?"

"Honestly?" Jimmy shrugged. "Yes, it's that easy. I love you and I always have, even when I didn't know you."

"Even when it—I—was a lie?"

"That was easy because I believed your lie. I thought I knew you. It got harder when I knew it wasn't the truth."

"Why?"

"Because my brain was screaming that I couldn't love you when I didn't know you. When everything had been an act and I'd been behaving like a power-crazed freak. It wasn't real and if it wasn't real, then anything I felt wasn't real either. I wavered for a while then but...no." He gave a soft snort of ironic laughter as he picked at the last few spots of cake crumb, collecting them up and putting them on the edge of the small table. "The trouble was," Jimmy said slowly, "that some little bit of me kept saying, 'you do love him'."

He looked at Nate, scrunching up his nose against the bright winter sunlight. "But I feel like I've fallen in love with you all over again, even though it never stopped. Which is stupid, I know. I loved fake-Nate, the hard bastard and, now, the real one. I've stopped trying to analyze it, stopped questioning everything. I do love you." He smiled, wide and bright. "And you got the long complicated answer anyway."

"You never could stop talking," Nate said softly.

"I know." Jimmy reached forward to take another piece of cake. "Eat your dessert. It'll build you up or stop me getting fat or something." He stood, pressing the plate at Nate, effectively forcing him to pick up the last piece. "You want coffee? I'm making some."

"Yeah." Nate nodded and suddenly Jimmy thought his eyes were too big, too intense for his face as he stared up. "You know I've never said it," Nate said. "I've never said I love you."

"I know." Now Jimmy's smile was smaller but more heartfelt. He ran a hand through the uneven cut of Nate's hair, the shorter strands on the injured side a constant reminder of what might have been. He flattened them, trying to hide the scarring. "I'll get the coffee, and then we can go into town or maybe get the boat out. We could drive down to the other end of the lake, if you want."

Nate stared at him. He seemed grateful.

Six days later Nate decided he was ready to go back to the city. Much as Jimmy didn't want to go, he thought it was probably time.

* * * *

"This is going to take ages." Jimmy moaned at the traffic jamming up the road. "I thought it would have cleared by now. It's nearly ten o'clock. Most people should be at work." He drummed his fingers on the steering wheel, the rhythm annoying, tuneless.

"Would you mind dropping me at the movement's headquarters?" Nate asked. "It's not far from here."

"Yeah, I guess so. But, are you sure?"

"Like you said." Nate glanced across at him, a hint of a smile on his face. "Most people will be at work, I think it's time I joined them."

"You don't have to, not if you aren't ready," Jimmy said, but he'd already pulled the car round, heading up a side street. "No one is going to think anything if you take a bit more time."

"Time for what?"

"I don't know, your head to heal? It wasn't so long ago you were unconscious and they weren't sure if you'd even live."

"But it's not my head holding me back now, is it?" Nate said quietly. "I have to get over what happened and get on with things."

"Maybe, but..."

"No, there's no but. It's time to move on. Now I have to go in and find out if there's anything for me to do."

"Of course you'll have things to do. Why wouldn't you? Last time I saw them, there was so much happening they were running round like headless chickens."

"I know but I'm not sure what I want to do." Nate suddenly snorted, the sound mocking. "Let's be honest. I'm not sure what I can do. There aren't any more physical fights but I'm not making speeches. Only, what else is there?"

"You'll find something. Just don't let them push you into anything you don't want." Jimmy pulled the car up in front of an imposing but battered building. He glanced at Nate as he turned off the engine. "There's a new country, a new way of living to be built. You're a hell of a man. You'll have more than enough to do."

"I just wish I knew you were right." Nate climbed out of the car, shutting the door carefully before he looked up at the headquarters.

"Hey," Jimmy leaned out of the car window. "When am I...? I mean tonight, what are you...?" Again he ran out of words. He tried again. "What do you want me to do with your things?"

"I was hoping you'd take them back to the house."

"You're coming back then?" Jimmy couldn't stop his grin.

"If you don't mind. If you want me to."

"Yes. No. Hell, yeah, I want you to and no, I don't mind. I just..."

"Go on. You can do it. You can finish a whole sentence." Nate grinned back at him. "After all, talking is one thing you're really good at."

"Shut up." Jimmy's cheeks were starting to hurt he was smiling so hard. "I want you to come home. I just didn't want to assume."

"There are other places I could go but..." The grin fell from Nate's face leaving something softer, warmer. "I'd like to come...home."

Chapter Twelve

Jimmy didn't know what to cook or what time to cook it or even if he should. He felt like a wife or a housekeeper or a... And that was the problem. He didn't know what he was or what he felt like. He tried to get on with his normal life but nothing was normal.

He rang the studio, only to be told that things were still shut down. There wasn't a time scale for restarting, not after all the massive upheavals, but it was thought to be sooner rather than later. They'd let him know when they needed him. Let him know in good time, so he could learn his lines and get his head round the idea.

That left him the rest of the day to fill.

After throwing the washing in the machine and watering his one plant, he stood in the middle of the living room, hands on hips, and thought. What did he use to do before? How did he spend his days off, before he started waiting for Nate? And there it was. That's what he was doing. He was waiting for Nate to come home. He couldn't, wouldn't, do that all day.

He went for a two hour run, sprinting as fast as he could on the way back, so his muscles screamed and his legs shook. Then he had a long, hot shower.

That left hours before... What time would Nate come back? If he didn't change his mind and go off somewhere with the others and... Jimmy rang his sister and managed to stay on the phone for almost ten minutes before she started talking about their mother and he had to cut her short. He thought about calling friends, meeting someone for a drink, but there wasn't anyone he wanted to see. Everyone looked at everyone else differently lately. They all knew Nate had been his slave, how he'd taken to that situation in a way that left him ashamed. Now people didn't try to keep how they felt about that off their faces. Anger and disgust he could take, envy and commiseration for his loss were harder.

He hadn't even bothered to explain to anyone how things had changed between Nate and himself. He wasn't sure he knew how to, didn't think they'd believe him anyway and, honestly, he didn't care enough to bother. What did it matter what anyone else thought?

He went to the supermarket, pushing round the trolley whilst he tried to work out what Nate really liked.

Nate got back at about seven that evening, a car pulling up onto the driveway and dropping him off. The driver didn't come in.

"Hey," Nate said, dropping his jacket on the back of a chair before washing his hands. "That smells good. What is it?"

"It's supposed to be chili but I didn't have half the ingredients it said in the book, so it's a thing."

"A thing?"

"A thing."

"Your thing smells good." Then Nate seemed to realize what he'd said, and they both burst out laughing. "And that sounded disgusting."

"You want a beer?" Jimmy asked, already getting a couple out of the fridge and handing Nate one. "How was your day? You look tired."

"Actually I'm not. I feel okay." Nate took a drink and sat down. "It was a good day, better than I expected."

"How so?"

"I thought it would be awkward, but it wasn't. They're used to me getting physically hurt and being laid up for a while, so that part was easy. As for the other... Well, I guess so many people there have been raped, my little two-man experience didn't warrant much attention."

"Nat... Nate." Jimmy corrected himself automatically. "Don't dismiss it, just because other people have suffered worse. You can't do that."

"No, it was good for me. There're other ex-slaves who got raped day after day, who got hurt, some badly. But they don't let it define their lives — who they are. That helped me get it in perspective."

"But what happened is important to you."

"That's the thing," Nate said, an empty fork already in his hand. "It isn't that important, not in the great scheme of things. You should hear some of those talk who've been to hell and back. Man, the jokes they tell about being raped. I thought you couldn't laugh about stuff like that, but they do."

"And that helps?" Jimmy started to serve up the meal.

"Yeah. About the only reference I got, the entire day, to what happened to me, was from one woman I've worked with for years. She patted me on the back and said, 'welcome to the club'. Her brother looked at me, confused and then realization hit and he said it as well."

"That seems kind of harsh." Jimmy put the plates on the table, sitting opposite Nate.

"But that's the point. She'd been raped, so had he." Nate stopped, first forkful of food half way to his mouth. "I'd forgotten that about them and that's what's important. I know they'd both had a bad time but it didn't change how I felt toward them. That was really good for me."

"Then I'm glad. Glad you've sorted out how you feel."

"Actually, I've sorted out how I feel about a lot of things," Nate said quietly, watching Jimmy. "You know, this isn't half bad." He pointed at his plate.

"So my thing tastes good?" Jimmy raised an eyebrow and Nate laughed.

"Shut up. When are you going back to work?"

"Don't know," Jimmy admitted. "There was this pesky, inconvenient uprising that's sort of got in the way."

"Pesky? Hell, you really need to stop watching kids' TV."

"Yeah, I know. So what did you do today?"

"Me? I"—Nate shrugged, the humor leaving his face—"I sat around a lot, got in people's way, answered some phones and even played cards."

"Wow, that was…" Jimmy shrugged.

"Yeah, it was. But I took your advice. I'm not going to be rushed into anything. I could have done a lot of important stuff today, but there wasn't anything I wanted to do. Anything that felt right."

"Wow, again." Jimmy raised both eyebrows.

"What? I can do nothing. I can."

"It wasn't that. I gave good advice? Me? You have to admit that deserves a wow."

"I'll give you that one. It deserved a wow." Nate smiled at him softly. "I'll find something and I'm going to take my time doing it."

"Good for you," Jimmy said.

* * * *

Jimmy spent the next few days running, cooking, going to the gym and even cleaning. Then word came through that filming would start up again the following week. A bike messenger delivered a script and Jimmy sat down to learn it. Then he made Nate laugh by practicing in front of the bathroom mirror.

"Shut up, dude." He pulled a face at Nate. "I've forgotten how to do this. I'm back to feeling stupid."

"You want me to go through your lines with you?"

"Are you going to laugh when I'm pretending to fight aliens and spouting made up science?"

"No, I wouldn't." Nate stopped, his bottom lip caught between his teeth, his eyes sparkling with a brightness Jimmy hadn't seen since before...in a long time. "Yeah, I probably will. But I'll try, I'll try real hard to do it properly."

Jimmy handed him the script. "If you turn out to be a better actor than I am, I will hunt you down and kill you."

Nate did his very best, on all counts.

The next night Nate got home early and had already started dinner when Jimmy got out of the shower after his run. They smiled, working easily around each other, not needing a lot of conversation.

Sitting at the kitchen table, Jimmy suddenly stopped eating, studying Nate. "You seem different," he said at last. "More... I don't know, more contented. Has something happened?"

"Not happened, but..." Nate wiped up sauce from his plate with a piece of bread, eating it before going on. "I've found a job, work that needs doing but isn't in the limelight."

"That's good." Jimmy smiled. "What is it?"

"Helping freed slaves. Sorting out secure, decent places for them to stay, organizing medical help, counseling and, hell, some of them are going to need that. Then, as time goes on, they'll need training, support getting work, setting up on their own."

"That doesn't just 'need doing'—that's really important."

"I think it is," Nate said and Jimmy noticed his eyes were completely untroubled. "It's also work that's going to need doing for a long time to come, years," he went on. "They're still freeing slaves daily, ones that their owners thought they could hide and keep."

"I bet some of the freedom fighters are putting them straight."

"Oh yes," Nate said with feeling. "They're also making sure everyone else sees what happens to those owners, that the message is clear and unmistakable. No exceptions and no excuses—all slaves have to be freed."

"That's important work as well."

"I know and Paulo wanted me to join him, but..." He shrugged, a brief movement of his shoulders. "That felt like the past, about the fight. I want to concentrate on the peace, the future."

"That's..." Jimmy smiled. "I'm glad that things are so positive. I really am pleased for you."

"So am I. I'm only doing positive things from now on, ones that are about the future." Nate put his knife and fork down. Pushing his plate away, he stared Jimmy straight in the eye. "Come to bed with me," he said clearly, no hesitation or uncertainty.

"I..." Jimmy's mouth had suddenly gone dry. "Are you sure that's what you want?"

"Yes," Nate said simply, standing up and holding out a hand.

"Now?"

"You want to wait?"

"No," Jimmy said heartfelt, the air rushing out across his teeth. He rubbed his sweaty palms on his jeans then took Nate's hand, letting him lead them up stairs.

Outside the door to the main bedroom—what had now become Nate's bedroom—Jimmy stopped. "Are you sure?" he asked again. "Because this feels different to me. Different from the weekend at the lake, from before you were hurt."

"It is different." Nate took a deep breath, letting it go slowly as he watched Jimmy. "That was about laying demons, sorting things between us. About finally accepting I'm not cliché-syndrome guy. I was scared of that for so long that I couldn't think straight. That time at the lake was about trusting my own judgment and admitting how much you've changed and that I believe in you. But it was still about the past. This is about the future."

"The future." Jimmy let the words hang out there, clean and fresh sounding, but also as scary as hell.

"Those people I work with, the ex-slaves," Nate said carefully, gaze still on Jimmy. "At the moment, they have no idea what their future is. They don't have anywhere warm to go home to, no one to go home to."

He paused and the air felt charged, the moment significant. "I'm hoping I do."

"You do. Trust me. You do. But that can't be why we do this." Jimmy waved at the bedroom door. "I want this so badly I haven't even let myself dream about it. But…" He ran a hand through his hair. "I can't believe I'm actually saying this, but it has to be right. It has to be what you really want, not just because you feel comfortable and safe here. You can have that without sleeping with me."

"It's not about that." Nate turned, standing squarely in front of him, confident and sure. "You know the real me. I also know you, now you've woken up and can see the world for what it really is, and I like this you so much better. You've kept what was good from before but you realize the world isn't just your playground. I look at you now and you're amazing and I want you so bad it hurts. But, if we're going to have a future, it had to be right. Now it is. Now you stop and think about what's right, even if that might prevent you getting something you want. Just like you're doing now."

"Are you sure? You have to be sure."

"Sure?" Nate pressed the tip of his tongue against his top teeth, shaking his head and giving an ironic snort that sounded like laughter. "Don't you understand how hard I've had to fight to get here, now, with you?"

"Paulo?"

"No, not him. Well, sort of, but mostly me. All the way along I've had to fight me."

"I don't understand," Jimmy admitted. "Cliché-syndrome thing again?" It seemed strange to be having this conversation standing on the landing, outside the bedroom with all the possibilities of sex just within reach. But Jimmy had to know what was happening before he could take that step across the threshold. Had to know how Nate really felt.

"I tried to explain it to Paulo, now I have to make sure you understand," Nate said, leaning back against the banisters, eyes assessing Jimmy. "I was supposed to hate you — you were my owner. Only I didn't, and I haven't for a lot longer than I was willing to admit. You…" He wrinkled his nose and shrugged. "You've fascinated me for a long time. I couldn't work you out and I tried so hard. Even in prison I couldn't pin you down. One moment you were kind and decent, protecting me, the next you were every bit the controlling owner. I used to think that you were playing mind games with me, to keep me off balance. It took me a long time to work out you weren't, to work out what you really were."

"And what am I?" Jimmy had to ask.

"Deep down you're decent, you just got lost with all the power and couldn't find your way. It only took a little nudge from me to make you stop and think."

"A little nudge?"

"Yeah. When I left, you could have sent the police after me, but you didn't. I heard you didn't tell them a damned thing about me."

"I didn't know anything to tell."

"But you didn't even file a runaway report," Nate said quietly. "They didn't know I was gone for a long time."

"I began to realize why you went."

"See? Just a little nudge." Nate tipped his head, still studying Jimmy. "Then, when I first started coming to see you, it was obvious you were thinking, changing, when you could've had me recaptured."

"I wouldn't."

"No, you wouldn't. But you could have said the right things to get closer to me, if sex was what you wanted—only you didn't do that either. You took everything I hit you with, and I deliberately hit you hard. I forced you to face all the lies, how you acted, hit you with rape. You took it, thought about it, struggled, but kept on thinking. I watched you do that, watched you hurting but keep on fighting to change, and I..." He shook his head, lips pressed together in a thin line. "That takes real guts and I admired you for it."

"You admired me?" Jimmy snorted ironically. "That doesn't seem right."

"Why not? You've done something pretty amazing and I admire and respect you." Again Nate shook his head, harder this time. "But it was more than that. You stirred all kinds of feelings in my belly that I wouldn't think about. I put it down to lust, and even that was hard enough to accept, but it wasn't just that. It was..."

"Go on." Jimmy pushed. "I need to know this."

"When we were living together, before I left, you used to mess with my head and confuse the hell out of me."

"I didn't." It was Jimmy's turn to shake his head. "At least I didn't intend to. I might have been deluded, but I think I was consistently deluded."

"You told me you loved me and I could see by the way you looked at me, the way you acted, that you meant it." Nate inhaled, long and deliberate. "But then you wouldn't let me cut my hair, would let me be me, and you'd demand sex. I didn't understand that and..." Again he stopped, eyes fixed on Jimmy. "I thought then that I really did have Stockholm Syndrome, because there were times I liked you. Even if it was only lust, it didn't seem right, and it's hard to admit something that everybody, including myself, thought was wrong. I might have wanted you, but I didn't want to want you and that made me so angry with myself. Does that make any sense?"

"Yeah, it does." Jimmy nodded. "You didn't want to want me. But it's good to know you did. For a while I wasn't sure if I'd got that wrong as well. I thought you did, but..." He shrugged, letting the implication hang.

"Oh I wanted you. I just didn't like myself for feeling that way. I got so screwed up in my own head about it all. I used to fantasize about pushing you across the bed and fucking you into the mattress, then tie myself in knots trying to work out if that was about power or desire." He sighed, a sound of pent up emotions.

"I didn't know you felt like that."

"It was one of the reasons I started seeing you. At first it was just to say a genuine sorry but then I saw you and...I thought I was as bad as you, wanting the body, not the man. But then you began to change and... No, it wasn't even changing. Your real character was fighting to get to the surface, the honesty and integrity that I admire. I wanted you and I didn't know how I should feel about it. I had no one to talk to — no one that would understand — so I kept coming back, kept wanting."

"Why are you here now?" Jimmy asked softly, but he didn't think there'd ever been a question that mattered so much.

"Because now I know what I want—you. Not for comfort or security or anything else, just for you. For who you are because you're good and gorgeous and I want you. I don't care how anyone else sees it. You and I know it's real, and that's all that matters." Again there was a pause, a crackle of importance in the air. "Now you know me. Do you want me as an equal?"

"As an equal? Oh God, yes," Jimmy said with no hesitation and with such feeling that it made Nate smile.

"Then let's go to bed."

Nate held out his hand and Jimmy took it.

It was different from anything Jimmy remembered. Different from anything he'd ever known with anyone, even that weekend at the lake. When Nate touched him, he didn't want him to ever let go, never let his skin feel naked, exposed, again. He'd thought Nate's hands were rough, a workman's, but now they felt strong—a fighter's hands—and he wanted them spread out on his body for the rest of his life.

When he touched Nate, he wanted to hold, to touch, but not to own or claim. Now he wanted to be part of him, his life. He wanted the world to know they stood shoulder to shoulder, that they were a unit, an equal part of each other.

Everything was different—from how he felt to the way Nate moved. He might recognize some of the noises Nate made but even they had a subtle, different edge to them. They were unrestrained, natural and Jimmy wanted to spend the rest of his life learning each nuance. Even Nate's skin, his mouth tasted different, warmer, more intoxicating, and Jimmy never wanted to pull his tongue away.

Nate rolled them until he was on his back, Jimmy between his spread thighs. Jimmy kissed him deeper, stroking with his tongue and the hand that wasn't tangled deep in Nate's hair. He felt Nate's hands running down his back, strong fingers pushing into his spine, grabbing at his arse, pressing it down so his cock slipped into place between Nate's legs.

Next second, without conscious thought or intent, Jimmy pulled up, away. "I can't," he said. "Not..."

"But I want you to." Nate stared at him, sure and steady, nothing but confidence in his eyes.

"It's too soon."

"No, it's not." Nate cupped his face, kissing him on the lips. "I've been better—ready—for a long time."

"Then it's too soon for me."

"You don't want to?" Nate stopped, his fingers still on Jimmy's cheekbone. "I'll never pressure anyone to do something they don't want."

"I do want." Jimmy huffed a huge breath. "I do. I guess I'm just not ready, just...not yet."

"Why not?"

"After they hurt you... Not yet." Jimmy didn't have any more of an answer.

Nate's hand fell away, his shoulders pushing back into the pillow as his face tightened. As he made connections. "You saw it, didn't you? You were there. I'd asked you to come to the rally. I'd seen you in the crowd, waved at you and..." His face changed, concentration etched across his features, as he obviously thought back over the weeks and months, over the missing chunks of his memory. "You were standing at the side near the platform, close to where I was. I was watching you. You were the other side of the fence, then everything started to kick off and..." He focused on Jimmy's face. "You didn't just hear about it. You saw me get attacked, saw me raped."

Jimmy thought it would be so easy to say no, to rub away the expression on Nate's face and put back the happiness and, oh God, Nate had looked happy. Happy and content and Jimmy didn't want him to lose that.

But if there was one person he could never lie to again, it was Nate.

"Yeah, I saw." He nodded briefly, going on as Nate's face closed up even more. "But it isn't important. It doesn't matter."

"Only now you don't want to fuck me and you really like fucking me. It doesn't matter, except now you see me as a victim." Nate pushed and, before he knew what was happening, Nate rolled Jimmy away and started to get up.

But he wasn't having that. He caught hold of Nate's arm, pulling him back around.

"Don't you fucking dare," Nate shouted, face tight and red. "You don't own me. You don't make me do anything."

"The only thing I'm going to do is make you listen, you moron." Jimmy had never called him names before and the surprise of it seemed to stop Nate. "I saw it happen. So what? You accepted I knew about it, witnessing it doesn't make any difference."

"Yes it does." Nate folded his arms over his chest.

"What, seeing is different from knowing? How? Now I suddenly see you as a victim? Why? Remember, I've seen you as a victim, a proper one. Hell, I was the one that raped you in front of a courtroom full of people. Yeah, I might have had to do it, but I did it calmly and slowly. Bruised your neck as I made you submit to me and everyone else there. That was a victim, not the man that fought with everything he had to get away. That was a casualty of war. If you don't know the difference, I do."

"But..." Nate wiped a shaking hand over his face. "You don't want to fuck me."

"That has nothing to do with seeing it." Jimmy shook his head. "To put it crudely, your arse got hurt.

I want to take as much care of that as I do of your head."

"My arse is better."

"So's your head. Doesn't stop me worrying, or telling you to sleep more, though."

"Okay," Nate said at last, sitting back down on the edge of the mattress, all the anger and fear seeming to draining away as fast as it had come. "I don't know what happens now," he admitted.

"How about you get back in bed?" Jimmy stroked along his spine. "We think of something else to do and forget all the complicated crap, just for a while."

Nate twisted round, the position awkward. "I'll never pressure you but are you going to fuck me sometime?" He kissed Jimmy, not tentatively or half-heartedly, but a full on proper kiss, his hand holding the back of Jimmy's neck. "I like being fucked by you."

"I know you do. You just don't like sucking cock." Jimmy grinned at him, pushing until Nate was flat on his back. "Soon," he promised. "When I've got to know the real you in bed again. Soon."

"What's this something else you got in mind?"

"Anything you want," Jimmy said, then stopped and smiled again. "Almost anything you want. Anything that makes you feel good. I want to make you feel real good."

"No." Nate shook his head, hand reaching up to rest on Jimmy's shoulder. "It can't be like that."

"Like what?"

"You making me feel good."

"I'm not allowed to make you feel good? That's crazy."

"No, it can't be just about you making me feel good. That smacks of compensation, of inequality, and that's wrong."

"But I feel like…"

"No, Jim. If we're going to make this work, we have to start off right and that isn't the way."

Jimmy held still, studying Nate for a long moment. "You want us to be equals?"

"I'm not doing this any other way."

"Okay." Jimmy exhaled hard through his nose. "I don't feel like your equal at times but, okay, you're right."

"I usually am." It was Nate's turn to smile.

"We do things that make us both feel good, only…" Jimmy wrinkled his nose up as he thought. "But you just called me Jim, only I'm not allowed to call you Nat."

"No one calls me Nat."

"So you can't call me Jim, right?" Jimmy's grin was wide, his eyes bright. "Remember, equals."

"All right." Nate grabbed a handful of Jimmy's hair, pulling him down for a hard, hard kiss. "You can get away with the occasional Nat, but you call me baby or sweetheart and I will fucking kill you in your sleep."

"Deal," Jimmy said and kissed him back just as hard, pressing him into the pillow. He rolled on top of Nate, driving his hips down again and again, moaning his appreciation into Nate's mouth as Nate met him thrust for thrust. "I could get off on just this, covering you in my spunk, getting you to smear yours all over me. Fuck, I want you to rub it in deep."

"You really are a weird bastard." Nate managed to laugh through his panting. "Smearing?"

"Nothing wrong with smearing, except…" He thrust down, catching Nate just right and they both had to stop talking to feel every moment of it. Nate pressed his fingers deep into Jimmy's shoulders, as his own hands held Nate's hips tight, not letting him move, creating a fixed target for himself. He thrust again and felt the resulting shudder through both their bodies. Again and Nate was pulling his hair once more, only this time he was pulling Jimmy's head away.

"Except?" Nate asked.

"This is amazing." He rolled his hips and, yeah, amazing. "But I want more, want to feel you inside me."

"We're not going to start doing it that way round every time. That's not right."

"Don't want to do it every time." Jimmy was already dragging Nate up, manhandling him up onto his knees. "I want to suck your cock, want to fuck you, want to do just about everything I can think of. But now I want to feel you inside me, see if that's different as well." He knelt with his back to Nate, dropping down onto all fours and wriggling backwards so they were almost lined up.

"Different?"

"Yeah." Jimmy twisted his head round so he could see over his shoulder.

"Please." Nate ran a hand along Jimmy's spine. "Just explain that."

Jimmy caught his bottom lip between his teeth for a moment, watching. "So far, since you touched me tonight, every damned thing has felt different, different to anything else we've ever done together, including that weekend at the lake cabin. I want to know if this is different as well." His eyes suddenly narrowed. "Or maybe you don't feel it?"

"Yeah, I feel it," Nate said very quietly. He leaned forward, running his hands up Jimmy's sides as he kissed along his back, lips and mouth gentle, to press his face into the base of Jimmy's neck. "Different."

"Fuck me," Jimmy whispered, rubbing back against Nate. "I want to feel you."

"Okay." Nate pressed his open mouth to the top of Jimmy's spine, holding there for a moment. Jimmy could feel the flutter of Nate's eyelashes against his skin, the dampness of his warm breath.

"Bedside cupboard."

"What?" Nate lifted his head.

"The lube. It's in the bedside cupboard."

"All right." Nate reached over, fingertips just catching the drawer. "I can take a hint."

He took his time, preparing Jimmy with a care that left Jimmy frustrated to near irritation point and begging obscenely for more. "Shut up and keep still," Nate said, his voice thick with warmth as Jimmy twisted on his fingers. "It's coming."

"Now would be nice. Two hours ago would have been better." Jimmy rubbed his arse back against Nate's body, knowing just what a reaction it would cause. He wasn't disappointed.

"Two hours ago we were sitting in the kitchen." Nate groaned, pulling his fingers out and settling himself, ready. "God, but you're a demanding bitch."

"But you lov— But you adore me for it." Jimmy could feel Nate's cockhead right where he wanted it to be. He wasn't about to let Nate stop and think, not now, not when it was all going so perfectly.

Not because of a stupid mistake he'd come so close to saying.

He pushed back, hard as he could and, oh yes, it was every bit as good as he'd hoped. Nate filling and stretching him, Nate exhaling hard over him, Nate clutching at his hips, his cock pulsing. Jimmy pushed again and Nate slipped all the way in as he fell to press his chest to Jimmy's back.

Jimmy heard the muffled, 'yes' and knew everything was good.

Nate's breath was coming hard, his mouth close to Jimmy's ear, as neither moved. But that was good, right, as well. It gave Jimmy a chance to catch his own breath and he needed to because everything was as different as he'd hoped. Free will and choice and all those important things had been there at the lake cabin but this…this was different. This wasn't about anyone exerting their rights or laying ghosts or even because they cared.

This was about building a future together.

The concept took Jimmy's breath away. Nate's dick in his arse made him pray to any deity he'd ever heard of for more.

"Move, please," Jimmy said, but it sounded broken, desperate. "I need you to."

"If you need—" Nate hefted himself off Jimmy's back, his hands gentle on his hips. He pulled out slowly before pushing back in faster.

"Oh God." Jimmy groaned, hanging his head down between his shoulders. "Oh God." Different didn't even cover it. The rub of flesh against flesh was new but weirdly familiar. He knew how Nate's hands felt on his skin, what they could do, the sensations they could cause, but this… He had no words for how this felt. Different and perfect and what he'd always wanted and no words that could do it justice. "Please." He panted, and he had no idea what he was asking for.

"It's okay. It's okay," Nate said over and over again as though it were some kind of mantra. He thrust in once more and again, each one a little deeper, a little faster, but never hard, his hands constantly skimming over Jimmy's back, sides, up to his shoulders. It was as if he wanted to touch all of Jimmy at once, touch and feel and be part of.

"Please." Jimmy felt broken, ripped apart in ways he didn't know could happen. His throat was raw, his body open for Nate to take—take all of him, every atom. He pushed back, trying to screw Nate in deeper, and reached round to pull himself further open, dropping to the other elbow as he did. And that was good, right, so fucking perfect he was in danger of hyperventilating.

But it wasn't about Nate filling him, about flesh and prostates and cocks. It was about Nate moaning softly above him, incoherent words of affection and admiration, all breathy and genuine. It was about the way Nate's hands seemed to travel over his skin with reverence and appreciation to the point of near worship.

It was about how much Jimmy loved the man who was fucking him slowly and thoroughly.

Suddenly Nate pulled out, pushing Jimmy so he fell on his side then rolling him onto his back. He lifted Jimmy's leg and pushed back in before Jimmy had even caught on to what was happening.

"What?" Jimmy managed to ask.

"Needed to see your face," Nate said, hips already back in their rhythm. "Needed to see you."

They came moments apart—Nate's hand safe on Jimmy's cock, his own dick still deep inside. A shudder, a broken gasp, hands clutching hard, they panted together. Nate eased out as he pulled Jimmy closer to him, wrapping them tightly as Jimmy lifted the cover over them. He pressed nearer and Nate threw an arm across his chest. Just as he wanted, needed.

He fell asleep with the thought that things couldn't get any better.

* * * *

The next morning Jimmy woke up with Nate kneeling over him, slippery hand working his cock as Nate lined them up.

"One word and I'll break your cock off." Nate threatened.

"Not one." Jimmy slid his hands up Nate's thighs to cup his hips. He couldn't control the manic grin that was making the muscles in his face protest. "Not even one asking what would you have done if I'd said no?"

Nate's eyes were fierce on his in a heartbeat.

"I'm not saying no. I'm not stupid. In fact I'm saying yes, yes, yes. I was just wondering."

"Jimmy," Nate barked.

"Not another word. Not a single one." Jimmy clamped a hand over his mouth.

Nate eased himself down, his eyes closing as he sighed and seemed to relax over and onto Jimmy. Jimmy pushed up experimentally once, twice, a third and, God, that felt different as well. Not a thing like every other time he'd fucked Nate. The pressure around his cock was different, the intensity, the feel, all new and wonderful. He put both hands back on Nate's thighs and that felt different as well. The man under his hands had changed. Relaxed didn't begin to cover it, Nate was letting himself go in ways Jimmy had never known.

He lifted Nate, pushing him onto his back and spreading him out against the sheet. "That's a hell of a form of stress relief you've got going there, but I think it's better if you lay down before you melt into a puddle."

"I..." Nate looked up with hazy eyes as Jimmy slid back into him.

"No worries, man. Trust me, we're both happy with this arrangement." Suddenly, as unexpectedly as if a falling meteor had hit him, Jimmy realized just how happy he really was. Happy to have Nate in his bed, but happier that it was all by choice, because they were equals — partners. That they could both do something for the other.

If this was what he could do to relax Nate, he thought it was a job he'd take on for life.

And rape? This had absolutely nothing to do with that. This really was about two people making love.

Jimmy canted his hips, gliding in and it felt so perfect, so right, it was in danger of taking his breath away.

"Hey." Nate reached up, gripping onto Jimmy's hair. "You aren't going soft on me, are you, man?"

"Soft?" Jimmy thrust a little harder, pushed a little deeper. "Is that soft?"

"No." Nate pulled him down to kiss him, the laughter in his voice making it sloppy. "And any wetness around your eyes is just because you're so freaking happy, right?"

"Yeah." Jimmy licked across his cheek. "Actually it is." His voice sounded raw, even to himself.

Nate studied him carefully. "Jimmy? Don't... I..." He gripped Jimmy's neck tighter. "I'm freaking happy as well."

Jimmy snorted out a laugh, almost collapsing down onto Nate, ignoring his protest as he made them both freaking happy.

It was a hell of a way to start one of his last days off.

* * * *

"Are you ready to go back to work?" Nate asked, as he pushed the cereal packet across the table toward Jimmy.

"Don't I look ready?" Jimmy didn't even glance up from his script, although they must have gone through it a hundred times the night before.

"Actually." Nate stood up, putting his plate and coffee mug in the sink as he searched for his jacket. "With your shirt buttoned up wrong and your hair sticking up like a six year old's, you don't even look vaguely ready."

"I feel weird," Jimmy admitted. "Like I don't know what I'm doing, even though I do. I'm nervous, I guess."

"You shouldn't be. You're good at your job."

"I know. It's stupid. Forget it. What are you doing today?"

Nate slipped into his jacket and started hunting for his keys. "I'm going to bully, and maybe threaten in a non-obvious way, a former owner into donating one of his tenement buildings to house ex-slaves."

"That sounds like fun." Jimmy put down his script, smiling up at Nate. "And I know you're good at what you do." He watched as Nate suddenly stopped, keys held tight in his hand, his face going soft as he simply stood there, staring at Jimmy. "You okay?" he asked at last.

"Yeah," Nate said quietly. "I'm good, really good." He dropped the keys and moved round the table, leaning in. Jimmy thought he was going to kiss him goodbye but he didn't. Instead he reached to the back of Jimmy's neck and started to undo the leather cord that was always tied there.

"What?" Jimmy asked, but Nate hushed him quiet as he took it off.

Carefully he slipped off the bonding ring. Jimmy remembered putting it on him so long ago and now Nate held it in his palm. He looked at it for a moment then picked it up and took hold of Jimmy's hand, holding the ring at the tip of his finger. "Yes?" Nate asked.

For a split second Jimmy couldn't think of a damned thing to say as his throat closed up and his mouth turned dry. Then a million combinations of words filled his mind, long winding sentences expressing undying love and need and all kinds of things. But Nate was waiting for him and Nate always said he talked too much. "Yes." He nodded. "Yes."

Nate pushed the ring onto his finger then looped the cord round Jimmy's wrist twice before tying it securely. "Yeah?"

Again Jimmy nodded. "Definitely yes." He didn't think he ever take either of them off.

Then Nate purposely caught up Jimmy's other hand, no hesitation in his actions, and twisted off the ring he wore there. He held it out to Jimmy and offered his hand. "Do you want to?"

"Oh fucking hell, yes." Jimmy couldn't help the thick want that colored the words. "But only if this time it means that we're doing it right, because you want to—we want to. That it means what it should mean."

"We've never stopped being legally bonded," Nate said. "But that didn't mean a jack shit to me. This, now... This is real."

Jimmy took the ring from his hand and stood up. It felt the right thing to do, to be able to look Nate in the eye. "Do you want to?"

Nate stared straight back at him, everything he was, everything he felt, showing in his eyes. "You bet."

Jimmy pushed the silver ring home. Just as he was about to lean in to kiss Nate, a car horn sounded outside.

"That'll be your ride into work." Nate grinned. "Your driver has such bad timing."

"We'll make up for it tonight," Jimmy said, and that was the great thing. They had tonight and tomorrow night and for as long as they got. The kiss was meant to be a brief peck on Nate's lips, but neither could pull away that quickly.

The horn tooted again and Nate pushed him back. "Go. Earn money, seeing as I hardly do."

"I will. I might even remember my lines now."

"Not nervous anymore?"

Jimmy stopped with his hand on the door handle. He stared down at the ring on his finger, the cord round his wrist. "No, not nervous."

"Hey," Nate called, as Jimmy was half way out of the door, making him look back. "I love you."

"I know you do," Jimmy said with a confidence that completely shocked him. But it was true. He did know. "Can't tell you what it means to hear you say it though."

"Took me long enough to get there, didn't it?"

"You like to be sure, of motives as well as feelings. There's nothing wrong with that."

"I've loved you for a long time," Nate said carefully. "I fell in love watching as you opened your eyes to the world. I fell in love and got scared down to my boots. What if it still wasn't real?" His gaze stayed fixed on

Jimmy. "Only it was, and you gave me the guts to see that, after my fight with Paulo. You made me trust myself. Thank you for that."

"You're welcome." Jimmy grinned wide and proud. "And I'm awesome."

"Go to work, fool," Nate said, sounding light and happy.

"I love you too, idiot."

* * * *

Jimmy tapped the phone against his knee. If he was going to do this, now was the time. It was all organized and ready. The timing was perfect—if he could get Nate to go along with it.

And he really, really wanted to do it.

"Hey," he called over to the director. "I'm okay to go for a couple of hours, right?"

"Yeah, sure." The guy nodded. He might not be so happy when Jimmy got back, but what the hell.

Jimmy hit speed dial and Nate answered after four rings. "Hi," Jimmy said, suddenly nervous. Not about what he was going to do, no, not that, but about Nate's reaction. "You busy?"

"Not especially. Why, what you got in mind?"

"Can I steal you away for an hour or two? There's something I want to do."

"Will I like it?" Nate laughed, a dark dirty laugh.

"I hope so. I'll pick you up in twenty minutes."

"I'll be waiting outside." There was the warmth in his tone again.

Twenty-two minutes later Jimmy pushed open the car door and Nate climbed in. "Where are we going?" he asked.

"It's a surprise. Wait and see."

"I don't like surprises. I—"

"Shut up. Don't be a spoilsport." Jimmy grinned at him.

"Okay, but this had better be good." Nate folded his arms over his chest, putting a foot up on the dashboard.

"I sure hope you think so," Jimmy said quietly.

Ten minutes later they parked outside a nondescript building and Jimmy led the way round the back. A thick-set man opened the door. Jimmy asked if they were all set and, when he nodded, they shook hands, before they all went in.

He left them in a small room and Nate raised a questioning eyebrow but Jimmy just smiled as he took off his jacket. Then the man was back and Jimmy knew for certain that Nate recognized the box he put on the table.

"Is that what I think it is?" Nate said, voice clipped and tight.

"Yep." Jimmy was sure of his ground.

"What the hell?"

Jimmy took the stylus from the top and held it out. Nate just stared at it. "You need to write your name."

"Why on earth would you even think of doing this?" Nate asked incredulously.

"Because." Jimmy picked up Nate's hand, running his thumb firmly over his own name on the back of it. "You want... No, we want to be equal, partners. I need this to make me equal."

"You want to be branded like a slave?"

"It's got nothing to do with slavery. It's everything to do with us. I want a level playing field."

"You want everyone to think you're an ex-slave? That's fucking insane."

"I don't give a damn what everyone else thinks." Jimmy kept a firm grip on Nate's wrist. "I only care about you."

"I don't need you to do this," Nate said, outrage thick in his tone.

"But I do. Don't you get it? You're a better man than I am—or at least than I was. I want this, because it means we'll be even but it's way more than that. I want this," he said, staring hard at Nate, "because I want everyone to know who I'm bonded to, that I'm taken and so fucking happy about it. Because I'm proud to wear your name, because it means I have less chance of losing you again, because it's so fucking hot seeing my name on your skin and I know it'll be even hotter seeing yours on mine." He dropped Nate's hand but kept hold of his gaze. "Because I want it."

"You don't have to do this," Nate said.

"No, I know I don't, but I want to. It's right for me, right for us. I want this."

"But…you need to think about this."

"I've done nothing but think about it for weeks."

"Then I need to think about it."

"No, you don't." Jimmy was sure. "You need to trust me to know what's right for us. I want this."

"What if I don't want it?"

"Then I don't do it. But don't say no for my sake. You wouldn't be doing me a favor. You'd be stopping me having something I really want."

Nate stood still and stared at him for long, long moments and Jimmy had the sense to keep quiet for once. "You're crazy," Nate said at last.

"But I want it."

"No." Nate shook his head. "It doesn't seem right. People will think…"

"People didn't think it was right that you fell in love with me. Fuck it. You didn't think it was right, but it happened. They might not understand this, but all that matters is that you understand and you do, don't you?"

"I..."

"You do. Admit it," Jimmy pressed. "This is about binding us tight and you know it. Trust me and forget what anyone else might think."

"But..."

"Nate, think, man. Not about anyone else, just us."

"Are you totally sure?" The uncertainty was still thick in Nate's voice.

"I am. Trust me."

There was a long pause then Nate nodded, just once.

Jimmy held out the stylus again. Nate's hand was shaking as he took it.

He moved over to the table, turning the box to face him. Without warning, he dropped the stylus onto the table and rubbed his palms hard on the back of his jeans before picking it up again. After taking a deep breath, he wrote his name on the top section of the box.

The man moved forward silently as Jimmy placed his hand flat on the table.

"It hurts like a bitch," Nate said suddenly, his voice scratched and drawn out.

"If you can do it, so can I." Jimmy smiled at him. "Besides I've got a stack of pain killers and a bottle of bourbon ready at home."

The box was fitted over Jimmy's hand. The man went to press the button.

"Wait," Nate called, and Jimmy sighed at him. "Are you sure, really sure? Totally, absolutely, completely sure?"

Jimmy could see him breathing hard, see how wide his pupils were dilated. "Yes, I am—totally, absolutely, completely sure." He was pleased his voice reflected how he felt, calm and confident. "It took a lot of organizing to find one of these boxes, to get this all arranged. I don't put that kind of effort into anything, unless I'm really sure. Trust me." He looked back at the box, ready to indicate for the button to be pressed.

"Stop." Nate grabbed hold of his arm and pulled Jimmy away.

"Hey." Jimmy took a deep breath. "If you really don't want me to do it then I won't but believe me, I want this."

"I wasn't going to say that." Abruptly Nate turned his head away. "I was going to say let me write it again, that first go wasn't good enough." He hitched a shoulder, his face sheepish. "It has to be right."

Jimmy kissed him, sweet and light but full on the lips. "Go on. Do it again." He pushed the box closer.

Nate cleared the first attempt, leaned in and kissed Jimmy, then wrote again.

"Happy now?" Jimmy asked.

"That's better." Nate nodded. "It looks the same as normal."

"Good." Jimmy turned to the man. "Do it quick, before he freaks again."

"I wasn't frea—" But before Nate could finish the sentence the button was pressed.

"Ouch! Fuck, shit. That fucking hurts." Jimmy pulled his hand out, holding the wrist with his other hand and waving them both about.

"Told you," Nate said.

"Yeah, but I saw you having it done. You hardly flinched. I didn't think it would be this bad. You must be some kind of fucking ninja." He gestured to the man. "Let's do the second one fast, before I embarrass us all by pissing myself."

"Whoa, you don't have to—"

"Nate, shut up and help me with my jeans." Jimmy carried on waving his hand around. "I don't think my fingers work."

"But..."

"Oh for fuck's sake, shut up. You can kiss it better later—just get on with it now." Jimmy pulled at the zipper on his jeans until Nate helped him out, easing both them and his boxers down just far enough. Then he moved behind Jimmy, holding him under his arms. "What are you doing?" Jimmy demanded.

"This hurts worse," Nate said, his mouth close to Jimmy's ear. "It's on your hip bone."

"Thank you so much for telling me that."

"You can always change your mind?"

"Not a fucking chance." Jimmy signaled to the man. "Do it."

The box was fitted and the button pressed as fast as possible. "Fucking—" Jimmy groaned, falling back into Nate. He panted hard and fast as Nate tightened the circle of his arms, holding him secure.

"Okay?" Nate asked softly.

"Yeah, but I could really do with that bourbon about now." Jimmy pulled himself upright, the sweat running down his face as he tried to drag his clothes back into place one handed.

"Where're the first aid supplies?" Nate asked.

Jimmy pulled a face. It felt like a million pulse points were beating under his skin. "At home?"

"You organized all this but no medical supplies?"

"Yeah, well...."

"Idiot." Nate smiled as he took over getting Jimmy dressed again.

Jimmy held onto the table, gripping the edge as Nate did up his jeans for him. From his wrist down, his whole hand was throbbing and his hip felt like it was on fire but then he looked down and knew he'd been right. "I can't decide if I'm going to throw up or pass out." He huffed.

It was worth it. It was all worth it.

On one hand was the ring, the leather cord tied around his wrist. On the other Nate's name was burned into his skin.

Nate caught him under his arm, hauling him up. "Let's go home."

Perfect.

About the Author

When Faith was clearing out her attic many years ago, she found a book she'd written as a ten-year-old. On rereading it she realised that it was the love story of two boys. Over the years her fascination with the image of beautiful young men, coiled together as they fell head over heels in love, became a passion for her.

Since that first innocent book—written in purple sparkly pen—she has written many stories, set in varied worlds, but always with two men finding their way to happiness.

Still nothing much has changed because now she can be found in a daydream, wandering around the supermarket, or sitting in a meeting at work still dreaming up stories.

Faith Ashlin loves to hear from readers. You can find her contact information, website details and author profile page at http://www.totallybound.com.

Totally Bound Publishing